UNWORTHY

Book One of The Blacksea Odyssey

J.A. Vodvarka

Book cover illustration and interior art by Chris Yarbrough.

Line and copy editing by The Editor & the Quill.

Proof reading by Markham Correct.

First edition 2024.

For those who cast their own shadow.

THE DESERTER

Quinn's hands trembled, working at the collar around her neck. Growling at the stubborn lock, she kept at it, ignoring the sweat coating her palms. She had practiced, successful over a dozen times, but now it mattered.

Now, it meant freedom.

The fork—her makeshift lockpick—slipped, jabbing her hand. "Fuck," she hissed, sucking the blood off her finger. Another cut. Another scar.

Just add it to the collection.

Quinn shook out her hands and exhaled, taking a moment to refocus before she tried again. It took months just to shave down the fork to fit the lock. And weeks to wait for the perfect night to escape, when most of the Citadel was preparing for Winter exams.

The fork tine slid home, the lock springing open, and a rare smile crept across her face. She slipped the void collar off, and her magick flooded back through her body, warm and electric, accompanied by a familiar wave of nausea. Magick thrummed at her fingertips, ready to use with just a touch.

She tossed the collar on the bed and double-checked her travel bag. Her meager belongings were all there, save for her favorite book of poetry that she had left on her desk in the library. A mindless error, but going back for it was out of the question.

She wrapped a scratchy wool scarf around her naked neck. Normally it hid the shame of wearing a void collar. This night, it hid her freedom.

Exhaling a long breath, she opened her door, and the guard—Felix or Francis or some other forgettable name to go with his forgettable face—turned to her.

"Past curfew, Quinn. Back in your room," he said, waving his hand as if shooing a fly.

"I require the bathroom," she said, softening her voice in an attempt to lull him into tranquility. A small dip in his shoulders gave him away.

"I suppose you ca—"

Quinn lunged, her hands flying to the man's throat. His legs buckled underneath him as she drove him to the ground. Twisting her magick inside him, she found his core of power and attacked, nullifying it.

The First Master had made her do it to other adepts before, and it always left them nauseated and disoriented. He would be fine in a few minutes, but she needed more time. Setting her shoulders, Quinn gritted her teeth and kicked the guard in the head.

Hurting another person always proved easier than expected.

She bent over and fumbled at his belt, stealing his knife and slipping it into her boot. His thin wallet held less than twenty gold marks, but it was better than escaping with nothing.

Back inside her room, Quinn pulled on her cloak, strapped her travel bag over her shoulder, and took one last look around her drab room, its walls dotted with charcoal sketches of her limited world, and even some from her dreams. She caught her reflection in the dull mirror, her dark hair falling around her shoulders in stark contrast to her pale skin and bright-green eyes. She tugged her scarf down. The sight of her neck without a void collar stilled her for a moment.

It had been almost ten years since First Master Ceril Anelos saw fit to put the collar on her, only removing it when he needed her magick. An equal mix of shame and anger plagued Quinn, but she had no power to stop him. Putting an adept in a collar was against all guild laws, considered inhumane, but no one objected. Other adepts and Masters turned a blind eye to how she was treated.

Best she not exist.

Best they not rock the boat.

Quinn left her reflection and ran through the hallway to a back staircase. Spiraling quietly down the worn stone steps, she stayed alert, thankful to hear nothing but the rush of blood in her ears. Dim orbs dotted the walls, many of them burnt out, not recharged for years. Dust hung in the air, musty and grim, stirred by her movement.

A dark door guarded the exit at the bottom of the stairs, and Quinn stopped before it and tried to slow her breathing, wiping the sweat pricking her forehead.

Cautious, Quinn waited, listening for any movement. Icy fear pooled in her stomach, and she expected the shouts of guards at any moment, alerting Arcton Citadel to her escape. But the only sound was her labored breathing. She placed her hand on the door handle and twisted, hoping that no one had found and fixed the one door in the Citadel with a wonky knob.

The hinges creaked, swinging open, and cold air rushed past the door. Winter was sinking its teeth deep into the mountain, and Quinn drank it in, taking the slightest of moments to relish her freedom. She slipped out and pressed against the cold stone of the wall. Her room was far from the heart of the Citadel, on the isolated outskirts of the massive, sprawling mansion where they saw fit to let her exist.

Scraggly, dead gardens lay at her feet, the musky scent of dirt invading her nostrils. Past that, across a long stretch of wild grass, a shadowy forest rose in the distance. A narrow path bisected the woods and led to a cliff.

Her way out.

With a deep breath, Quinn pushed off the stone wall, swearing it would be the last time she ever touched anything connected to the awful place, and ran toward the forest. With freedom so close, she kept checking over her shoulder to see if anyone was giving chase.

Failing now, failing to be free, would break her.

When she reached the tree line, she pressed herself against a trunk and glanced back. Moonlight bathed the grass and the gardens, a stiff, icy breeze stirring the desiccated branches of dead flora. Quinn's ragged breaths came in bursts, on the verge of panic. Despite needing to run, she waited for the hammering in her chest to slow.

Arcton Citadel loomed in the distance, its eerie white stones etched with runes to fortify the building against outside dangers. It was perhaps the most protected building in the world with ward upon ward layered on top of each other, ready to be activated to keep intruders out.

And keep unspoken things in.

Its bone-white visage glowed against the night, and distant windows lit up. The part of the Citadel that Quinn lived in, however, was dim, bereft of occupants save for one lonely woman, now escaped into the dark.

Quinn swallowed the cold lump in her throat, pushed away from the tree, and jogged through the underbrush, the pine needles crunching underfoot. The scent of dirt mixed with the strong sting of pine, a welcome change from the smell of dusty books. Branches and brambles pulled at her clothes, slowing her down, and she tripped over tree roots several times.

What if she fell and busted her head? Just bled to death in the cold night? Morbid thoughts had plagued her of late, some darker than others. Some she dare not dwell on for more than a second.

Quinn hissed as thorns tore at her hands pushing through unruly bushes. They'd heal over, more scars to add to the smattering of old injuries—a sordid record of the work First Master Anelos forced her to do for the Citadel. Her magick made her a useful tool to the guild. A tool that they locked away so she wouldn't hurt anyone. An irony that was not lost on her.

The path to the cliff was easy to spot, and she ran parallel to it, remaining under the cover of the trees. Every step got her closer to freedom and away from the nightmares that threatened to erode her sanity.

Of late, her dreams punished her. They had turned frantic and cruel. Black fingers forced themselves inside her mouth, down her throat, and choked the life out of her, wrenching her ribs apart until they snapped. There was darkness in the Citadel. Darkness that she had touched. And it was leeching into her dreams, a bleak presence trying to sink in and take hold.

So, Quinn ran.

She was not willing to sacrifice her sanity to obey the First Master; to grant him access to places he didn't belong. She knew that getting captured meant execution, or worse—being marked as Unworthy, a traitor to the Empire. Death or cursed exile, both preferable to living one more second in the Citadel.

The forest path wound to a clearing of rock that led to a cliff face. Quinn carefully approached the two squat, stone pillars etched with runes that sat on its edge. She stretched out her hand, cautious, her fingers buzzing in the icy wind. A quick peek over the edge made her stomach drop—a plummet of ten thousand feet into the darkness awaited. Bracing herself against the cold, she made sure her bag was strapped fast against her body.

Quinn closed her eyes, took a deep breath, and jumped.

HAPPY BIRTHDAY

As bar fights go, this one was magnificent.

Nyssa roared with laughter and dodged an errant beer glass set to collide with her head. It shattered against the back of the bar, shards of glass pinging against bottles of dark liquor. Impressed with her drunken reflexes, she turned back to her drink. A fist slammed into her chin.

"Shit," she grumbled, her beer sloshing in her hand.

Staggering back, she searched for the owner of the fist as bodies flew past her. The chaos made her giddy. Instigating a fight was the perfect way to kick off her twenty-fifth birthday.

Nyssa shook her head and drained the rest of her beer, tossing her glass to the unhappy man behind the roughly hewn wooden bar. "Another!"

Someone stumbled into her, and she reared back, cocking a fist, ready to throw a punch. "Oh!" She grinned and raised an eyebrow at the man's handsome features. "I like your face. What are you doing after this? Would you—"

A group of men crashed into her, shoving her back into a rickety table. Nyssa howled with delight as she spotted a face she deemed punchable. She raised her fist, ready to let it fly, but strong fingers clamped over her wrist and an arm wrapped around her waist. Her beaming smile turned into a deep frown.

Rude.

She was hauled outside the bar and dumped on her ass in the middle of the dusty street. The bright, blinking neon signs dotting the storefronts of nearby businesses assaulted her eyes.

"Hey, asshole! I was tryin' to enjoy a rather rousing fight, if you don't mind." She squinted up at her assailant. Her heart leapt. Popping to her feet, she listed a few steps to her left—the ground surely slanted that way—before flinging herself at the tall man who dragged her out of the bar.

"Athen!"

A massive man with golden eyes and a shaggy brown beard wrapped her up in his arms and lifted her off the ground in a warm embrace. It had been too long since Nyssa last saw her best friend.

"I've missed you," he rumbled into her ear before putting her down. "What have you done, Nyssa?" He jerked a thumb back over his shoulder at the bar, his breath clouding the crisp night air.

She shrugged. "It's my birthday. I'm celebrating." The ground seemed unwilling to remain steady, and she stumbled into Athen.

"Technically, your birthday is tomorrow, idiot."

Nyssa stuck a finger up in the chill air. "*Technically*, my birthday's whatever day I say 'cause no one knows my actual birth date. Tha's the benefit of being made to pick jus' any ol' day. I can change my mind. No one cares!"

"You're drunk."

"Cooooorrect."

A bald, rotund man burst out of the bar, his face red and sweaty. "Blacksea! What the hell did you start in there?"

Nyssa tried to whistle, but only blew out air. "Tha's a glorious fight, you have to admit," she said, gesturing wildly. She stumbled toward the man and threw an arm around him. "You're not going to bar me from your bar, are you, Haffo?" Nyssa giggled. "Ha, wordplay!"

Haffo peered behind Nyssa. "Athen Fennick! It's been awhile. Please tell me you're here to take her back to the guild. She's usually the one breaking up the bar fights, but the last couple of weeks, she's been..." Haffo shook his head.

"What?" Nyssa asked, still hanging on to him. She pet his head. "I've been perfectly lovely."

"I like you when you're flirting with my patrons and buying drinks, not causing a ruckus. Please, Athen, take her back to the Order. Let her sleep this off."

"You're zero fun." Nyssa let go of the bartender and stumbled back toward a wooden hitching post, getting tangled up in the wheels of several bicycles that had been haphazardly leaned up against the post. She wrapped her arms around the wood to steady herself. "You're the exact opposite of fun," she grumbled.

Athen sighed. "I'm sorry, Haffo. What does she owe you for the drinks and the damage?"

"Don't worry about it, son. I don't mind having an Order adept to keep things tight in there, but I can't take her like this. She's gonna hurt someone. More than a bump and a bruise. I've seen you adepts break bones over less."

"I pull my punches and don't have a lick o' magick, so I'm tame compared to the rest of 'em," Nyssa objected, frowning. She lolled her head back and stared at the night sky. "Stars...do you see 'em? S'pretty," she whispered to the hitching post.

Athen patted the man's back. "I'll take care of her. Have yourself a good night, Haffo." He then walked up to collect Nyssa. "You're a handful tonight," he said while she continued to chat up the post holding her upright.

"I think I'm drunk." She smiled at him as he towered over her, imposing and impressive. "When did y'get so tall?"

A delicious aroma drifted her way—Ozai's food cart full of perfectly charred chicken, basted in a sweet and spicy marinade and impaled on a skewer. Her favorite post-drinking food.

"Meat," Nyssa said, pointing.

Athen shook his head. "No. Sleep."

Squinting down the street, she asked, "What about a hangover cure from Grandy's shop?"

"Nope."

"But...it's m'birthday."

Athen patted Nyssa's cheek before picking her up and slinging her over his shoulder. "A hangover is a perfect twenty-fifth birthday present. Now, let's get you home."

"Happy birthday."

Athen slid a cup of coffee next to Nyssa as she watched the guild adepts at their morning practice from her perch on a bench. Athen had roused her out of bed early so she could visit the healer to deal with her headache, but her body still dragged and her tongue lay thick and fuzzy in her mouth. A hangover cure enchantment would have worked so much better.

Nyssa sighed and drummed her fingers along with the predictable rhythm of the students' footfalls as they moved through the First Form of Ithais-Toru. She could close her eyes and picture each form in her mind and feel them echo through her body. Years of practicing the martial art had etched the movements deep into her muscle memory.

Icy winds drifted off the Ashen Mountains, and Nyssa shivered, drinking in the chill. Winter cherry blossom leaves blew across dark gray stones, shed from the trees edging the courtyard. She would forever associate their faint sweet scent with the Emerald Order, along with the smell of sweat and blood.

"Did Eron send you after me last night?" Nyssa asked, picking up her coffee, thankful for the sweet, hot liquid.

"No. He told me you went into town, and I know your usual haunts. I didn't expect to find you throwing fists, though," Athen said before biting into a pastry snagged from the dining hall. He broke off a piece for Nyssa, and her empty stomach growled. She popped the flaky morsel into her mouth, groaning at the buttery, sugary goodness.

"What's going on with you? Starting fights?"

"It's nothing. Just restlessness, I suppose," Nyssa mumbled, sipping her coffee and avoiding eye contact. She scanned over the courtyard and the sprawling estate of the Emerald Order. The blue-green tiles on the curved roof glinted in the morning sun, reminding her of the stones in the nearby Emerald Lakes that would sparkle with vibrant colors as the light danced across the water. Wolf-head carvings at the corners of the roofs snarled down, warding off forbidden magick and ornery gods—not that Nyssa believed in such superstitious nonsense.

Athen poked her arm. "I know your moods. Your birthday is always a sore spot."

"I wish I knew my actual birthday. Just picking a random date feels so...meaningless." The only thing anyone knew about her birth was she was born in winter on the Black Sea. As a child, she chose the first day of winter because she loved the ringing of the bells to signify the coming of the long, cold winter, an arbitrary way of picking a date that made her cringe as an adult.

Athen looked into the sky, squinting in the sun. "You think Eron will make you an Ashcloak?"

Nyssa had begun to hate that word. Adepts were either elevated to the honored status of Ashcloak or were politely asked to leave the Emerald Order. Nyssa hung about in a frustrating stasis, neither put to service nor kicked to the side.

If she were honest with herself, she never belonged in the first place. She was the only member of any guild in the history of the Areshi Empire to not have magick—a fact that continued to bite her in the ass. After Eron took her in as a baby, became her adoptive father, he raised her in the Order. Whenever she asked why he'd adopted her, the answer was the same: *"When you save others, you save yourself."*

"I'm three years past when Ashcloaks are named. I'll be stuck here forever," Nyssa grumbled.

"You're frustrated, but starting bar fights?"

"It was one night that got a little out of hand."

Athen's eyebrow shot up. "One night?"

Nyssa rolled her eyes and yawned. That eyebrow called her out on her bullshit more times than she cared to remember. She stood and stretched, her back popping as Athen smiled at her, his golden eyes twinkling.

"What?" Nyssa asked.

"I've missed your morning grumpiness when I would drag you out of bed to spar in the morning. Now, I get up and head straight to my mother's office to start the business of the day."

"Your messages make it seem like you're getting on well."

He sighed. "I'm knee-deep in bureaucracy. Keeping city factions happy. Looking over tax records until my eyes roll back in my head. My mother is obviously grooming me to succeed her as Regent of Ocean's Rest. Some great Ashcloak warrior I am."

"You're unhappy."

"I'm...adjusting. Trying to figure out my place."

Nyssa laughed. "Welcome to my life." She leaned forward and tugged on Athen's beard. "I meant to ask last night but I hear I might've been a *wee* bit drunk—what in the name of a billy goat is this thing growing on your face?"

"You like it? I'm told women find me handsome with a bit of facial hair," he said, raising an eyebrow at her. She had to admit, he did look good with the beard. With his short, spiky brown hair, it made him look every bit the man he had grown into.

With a squint, Nyssa leaned back and nodded. "It suits you, I guess."

A young woman ran up to the two of them and stopped, standing at attention. Nyssa smiled at her. "Juliana?"

"First Master Greye has asked to see you both."

Nyssa's shoulders drooped. "It's time for my punishment, it seems."

THE FIRST MASTERS

Raised voices carried through the cracked door of First Master Greye's study as Nyssa and Athen arrived. Nyssa wasn't a stranger to being called to her father's office. She had spent many an hour being scolded for some transgression or another as a child. And as an adult.

Nyssa was about to knock when she heard her name mentioned, stopping her cold.

"I don't want Blacksea on this endeavor. You continue to bend the rules for that magickless girl," a reedy, unfamiliar male voice said.

"Who I send from my guild to retrieve the runaway is not your choice, Ceril," Master Greye said, his voice a welcome calm to the other man's anger.

"Blacksea was worthless as an infant and is worthless now. You make a mockery of guild law with that girl."

Nyssa's hands balled into fists, and Athen moved past her and rapped on the door. The arguing ceased.

"Enter," Eron said.

First Master Greye sat at his desk when Nyssa and Athen let themselves into his sparsely decorated study. The surface was uncluttered, save for a few books in a tidy pile, a pen and pot of ink, and two carvings that sat on the outer corners. One was of an armored Emerald Order warrior, the other a white wolf—the Order's sigil.

The walls were lined with inked art depicting each starting pose of the nine forms foundational to Ithais-Toru. Nyssa spent a lot of time in the study and had committed the art to memory. She loved the sweeping black brushstrokes, bold and fearless.

Eron greeted Nyssa and Athen with a strained smile. Nyssa eyed the tall man standing in the back corner of the study, his pale-blue eyes looking her up and down. She suddenly became keenly aware of her partially tucked shirt and half buckled boots—victims of her hangover.

"Thank you both for coming so quickly," Eron said. "And Athen, while it's good to have you back at the Order, I'm afraid I'm going to ask you to return to Ocean's Rest."

"I planned to stay at least a month to catch up with Nyssa."

Eron held up his hands. "It's good news. I have an assignment for the both of you."

A burst of excitement filled Nyssa. Finally leaving the Order to *do* something. She had been waiting for a chance to prove herself, having watched adepts leave when they were named Ashcloaks, most half the fighter she was. And that was being generous.

"What is the assignment?" she asked, trying to keep the tremor of nervousness out of her voice. Barely succeeding.

"First Master Ceril Anelos of Arcton Citadel will give you the details," Eron said, gesturing to the man in the corner.

Nyssa's blood turned to ice. Some members of the various guilds protested her inclusion in the Order, but the derision of a First Master was worrying.

She straightened up and bowed her head slightly to Ceril. "A pleasure to meet you, First Master."

Ceril offered her a slight smile, but it didn't reach his eyes. His skin was smooth and taut, save for a few small lines creasing the corners of his mouth and eyes, uncharacteristic for a man his age. Ceril was well into his seventies, if Nyssa remembered correctly. She guessed he employed some kind of magickal cosmetic enhancement. A trifling vanity.

"Master Greye's magickless adept," Ceril remarked.

Nyssa hooked her thumbs under the black leather of the sword strap slung across her chest that held her blade to her back. "Nyssa Blacksea, of the Emerald Order. I find 'magickless adept' to be rather informal for polite use," she said, cocking her head at the man.

"But it is what you are—magickless. First of your kind in any guild."

"Yes, I am indeed a rare beast." Nyssa smirked at the man and felt Eron's eyes boring into her. She didn't do well in the face of blatant disrespect.

"You have a mouth on you. Your Order peers must find you amusing."

"I assure you, they do not."

"Your First Master insists on your involvement in a task the Empress has requested personally. However, I'm not sure you're qualified."

Nyssa reached over her shoulder and quickly drew her sword, a small, satisfied grin curling one side of her mouth when Ceril flinched. She grabbed the flat of the blade and rotated the hilt toward him. "The toldoku you see woven into the grip of my sword says I'm qualified," she said. "You're familiar with the system of recognition in Ithais-Toru?"

Ceril glanced down at the hilt, its thin colored threads intricately interlaced in the grip of her sword. Over the years, Nyssa patiently collected the colored toldoku threads after being awarded each one. She had a blacksmith take pieces of each and intricately interlace them into the hilt of her sword. They were a significant source of pride for her, proving her excellence as a fighter.

"Which one of those toldoku is awarded for magickal aptitude?" Ceril asked, raising his eyes to meet Nyssa's.

She blinked and swallowed, the tips of her ears growing hot.

"Nyssa," Eron said, a tone of caution—all too familiar to her—lacing his words.

She stepped back and returned to her place next to Athen, sheathing her sword. Her jaw flexed as she bit down to stop herself from saying anything that would lead to real trouble.

Eron cleared his throat. "Ceril, this is Ashcloak Athen Fennick, currently posted in Ocean's Rest with his mother."

Ceril looked him up and down. "I know your mother. She is a force."

Athen nodded. "That she is, sir."

Ceril pulled a chair next to Eron's desk and sat down, smoothing his cloak and the dark tailored suit underneath, picking a small piece of lint off his knee. "Down to business. Arcton Citadel has a deserter. She's been gone almost a week now."

"A week? That's quite a head start," Nyssa remarked.

"We thought she would be easy to find on the mountain path leading down from the Citadel. We miscalculated. She took another exit."

"Another exit?" Eron asked.

Ceril cleared his throat. It was obvious to Nyssa that the escape of this adept rankled him. "There is an old free fall enchantment off a cliff east of the Citadel. An alternative route off the mountain, if you will, in case of emergencies. No one has used it for decades. To be honest, I thought parts of it would have decayed by now. But we tested it, and it is fully intact."

"Tested it?" Nyssa asked.

Ceril's eyes settled on her. "A guard volunteered to take a leap of faith. A five-minute fall. But controlled, safe."

Nyssa blinked. *Volunteered my ass.*

Ceril continued, "I suspect my adept is in Ocean's Rest awaiting passage off the continent or is already at sea. I need her brought back."

Eron cleared his throat. "*We* need her brought back. Empress Kalla is keen on her safe return."

Ceril shot Eron a look that made Nyssa tense, pricking up her instinct to protect her First Master.

"Brought back safely?" she asked, looking at the two Masters. "By guild law, deserters are executed. Or marked as Unworthy." Nyssa knew no one had been marked as Unworthy—a punishment used for traitors—for a hundred years.

Laughing softly, Ceril pulled his black cloak tighter around his narrow frame. "This adept is special to us. I will not hand her to the Justiciars to be killed or marked. Her ability allows her to negate magick for a short time, a gift that is quite rare." Ceril paused and licked his lips. "We have several items in the Citadel that we could not touch or study if not for her ability, so as you can imagine, she is highly valuable to me. But be wary of her effect on flesh. If she uses her magick on you, Athen, you'll find your strength and toughness sapped. But she can't affect you, Nyssa."

She smirked. "I guess not having magick is an advantage in this situation."

"How nice at the age of twenty-five to finally have a modicum of value."

A burst of anger ignited in Nyssa's chest, and she swallowed, trying to calm herself.

"Yes, Nyssa, you are uniquely suited to this task," Eron soothed.

"How do we find her?"

Ceril sniffed. "There are no Hounds available at the moment from the Obsidian Rule. There is a tracker of sorts at the Wayland Conservatory, though unconventional in her abilities. Apparently, she uses a personal object belonging to her target to find them. My adept kept a book close to her, always scribbling in it. I will send it along to Ocean's Rest. The tracker will meet you there."

Wayland? We're getting a bookworm to help us?

Eron stood up. "I want to impart upon you the importance of this assignment. This runaway is valuable. The Empress is making a rare exception for her and make no mistake, she and her Justiciars are paying close attention. You need to bring the escapee back safely, and you must be very careful with her."

"Understood, First Master Greye," Nyssa said. She was unsure who scared her more—the Empress or her Justiciars.

"Will we get a void collar for her?" Athen asked.

"No," Ceril replied. "Those collars are inhumane. Just be wary of her hands and avoid skin contact. Gloves will do."

"Ensure she understands you do not mean her harm, nor are you returning her to be executed. She is still a guild sister, so do not injure her. Be aware, she will be afraid of you. Ease those fears," Eron advised.

Nyssa smiled. "No worries, I'll charm her. This adept, what is her name?"

"Quinn."

THE ORDINARY ADEPT

Nyssa hit the dirt. Cheers echoed off the courtyard's stone walls. She smiled up at Juliana standing over her, pride written on the young woman's face. Her peers clapped the short, blonde girl on the back as Nyssa stood and brushed the dirt off her black leather pants.

"That was perfect, Juliana. You were patient and waited for the moment to put me on my ass. Now you see how powerful counterattacking can be. Many fighters want to make the first move and land the first blow..." Nyssa paused for effect, making eye contact with several of the students, and a tittering of nervous laughter spread through the group. "...but you get more information from someone's opening move and give them nothing in return if you simply wait. All you have to do is wait," Nyssa explained, slowing down her cadence to drill home her point.

Beyond the circle of students, Eron approached.

Nyssa stood straighter. "Also, remember your stance. As First Master Greye has told us a million times, a solid stance is your foundation. Extend your body into the ground and draw your strength from the earth, like you learned in the Bamboo Form. Did you all notice how Juliana always reverted to her stance when fighting me? Everything comes from that stance. Her power, her speed. Everything."

"Can her stance stop these?" a girl called from the back of the pack, holding her hands up as they burst into bright-yellow flames. The surrounding adepts snickered.

Nyssa rolled her eyes. The Order was rife with corporeal magick users able to call forth their powers with a thought. And always eager to show off, especially the younger ones.

"Stand down, adept. Save your magick for your practical application courses. I'm sure they'll find you far more impressive than I do." Nyssa placed her hand on Juliana's shoulder and leaned into her. "Now, what are the six pillars of Ithais-Toru, Juliana?"

"Courage, compassion, loyalty, justice, integrity, and honor."

An older boy at the front of the group groaned. "Not that crap again."

A clearing of a throat snapped all the young adepts to attention. Eron was rather good at sneaking up on students. He shook his head. "Ithais-Toru is more than a martial art. I see most of you slept your way through my class covering Sakei's philosophy and its six pillars."

Nyssa sighed and clapped her hands, the crack echoing through the courtyard. "You are all now late for your morning classes. Do not make your Masters wait, they will yell at me for keeping you!" her voice boomed. The adepts scattered, taking a wide berth around Eron.

He walked up to Nyssa. "You're good with them."

She shrugged and bent over, trying to catch her breath. Sparring with the younger adepts was invigorating, but they were relentless, each one wanting to take a turn to best a fighter ten years their senior. Their exuberance was exhausting.

"Gods, they love to beat the shit out of me if given a chance. I let them win from time to time. Good for the ego." She stood up and stretched out her back. "Where's First Master Anelos?"

"Gone already. Off on Citadel business, likely has a line on some rare items to add to its collection."

"I will miss him dearly." Her voice dripped with sarcasm.

With a warm smile, Eron ran his hand along his cropped hair. Over the years, it had flipped from being black with a touch of gray to gray with a smattering of black. The tattoos marking his temples had faded, though he swore to Nyssa he would get them re-inked someday.

"Before you leave for Ocean's Rest tomorrow, I wanted to let you know that you will be made an Ashcloak after you bring Quinn back to us."

Nyssa's stomach jumped, and she fought back a smile. Her lack of magick made her future murky, and each glance or whisper added to the dark kernel of self-doubt that festered in the back of her mind. Her peers had always let her know she wasn't worthy of being in the guild and had bullied her to demonstrate their disdain.

"You are allowed to smile," Eron said softly. "You will honor this guild with your service. I know how much you want this and how frustrated you were when Athen became an Ashcloak. I know you felt left behind."

"Well, he wasn't exactly happy either." The memory of his protests were still fresh. The two of them had been friends since they were ten. When Athen first laid eyes on Nyssa, she was on her back in the dirt, taking a beating from other students, doing her best to fight back. Athen bloodied his knuckles in Nyssa's defense and had stuck by her ever since.

"The Order will be a less interesting place without you here."

"Oh, I doubt that. You'll find someone to latch on to and talk their ear off about Sakei's pillars."

Eron chuckled. "You were always in my books, learning everything you could. I'm proud that you take the code of the warrior to heart. I try to instill it in all adepts, but as you see, not all take to it."

Nyssa loved reading about Sakei and his code. It made sense to her, gave her a larger context for the martial art. She liked that Ithais-Toru wasn't just about hitting things. Moreover, like her, Sakei was magickless, making a name for himself as an honorable warrior. His students called themselves Ashcloaks after the dark cloak he once wore.

A stiff breeze surrounded Nyssa and Eron with the sweet smell of winter cherry blossoms.

"Do you remember when you were small and we would walk the grounds of the estate together? You would point at things and call them all a tree," Eron laughed.

"I would like to think I was far smarter than that."

"Ah, but you weren't, Daughter."

Nyssa laughed and shook her head, brushing back the auburn hair falling over her shoulders. Looping his arm in hers, Eron smiled up at her.

"Let's walk like we used to," he said.

As they strolled the courtyard, Nyssa felt lighter and freer than she had in years. She finally had direction.

"I remember we would hike into the mountains and you let me play in the Emerald Lakes. I still have all the rocks I picked up." She would fill her pockets with as many of the smooth, multicolored stones as she could fit.

"I recall you throwing a tantrum when I tried to teach you how to swim in those lakes."

She raised an eyebrow. "I don't enjoy being in water I can't see the bottom of."

Eron sighed. "Your surname is Blacksea, yet you can't swim a lick. At some point, you'll have to learn."

"Well, that day isn't today." She chuckled and drew in a deep breath of mountain air.

A smile settled on Eron's face. "You were so small then. Your eyes were as blue as the water of the lakes. Still are. You've grown into quite a woman."

"I attribute my physique to pastries."

Eron laughed. Nyssa wasn't shy of her height or muscles. She was proud of her fighter's body, confident of the space she took up in the world. Being a few inches shy of six feet intimidated a few people, and she didn't mind one bit.

Eron slowed to a stop. "I have another bit of news. The Arch Master has announced his retirement, and the Empress is considering me for the position."

Nyssa broke into a bright smile. "Arch Master? Eron, the Empress would be lucky to have you!"

Holding up his hand, he slowly shook his head. "Now, no guarantee I will be offered the position, and certainly no guarantee I'll take it if I were. I just wanted to share the news with you. And only you. Keep this to yourself, Daughter."

"Yes, sir," Nyssa said. "But if you leave, who would take your place? Please don't say Master Ruggen."

"No, Ina is too young. But perhaps one day her turn will come."

"Yeah, fuck that," Nyssa grumbled.

"She's grown up, like you, and I think has learned her lessons."

Nyssa had many enemies as a child—but Ina Ruggen was notably persistent and cruel. When Nyssa was nine, Ina, three years her senior, cornered her and gave her a beating. It wasn't the first or the last time to be sure, but she vividly remembered Ina wrenching her arm behind her back and using her magick to shatter it. The sound was the worst part—the crack of her bones giving way under senseless cruelty.

Nyssa had stumbled to the healer on her own, bloody and broken. That was before Athen arrived at the Order; back when she had to face her bullies alone.

The last time Ina came for her, Nyssa was fourteen, and she put three of Ina's friends into the dirt before pinning her down and breaking two of her fingers. The Masters had to pull Nyssa off before she could snap a third. Ina howled like a dying wolf.

She'd maintained a respectable distance from Nyssa since.

Eron closed his eyes and breathed deep. "You are about to go into the world to cast your own shadow."

Nyssa grew serious. "I've only ever wanted to make you proud."

"I'm already proud of the woman you've become. And once you are an Ashcloak, no one can take that accomplishment from you."

"If you're trying to make me cry, it's not going to work." Nyssa flashed him the half smile that she so often used to charm him, especially when she got into trouble. The slight tremor in her voice gave her away, though.

"I'm a sentimental fool. I think I'm more likely to cry than you." Eron stepped away from her. "I intend to follow you and Athen to Ocean's Rest in a few days. I want to make sure this tracker from Wayland is capable."

"So, this isn't a goodbye after all, old man?" Nyssa asked, smiling.

He straightened. "I'm still your First Master, adept. Address me with respect."

"Yes, sir," she replied, giving him a wink and a light kiss on the cheek before he took his leave of her.

Leaves tumbled through the courtyard, the soft hush of their touch against stone a familiar sound to Nyssa. Winter moved into the Ashen Mountains and the valley occupied by the Emerald Order, displacing autumn. The late morning sun moved behind the clouds, casting giant shadows over the Order.

The promising scent of snow gently teased Nyssa's nose. When winter descended on the Empire, it would come swiftly and wouldn't release its icy grip until spring. The changing seasons were familiar friends, settling into Nyssa with a slow, predictable cadence.

She would miss the cherry blossoms blooming again in the spring once she became an Ashcloak. She wondered where she might be sent. It was far too much to hope to be assigned to protect the Empress, but she would be happy anywhere, even if sent to protect a city in the barren Northern Wilds.

A strange pang of melancholy struck her, the lump that formed in her throat surprising her. She had not expected to feel sad about leaving a place that held so many bitter memories.

Alone with her thoughts, she closed her eyes and stretched her back out, feeling her muscles expand and bones pop. She bounced on her toes, trying to stay warm and loose in the chilly morning air.

"Blacksea!" Athen's deep voice called as he strolled over to Nyssa. "Spending one last day training in the old courtyard?"

"Enjoying the slow creep of winter. You know how I love it."

Athen chuckled and shook his head. "I remember how the Masters would make us practice our forms in winter while wearing our summer uniforms with no shoes. You were always the last one to run inside to get warm."

Staying out in the cold and demonstrating her sheer force of will had become a source of stubborn pride for Nyssa. No one could ever outlast her.

"What's Winter's Fire like in Ocean's Rest?" she asked.

"Two weeks of food, drink, and parties. It gets bigger every year. The city will be crowded."

The holiday was Nyssa's favorite, paying homage to winter—a time of death and rebirth. Renewal. Celebrants would whisper their desires into paper lanterns to release into the night sky on the first night of Winter's Fire.

"I suppose we won't have much time for parties, given our assignment." Nyssa turned her face to the sky. "What do you think she's like, this runaway, Quinn?"

Athen shrugged. "Arrogant. Citadel adepts have a reputation for being..."

"Assholes?" Nyssa smiled and stretched her arms above her head. "Kinda like their First Master?"

"Well, yes."

"I wonder why she ran."

"Does it matter?" Athen asked. "We have a job to do, we do it, and you become an Ashcloak."

"I've earned it." Nyssa ran her hands over the top of her hair, feeling the long braids scattered throughout her curly auburn locks. She shook her head to knock out the dust of the morning sparring session with the younger adepts. If only it were as easy to knock the soreness out of her body. "I'm just curious why someone would abandon their guild."

"Her reasons aren't our concern."

Nyssa sighed. "I suppose not."

"You think anyone in Vane will miss you when you're gone?" Athen smiled and gave her a wink.

"You know better."

The town had been Nyssa's respite, and she spent many nights there, occasionally in the company of whatever man or woman piqued her interest. She wasn't very good at making friends, but flirting was never difficult for her. Lovers came and went out of her life by her own choosing.

Athen cocked his head. "I've been perfecting my lemon tart recipe while in Ocean's Rest and made a batch while you were letting the adepts beat on you." He cracked his neck and puffed his chest out. "There is one lemon tart left that I barely saved from those same ravenous guildies. Fight you for it?"

Despite Nyssa's tired muscles, sparring with Athen would be fun. She bounced on her toes. "Let's dance, big boy. And make this quick, I'm hungry." Nyssa grinned and beckoned him forward. She had a pastry to win.

THE CLOUD CRASHER

"Oh, fuck no," Nyssa swore under her breath.

The Cloud Crasher loomed in the distance—a massive airship, long and fat with a flat bottom designed to land and anchor to the ground. Its sails mimicked those of a seaworthy vessel, but the cloth was light and translucent, like dragonfly wings. A myriad of colors shimmered off the fabric as it danced in the wind. Nyssa would have found it beautiful if it didn't make her stomach lurch.

Athen grinned at her. "It's going to be fine."

"Nothing about this is *fine*."

"I've gone to Ocean's Rest and back dozens of times on it," he insisted. He had already given her the rundown: The Cloud Crasher was a storied vessel, once the personal transport of the Areshi Emperor for generations, until they decommissioned it as an Imperial Air Navy ship. It had changed hands a few times before the Legrand family purchased it and turned it into a passenger and cargo transport that hopped between Areshi cities.

Though Nyssa wasn't looking forward to flying, airships were a marvel of technology and magick, perhaps more impressive than trains, streetcars, and the myriad of enchantments available for purchase at corner shops. Though magickless herself, Nyssa never begrudged the advantages that magick mixed with technology bestowed.

While she could do without flying ships, the enchantment that forced water through pipes to provide a steaming hot bath was a luxury she'd never abandon. She also had an affinity for the enhanced bath salts that soothed muscles and created a short burst of euphoria. Oh, and the small wafers that tingled in her mouth and smoothed the very rough edges off a hangover were a special, though expensive, treat. A treat she couldn't afford much of after spending all her gold—most of it earned playing cards—on a sword.

Worth it, though. A proper sword for a proper Ashcloak.

A short older woman with a shock of white hair called out to them, her voice booming as Nyssa dismounted from her horse.

"Athen! We just dropped you off! What are you doing back here?"

"Quicker turnaround than I expected, Captain."

"Eh, I still want a hug!"

The woman approached them, and Athen bent down to give her a hug, though the height difference made it awkward. He put his arm around her and motioned toward Nyssa.

"Captain, this is Nyssa Blacksea. Nyssa, this is Anna Legrand, Captain of the Cloud Crasher."

Nyssa extended her hand out, and Anna grabbed it, giving it an enthusiastic shake, her warm smile extending up to her pale-blue eyes. She looked more like a deckhand with her mussed-about short white hair, dark-blue overalls, dusty boots, and a tight white shirt.

"This is Nyssa? Oh, Athen, you were right about the nose, a little out of place, but she's got a fine visage. A warrior's carriage too. Strong. Like the Black Sea you're named after, girl."

"I guess Athen has spoken of me?" Nyssa raised an eyebrow at Athen, who only offered her a shrug and a smile.

"Oh, not to worry, Nyssa. Athen has said nothing but lovely things. I know you two are the best of friends. Bees in a blanket and all. He's been traveling with me to Ocean's Rest and back since he was a pup. We're old friends now."

Anna reached up to pinch Athen's cheek, which drew an exasperated "Hey!" out of him, but his smile gave away his delight. He must have been the least intimidating Ashcloak in the history of the Emerald Order.

"Now, Nyssa, am I to understand you're a bit scared of air travel? I can assure you I've only had but a handful of incidents over the years. Me and my boys will make sure your trip is the tops, true up!" Anna took Nyssa's hand and pulled her toward the airship. She stopped and spread her arms wide, gesturing at the ship before her with pride. "The Cloud Crasher's the best ship to skip the skies, my girl. I'm a third-generation captain in my family on this bird. She's old but sturdy, just like me. And the boys are the best crew of any airship in Areshi, hands down."

Nyssa eyed the crew, who were definitely not all boys, despite Anna's words. Quite a few women, in fact. "You have a fine-looking crew."

"I do, I do. Tops in the skies." Anna turned to face Nyssa and stuck a stiff finger in her chest. "Now, Athen's told me about you. I don't have a strict crew-and-passenger-relations policy, being you're adults and all, but don't break any hearts, you hear? I can't have anyone on my crew crying their eyes out over you, Nyssa."

"Oh, Athen," Nyssa said, slowly turning her head toward him. "What exactly have you shared about me with Anna?"

"Oh, only the best stories, girl," Anna said with a wink. "Now, let's get your luggage so we can board ya, right?"

Anna stuck two fingers into her mouth and let loose a shrill whistle. Two deckhands came jogging up. "Take our guests' belongings to their cabins—master suites one and two." She turned back to Nyssa and Athen. "Your rooms will be ready shortly. A last bit of sparkle to spark, as it were."

The deckhands grabbed the bags, smiling at Nyssa and Athen, and Nyssa grinned in return.

"Heartbreaker." Anna chuckled, shaking her head. "You have this thing about you, child. Athen was right."

Nyssa shot her friend a look. "I'm not a heartbreaker. More of an asshole, I'd say."

Anna barked out a laugh. "Oh, no one says you can't be both. Now, get your asses on my beautiful ship."

The Cloud Crasher's crew rushed about, getting the ship ready to take off—polishing brass, cleaning windows, handling the sails, attending to passengers and cargo alike. The boatswain called out orders, ensuring the crew buttoned everything up and prepared for flight.

Nyssa and Athen walked around the front of the ship on their way to the gangway. Nyssa looked up at the figurehead at the bow—a rotund woman cloaked in robes, her outstretched arm reaching forward as if she were flying and pulling the ship behind her.

"Why is she blindfolded?" Nyssa asked, pointing up at the carving.

"According to Anna, she embodies the spirit of adventure. Just pick a direction and go."

"I'd much prefer something that embodies the spirit of not falling out of the sky."

Athen rolled his eyes. Nyssa had missed their easy rapport. Without him at the Order, she had no one to really talk to except for Eron and one scraggly tabby cat that occasionally slept on her bed whenever it pleased.

Nyssa and Athen reached the gangway and found a pair of crewmen struggling with a massive crate.

"Let me get that," Athen said.

"Oh, no, Ashcloak Fennick, you needn't—"

Athen stooped over and in one smooth motion, effortlessly lifted the crate and carried it up the gangway. He was met by a steward waiting with a trolley, and he placed the crate on top.

Another steward strode over and bowed, handing Nyssa and Athen each a mug of dark, sweet tea. "Ashcloak Fennick, let me show you to your cabins. We expect to be off the ground in about a half hour."

The young man expertly wound them around passengers milling about on the deck, guiding them into the ship's interior. They ascended the upper decks to the master suites and captain's quarters before the steward stopped in front of side-by-side doors. "Your suite, ma'am"—he swept his hand to the door on the left—"and, sir, you are here." He then opened both doors at the same time and gracefully moved aside.

"Lee, I've said you can call me Athen. No need for formality."

"Yes, sir."

"Lee..." Athen playfully chided.

Lee turned a little red. "Sorry, it's a habit!"

Athen clapped him heartily on his shoulder, and Lee stumbled a bit to recover his balance before nodding to the two of them and hurrying away.

"Go check out your room. This ship may be old but it has its luxuries."

Nyssa nodded and walked into her suite. Athen followed her.

Nyssa instantly fell in love. The dark wood walls were etched with delicate, intricate circular symbols that swirled and repeated, over and over, in and around themselves to the point she couldn't tell where the designs began or ended. Tiny leaves and ivy wove around the circles carved into the walls. She dropped down on the massive bed and smiled at its softness. At least she could hide under the covers and ignore the fact she was aboard a ship racing through the clouds, thousands of feet above the ground.

She reached over to run her fingers along the scene carved into the headboard—two massive bucks locked in combat, their antlers twisting around each other's heads. When she looked closer, she noticed the deer had two sets of eyes. *A Caracor?* A long-dead mythical beast that Nyssa remembered from a few childhood tales.

As Nyssa stretched out on the bed, she cocked her head to get a better look through the cracked door that led to the suite's adjacent bathroom, delighted to see a small tub inside. The true heroes of the Empire were the engineers and enchanters using their magicks to build marvels like the Cloud Crasher.

Two high-back leather chairs sat across from the bed, a steaming pot of tea on the table between them. Nyssa smiled at the plate of assorted sweets, finger sandwiches, and luscious-looking strawberry tarts, their bright scent lightly permeating the air. Her stomach rumbled. Skipping breakfast had not been her best idea.

"What do you think?" Athen asked, leaning in her doorway.

"It's much nicer than I could have imagined. At least I can be terrified in comfort."

"I'm going next door to wash up a bit, but I'll be back over for those." He pointed at the plate of treats and tea. "Don't you dare eat them all!" he warned, closing the door behind him.

Nyssa stood and grabbed a finger sandwich before moving over to the suite's portholes, their curtains open to let in the midday light. Oranges, reds, and browns painted the valley forest and the Ashen Mountains rose hazily into the clouds in the distance. The sight of such beauty made her throat catch. She would miss how the mountains embraced the seasons and the crisp, chill air of winter lazily overtaking autumn.

A mixed set of drawers, bookcases, and storage nooks lined the wall under the portholes, and Nyssa scanned the books, popping the finger sandwich into her mouth. Several tomes sparked her interest, as if calling her to draw a bath and dive into them.

Venturing into the bathroom, she peered into the mirror above the small sink and sighed when she saw a trace of pain on her face. Sparring with the adepts had left her sore. Beating Athen took the rest out of her.

The lemon tart was worth it, though.

Nyssa turned the faucet on and splashed water on her face, absent-mindedly brushing against the scar that slashed from her forehead down through her cheek, sparing her left eye—a terrible reminder of a shameful mistake. Of hurting someone she cared deeply about because she got cocky.

With a shake of her head, she banished the past out of her mind.

Returning to the main room, she swung her sword off her back, running her fingers lightly along the gently curved black sheath. The weapon was a single-edged sword, her preference after cutting herself too many times on double-edged swords. She gripped the hilt—her toldoku woven into the silk—and tugged the black blade out. The guard was a simple oval, etched with waves. Given her lack of a family sigil, the waves made sense. She had an orphan's name and embraced it.

Forged of sun steel folded over itself countless times, the sword had cost her a small fortune, but she figured better to have a blade that never shattered than cheap out. When Nyssa first wrapped her hand around the hilt and drew her new sword, she forgot to breathe, its beauty enraptured her so. The heft of the blade felt *right*, like an extension of her body.

She moved her sword to a shelf that lined the windowed wall, within reach of a quick roll out of bed if need be. With her sword accounted for, her fingers lit upon the zipper of an interior pocket in her black jacket. A small, leather-bound notebook was stored inside. An indulgence for when inspiration struck so she could jot down a verse or two of a poem. Her poetry was a carefully hidden secret from everyone, even Eron and Athen. The thought of them finding her writing mortified her.

A vanilla cream pastry proved too tempting, and she sat down, munching on it, thinking about the task at hand. Finding and securing a runaway adept seemed an easy enough assignment. A mage whose particular power couldn't hurt her. Oh, the irony of being the perfect foil.

Athen knocked on the door and let himself in. "We're going to take off soon. I assure you that we need to be on deck. I don't want you to miss the spectacle."

Nyssa groaned. She'd likely break into a sweat soon. But dealing with her fear of heights was the price she'd gladly pay to get closer to capturing Quinn. And get one step closer to her future.

A GIFT AND THE BLACK SEA

The Cloud Crasher creaked and groaned as it slowly lifted off the ground, climbing into the clouds. Nyssa clung to the handrail on the port side of the ship, her stomach lurching along with the boat's soft rocking.

Athen was right, though—it was a spectacular experience, and she was glad she was on deck to watch the ground grow distant. Athen was also kind enough to hold on to her belt while she emptied the contents of her stomach overboard.

A crew member appeared at her side with a small vial of pale pink liquid. "This will settle your stomach for the journey."

"You couldn't have mentioned this before we took off?" Nyssa moaned.

The crew member bowed and hurried away as Nyssa drank the thick liquid, scrunching her face at the taste—salty and bitter. But she immediately felt better.

The gossamer sails above their heads billowed gently in the wind, rustling like thin, delicate paper. The crisp air was refreshing, and Nyssa had to pull her jacket closed from the chill of it.

Passengers milled about on the deck and lounged in seating areas that afforded amazing views of the sky, braving the cold for the spectacle. Glasses clinked together, travelers toasting the start of their journey. Stewards were quick with refills of ale, wine, or tea, while plates of small, delectable treats floated around the deck. Nyssa eyed a crew member intricately moving his hands and fingers, casting a glimmering, soft-blue light that rose up and across the ship, creating a dome to buffer against the wind.

"Ethereal magick like that doesn't come cheap," Nyssa remarked to Athen. "How does Anna afford a spellweaver?" Magick users were in the minority—about one for every fifteen people. Truly talented mages even rarer.

Athen chuckled. "Cheaper than you'd think. There are plenty of jobs for ethereal and corporeal mages. Not all magick users are lucky enough to be in a guild and get a cushy Imperial post. Lots of work of all types, and it pays."

Nyssa shrugged. "Can you imagine weaving light orb enchantments every day? How tedious."

"Low-level magick isn't sexy, but it makes shit work. My mother brings engineers into the Keep twice a year to check on all the plumbing and reweave any enchantments that need refreshing. You'll appreciate that when you take a hot bath to ward off the chill of that drafty old place."

"I do like a good soak." Nyssa winked.

"Let me show you the rest of the ship."

Slipping her hand in the crook of his arm, she smiled. "Give me the grand tour."

The tip of Nyssa's tongue peeked out of her mouth ever so slightly. Stillness blanketed the room as she concentrated on the spinning cup suspended no more than twenty feet away.

Exhaling, she let her coin fly. It arched through the air and sank into the cup. Cheers erupted around the room.

"Drinks on the house!" the dealer yelled with a wink and a lingering smile for Nyssa. She had been in enough card rooms to know he was angling for tips, but something about his smile suggested an interest that she wasn't exactly averse to. A long soak with a book was still on the top of her list of priorities after the casino, but she always liked a good flirt.

The players at her table clapped her on the back, happy for their free drinks regardless of how much money they were losing to her. They were cautious at first, having two Order guildies in their midst, but buying her table companions a few rounds and learning their names loosened them up.

"Even for you, that was a helluva shot," Athen said.

"Yes, it was." Nyssa shoved a portion of her coin pile in front of Athen, who pretended to object. "How are you still this bad at cards?"

He screwed his face up at her. "I've gotten a bit better. The late-night games at Ocean's Keep are brutal. I think one of the guards won enough from me to pay off her mortgage."

Nyssa laughed and tipped her beer mug against his short glass of whiskey, her mood soaring much like the ship under her feet. "To your generous heart."

Athen stood and motioned to her. "Come on, I want to show you something."

She shot to her feet and pointed at a man across the table. "You have a short reprieve, Xoas. I'll be back to take the rest of your gold in a moment."

She followed Athen to a set of doors at the end of the card room. He opened them to reveal a sizable deck extended off the back of the Cloud Crasher's intimate casino. A sea of stars peppered the night sky, the cold, crisp air bracing her when she stepped out. The vista was simply breathtaking—clouds and stars mixing as if they were comfortable, longtime friends.

Scattered about the deck were a few tables and chairs softly lit by light orbs. Two women sat off in the corner, passing a thin cigar between them, and they nodded at Nyssa and Athen as they sat down.

"This is one of my favorite places in the world," Athen said, breathing in the night air, a smile firmly planted on his face. "A nice reprieve before you're dropped straight into Ocean's Rest."

"Should I be worried about meeting everyone?"

"Well, my mother is intimidating, but you'll be fine. Pol is...Pol. And I think you'll like Reece."

"You haven't told me much about any of them. I know Pol is your mother's right-hand man, but what does Reece do?"

"She manages The Feather. We were partners in crime before I left for the Order. I've told her a lot about you. She's eager to meet you."

Nyssa frowned. "Eager?"

"Give her a chance," he gently chided. "You gave me one."

"Yeah, I finally warmed up to you slightly after about six months." Nyssa smiled. She had taken her time accepting Athen as a friend. Her experience with the other Order children had soured her outlook toward strangers, and she wasn't quick to trust anyone. People can't hurt you if you don't let them get close.

"Life is different outside the walls of the guild. You start to see where you fit into the world."

She sighed. "It's hard to believe that. I never really fit in anywhere."

"Yet you always manage to carve out a place, all sharp elbows and attitude."

She chuckled. There was truth to that statement.

Athen leaned forward in his chair. "Nyssa, I know you hate this type of thing, but happy birthday." He placed a small package adorned with a simple blue ribbon on the table. While he'd always made it a point to acknowledge Nyssa's birthday, he'd never gotten her a present. No one ever had. Not even Eron, who'd honored her wish to not celebrate turning another year older.

This was her first gift.

A lump rose in her throat. "You didn't have to, I—"

"Just open it, Nyssa," Athen said, his smile soft and warm—a perfect defense to her rougher edges.

She pulled off the ribbon, tossed it aside, and tore at the plain wrapping paper to reveal a small box. Inside lay a thick, silver ring with an intricate Kraken etched into the metal, its eight tentacles flowing around its body and back around the band.

"It's made out of gradient metal, so the deeper the etching, the darker the metal gets," Athen explained. Nyssa turned the ring over in her fingers and examined it next to the soft light of the glowing orb. The artistry was stunning, and the silver-to-black tint gave the Kraken depth and dimension.

"I know you don't have a family sigil," Athen said, "but I took a chance you might like this. The Kraken is the most feared thing in the Black Sea...until you sail out there, I guess."

Nyssa knew he was taking a significant risk with this gift. Conversations about her place of birth or her parents usually darkened her mood.

"Uh...is it okay? Do you like it? You don't have to keep it if you hate it, I just..."

Nyssa exhaled. The ring was stunning. She slipped it onto the middle finger of her left hand, and it warmed against her skin, forming itself to her finger. The sizing enchantment alone must have cost him a good chunk of money.

"It's beautiful," she whispered. She tried to thank him, but her voice failed her and cracked. The nervous smile on his face belied a man that was convinced he had a good chance of being murdered right then and there for making her cry.

"I just thought you deserved a personal sigil. Usually these things are determined by blood, but I know for you it's different, with your family missing and all..."

Nyssa sighed. "You're my family."

"And you're mine. It's also a reminder of my promise to find out more about your parents. When you're ready."

She had been told her parents—Shana and Mikel—were pirates who lived in the shadows of seafaring society. They had left Nyssa in the care of an innkeeper on what would be their last visit to Ocean's Rest before sailing out to sea and never returning.

"They could be anywhere."

"You're my mother's ward. Eron isn't the only one responsible for your well-being. She'll look after you in Ocean's Rest. Maybe she has some information on your parents."

"Maybe." Nyssa had wrestled with her parents' disappearance her whole life. As an orphan of pirates, she had been mercilessly bullied by adepts who viewed themselves superior to her.

She shook herself out of her dour thoughts. "Thank you for the ring, Athen," she whispered, holding out her hand and admiring the band on her finger. "I love it."

As she relaxed into her chair and rubbed her thumb against her new ring, feeling the Kraken engraving under her fingertips, something among the distant clouds caught her eye.

It looked as though a city had been ripped from the ground and flung into the sky. It hung in the ether, its hazy buildings piercing the clouds. "Is that a floating city?" she asked, pointing toward it.

"It sure is," Athen replied.

From her studies, she knew that sky cities had been long abandoned after they started falling from the sky, the enchantments meant to hold them up decaying. Scavengers had likely picked apart and stolen anything of value, the city left to crumble until it eventually crashed to earth. "Does Anna ever visit them?"

"Doubtful. Rumor is they're haunted by Cursed Gods."

Cursed Gods? Nyssa chuckled. More like Cursed Assholes. According to the history books, their misdeeds were stuff of legend.

"It would be exciting to explore them. I wonder what got left behind when the people fled," Nyssa mused.

Athen shrugged. "Every time I see one, I get a bit of a chill. You know I'm not superstitious, but something about them sets me on edge."

Nyssa gave his beard a playful tug. "C'mon. I feel the need to take more money off these strangers. And you need to keep flirting with that barmaid."

"You think she likes me?"

"Athen, are you blind? If you don't make a move, I'm half tempted to. She's cute!"

Athen stood up and held his hand out to her. "Happy birthday, you idiot."

Nyssa smiled and took his hand, ready to play cards deep into the night.

Sails unfurled overhead, the cloth swaying gently above her slicing shadows and moonlight rhythmically across Nyssa's face. The thumps and dings of metal against wood pinged her ears as she tilted and dipped in the wind and waves, the ship cutting through icy, blue water.

Her eyes roamed the black sky. Flickering red dots floated in her vision, and beyond them, a sea of stars stretched in all directions. An infinite darkness.

The scent of sea brine, winter orchids, and juniper tickled her nose in the chilly nighttime air, and the gentle hum of a woman's voice vibrated in Nyssa's chest, lulling her, warm and comforting. She desperately tried to see where the voice came from—glimpse anything that connected her more deeply to this time and place; to bind her to this person watching over her.

The dream shifted, as it always did, and Nyssa tumbled into the sea.

It wrapped her in an icy embrace, and she drew a breath, her lungs filling with water. Pushing through the panic, she drew another breath, and a deep, buzzing drone of an ancient song moved through her body, burrowing itself into her bones as the waves consumed her, dragging her down into its bottomless blue maw.

Nyssa floated down, shedding her fear. Darkness enveloped her before the sea shuddered and burst into a field of stars—emerald and azure specks twinkling in the dark water. A warm hand slipped into hers and held fast before the cold shattered her into a thousand pieces.

Nyssa shot up, gulping for air, panting in the darkness of her stateroom. The dream that had subsided for a year was back, taunting her from the edges of her consciousness. She felt certain it was a memory of her birthplace.

Her chest rose and fell as she tried to calm down. Traveling to Ocean's Rest was drudging up old dreams. She was getting close to her past. Closer than she'd ever been.

Nyssa swung her legs off the bed and braced her hands next to her, raising her head to look out through one of the portholes. The moon peeked out from billowing clouds as the airship raced through the sky, drawing closer to Ocean's Rest and the questions Nyssa dreaded to ask about the pirates who left her behind.

THE CITY BY THE SEA

The Cloud Crasher touched down outside of Ocean's Rest. Two other airships sat in the expansive airfield. The crew jumped to life, deboarding passengers and their luggage while a buzz of activity around the ship signified the unloading of cargo, new shipments taking its place to be transported inland. It seemed a well-worn routine, and Nyssa couldn't help but be amazed by its efficiency.

Captain Legrand met her and Athen to say farewell, kissing Nyssa on each cheek. "It was such a pleasure having you aboard. I'm so glad to have met you."

"Thank you so much, Captain."

"You caught the hang of flying, dear. You're tops at it now!" Anna patted Nyssa on the back, much to Athen's amusement.

"Tops of the bottom, I'd say," he said with a wink, then pulled Anna off her feet in a giant bear hug.

"I can't wait to see you again! And I daresay I'm not the only one." Anna laughed and nodded toward the casino's barmaid. When she caught Athen glancing over at her, she gave him a quick wave. Athen smiled and waved back.

"She's been flirting with you for years, and you finally noticed!" Anna said, playfully slapping Athen's arm. Nyssa barked out a laugh. "Now get off my ship and say hello to that mother of yours for me."

As they walked down the ramp, a tall, skinny man with dark skin and hawkish features held his hand up. As the pair met him on the ground, he gave Athen a shallow bow.

"Lord Fennick, it surprised me to hear you'd be returning so soon." His voice was smooth and deep.

Athen nodded. "Interesting change of plans. Nyssa, this is my mother's advisor and second-in-command, Pol Cress."

Pol's pale-gray eyes slid over to Nyssa, and he gave her a tight smile. "Welcome back to Ocean's Rest, my lady. I remember you as a baby. You were a rather loud little thing."

"I don't think a lot has changed since then," Athen replied.

Nyssa barked out a laugh, eyeing her friend before nodding to Pol. "Pleasure to meet you."

"Shall we, then?" Pol walked to the horses and quickly swung himself up on one. Athen and Nyssa followed suit, and they made their way toward the massive city gates.

Ocean's Rest sprawled before Nyssa, a marvel to behold from her vantage point. Buildings, packed in tight, stretched across the rolling hills next to the Areshi Ocean, following the contours of the landscape, rising and falling like the waves of the ocean. Structures of stone, brick, metal, and wood poked up at the tallest points.

Broad, curved roofs extended out in all directions, covered in tiles of deep red, green, and blue, featuring intricate carvings along their edges, with the sharp corners of many roofs home to small sculptures of protective spirits and demons. As they entered the city, Nyssa's eyes darted from building to building, marveling at the different colors, etchings, and sculptures. Artisans had made their mark across the city, filling it with endless details.

The streets burst with people flowing in and out of shops, glowing in their neon lights, a cacophony of voices and sounds of the city filling

Nyssa's ears. Tram tracks lay in the middle of the street, pulsing with a soft yellow light indicating the streetcar was still a way off from their location. Nyssa had only read about the tram systems in larger cities, and she secretly wanted to ride one someday—not that she'd admit that desire to anyone. Athen had promised her a trip to the symphony and The Bent Page, the biggest bookstore in the region, after they settled their business with retrieving Quinn. She was giddy at the mere thought of hearing a live symphony or leafing through endless books.

A rich, yeasty scent filled the air, one Nyssa was intimately familiar with, having watched Athen bake in the Order's massive kitchen over the years, and being his taste tester. She ran her eyes up the street, each side lined with bakeries and pastry shops. The mouthwatering aroma of cinnamon hit her, a sure sign the city was preparing goods for Winter's Fire. Small white pastry boxes flew through the air, held aloft by levitating orbs—deliveries on their way to customers. Tiny solitary orbs zipped along the city's rooftops, bearing messages sent throughout Ocean's Rest.

After growing up at the Order and traipsing around Vane, Ocean's Rest was almost overwhelming in its size and activity. The mere din of the place buzzed in Nyssa's ears and its colors and shapes filled her eyes with so much variety it took her breath away.

"It's really quite beautiful, isn't it?" Athen mused.

"It's amazing."

"Don't let the outside fool you. There's a beating heart of a scoundrel underneath. This city's as scrappy as my mother."

Pol eyed him. "Your mother is the first person to rule over Ocean's Rest in hundreds of years. Scrappy is an insufficient word to describe that woman."

"How long have you known Lilliana?" Nyssa asked.

Pol smiled and narrowed his eyes. "Going on forty years. She hired me as protection when The Feather was just a five-room shack in the Shallows. She quickly saw the folly in thinking me a proper bodyguard and made me her accountant instead. Eventually, I became her advisor."

"So you know all her secrets," Nyssa ribbed.

"No, my dear lady. I quite think Lilliana knows everyone else's secrets."

Athen was always forthcoming about his mother's history. Lilliana had started as a brothel mistress and turned her workers into confidants, making sure they chatted up the men and women who visited her doorstep, learning their secrets. She leveraged those secrets to gain money and power, powerful enough to wrest control of the city from its five factions.

And she earned the factions' loyalties through her tireless defense of Ocean's Rest during the Mire War. The Thu'Dainian king, Teodor Rell, died by Lilliana's own hand, effectively ending the conflict. His armies limped back to their country under the command of their new queen, Suvi Rell, barely twenty-three at the time. That victory elevated Lilliana in the eyes of the city's factions, knowing that perhaps it was best to bow to her than continue their endless jockeying for position as the top dog.

"Ocean's Rest is so busy. How does Lilliana keep track of it all?" Nyssa asked.

"Men and women like Pol and Reece," Athen replied.

"And what of you?"

He shrugged and frowned. "I do my part."

"Lord Fennick is modest," Pol said. "He is not his mother yet, but he is learning."

Athen pointed at a building that bore the symbol of the Ellanholme guild, home to weavers of enchantments. "Some guilds are establishing a presence here. Ellanholme intends to open a storefront and offer all manner of enchantments to our citizens. Almost all goods—legal and illegal—pass through this city. Lots of money to be made, and the guilds want a taste."

"I thought the Empire kept its hands off Ocean's Rest?"

Pol spoke up. "Ocean's Rest is a delicate machine, one that needs a firm hand in control. The Empress understands Lilliana's value—the city doesn't function without her. We pay taxes and the business that runs through this city makes money for a great deal of people. So the Empress keeps her hands off. It is a symbiotic relationship, my lady. One that is lucrative for everyone."

"A complicated system, I imagine."

"Indeed. One that Athen will one day maintain."

Athen mumbled something under his breath, and Pol gave Nyssa a smile. "Lilliana is very much looking forward to seeing you again, Nyssa."

She nodded. She often forgot that Lilliana had already met her as a baby, a time she herself didn't remember. They rode the rest of the way to Ocean's Keep in silence, the massive stone structure rising above them as it looked out over the city.

OCEAN'S KEEP

Nyssa, Athen, and Pol approached Ocean's Keep, its high, white walls stark and imposing. Protective wards covered the stone, remnants of its time as the city's military stronghold. It had since been tamed and turned into a massive mansion looking down upon the city proper.

The broad gates of the Keep were open, revealing a large courtyard within and a gravel driveway lined with towering oak trees and tidy rows of bushes that led to the front door. A garden in the distance full of winter flowers and spruce bushes filled Nyssa's eyeline, the unmistakable smell of pine mixing with lavender and orchid.

Attendants spilled out of the doors to tend to the horses and bring Athen and Nyssa's bags inside. Pol gave a stiff bow and disappeared in the Keep.

"Athen, so glad you're back!" a woman called from the garden, walking toward them. Behind her, a man slid shiny squares of metal into a small black box sitting upon a tripod.

"I couldn't stay away," Athen replied.

"Ah, liar. Eron sent word of a change of plans," she said.

He laughed. "What's this?"

She glanced behind her. "Your mother bought a simulachrome to capture images of the Keep, the city, and our family. An affectation of the rich, but Lilliana wanted to splurge on something ridiculous."

The imageer behind the simulachrome bent to peer into its viewfinder and held up his hand. A moment later, a square of red energy burst out of it, and flowed through the flowers, plants, and trees before coming to a stop. The red magick hung in the air for a second, then retreated back to the simulachrome just as quickly as it shot out. The man stood up, pulled a paper-thin, square piece of metal out of the device, and examined it.

"It captures images of the physical world, right?" Nyssa asked. *Amazing.*

The woman gave Nyssa a big smile. "It does. An expensive little toy. You'll have to sit for a chromoimage portrait."

Athen smiled and put an arm around the woman. She was petite, at least six inches shorter than Nyssa, and only hitting Athen mid-chest.

"Nyssa, this is my oldest friend and sister, Reece Ae'Shen. She works for my mother. And Reece, this is—"

"Nyssa! Finally, I get to meet you!" Reece squirmed out from under Athen's arm and excitedly grasped Nyssa's extended hand in both of hers. Her grip was impressive.

"Let me get a proper look at you!" Reece ran her dark, piercing eyes up and down Nyssa, who stiffened under the scrutiny, becoming keenly aware of the meandering line of her nose, the scar down her face, and the road dust in her hair.

Reece ran a hand through her silver-white locks, moving them out of her face. She wore thin strands of cloth woven through her hair and her bulky cobalt sweater made her ivory skin stand out. Nyssa smirked at her rolled-up pants, one leg longer than the other, finished off by scuffed brown boots. Reece was undeniably attractive, a thought Nyssa tried to purge from her mind unsuccessfully. A smile crept up on Reece's face, her eyes not wavering from her own.

"I'm a bit of a mess from the journey," Nyssa said, shifting from foot to foot, feeling her spine pop.

"Nonsense," Reece said. "You look good. Rather good."

Is she flirting with me?

The back of Nyssa's neck grew hot. She did the flirting, not the other way around. Reece's smile only grew wider.

"I would like to freshen up if I could."

"Oh, we arranged a room in the family's wing when we heard you'd be coming. Across the hall from you, Athen." Reece turned to Nyssa once again. "I hope we can have tea together this evening, if you're up for it?"

"Certainly," Nyssa replied, trying to be polite. Reece's casual ease made her fidget, wondering what to do with her useless arms and hands.

"Your mother is out, Athen, but she will be here for dinner."

"Will you be joining us?" he asked her.

She shook her head. "No. I think it best the three of you catch up in private." Her eyes flicked over to Nyssa and back to Athen.

"Of course," Athen said, gesturing to the front door.

Tiny, elongated light orbs suspended in the ether to look like twinkling raindrops lit up the entryway, stealing Nyssa's breath. The room spilled into an open foyer, its bones made of stone but warmed up to feel like a home with furniture, tapestries, and eclectic art.

Everywhere Nyssa looked offered something new and interesting to marvel at. The Emerald Order was sparse and uniform in its design compared to the massive Keep.

Athen and Nyssa ascended the staircase to the upper levels of the Keep. A deep-red rug stretched down the long, wide hallway that led to the Fennick family wing.

Nyssa quickly glanced into the first room, its broad wooden doors flung wide. Massive and impossibly tall, the room contained shelves upon shelves of books, stacks of paper, and all manner of ephemera. A library! She smiled with excitement at the idea of spending some time rifling around in the books after they caught Quinn.

Athen came to a stop in front of a large door and waited for her to catch up with him, her mind still on the library. "This is your room. I'm across the hall."

He opened the door, and Nyssa pulled him across the threshold. She rounded on him, preparing to question what he had shared with Reece about her, but she stopped cold upon seeing her surroundings.

Calling it a room was underselling it. The expansive apartment dwarfed Nyssa's room at the Order. Bookcases lined the right wall, containing hundreds of books and bits of art with a broad, worn writing desk in the middle. Light orbs dotted the shelves to illuminate its contents.

Forget the library. She could lose herself for a year just with the books here.

The opposite wall had a massive bed covered by a fluffy, down-stuffed comforter with matching pillows piled on top. Couches, chairs, and tables filled the room and rugs crisscrossed the suite's stone floors—some looked ancient and threadbare, while others contained lush, vibrant colors.

The back wall of the suite featured a fireplace in the middle, flanked by expansive floor-to-ceiling windows and a set of doors that led out to a balcony that overlooked the city and the Areshi Ocean beyond. Nyssa eyed a little alcove in the far right corner of the room and poked her head in to explore. She found a spacious bathroom, wardrobe, and dressing area, tucked away and private.

"Shit," she whispered, taking it all in. The bed looked like a dream. She could lie in it and stare at the stars before drifting to sleep.

"Does it meet your approval?" Athen asked.

"I don't know what I expected, but it wasn't this." She walked over to a black leather chair and dropped into it. "I knew you were rich, but this is *rich* rich." She picked up a candle from the table next to her and sniffed, the scent of pine trees and warm, earthy cardamom and cinnamon filling her with warmth. Similar candles dotted the room, along with incense burners to welcome the coming of winter—the scent of sweet, spicy smoke a reminder of her favorite season. A delicate white vase containing fresh-cut winter-blooming flowers sat on a large table near the middle of the room. *Fancy*.

"I guess I'll have plenty to keep me busy while we wait for the Wayland adept and that damned book to get here so we can hunt for our fugitive," Nyssa said, gesturing at the full bookshelves.

"Impatient?"

"I just hate waiting knowing Quinn might still be in the city. I want to catch her. Prove I'm a true Ashcloak."

"Well, we don't have what we need yet to go after her, so settle in. When the tracker gets here and we get Quinn's book, we'll scoop her up," Athen replied.

"We should look for her now."

"Ah yes, a woman with dark brown hair and medium build should be easy to find in the crowds here for Winter's Fire."

Nyssa rolled her eyes. "The description Ceril sent along left much to be desired, I'll give you that. Hell, I'm surprised he even remembered her hair color. He doesn't seem like a man who takes an interest in anyone but himself."

Athen snorted and sat opposite Nyssa, a grin spreading across his face. That grin was waiting to say something. She arched an eyebrow at him. "Out with it."

"Reece seems to like you."

"Uh-huh."

"You don't know what to make of her, do you?" His smile widened.

Nyssa scowled. "I'm sure she's nice."

"Like I said, give people a chance. I think they'll learn to like you despite, you know, you."

Nyssa shook her head and laughed.

Athen's smile receded. "Reece is my only friend here, really. I have my mother and I guess Pol, but she's been my support here, especially after I returned home to take up my post. It was a hard adjustment, leaving you and the Order."

Looking down at her hands, Nyssa sighed. "And I never came here when you invited me..."

"I know being here isn't easy for you. I'm here for you. Always. And maybe get to know Reece? She's good people."

Nyssa stood up to stretch. "No promises," she fibbed, more than slightly curious about Reece. "But thank you. And about dinner later...your mother and I will undoubtedly have a long overdue conversation about my parents, and I'll need you there."

"I wouldn't be anywhere else."

"Now, I need a bath. Off to your room, Lord Fennick." Nyssa smiled and offered an exaggerated bow.

"Oh, fuck off with that," Athen groused.

THE DEMON'S WAIL

Nyssa stared in awe at the enormous Kraken relief above the fireplace, its black tentacles wound around a ship, dragging it below the surface of the sea. Small men and women dotted the deck, all destined to share the same fate. The angry blue eyes of the beast stared back at her, a storm raging above its head and bright azure lightning coiling around its tentacles. She twisted her ring, feeling the imprint of its own Kraken etched into its metal under her fingertips.

The relief, carved from a giant piece of wood and meticulously painted, made a stunning centerpiece. Nyssa turned around. She was early to dinner, and the attendant who had accompanied her had disappeared.

The room was daunting, large and cold, with a long table that could seat at least twenty people. Two thirty-foot tall, floor-to-ceiling windows flanked the fireplace at the back where Nyssa stood.

The space dwarfed her, and she felt a little underdressed for such formality. After her bath, she had explored the wardrobe and its collection of clothes, many close to her size. It must have been stocked for her. She chose a pair of black leather pants, a loose white shirt that she left open at the collar, and a tailored, scarlet jacket with gold accents. Fennick colors. The jacket complemented the deep-red tones in her hair. Nyssa put her own black boots back on—they fit her perfectly, no need to find something new.

Now, feeling small in the formal dining room, she wondered if a gown would have been more fitting for dinner. She turned back to the carved relief, narrowing her eyes to inspect the piece.

"An Ancient God dragging interlopers into the Realm of the Deep," a voice rang behind her, making her jump.

She turned, taking in a tall, well-built woman with black hair interlaced with streaks of gray that fell just to her shoulders. As she approached, Nyssa admired the long scarlet dress she wore, a pin of a lion affixed on her chest. The woman carried herself like aristocracy, holding her head high. Her presence was intimidating, her air of confidence coming off in waves.

"I seem to have startled you, Nyssa. I apologize. You don't remember me, surely, but I'm Lilliana."

Nyssa swiftly offered an awkward bow. "I am honored to meet you, Lady Fennick."

"Please, no need to bow. You are a treasured family friend." Lilliana stepped forward to take Nyssa's hand, her light-green eyes meeting Nyssa's. "It is so nice to see you again, finally. You have grown into quite a striking woman. I see the clothes Reece stocked for you fit rather well."

Nyssa's face grew warm, and she ran her hand self-consciously over her hair. She wondered if she should have taken her braids out for this occasion, fearing herself rough around the edges.

"Yes, my lady, they fit very well."

Lilliana looked at the relief above the fireplace. "This manor is a thousand or more years old. It's acquired much of its character as ownership of the Keep has changed. But this artwork here is as old as the bones of this place."

"What does it depict?" Nyssa asked.

"Narileh the Protector, Ancient God of the Realm of the Deep."

The Realms had long ago pulled away from the world, though Nyssa heard rumors of travelers accidentally stumbling into the Realm of Night along the dark fringes of haunted forests. Tales mostly told by drunks in Vane's taverns at the end of the night while they nursed their last drink.

"You think the Ancient Gods are still around?" Nyssa asked.

"They're ageless. I believe they're waiting, observing us, adjacent to our world. They're what you see out of the corner of your eye, just darting out of view."

"I wonder if they're lonely," Nyssa mused.

Lilliana peered over at her. "What an odd thought, gods being lonely. I think they're endlessly amused and horrified by what they see of our world."

The women regarded each other, the painful awkwardness of the moment hanging in the air as Lilliana looked Nyssa up and down. Nyssa tried to read her face, but it was impossible. Nothing leaked through her controlled expression.

Lilliana broke the silence. "So, what are your thoughts?"

Nyssa cleared her throat. "Thoughts, my lady?"

"The relief above the fireplace. Why do you suppose Narileh is destroying that ship and dooming its crew?"

"Oh. I'm afraid I know very little about the gods to know what her motives may be."

"Narileh is the Protector. She's said to be the guardian of truth and righteousness. Whatever that ship's crew did, those souls will sink to the deep, every last one of them drowning in her rage."

"Mother, your topic of conversation before we eat leaves a lot to be desired," Athen said, walking into the room. Nyssa let a breath out, grateful for the interruption.

"Sorry for eavesdropping." He bent over and gave Lilliana a kiss on the cheek. "I keep trying to convince my mother to have her victory over Teodor Rell painted to hang above this table so when Imperial officials dine here, it will remind them of why the Areshi Empire still stands."

"I daresay the Empire is far more impressed with the money it makes off the goods flowing in and out of this city than a thirty-year-old war best left in the past," Lilliana said. "Warriors don't get ahead in the world, powerful people do."

Athen sighed. "You mean bureaucrats."

Lilliana addressed Nyssa. "My son thinks I built our power and fortune on the death of a Rell king. Information and influence, that's true currency, which I used to tame this city. Along with spilling some blood."

"Mother."

"He doesn't like to be reminded of the uglier side of leadership."

"You and I just have different styles of leadership," Athen said, a strained smile on his face.

"That's a rather polite way of putting it. In time, my dear, you'll come to understand that a gentle hand gets bitten."

A moment of silence passed, and Nyssa fidgeted, tapping her fingers against her thigh as mother and son stared at one another. Athen cleared his throat. "Regardless, I still think you should commemorate your victory in the war. You saved this city from falling to Thu'Dain."

"The fantasy of battle and the reality are starkly different, Athen. You would have someone paint pure romantic drivel," Lilliana replied, waving dismissively. "War isn't heroics and myth. I watched my compatriots fall in battle only to be raised by forbidden magick and turned into wraiths by Teodor Rell and his spellweavers. Thankfully, a wraith hasn't darkened our shores in the thirty years since."

Lilliana offered Nyssa a thin smile. "Apologies for broaching such a grim topic."

"No worries," Nyssa politely said.

"Let's sit, shall we, and I'll have dinner brought in." Lilliana leaned over the head of the table and plucked up a small orb the size of a grape. She whispered into it, and the sphere lit up with a dim green glow, rose from her hand, and darted out the door.

She sat at the head of the table, with Athen and Nyssa flanking her on each side. Athen caught his mother up on their travels before the servants came in carrying enormous bowls of soup and a basket of freshly baked bread and poured large glasses of wine to start the meal.

The food that followed was robust with flavor—filleted fish basted in butter and fragrant herbs, its delicate white flesh sweet and delicious, paired with fresh marinated vegetables, smoky from the grill and served with a rich mushroom tart.

As they ate, Lilliana brought up the Emerald Order. She and Eron had been old friends for decades, and they fought alongside one another in the Mire War, defending Ocean's Rest.

"Eron sent word that you would be coming, Nyssa. I hear you and my son have an assignment for the Order."

Nyssa nodded. "Eron and First Master Anelos tasked us with capturing a runaway from the Citadel."

"Ah, Ceril Anelos. So much ambition in one man and nowhere for it to go."

"I don't wish to speak ill of him, but I get the impression he doesn't like me."

Lilliana picked up her wineglass and took a long drink. "Steer clear of him. He is more trouble than he's worth."

Nyssa nodded, finding comfort in Lilliana's advice. Ceril was a deeply unpleasant man, haughty and insulting.

Over dessert, the talk turned to the city's planned activities for Winter's Fire. Nyssa wasn't hopeful that she'd get to enjoy any of them with Quinn being her focus, but from what Lilliana described, Ocean's Rest put on quite the party.

After plates were cleared, Lilliana smiled and folded her hands in front of her. "Enough about city business. Nyssa, I know you have questions for me about your past, questions you've been waiting years to ask, and you have been very patient."

Nyssa put her wineglass down and cleared her throat. "Yes, I do," she said, dread creeping over her. "Is there anything you can tell me about my parents?"

Lilliana paused, her demeanor palpably changing. "I have been expecting this conversation for a long time, and I hope you understand why what I'm about to share was withheld from you until I could speak to you myself. I'm afraid this will be hard for you to hear."

Nyssa's stomach dropped.

"You're now a grown woman, and I think enough years have passed to disclose the truth. Two Thu'Dainian warships attacked your parents' ship, the Demon's Wail, and put it at the bottom of the sea."

Nyssa swallowed hard. "I...I don't understand. Why would Thu'Dainian ships attack them?"

"Nyssa, your parents were pirates. On the sea, that often means making dangerous enemies. Thu'Dainian warships daring to come into Areshi waters would mean that your mother and father made a powerful enemy of their queen, Suvi Rell. Perhaps they stole from her or broke a business arrangement? It was clear, she wanted them dead."

Nyssa glanced down at her hands, clutching the edges of the dining table, her knuckles white.

"Did Eron know?" she asked, her voice low.

"I told him when you turned twenty but asked him not to tell you. That was my burden," Lilliana replied.

"Why didn't you tell me before now?"

"Thu'Dainian warships in Areshi waters directly violates the Mire War Treatise. Telling anyone could have meant war."

Nyssa narrowed her eyes at Lilliana, fighting back tears. "So, you lied...you let me believe they had disappeared."

"A very necessary lie to keep a vulnerable nation from rushing headlong into another war and unraveling at the seams," Lilliana stated firmly.

Nyssa ran her hands through her hair. "All this time, I thought they could still be alive. That they abandoned me in this city and never saw fit to come back. I hated them for it. I thought they didn't want me. Do you know what that was like?"

Lilliana's face didn't change. "They *did* leave you, Nyssa. Doing so saved your life, but they left you with strangers and no word if they'd return. They suffered the fate of so many of their ilk."

"Their ilk?" Nyssa breathed.

"Criminals."

"Mother!" Athen hissed.

Nyssa pushed back from the table and stood on trembling legs. When she spoke, her voice was barely a whisper. "Excuse me, I need to get some air."

She turned from Lilliana, walked away from the table, and fled the dining room. Head swimming and heart pounding, she made it thirty feet down the darkened hall before she needed to lean against the wall to catch her breath. From within the dining room, Athen raised his voice, and it was quickly followed by a lower, calm murmuring from Lilliana.

Criminals.

They were pirates, of course they were criminals, but Nyssa didn't ever dwell on that detail for long, choosing to believe they were somehow...better than that label. All the books she had read, the adventures at sea, cast pirates as savvy and charismatic, though often reluctant, heroes. Her heart pounded in her chest, and she felt like she couldn't get enough air.

Criminals.

How stupid she had been, romanticizing her parents. She leaned her forehead against the cool, dark wood of the wall, thankful for its steadying presence. She heard footsteps behind her and turned, putting her back to the wall as Athen approached. She slid down and sat on the floor, her head hanging.

Athen slowly sat down beside her. "Nyssa, I'm so sorry. About my mother. About your parents. All of it." His voice was low and soft, a stark contrast from the anger she heard in the dining room moments prior.

She looked over at him. "You don't have to apologize. At least now I know the truth."

He leaned his head against the wall and stared up at the ceiling. "Now you have someone to blame."

For so many years, she'd tried to imagine what her parents might look like. Did she have Shana's eyes or Mikel's nose? She didn't even know their surnames. Eron told Nyssa that she was called Blacksea because stories had circulated of the pirate Shana giving birth to a daughter on the rough winter waters of the Black Sea.

"I've been filled with anger for so long. I've hated them for leaving me. But I thought maybe they were doing something...good out on the sea. Like the damn pirates in the books we read growing up. I'm such a fool."

"Nyssa, don't—"

A low sob escaped her throat. "They left me here alone. Then they were hunted down by Thu'Dain and killed. I'll never know if they intended to come back for me..." The reality of her parents' fate sank in like a dark shroud threatening to smother her. Her heart began to race, and her breathing quickened.

Athen put his hand on her knee, giving it a gentle squeeze. He wrapped his arms around her as she turned and collapsed into him, silently crying into his chest. She seldom gave in to tears. Only ever with him.

After a few minutes, Nyssa sat up and smoothed out her hair. She was twenty-five now and shouldn't be crying like she often did as a little girl in the darkness of her room, wondering what she did to make her parents leave her forever.

"Sorry about that," she said, wiping the tears from her cheeks with the back of a sleeve.

"Don't apologize."

"I hate feeling like this. Just...helpless. I can usually hit someone or something to feel in control."

"Promise me you will not go riding into Thu'Dain looking to put Suvi Rell's head on a pike," Athen joked, drawing a snort and a small smile out of Nyssa. "There's my girl."

She sat silent for a moment, the smile leaving her face. "I'm never going to know why they were murdered, am I?"

He looked down at his hands, rubbing his thumb on his palm.

"I'm sorry, I don't think you will. But in fifty years, if you decide to ride a warhorse into Thu'Dain, howling to the nine winds and intending to take your revenge, I'll be by your side. Likely arthritic and half blind," Athen chuckled, "but I'll be there to watch your back."

"Always my protector, huh?"

"Someone's got to look out for you."

Nyssa took his hand. "You are better than me, Athen. Any goodness I do is because of your example. You know I love you, right?"

He squeezed her hand. "Yes. Yes, I do." He glanced towards the dining hall. "Listen, I'm going to chastise my mother a bit more for being so blunt with you. I have to remind her that being a little softer can be a virtue. Head back to your room and take some time for yourself."

"Thank you, Athen."

He stood and smoothed out his clothes, then offered a hand to her, hauling her to her feet. "I'll send up a pot of tea. Go relax. Get some rest. The adept from Wayland will be here soon and then we'll get after Quinn. I'll need you focused."

"I promise I'll be ready." Nyssa stood on her tiptoes and gave him a soft kiss on his cheek. "Thank you."

He nodded at her and turned back to the dining room, passing through the shadows dancing in the hallway from the firelight within.

THE EMPATH

Nyssa flung a book across the room, letting out an angry roar. The book was a poor distraction, her thoughts and emotions tumbling around inside of her. Crying had proved to be a temporary bandage. The frustration of not understanding why her parents were dead burned bright. She wondered if Lilliana was right.

Had they gotten themselves killed?

A soft knock on the door startled her, and she hastily wiped her face as she walked to the door and opened it to find Reece carrying a small tray containing a teapot, a couple of mugs, and a plate of pastries.

"Athen asked the kitchen to send this up, but I intercepted on the way here."

Nyssa stared at her.

"Do you mind if I come in?" Not waiting for an answer, she gently pushed past Nyssa, leaving a light scent of lavender in her wake.

She placed the tray down on a table and turned, gaze attentive and piercing, despite the warmth of her smile. Reece looked effortless and beautiful, a light-blue dress hugging her curves, flowing freely to her knees.

Nyssa cleared her throat and crossed her arms. "I'm not good company tonight."

"I know." Reece sat on the bed. "I could feel you from across the Keep."

"Excuse me?" That Reece felt comfortable enough to sit on her bed annoyed Nyssa. She was too forward. Pushy.

"You're radiating pain and anger, and I could barely concentrate on my work with that energy coming off you."

Nyssa scowled. "I don't understand."

Reece offered a smile. "I'm an empath. I can sense the emotions of others, especially when they're strong. You're glowing like a sun, Nyssa. Usually, I can block people out, but tonight, it seems you're not to be ignored. You're so...bright. I've never experienced—"

"What do you want?" Nyssa growled.

Reece stood and walked over to her, holding her gaze. "I'm sorry, I don't mean to impose, but I can feel your pain, your chaos, and I want to help. We can talk about what's causing this storm within you."

She stared at Reece, speechless, stomach sinking. This woman could sense her pain, fear, anger—everything, including her attraction.

Nyssa instantly felt naked and defenseless.

Her shoulders went slack. "I don't want to talk," she whispered, dropping her eyes from Reece's. She exhaled a shaky breath, and a tear rolled down her cheek.

Dammit.

She balled her hands into fists, trying to will the tears away. The last thing she wanted was to fall apart in front of a stranger.

"We don't have to talk—"

"You need to leave," Nyssa breathed, barely able to speak without her voice cracking.

Reece scowled but nodded and let herself out. Nyssa sat on the edge of her bed, the air still lightly scented with lavender. Part of her wished she hadn't sent Reece away, but her magick was unnerving. She didn't know how to navigate a conversation with someone she couldn't hide her feelings from.

Eron had often warned Nyssa that keeping people at arm's length was untenable. She would have to change once beyond the walls of the Order.

He assured her she would figure out her place in the world. Find friends. Find a family.

She just didn't know *how*.

Flopping back on the bed with a sigh, she laced her fingers over her belly and stared at the ceiling. Her thoughts kept drifting back to Reece and what she'd said.

I could feel you from across the Keep.

Nyssa dropped her head, cursing under her breath.

Fuck!

She walked back to the center of the small courtyard for her fourth try at the Ninth Form of Ithais-Toru—the Sea Form. It was a lengthy exercise, slow and deliberate, one movement flowing into the next, and she kept losing her balance or moving through it too quickly, throwing off her timing.

She'd found an out-of-the-way courtyard to practice in while exploring the massive Keep. The enclosure was quiet and peaceful with a few trees swaying gently in the cold air of the afternoon, holding onto their very last leaves of autumn as if they could fend off winter. It was the perfect environment to distract herself for a time—or so she'd thought.

Her feelings from the previous night had crept back in as she considered her parents and their fate.

And then there was Reece. The woman's casual familiarity with Nyssa threw her off. She got angry at herself for letting the woman rattle her. Nyssa had read about empaths. Their magick was rare, and they could dive into someone's emotions and know them in ways a person couldn't even know themselves. That wasn't something Nyssa could fight.

The emotions swirling inside of her affected her concentration. She would need her focus to go after Quinn. What if Quinn proved far more wily than they expected? Or hurt one of them?

One mistake could cost Nyssa everything.

Nyssa shook out her arms and got into the Ninth Form's beginning stance again. The inability to get her body to obey frustrated her beyond measure—turning it into a precise weapon was the one thing she could always control. She rarely felt so disjointed, and her body exposing her inner chaos felt particularly cruel.

Slowing her breathing, Nyssa paused a moment before she moved. Almost immediately, she got out of rhythm and slid her foot too far in the opening movement.

"Fuck!" she yelled, voice echoing off the walls of the small courtyard. She hopped up and down, trying to loosen her muscles, but the problem was her mind. The capacity to concentrate eluded her. And it didn't help that the courtyard smelled of lavender.

Like her.

Nyssa groaned, angry at herself for being so easily distracted by just the scent of the empath.

Eron would be disappoi—

"This is painful to watch," a voice said, and Nyssa turned and followed it to an archway bordering the courtyard. Reece stepped out from the afternoon shadows.

"Are you stalking me?" Nyssa asked.

Reece seeing Nyssa in two vulnerable moments was galling.

"No, a message arrived for you, and I came to deliver it. You're burning bright once again. And I owe you an apology for last night. I can be a little too pushy."

Nyssa searched for a response, but Reece saved her by speaking again. "Athen has told me a lot about you. I know you're different," she said. Nyssa noticed how she avoided mentioning magick. "Says you're a superb fighter, though he's bested you enough—your nose a testament to that fact."

Nyssa self-consciously touched her nose. "Is it that bad?"

What am I doing?

"No, it makes your face more interesting. Tells a tale straight away without you having to utter a word."

The back of Nyssa's neck warmed, but strangely, she didn't feel judged.

Reece's smile reached her eyes, brilliant and dark. "You know, Athen and I have been close since childhood. I cried when he left for the Emerald Order. I was inconsolable. A grump for weeks. And a holy nightmare for Pol and Lilliana for a time. I'm surprised they didn't throw me into the harbor. I was overjoyed when he finally returned, but he's missed you."

Nyssa cleared her throat. She knew how Reece felt. Athen leaving the Order made her miserable for quite a while. "He tells me you manage The Feather?"

"Yes. You know what it is?"

Nyssa nodded.

"Are you going to ask me the question you're dying to ask?"

Nyssa grinned and crossed her arms. "I don't suppose there's a polite way to ask if you're a consort?"

Reece laughed. "No, there isn't, and no, I'm not. It's hard work, and I'm not suited to it. My magick pushes me in another direction. I counsel people—help them work through their thoughts and feelings. I take them into my confidence, and they pay me for it. Handsomely."

"And how much do I owe you?" Nyssa asked, cocking an eyebrow.

Reece frowned. "This isn't a job. You're not a client. I will never treat you like one." Her tone belied disappointment.

Nyssa stood silent, kicking herself for insulting the woman.

"I was hoping we could be friends," Reece explained, reaching forward to lightly touch Nyssa's arm. "I know you don't have many of those."

Nyssa pulled away. "Wow, really?"

"I didn't mean—" Reece let her hand fall to her side. "Look, you're important to Athen. And he's important to me. He told me you could be difficult, but you'll find I'm persistent."

"Yes, you are."

"Honestly, aside from Athen, I don't have many friends myself," she admitted, stepping back and crossing her arms. "It's hard for people to trust me. They always believe I'm prying into their feelings. They don't know how distracting it is to let my barriers drop, to let everyone just wash over me. It's..." Reece dropped her eyes from Nyssa's face.

An instant pang of pity resonated within Nyssa. She didn't consider how isolating Reece's magick might be for her. "I'm not exactly good with people."

"I suspect that's not entirely true," Reece replied, a twinge of a sly smile pulling at her lips. "Athen has told me stories."

Nyssa had to distract herself by looking at her hands, trying to ignore how her pulse quickened. She had never been this useless around anyone.

Reece cleared her throat. "Anyway, a message arrived for you. The adept from the Wayland Conservatory is arriving tomorrow at The Feather. I'll take you in the morning. I think you will enjoy seeing the business that made all of this possible," she said, gesturing toward the Keep.

Nyssa rocked back on her heels. "What about Athen?"

"He has city business to attend to and told me you'll be fine on your own. Is that not the case?"

Nyssa frowned. Reece seemed to enjoy poking at her. "Fine. I can handle meeting our tracker without him."

"Tomorrow morning, then. Early. Don't be late. I know you're not a morning person," Reece said before walking away.

It took Nyssa a good minute to compose herself. "That cheeky woman," she whispered to herself with a grin.

THE FEATHER

"Welcome to The Feather," Reece announced, exiting their rickshaw. The ride had been mostly silent, Nyssa watching the city pass by, doing her best to tamp down her emotions with Reece's eyes on her.

The doors of The Feather stood open with men and women coming and going freely. Several guards in finely tailored suits stood outside, swords and daggers at their hips. The building itself was wide and tall, painted a deep scarlet and made of carved stone and wood, images of birds and feather patterns throughout. A nod to the establishment's name. Its sign was tasteful, just a large, glowing white feather. Nothing else.

Nyssa smiled. A place like The Feather needed very little to entice visitors—everyone knew of the infamous entertainment house. People came to the city just for a spin around the place.

"This isn't the original Feather, of course," Reece remarked. "It started off small in a ratty house in the Shallows."

As Nyssa started to cross the street, Reece grabbed her arm and pulled her back as men and women on bicycles whipped past, expertly dodging pedestrians.

"Keep your head on a swivel, Nyssa. Ocean's Rest is incredibly busy this time of year."

She nodded, and they continued toward The Feather, the guards that had accompanied them from the Keep sticking close by. "You are well guarded."

"Lilliana insists. The façade of civility this city wears doesn't make it less dangerous, especially for those associated with the House Fennick. The old factions remain and some of them could hazard a shot against Lilliana."

"Could any of them actually succeed?"

"No. She would crush them." Reece pulled Nyssa aside before they entered The Feather. "Lady Fennick would do anything to protect this city and her family. And you are a part of that. You were the moment she made you her ward."

"Lilliana doesn't have to be responsible for me. I belong to the Emerald Order."

Reece frowned. "You belong to no one but yourself."

Nyssa narrowed her eyes. "Do you belong to yourself, Reece, or are you beholden to the woman who raised you?"

Reece scowled and took her time answering. "My mother was a consort and died giving birth to me. Lilliana took me in as her ward without thinking twice. She and Pol raised me, and yes, I feel obligated to repay their kindness, but I cast my own shadow."

Nyssa arched an eyebrow. Reece was quoting the philosophy of Sakei.

"Oi, layabout! Move your ass!" a man shouted.

Reece took Nyssa's arm and pulled her out of the way of a streetcar idling behind them, its driver eyeing her. The tram passed on its magick-powered track, crammed with people. A ruddy boy hanging on to the back, his arm wrapped around a stack of books, stuck his tongue out at Nyssa. She returned the favor, chuckling under her breath.

"Head on a swivel." Reece smiled and turned toward The Feather. "Come, let's go inside. I think you will be impressed."

As they entered The Feather, Nyssa's eyes darted around, trying to take in the spectacle. A long bar, occupied by patrons and bartenders, spanned the width of one wall, row upon row of bright bottles of liquor behind it. Exuberant gamblers smiled and shouted at the gaming tables at the end of the room. Nyssa's heart beat a little faster at the sound of chips clinking on the tables. She loved a good game of cards. *I'm here on business, not for gambling.*

Glass doors leading beyond the main room teased a restaurant, servers hustling between tables. Waitstaff hurried around the floor, delivering drinks and skewers of grilled meats and vegetables to patrons who were too engaged with their gambling to pull themselves away. The servers were all dressed smartly in sleek black suits with small lion head pins on their lapels. Reminders of House Fennick were everywhere. A number of men and women—all attractive and finely dressed—dotted the room.

"Wondering which ones are consorts?" Reece asked, drawing close. She looped her arm through Nyssa's, her touch warm, a heat that Nyssa could feel through her jacket. It was distracting.

"Some are on the floor, mingling. Many of our companions are by appointment only. We have a lot of repeat customers. But The Feather is not just about sex, as I've told you. As you can see, we have gaming tables—the high-stakes rooms are upstairs, if you want a private game with some very, *very* rich patrons—and we have suites for rent if anyone wishes to conduct meetings here. The Feather serves as neutral ground, offering safety and discretion. For all things legal...or not." Reece smiled. "We'll wait in my office for your tracker."

Nyssa trailed Reece through the lounge to the wide staircase, her eyes darting from person to person before settling on a man with a short beard and bright-green eyes. His tight pants and loose, unbuttoned shirt left little to the imagination. He smiled at Nyssa, and she couldn't help but smile back.

"Benedict is rather handsome. Let me know if you wish an introduction."

Nyssa set her jaw, refusing to humor the woman, but heat blushed her cheeks despite herself.

She followed Reece up two flights of stairs to her office, spacious and decorated with diverse pieces of art and furniture that didn't match. An ornate chair made of carved wood, its gold paint chipped and worn, sat opposite of a black leather couch, colorful pillows strewn about its surface. A low table was arranged between them, covered with books and a bowl full of bright glass beads that reminded Nyssa of her river rock collection back home.

Reece watched Nyssa intently. "What do you think?"

"It's...interesting. Is this who you are? A bunch of mismatched things?"

"I like what I like. I give no mind to if they all fit together aesthetically."

"My room at the Order is like this," Nyssa admitted, absentmindedly picking up a small sculpture from a nearby table. It depicted two women tangled together in the throes of passion. Nyssa cleared her throat and put the sculpture down, noting Reece's soft chuckle.

Reece moved over to the window and attended to the plants that lined the windowsill with a small watering can. She bent over and whispered to one of the shorter ones with wide green and blue leaves.

"Are you...talking to your plants?" Nyssa inquired, fighting back a smile.

"I was telling them who you are."

"And what did you say about me?"

Reece straightened, cocking her head. "You want to know, ask them yourself."

Nyssa laughed under her breath and strolled around the room, taking in the collection of art and books. "Before, when you said that you cast your own shadow, you were quoting Sakei."

"An admirable man," Reece replied. "The Emerald Order adopted his fighting techniques, but sadly left most of his philosophy by the wayside. A shame."

"You really have a problem with my guild, don't you?"

"The guilds have a sliding scale of merit. Tell me, do your Masters and peers make you feel valuable, or does your lack of magick color all of their decisions regarding you?"

Nyssa browsed Reece's bookcase, running her fingers over the soft leather spines of a collection of tomes, and ignored the question. Answering it would only result in anger. "So you manage everything here?"

"Honestly, aside from seeing my clients and the administrative tasks, this place runs itself."

"Sounds boring," Nyssa said. If Reece poked at her, she would poke back.

"That's rather presumptuous of you." Reece looked annoyed.

"Oh, you can criticize my guild but your work is off-limits?"

Reece stared at Nyssa before breaking into a smile. "You're sparring with me. Is this fun for you?"

"A little. Did I offend you?"

Reece pushed off the desk and approached her. "You'll have to work far harder than that to offend me," she replied, dark eyes unwavering.

Nyssa tried to ignore how her stomach tightened when the empath got closer. She wanted to believe Reece wasn't actively reading her emotions, discovering how intrigued she was. Not just intrigued—excited.

Three rapid knocks drew Reece's attention, allowing Nyssa to exhale.

"Come in."

A tall, lithe man sauntered through the door, his eyes darting about. His manicured, black beard and straight black hair, neatly tied at his nape, indicated a careful attention to personal appearance. His deep-emerald jacket adorned with intricate silver embroidery denoted money.

A shorter woman followed him, a smile growing on her face as she took in the contents of Reece's office.

Reece stepped forward. "Welcome to The Feather. I am Reece Ae'Shen, and this is Nyssa Blacksea of the Emerald Order."

"Master Vykas Devitt." The man's eyes lit upon Reece before narrowing on Nyssa.

Nyssa recognized the surname immediately. The Devitts were the royalty of Frosland, a sovereign nation within the Empire.

Vykas turned his attention from Reece to Nyssa, frowning. "Nyssa Blacksea. The adept with no magick—a failing that should disqualify you from even being in the Emerald Order, yet here you are. I'm not comfortable with your inclusion on this endeavor."

Arrogance wafted off of him like perfumed bath oils.

A familiar stirring of indignation roused in Nyssa's chest, and she clenched her jaw. "Your concern is noted. Shall I inform my First Master of your displeasure at my presence, or would you prefer to express that to him yourself when he arrives in Ocean's Rest?"

It suddenly struck Nyssa that she was speaking to the future King of Frosland and certainly not winning any favor. Vykas inhaled sharply before turning to the woman beside him. She nervously shifted from one foot to the other under Nyssa's inspection. She had the same warm-brown skin as Vykas, her straight black hair was pulled into a high ponytail, revealing the shaved sides of her head. Her pair of scuffed, black leather boots didn't seem to match her expensive-looking fur-lined coat and long, dark purple dress.

A bright smile crossed her face, and she stuck her hand out in the middle of their small gathering to no one in particular, announcing herself. "Aryis Devitt, very pleased to meet all of you." Her light-brown eyes darting between Nyssa and Reece.

Their tracker was royalty? Nyssa's stomach dropped. The last thing she wanted was to babysit a royal while chasing their fugitive.

Reece leaned forward, looking from one Devitt to the other. "Brother and sister, I gather?"

"Yes," Vykas replied. "Twelve years my junior. She has the tracking abilities for this assignment."

"Hello." Aryis grabbed Nyssa's hand and gave it a firm shake, introducing herself again. "Aryis Devitt."

"Yes, you are." Nyssa arched an eyebrow, her eye drawn to the small osprey brooch pinned on her cloak—the sigil of House Devitt.

Aryis grabbed Reece's hand and gave it a hearty shake. "You're the empath I've heard about! How fascinating. I would love to talk to you more about—"

Vykas cleared his throat. "A word alone, Blacksea?"

Nyssa followed him out into the hall, and he closed the door.

"Aryis is the daughter of the King of Frosland. You will treat her with respect and care. She is clever and, as you can see, eager, but she's also terribly naïve, and I would caution you against anything that would put her in danger."

"She will be fine with—"

He waved her off. "Her safety is your number one priority."

Nyssa crossed her arms. “No, capturing and returning the fugitive is our number one priority. Not babysitting your sister.”

“Watch your tongue. Do your best to remember she’s royalty.”

Vykas was quickly becoming one of Nyssa’s least favorite people, now neck and neck with First Master Anelos. His disrespect for her was galling.

“If you’re so protective of—what’s her name again?”

“Aryis,” Vykas hissed.

“Right. If you’re so protective of Aryis, why send her on this task?”

He offered a strained smile. “She volunteered. Rather insistently.”

Nyssa smiled back. “Well, I will do my best to keep her out of harm’s way, but as an adult, she will have to look after herself. Is she able to do that or will I need to hand-feed her to ensure she doesn’t starve to death?”

Vykas exhaled through his nose and brushed past Nyssa to reenter Reece’s office. Nyssa smirked. Standing her ground against men like Vykas had become a secret delight of hers.

The two of them rejoined Reece and Aryis, who were smiling and chatting, Reece no doubt making Aryis feel at ease.

“I have some business at our guild residence here in the city,” Vykas said to his sister, “but I will meet you at Ocean’s Keep this evening.”

She didn’t hesitate to give her brother a hug goodbye, which he awkwardly returned. “Mind yourself,” he said to her.

She pulled away and patted his cheek, which drew a wincing smile from him. “I will be fine. I have Ashcloaks to protect me and, of course, Splinter.” She turned to the others, gesturing toward the small dagger on her belt.

“Aryis, I’ve warned you about wearing a weapon,” Vykas scolded. “The other Wayland Masters would be—“

“A woman needs protection, Vykas. Don’t fret.” Aryis turned to Nyssa. “I see you wear a sword. What’s it called, Ashcloak Blacksea?”

Vykas interjected. “Blacksea is not an Ashcloak as yet.”

Nyssa opened her mouth, annoyed, and ignored Vykas. “I don’t call my weapon anything. It’s just a sword. You...named your dagger?”

Aryis shrugged. “It seemed impolite not to. You are a very fit woman.” She turned to Vykas. “I think I will be fine with her. She appears capable.”

Nyssa huffed and exchanged a look with Reece, who appeared amused. *This woman...*

Vykas cleared his throat. "I'll see you later, Sister," he said, before leaving Reece's office.

Aryis wandered about the room. She bent over to examine the same small sculpture that Nyssa had picked up earlier. Her eyes widened before she straightened, a smile on her face.

"I didn't know what to expect of The Feather, but it's rather delightful," she said. "A fascinating study of power brokering, a storied part of Lilliana's rise to the Regency. I should hope to have some time to chat with her, if that could be arranged."

Reece smiled. "Of course."

"I'm not so sure we'll have time for you to have tea and finger sandwiches with Lilliana," Nyssa remarked. "We have an adept to recover."

"Yes, we do. Has a personal item of this runaway been sent along yet?" Aryis asked, scanning the books on Reece's shelves.

"Not yet, but—"

"So, until then, I can't track her. I am just as eager as you to complete this assignment. Apologies for earlier, I just assumed that since you're twenty-five, you had already been made an Ashcloak."

Nyssa frowned. "How do you know how old I am?"

"I read a fair bit at the Conservatory. I'll read just about anything, including the rolls for the Emerald Order—we keep a copy of every guild's rolls. So, I looked you up. Nyssa Blacksea, parents unaccounted for, age twenty-five—happy belated birthday, by the way—and no identified magick," Aryis recited from memory. "Quite fascinating, really, you being the first and only member of any guild to ever be accepted without magick. I'm sure..."

Aryis trailed off as Nyssa's frown deepened.

"I'm sorry," she continued. "I don't judge you for not having magick."

Nyssa scowled. "Unlike your brother, you mean? I'm sure you will at some point. Everyone does."

"I assure you, I will not! The Order wouldn't have sent you if you weren't up for this task. I think you and I can learn a lot from each other while—"

"Could you cease chirping for a moment, Little Bird?" Nyssa asked, pinching the bridge of her nose.

Aryis looked about to reply when a knock on the office door interrupted her.

"Yes?" Reece called out.

An older man popped his head in. "Reece, we've got Obsidian Rule downstairs."

Nyssa turned to Reece, concerned. "Is this a problem?"

Reece shook her head and tugged on the bottom of her jacket. "No. They occasionally come here, like any other guildies. I just like to know when I have assassins and spies under my roof. I suppose I should go give them a little personal attention."

Nyssa stepped next to her. "I'll come with, just in case."

"Me too," Aryis piped up with a broad smile.

MEASURING UP

Reece walked through The Feather with Nyssa at her side and Aryis trailing behind, unsure if bringing Nyssa along was a good idea. She pulled her defenses up high, blocking out the emotions from her patrons so she could attend to the matter at hand. She didn't care for guild politics—the tenuous nature of guild alliances and their rivalries bored her—but potential conflicts concerned her. Athen had told her enough about Nyssa to know she wasn't one to back down from a fight, and Obsidian Rule adepts were arrogant and unpredictable.

Seeing how Nyssa would respond if provoked intrigued Reece—she had an affinity for troublemakers.

"Which ones are the consorts? Should I be able to tell by looking at them?" Aryis asked as they passed through the main lounge.

Annoyance simmered within Nyssa, making Reece smile when she sensed it. Even with her walls up, the woman's chaotic emotions poked through. Nyssa was going to have her hands full with Aryis—so eager and chatty in a way that made Nyssa delightfully uncomfortable.

Reece shouldn't revel in it but, damn, she couldn't help herself.

The Obsidian Rule adepts stood at the bar, obvious in their dark green leathers, daggers at their hips. The two of them, a man and a woman, turned to Reece as she approached. Their eyes darted to Nyssa, their attention no doubt drawn by her sword and the black leathers of the Emerald Order.

Dammit. This could be trouble. Reece dropped her walls, letting their emotions in. What she sensed confirmed her suspicions—these adepts were looking for a fight. Obsidian Rule were almost always prickly and troublesome, her least favorite guildies to deal with.

"Adepts, what a pleasure it is to have you here at The Feather. I'm Reece Ae'Shen. Whatever you need, or want, I'm at your disposal."

The man smiled at her and stepped forward to take her hand. "Reece, I've heard about you and your interesting abilities. I'm Tann Eld'on and this is Efla Eld'on." He gestured to the woman behind him with the matching black hair, dark eyes, and hawkish nose.

"Brother and sister, I take it?" Reece asked, her eyes shifting to the woman. Efla studied Nyssa's face intently, gaze unmoving.

Discomfort radiated off of Nyssa.

"By blood and by guild," Tann replied.

Reece nodded at them both. Efla looked a bit more put together than her brother, her long, black hair tied at the base of her neck. Tann's hair was unruly, falling well past his shoulders; his face unshaven for days.

"Brother and sister! How lovely. My brother and I are Wayland adepts," Aryis beamed.

Efla glanced at her with disdain. "Politicians and librarians who lack the talent to attend the Citadel. How dreary."

Aryis let out a soft gasp.

"And who is your Ashcloak escort?" Tann asked Reece, his eyes settling on Nyssa.

"Is the Emerald Order renting itself out as brothel security now?" Efla asked with a wolfish grin, dark eyes still boring into Nyssa. "Seems fitting for a lesser guild."

An intense, fiery anger spiked in Nyssa, and Reece swallowed. She reached out to sense Efla and Tann, not liking what she found.

Disdain.

Arrogance.

Aggression.

Nyssa hooked her thumbs under the sword belt across her chest, lightly tapping her index finger on the leather. "I'm here as a guest," she said, her voice steady, despite her anger.

Tann regarded her. "I hear the Order has a magickless adept. Is that true?"

Reece sensed Aryis was about to object. She put her hand on the young woman's arm and shook her head. Something was strange about Tann's question, his emotions not matching the curiosity behind his inquiry.

Nyssa chuckled. "Yes, unfortunately it's true. She's rather pitiful, though you didn't hear that from me."

Reece bit the inside of her cheek. Aryis gave Nyssa a curious glance.

Tann looked at his sister. "What's she like?"

Deception. He was lying. He knew perfectly well who Nyssa was. *What is he playing at?*

Nyssa stepped forward, a range of emotions radiating off of her.

Anger.

Pride.

Excitement.

An intoxicating and dangerous mix.

"She believes herself to be a good fighter, but she's hardly passable, in my opinion," Nyssa replied. "Far too cocky for her own good. Lovely head of hair, though, if I'm being honest. Long and curly, a bit of a reddish tint to it. But she has this hideous scar on her face. Very off-putting."

Aryis let out a small giggle before clamping a hand over her mouth.

Nyssa offered Tann her hand in greeting. "Nyssa Blacksea, the Order's magickless adept. I'll try not to hold your ignorance against you."

Tann stepped up to her, ignoring the offered hand. "I came here for a drink and a lay, not to be disrespected by the likes of you. You're not even an Ashcloak. It's only a matter of time before they kick you out."

Nyssa cocked an eyebrow at him, an impish half smile creeping onto her face. "A drink and a lay, huh? Well, I can't pour a decent beer to save my life, and I'm afraid you're a bit too unkempt for me to consider fucking." She turned her attention to Efla. "Now, your sister on the other hand, she at least looks clean."

Reece instinctively put her hand on Nyssa's arm when an explosion of Tann's anger slammed into her senses. He wanted to hurt Nyssa. Efla, too, burned with a simmering disdain. The situation could turn dangerous quicker than Reece could control.

One of her barmen signaled for security.

"I would really appreciate if this didn't turn bloody," she said with a strained smile. She especially didn't want Aryis caught up in a scuffle. She imagined Vykas would erupt if he got wind of his sister being anywhere near danger.

"Shall we take this outside?" Nyssa asked Tann. "No magick, no weapons. Just fists."

Tann smirked. "And no Justiciars if there are any hurt feelings or broken bones."

"Agreed."

Reece ground her teeth. "You two will not bloody each other on the street in front of my business like a pair of drunks. Back terrace. Now." She walked around Tann and gestured for them to follow her. A hallway behind the bar led out to a large courtyard surrounded by a high brick fence.

"We prefer to host private parties back here, but you can beat each other bloody if you prefer," she said. A handful of Feather guards followed them and fanned out, two of them flanking her.

"This will be the perfect place to teach you a lesson," Efla said to Nyssa. "Your blood will stain these stones."

Nyssa smirked before the brother and sister strolled to the middle of the courtyard. Tann stripped off his jacket and rolled his shoulders to warm up. Efla kept her eyes trained on Nyssa, studying her.

Waves of nervous excitement wafted off of Aryis, and Reece shut her out, turning to Nyssa. "Are you sure about this? Won't you get in trouble with Eron?"

Nyssa shrugged. "Eron's not here, is he?"

Aryis smiled. "I must say, this is all rather exciting. Does this happen here often? Oh, Nyssa, do mind yourself, though. Don't get hurt. We have a mission to complete."

Nyssa frowned down at the young woman, who took a cautious step back.

Reece let out a frustrated sigh. "Have you ever fought a Rule adept before?" The slight spike of doubt Reece sensed was all she needed to know. "Nyssa, have you fought anyone other than your guildmates?"

"Do bar fights count?" she asked with a grin. "Oh, and there was that one time at—"

Reece cut her off with an exasperated groan. "Nyssa, if you get hurt, Athen will absolutely kill me. And Lilliana is going to question my judgment no matter what happens."

Nyssa crossed her arms. "And if I win? A little faith, Reece."

"Tann will not pull any punches. I sense he wants to hurt you. And they faked ignorance before. They know exactly who you are."

"Of course they know who I am. The Rule makes every guild's adepts their business. No worries."

Reece frowned at Nyssa and shook her head, chest tightening with apprehension, even though Nyssa's confidence was wildly attractive.

"I said, no worries. Have a little faith, okay?" With a smirk, Nyssa patted Reece gently on the cheek before swinging her sword off her back. Aryis held her hands out excitedly, and Nyssa sighed, handing her weapon to Reece for safekeeping.

Nyssa bounced on her toes and rubbed her arms to keep warm, pushing her sleeves up over her elbows. She had shed her jacket, but the cotton shirt she wore underneath offered little protection against the wintry day. A mix of nerves and excitement jostled within her, and she kept her eyes on Tann and Efla while she warmed up.

Tann stretched out his arms and his sister stood to the side, watching Nyssa.

Reece stepped forward, her face beset by worry—a far cry from the cheerful mood earlier that morning.

"No magick or weapons, that was the agreement. I urge you all to honor your word. I won't hesitate to have my guards remove you," she said, walking back to the edge of the courtyard, crossing her arms.

Nyssa cracked her neck. "Are you done preening, Tann?"

He smirked. "You'll be easy."

"Let's dance, asshole." Nyssa stopped bouncing and let her arms and shoulders go slack, foregoing a fighting stance, looking as disinterested in him as possible.

A flicker of confusion crossed his face.

There it is.

He took the bait and advanced on her, but she backed away from him, twisting out of his path with a chuckle. He turned toward her and advanced again, throwing a jab at her head. She deflected his blow with a forearm and moved away again.

Nyssa grinned and bounced. "This is fun!"

"What are you playing at, girl? Stop running. Fight me!"

She shrugged. "You fight your way, and I fight mine."

Another flicker of anger crossed his face, and she smiled.

"Your way is cowardly."

"Rude," she grumbled. She found pleasure in taunting her opponents and watching their frustration grow. Every little advantage counted, a concept drilled into her at the Order. Words were weapons, sometimes more effective than a blade. It also didn't hurt that Tann was an arrogant prick and his irritation was delicious.

Nyssa relaxed and resumed her casual stance, shaking out her fingers numbed from the cold.

Tann closed the distance between them. As he threw a high punch, she ducked and crushed her knee into his ribs. He grunted and spun away from her, catching her jaw with a well-placed backfist.

Stars filled her vision, and she stumbled backward, shaking her head, trying to regain her composure. She spat blood on the ground and caught a worried glance from Reece. A calm exhale chased the stars out of her eyes.

"That was a passable backfist."

Tann smiled, though a twinge of pain on his face gave him away when he took a breath.

An injury to exploit.

"How are those ribs?" Nyssa asked.

Tann came at her again, glancing a hard elbow strike off her chin, but he left his torso vulnerable, and she buried a fist in his midsection. He stumbled away from her and put his hand to his side, his face grimacing in pain.

"And how are those ribs now?"

Nyssa lunged forward, catching Tann by surprise with her aggression, and feinted a punch to his stomach. Predictably, his arms snapped over his midsection to protect his injured ribs.

Almost too easy.

Rule adepts were assassins, not true fighters. Not like Nyssa.

She caught him with a vicious elbow to his temple, dropping him to the ground. His body tensed up for a moment, his eyes fluttering open after a few seconds, and Nyssa stepped back.

"Yield," she said, standing over him. She'd finish him off with a kick if she had to, but she was taught to offer mercy in a meaningless fight. He swept an arm at her leg, a weak effort, and she kicked it away. "Yield!"

Tann rolled over on his side with a groan. "I yield."

Nyssa exhaled, her whole body buzzing with energy and tension, the rush of winning creating its own exhilaration. A cocky smile, one she couldn't help, spread across her face, and she turned to Reece and Aryis.

Sharp, shocking pain seized her heart, ripping away the excitement of victory. She fell to her knees, clutching at her chest and crying out. Reece ran to her and sank to the ground, bracing her shoulders.

Nyssa grabbed her wrist. "I...can't...breathe," she choked, her heart beating wildly, like it was about to leap out of her chest. Every ragged breath she inhaled burned like acid.

Tann's hand was raised toward her, surrounded by a soft-green glow that extended up his arm.

"You're cheating!" Aryis yelled.

"Stop this! Stop this now!" Reece ordered.

After an excruciatingly long moment, the pain dissipated, and Nyssa fell forward. She balled her hands into fists and tried to stand.

Tann had earned himself an extra beating.

"Nyssa, no!" Reece hissed, pulling her back.

Efla stood Tann up, putting her arm around him for support. Nyssa was certain she bruised a couple of his ribs. She would have preferred to break them.

A cruel grin graced Efla's face. "You may be a good fighter but without magick, what are you really? Just another body made of flesh, easy to hurt."

"Get them out of here," Reece ordered, and her guards surrounded Tann and Efla. "You are not welcome back in this establishment."

"Enjoy your Winter's Fire," Tann snarled at Nyssa, voice dripping with sarcasm.

Aryis eyed the siblings as they walked away. "What a thoroughly unpleasant man." She turned to Nyssa, and her face lit up. "Nyssa, that was amazing! The fight, that is, not the cheating. Could you maybe teach me how—"

"Aryis, please." Reece shook her head before focusing on Nyssa. "You could have been seriously injured."

Nyssa sat back and exhaled, draping her arms over her knees. "I'm an Emerald Order warrior, Reece. I'm bound to get hurt at some point. A throwing knife from my weapon belt would have put an end to Tann's magick."

Distract the mage, disrupt the magick, just like Eron had taught her.

Despite her words, falling so easily to Tann's power was an unpleasant reminder that she wasn't like any other adepts. Even with tactics to use against magick, she was vulnerable.

She always would be.

Nyssa pushed those thoughts away.

I fought an Obsidian Rule and won. Athen will be pissed he didn't get to see it. He owes me a beer for this.

"I won," she murmured to herself with a smile, allowing herself a moment of pride. She felt Reece's eyes on her.

"You were...impressive," Reece said, her dark eyes not leaving Nyssa's face.

Nyssa's stomach tightened at the compliment.

"They could have hurt you," Athen chided. "Obsidian Rule plays dirty, and they baited you. You should have ignored them."

Reece, Aryis, and Nyssa sat in Lilliana's office, recounting the events at The Feather. Athen hadn't responded the way Nyssa expected.

She frowned up at him. "You should be proud of me."

"She was really rather formidable," Aryis added. Nyssa scowled at her, not needing the extra input. She was like a gnat buzzing about. A distraction.

"Everything the Rule does is for a reason. I've had run-ins with them myself, and it's best to avoid conflict," Athen said.

Nyssa scoffed. "I'm surprised to hear you advocate backing down from a fight, Ashcloak Fennick."

"There's not a fight to back down from if you never start one."

Lilliana sat expressionless at her desk, cutting Nyssa's reply off with a wave of her hand. "I can appreciate Athen's concern. The Obsidian Rule continues to push boundaries of late. Protecting this city sometimes means from the people who claim to be our allies."

Nyssa shrugged. "I did sort of provoke them."

"Eron warned me that your mouth often precedes your blade. But we use all the weapons we have at our disposal, Nyssa. You don't have to bow your head to those who would denigrate you. I never would have gotten anywhere if I was afraid to strike back when pushed. But my son is far more measured than I."

Nyssa looked at Athen, understanding he had to balance his willingness to bloody his knuckles with his responsibility as Lilliana's successor, but she didn't expect him to take issue with her standing up for herself.

"Reece, thank you for coming to me straight away. I'll discuss this with First Master Greye when he arrives tomorrow, Nyssa. I don't think he'll be angry, but I will smooth the way, just in case," Lilliana said, standing. "Now, if you all would give Nyssa and I a moment?"

Reece glanced at Nyssa before standing and following Athen, Aryis, and Pol out the door. Before it closed, Aryis asked Athen for a tour of the Keep. Nyssa smiled to herself.

Let Athen deal with the little bird for a while.

Lilliana sat back down. "I wanted to apologize for our exchange at dinner the other night. Athen has pointed out that I can be rather indelicate at times, and speaking that way about your parents was uncalled for."

"Thank you, Lady Fennick, but an apology isn't necessary."

"Sincerity requires effort, not just intention." Lilliana leaned back in her chair. "You came to us so young. I was six months pregnant with Athen. I asked Eron to raise you, but you were my ward first. You will always be my responsibility, Nyssa. I want you to remember that. Athen probably never told you this, but before he left for the Order, I asked him to find you at the guild and look after you. I thought you could protect each other."

Nyssa let out a quiet laugh. His persistence in watching over her suddenly made sense. She would have been mad, thinking Athen fake in his concern for her so long ago, if the boy wasn't so decent and earnest. His heart had changed little in fifteen years.

"That explains it. He was my shadow after he arrived, almost scared to lose sight of me. I guess I should thank you for that," Nyssa said. "If I may ask, do you know why Eron made me a part of the Emerald Order? He never gives me a straight answer. Certainly he had to know it would cause trouble for him. And for me."

Lilliana took her time before answering. "Eron knew with a baby coming, I'd have my hands full. And Reece—" Lilliana laughed. "Reece was, frankly, a pain in all of our asses. She was three years old at the time and couldn't stop herself from sensing the emotions of those around her. She would not cease talking about it either. Let me tell you, those were some trying years."

Nyssa smiled at the thought of Reece as a little girl, providing constant commentary on the inner workings of those around her. It sounded like a nightmare.

"Eron took you in, gave you an education, and trained you as a warrior. He never cared that you didn't have magick. Eron is not like the other First Masters—he's not like most people in our Empire. He believes the ideals and skills taught in the guilds shouldn't be available only to those with magick, and I've come around to his way of thinking over the years. Magick can't give you ambition or fearlessness or a steadfast heart. Plenty of magickless men and women fought by my side in the Mire War, facing down legions of wraiths, and they didn't back down. I daresay many of those who gave their lives to protect this city were worth ten Obsidian Rule assholes."

It was a surprise to hear such an admission come from Lady Fennick. Nyssa always had a healthy respect for her, mostly because of her reputation. She stood more as myth in Nyssa's mind than flesh and blood before meeting her.

Lilliana waved a hand. "Ah, ruminations of a retired warrior. You don't need to hear me drone on. Just know you are among family in this house. You will be off after your fugitive soon enough, so go enjoy your evening."

Nyssa strolled back to her room, her head swimming from her conversation with Lilliana. The woman's words made her buzz with confidence. She winced and rubbed the back of her neck, trying to work out a bit of stiffness.

"Fancy a drink?" Reece's voice drifted toward her as she leaned against the wall near Nyssa's room, casually flipping a dagger in her hand.

Nyssa grinned, a flutter of excitement sparking in her stomach. She drew close to Reece and stopped, watching the dagger flash when she tossed it up and caught it in one smooth motion.

"Where do you think this is going to lead?" Nyssa asked, no longer wanting to be evasive. She was too intrigued to play games, willing to set aside her fear of Reece's magick.

"I was hoping to your bed," Reece replied.

Nyssa hummed. "You're rather forward."

"I know what I want."

"Is that right?" Nyssa stepped toward Reece and grunted softly when the dagger pressed against her chest. She glanced down and smirked.

"I could barely breathe while watching you fight today," Reece whispered, her dark eyes dancing in the low light of the hallway.

Nyssa ignored the dagger and pushed Reece against the wall.

"Do you want to put that dagger away," Nyssa rasped, "or do I need to take it from you?"

Reece's gaze fell to her lips and back up to her eyes, a mischievous grin on the empath's face. "Are you trying to flirt with me?"

Tipping her head forward, Nyssa whispered into Reece's ear, "Oh, I'm far beyond flirting now."

She turned and grazed Reece's lips with her own, teasing a kiss before pulling away. Reece raised her eyebrows and tried to close the distance between them, but Nyssa forced her back against the wall. She studied Reece's face, enjoying the mix of frustration and desire.

Wanting to leave little doubt of her intentions for the evening, Nyssa slowly leaned in and gave Reece a deep kiss that was eagerly returned. The sweet taste of whiskey lingered on her lips, and Nyssa had to pull away to stop herself from going further right there in the hallway. Her pulse pounded in her ears as the smell of lavender clung to her. She stepped back and held her hand out.

Reece smiled and took Nyssa's hand, her eyes dark and dangerous. Nyssa led the empath back to her room, eager to spend the night exploring each other.

A FIRST

Reece watched Nyssa blink in the bright light, groaning as the morning sun streaming through the windows roused her. She savored the frown that crossed Nyssa's lips when she looked over and found her bed empty.

"I'm still here, grumpy," Reece said, leaning against the alcove entrance that led to the bathroom. "Get up, I drew you a bath."

Nyssa rubbed her eyes. "You stayed the whole night?"

"Yes. Your first time actually waking up next to someone?"

"Technically, I didn't wake up next to you. You were already up. And it's hard to sneak out of my own damn room."

"I hope my staying was okay." Reece was purposefully blocking out emotions, keeping her walls up high and strong, wanting a sincere moment untouched by her magick. It was hard, given the intensity of Nyssa's feelings.

Nyssa covered her eyes with her forearm to avoid the sun. And perhaps to avoid Reece's gaze. "I...I don't mind."

Reece smiled and carefully maneuvered her way across the room, trying not to step on Nyssa's discarded clothes, weapon belt, and sword. "Get up, lazy."

"It's early," Nyssa complained. "Are you...are you wearing my shirt?"

"Don't whine. Get your ass in the bath. I don't want to miss breakfast because you slept in." Despite the gruff tone she tried to put into her words, Reece found Nyssa's grumbling endearing.

Nyssa stood and stretched with a lazy yawn, and Reece put a hand on her shoulder, pushing her gently toward the bathroom. Once inside, she directed her to get into the bath.

"Are you getting in here with me?" Nyssa asked suggestively, sliding into the water and flashing Reece a cocky smirk. That damn smile was an invitation to trouble.

"I already bathed. The benefit of waking up early."

Reece pulled a jar of salts down from a shelf and walked back over to the tub. She bent over to give Nyssa a soft, slow kiss that lingered on her lips long after she pulled away. Kneeling next to the tub, she shook the salts into the hot water.

"Bath salts with verbena, lemon oil, and a little soothing enchantment to heal sore muscles and any aches from your fight...or from other strenuous activities," Reece teased, resting her arm on the edge of the bath.

She smiled and studied Nyssa's face as she laid back and relaxed. The silence grew between them before Reece spoke again. "Last night was unexpected."

Nyssa laughed and narrowed her eyes. "Unexpected? Really? You very clearly stated what you wanted, as I recall."

"Yes, but I thought you were going to keep dancing around me for a while before finally giving in to my charms."

"Bullshit. You and I both know I was attracted to you from the moment we met. I saw you smile when you sensed it. I was doomed from the start. You turned me into a blushing idiot."

"Blushing and breathtaking, I'd say," Reece countered, smiling at the color rising on Nyssa's cheeks. She wondered if anyone else got this response out of her, or if Nyssa was always the one in control. "Tell me, Blacksea, have you ever been in love?"

She raised her eyebrows. "That's a rather loaded question this early in the morning."

"It's not early, and if you don't feel comfortable answering, I understand."

Nyssa paused. "No, I haven't," she answered, her voice soft. "Why do you ask?"

Reece offered her a small smile and moved a strand of hair away from her face. "Just curious, I suppose."

"Please tell me this isn't leading to a declaration of love," Nyssa said, her tone cautious. "I knew letting someone spend the night was trouble."

"We are two people getting to know each other and having some fun while we do it. Nothing more. I'm not looking for a girlfriend."

Nyssa breathed deep. "It's just that...people have a habit of getting more attached to me than I am to them. I break hearts, I'm told."

Reece grinned and leaned in closer. "Oh, is that so? I'm sure you have stories." She was suddenly very curious and quickly licked her lips, noticing how the gesture drew Nyssa's eyes.

Nyssa chuckled, shaking her head. "Nothing too salacious."

"Give me an example."

Nyssa sat for a moment before speaking. "Well, there was this one time while I was doing a bit of gambling. I'm very good at cards, I'll have you know."

"Oh, are you?" Reece asked, raising an eyebrow.

Nyssa splashed water at her. "Yes, I am. How do you think I could afford a blade made of sun steel? The guild stipend is generous, but I have expensive taste."

"In swords."

"Yes. I also happen to like a good pair of boots and a jacket that holds up to the elements, but that's about it. I'm pretty easy past that."

Reece laughed. Nothing about Nyssa was easy. "The story?"

"So, I was in a card game in the back room of a bar, doing rather well. The bartender, Rikard, thought he could take me at cards. Bad idea. He got in over his head and couldn't cover my bet. Instead of pulling money back, I told him to put up his jacket. He did. And I took his money and his jacket off of him."

"Oh, really?"

"Things got heated when he refused to give me his jacket. And then they got...heated in a different way. Rikard had a little place above the bar. He was extremely handsome, and I was, well, extremely horny, so I didn't waste any time getting him into bed. I literally took the jacket off of him...and his shirt and pants. You get the picture," Nyssa said, winking. "He's one of the few men I've been with who was utterly obsessed with making sure I thoroughly enjoyed myself. He was very giving in bed." She sat back in the bath and sighed. "*Very* giving."

"I get it!" Reece laughed and slapped Nyssa's leg. "Wait, is that his jacket that you wear?"

Nyssa cleared her throat. "It's mine now, thank you. And it's one hell of a jacket. High-quality leather, good stitching, lots of secret pockets. And it's waterproof. Looks identical to guild leathers too."

Reece shook her head and exhaled. "You are...an interesting woman, Nyssa."

"I was a holy terror back then. Fearless. I went after whatever I wanted and whoever I wanted."

Reece got the impression that not much had changed. "What happened to Rikard?"

"He warranted a couple more visits, but I stopped that affair once his feelings became something more than what I wanted. Broke another heart, as I always do," Nyssa said, becoming a bit more somber.

"You can't reciprocate feelings that aren't there, Nyssa."

She met Reece's gaze and held it. "I don't know what to do about feelings, it seems. I just run."

Reece studied Nyssa's face and reached out to sense her emotions.

Sadness.

Uncertainty.

"Nyssa, if you're worried I'll fall in love with you, don't be. I'm a grown woman who doesn't mistake good sex for love. And I don't fall in love quickly or easily either. My record with partners isn't...great. It's wonderful feeling people fall in love with you, but devastating when you feel them slowly fall *out* of love."

Reece cleared her throat, putting the thought behind her. She considered her words before continuing. "I don't think you run from love, Nyssa. Athen is proof of that. I think you run when you can't give people what they want. But you'll find someone one day who asks nothing of you that you aren't willing to freely give. Someone who it hurts *not* to love." Reece's voice caught, and she swallowed hard, looking away for a moment. "I believe you would burn the world down for love, Nyssa. You have that in you. I feel it. And it's almost overwhelming."

Nyssa didn't respond. Did it scare her to see herself through someone else's eyes, especially those of an empath? There was no hiding emotions from Reece, a fact that kept a great deal of people at a polite distance.

"Now," Reece said, standing, "you need to scrub up and get dressed. First Master Greye will be here this afternoon, and I suspect you'll be after your poor runaway soon."

"Good." An intense spark of excitement from Nyssa washed over Reece.

"I'll gather your clothes and have them cleaned. You'll find fresh ones in the closet, which I look forward to removing from you tonight."

Before Nyssa could respond, Reece winked and exited the bathroom, shutting the door behind her, then leaning against it to catch her breath. She had to be careful with Nyssa's emotions. They were bright and loud and sharp. The previous night, she'd lowered her guard and let Nyssa wash over her. It was intoxicating to feel such raw desire, and Nyssa's emotions tumbled into Reece until she couldn't feel the edges that separated the two of them.

Her whole body had vibrated in tandem with Nyssa.

Reece knew it was dangerous to get so entwined. She had been warned of diving too deep into another person's feelings. Maintaining a strict boundary—a safe distance between herself and others—was imperative, reaching out instead of letting others in.

But it was hard to keep Nyssa out. And Reece feared she might lose herself again.

THE LITTLE BIRD

Aryis woke up excited for a new day with new possibilities. Vykas caught up with her after breakfast, frustration evident on his face, while she looked around the Keep for Athen and Nyssa.

"I heard about the run-in with the Obsidian Rule. I'm to understand Nyssa provoked them?" Vykas asked, taking a scolding tone of voice that she had come to hate.

"It wasn't like that, they—"

"I don't want you on this assignment. It isn't safe." Vykas crossed his arms.

Aryis's stomach dropped with disappointment, but there was something roiling underneath—anger. "You don't get to give me orders. I want to experience a little of the world before I'm shipped off to Cardin."

"I will not see you hurt. This mission is a frivolous distraction."

Aryis glowered at her brother. "Enough," she said, injecting a little bass into her voice, surprising herself. "Nyssa and Athen need me, and the Empress is watching. I will not let anyone down."

Vykas sighed. "You are the only sibling I have left. I...worry about you."

"Your concern is understandable, but I want to do this."

"I worry because I love you, Sister."

"I know," Aryis replied, "but trust me on this, okay?"

She left Vykas and continued her search for Athen and Nyssa, poking her head in countless rooms and courtyards before finding them in one of the Keep's interior courtyards. She took a seat on a stone bench, watching them spar, fascinated by the way they moved. It was as if they were dancing with one another. Strikes met blocks, counterstrikes landed infrequently. Athen was regimented and precise, his stance well-practiced. Nyssa appeared lackadaisical waiting for Athen to attack, much like the previous day when fighting Tann.

But as soon as she began moving, Aryis could not peel her eyes away. Nyssa wasted no movement. There was something instinctual and primal in the way the woman fought, her martial art ingrained into her body through years of training. An intense desire to learn a small fraction of what Athen and Nyssa could do burned within Aryis.

Her life at the Wayland Conservatory was rote and predictable, much of her time spent researching and writing papers on subjects that interested her, particularly the nature of ethereal and corporeal magick. An associate advisor post waited for her in Cardin—considered a prestigious position. She knew it was temporary until the Empress was comfortable moving her up. Years of studying under the Empress stretched before her, and she wanted to experience as much life as she could away from her guild before buckling down.

This assignment was Aryis's chance.

Hunting down another adept wasn't exactly in her wheelhouse, but her magick lent itself well to this mission, and she was eager to prove herself as more than just a scholar. Aryis just hoped they wouldn't have to hurt Quinn. She seemed an intriguing woman, her magick fascinating in and of itself, but what was the motivation for running from her guild? Aryis was brimming with questions for this runaway and couldn't wait to have a moment with her. And not just to study her and her magick, but maybe to make a friend?

Over the years, books proved to be far greater companions than Aryis's peers. Those connected to the Great Houses looked down on her, and those of middling or lower Houses thought her arrogant. There was no winning any of them over, so Aryis didn't socialize with the other adepts and made a promise to herself that once outside the confines of the Conservatory's walls, she would endeavor to make at least one friend.

Already she was meeting new people. Wonderful and frustrating new people.

Unexpectedly, Athen was warm and welcoming and not at all what she thought she'd find in such a large, imposing man. In his tour of the Keep the previous night, he was kind to her in a way that made her feel seen—a welcome change to being invisible at the Conservatory. It didn't hurt that he was rather lovely to look at and made her blush when he laughed. She cringed a little, remembering that she'd barely let him answer a question before she asked another one. He had been patient with her and, upon reflection, she wondered if she came on too strong.

On the other hand, Nyssa was fearless and cocky, though cold to Aryis. Aryis admired Nyssa's confidence, but she struggled to decide if it bordered on arrogance. The Order adept seemed rather annoyed by Aryis in the little time they had interacted. But Aryis was determined to be patient with Nyssa. She lacked female friends, and Vykas was a poor substitute for a confidant. It was time to get out from under his protective glare.

She desperately wanted to understand how to make friends.

Athen and Nyssa had an easy rapport. Studying them would help her better fit in, of that she was certain.

So, she watched and waited for her moment.

Nyssa dodged Athen's strike, sidestepping and throwing a punch into his kidney. She hopped back on the balls of her feet and laughed, shaking out her hand and flexing her fingers. "Anyone else would be on the ground moaning, but I'm the one with the sore hand."

"I sort of felt that, I guess?" Athen smiled. He raised his arms above his head and stretched with a yawn. "You're angry at me, aren't you?"

"Your criticism about me fighting Rule adepts was condescending, as if I didn't know what I was doing. I'm not a kid anymore, and I can take care of bullies on my own now. That's all those assholes turned out to be."

Athen put his hands on his hips and frowned. "Nyssa, I didn't mean to—"

"This is what I trained for, Athen. You can't protect me or chide me for standing up for myself," she said. It was odd having him on the opposite side of her the previous night. They were always of one mind back at the Order.

Things were proving different away from the guild.

Athen slowly nodded. "You're right. But you know I'm always going to have an eye out for you. We have each other's backs. Always."

"Always. I love you for looking out for me, but it's an old habit that you need to break. Give me some room to figure things out for myself outside of the guild."

"I get it."

Nyssa put her hands on her hips and stared at him, popping one eyebrow to drive her doubt home.

Athen sighed. "I get it!" he repeated with a smile. Nyssa punched him lightly in the stomach, and he rolled his eyes.

Her eyes shifted over to a bench in the corner where Aryis Devitt sat watching them. "She's an odd one."

Athen shrugged. "She's just enthusiastic. Intensely curious."

Nyssa looked at him and smirked. "Also rather attractive."

"Really? I hadn't noticed."

She chuckled. Did he really think she'd fall for that? "Lies! I take it you two got to know each other while you showed her around the Keep last night?"

"Hardly. She wouldn't stop asking questions about the Keep, my mother, me being half Koja, the city...she wants to know everything. Everything, Nyssa."

She grunted softly. "We'll have to keep a close eye on her. The last thing I need is to get a Devitt scion hurt on a mission for the Empress. I'll have a Justiciar's blade at my neck."

"Aryis may be inexperienced, but she's smart."

"She doesn't have a post outside the Conservatory yet. Don't you find that odd?" Nyssa asked.

Sudden movement next to her made her flinch. Aryis appeared at her elbow. "Wayland doesn't kick us out the minute we turn twenty-two," she said. "I want to feel like I earned my post in Cardin, not have it handed to me because of my last name. I imagine you feel much the same way."

Nyssa took a step toward her. "I have the surname of an orphan. Nothing will ever be handed to me."

Aryis held her hands up. "I meant nothing by it, just that you strike me as a woman who takes pride in earning your rewards."

"I'll let you know when I actually get rewarded for anything," Nyssa mumbled, and Athen raised an eyebrow at her.

"Would it be possible for you to teach me how to wield a blade?" Aryis pointed to the dagger on her belt, smiling.

Nyssa shook her head. "Absolutely not. We are not here to tutor you on the art of fighting. Do you even have one clue how to use this?" She yanked the dagger out of its sheath, testing its heft and balance in her hand.

Aryis put up her hand. "If you could just be careful with Splinter, it's a good—"

"Your dagger is shit," Nyssa remarked.

Aryis huffed, offended. "It is a finely crafted weapon, perfect for a woman of my stature."

Nyssa flipped the dagger over and caught it by the blade, then drew her arm back and let the dagger fly. It hit a tree across the courtyard with a *thunk* before it shattered, clattering to the ground in pieces.

Nyssa held her hand out in the tree's direction. "Your dagger is shit."

Aryis deflated.

Athen grimaced. "Oh gods, please tell us that wasn't a family heirloom."

Aryis shook her head. "I got it from the Conservatory armory. They said it was one of their finest blades."

"Well, at least you named it appropriately." Nyssa smirked, drawing a frustrated grunt out of Aryis.

"We will find something sturdy and suitable for you in the armory, I promise," Athen said, and Aryis perked up at the offer.

Nyssa considered Aryis with a scowl. "You should go inside. There are any number of rooms in this place where you could lose yourself with a thick book and a pot of tea."

Aryis put her hands on her hips and squared up to Nyssa. "There are endless books at Wayland. If I wanted to sit and read, I would have stayed home."

"And why didn't you?" Nyssa asked. "You're hardly qualified to run down a fugitive."

"Have *you* ever run down a fugitive?" Aryis countered.

Nyssa spied Athen fighting a smile.

"No, but that's not the point—"

"Then you don't have experience either," Aryis said, her self-satisfied grin further irritating Nyssa.

"And if this runaway gets the jump on you? Are you even physically capable of holding your own?"

Aryis frowned. "I'm very fit and—"

Nyssa quickly stepped toward Aryis, grabbing the front of her jacket and sweeping the legs out from under her. Aryis let out a surprised yelp as she started falling, but Nyssa's grip stopped her from hitting the ground. Her muscles groaned with the extra strain, but she yanked Aryis back up onto her feet. "We're going to end up babysitting you."

An excited smile burst onto Aryis's face. "Not if you teach me how to do that! Show me how to fight. You're pretty strong, by the way."

Nyssa glared at the woman. "You have got to be kidding—"

"Ashcloak Fennick!" One of the Keep's attendants jogged toward them. "First Master Greye has arrived and wishes to see the three of you in your mother's office."

Nyssa let go of Aryis. "Good. The sooner we find Quinn, the sooner I'm free of you."

"You are exceptionally rude," Aryis replied. "But I'm willing to overlook your behavior if you would teach me a little of your martial art to aid me—"

Nyssa walked away, eager to see Eron and leave Aryis for Athen to contend with.

Eron sat at Lilliana's desk, his hand on a small book in front of him, when they entered the office. Nyssa was rather happy to see her father again, even after a short absence.

Aryis burst with excitement, shaking Eron's hand. "It's an honor to meet you, First Master. I've often dreamed of visiting the Emerald Order, to see the grounds and experience what it's like to be in a place that produces such fine warriors."

Nyssa fought back an eye-roll.

"It's good to meet you too, Miss Devitt. I hold a great deal of respect for your father," he replied. "Now, I understand you need a personal item that belongs to the escapee. First Master Anelos sent this from Arcton Citadel. Are you a spellweaver?"

"No, my magick is corporeal, not ethereal, though I have memorized quite a few spells and enchantments. Don't know why, though, I can't cast them. Studying all forms of magick is one of my great loves. But as to my own abilities, I'm able to find people through their personal objects. I can also summon books I've read to myself. I call it blinking. It's a bit confusing for my Masters. They don't know if it's two manifestations of one type of magick or—"

"Aryis, will the book do?" Eron interrupted, drawing a smirk out of Nyssa. He held the book up, and Aryis took it.

She stepped back and cradled the book in one hand, hovering her other over it. She flexed her fingers and closed her eyes. The book began to glow red, and a small tendril extended out of it, turning toward the big window behind Lilliana's desk overlooking the city. Aryis opened her eyes. The tendril dissipated, and the glow around the book receded.

"Oh yes, the book will do nicely. I sense she's close. Still in the city, in fact."

Eron turned in his chair to the wide window and looked out over Ocean's Rest, the sky painted in the oranges and reds of dusk. "It's the first night of Winter's Fire. It's riskier to chase after her with so many people about celebrating, but we must seize the opportunity," he said before looking back at the three adepts.

Nyssa grinned, rocking on her heels and tapping her fingers against her thighs.

So close.

Maybe she would get to celebrate Winter's Fire after all once they had Quinn in custody.

Eron stood. "Get a quick dinner and then get dressed. Nyssa, find something appropriate for Aryis to wear—something she can run in if needed. Dress her like...well...you."

Nyssa frowned and Aryis bounced a little on the balls of her feet, her excitement palpable. Like a damn puppy.

"And perhaps a dagger from the armory that doesn't shatter upon looking at it?" Aryis asked, glancing up at Athen. He smiled down at her and nodded.

Nyssa rolled her eyes. This time she couldn't fight it.

"Take Reece with you. Lilliana wants her along to smooth over any issues with the locals," Eron instructed.

"I can do that," Athen objected.

"You are an Emerald Order Ashcloak on an Imperial mission tonight, not Lilliana's son. Any other time, I would ask you to balance both responsibilities, but I need you focused on capturing Quinn."

Athen nodded.

"Go. Find her."

As the trio headed out of the office, Nyssa pulled Quinn's book out of Aryis's hands—a collection of poetry called *Songs of the Sea*. She flipped through it. Page after page was full of charcoal sketches—in the margins, on blank pages, anywhere there was room for a drawing. Trees, flowers, faceless figures, animals, hands—it seemed their fugitive was a bit of an artist. And not a bad one, at that.

"We can take the underground passageway on your balcony down to the city. It'll get us there quicker without drawing attention," Athen said to Nyssa.

She stopped in her tracks. "There's a secret passageway on my damn balcony?"

He grinned at her. "Of course there is."

WINTER'S FIRE

"Ho there! Big man! I bet you can drink your share of ale! Come spend the first night of Winter's Fire at The Masthead," a barker shouted at Athen as the foursome walked up to the alehouse. "First tapping of Lessek's Spiced Ale, straight from their brewery in the Ashen Mountains! Exclusive to our humble establishment!"

Reece peered beyond the open doors of The Masthead. There was a good crowd inside, the Winter's Fire celebration in full swing. Aryis had led them here, where they spotted a lone figure in a dark, hooded cloak before she disappeared inside.

Reece wasn't too happy about capturing an adept in one of her favorite bars, but guild business trumped local concerns. She sighed and concentrated on keeping her walls up. There were far too many people, and their emotions would be crushing and overwhelming if she didn't block them out.

The surrounding streets teemed with revelers and merchants hawking their wares. Glowing lines, arrows, and words littered the ground, running in all directions—magickal advertisements to draw customers to the bars, music halls, eateries, and shops. When Aryis had sent out her tendril of her magick, she smartly used the ground to mask the glowing red ribbon—it looked like just another neon trail leading to a nearby business.

The scent of grilled meats, spun sugar, and baked pies hung in the night air. Normally, Reece would love to wander about and buy some Winter's Fire sweets or crafted jewelry, but celebrating would have to wait for another night.

"Let's go," Nyssa said.

The trio followed her into The Masthead. The alehouse was lively and inviting with fires lit in several fireplaces throughout the large tavern to keep the patrons warm and happy. Bartenders boisterously shouted over one another, each insisting they pulled a better mug of ale, vying for tips. A loud mix of conversation and laughter filled the place, and servers hurried about with steins of frothy ale. A spit full of chickens roasted behind the bar while a woman cut hunks of the meat onto pieces of flat bread and slathered it with a creamy white sauce for hungry patrons.

Nyssa held a hand in the air to flag down a server.

"What are you doing?" Aryis asked.

"We're the only ones in here without a drink in our hands. Let's at least blend in," Nyssa explained before she caught a server's attention and ordered four mugs of Lessek's Spiced Ale.

Athen nodded and put his arm around Aryis, but his attention was over Nyssa's shoulder. "I have eyes on her. She's headed out back."

"She's trapped, then," Reece said, sad for the woman. Quinn didn't know what was about to happen to her. "The rear courtyard is bounded by a high wall. The only way out is back through the building."

Nyssa laughed and smiled at her. "You're thinking like an Order adept."

Athen engaged Aryis in a conversation, his eyes scanning the room as he chatted her up. Nyssa insisted they be cautious. Wait and watch. None of them wanted bystanders hurt. That Quinn didn't have ranged magick was a small blessing. Only her touch was dangerous.

Reece put her arm through Nyssa's and pulled her close. She couldn't ignore the spike in Nyssa's delight at her touch. She was almost impossible to block out. Before they'd left the Keep, she let Nyssa's emotions wash over her—a nervous excitement that vibrated across her body. It was still so odd, the intensity of her mere presence.

"I don't understand the need to capture this adept. She ran away for a reason. Perhaps you should let her stay gone?"

"You start in on this now, when we're trying to catch her?" Nyssa scowled at her. "You really dislike the guilds."

"Do you know what the Empire would have done with someone like me? Stuck me in Ambershine and forced me to don a Justiciar's mask. Lilliana protected me from that, refused to let the seekers near me. I can understand why some adepts choose to flee. Choose to be *free*."

"My guild trained me and gave me purpose."

Reece shook her head and smiled sadly. "You should give yourself purpose, Nyssa."

She sighed. "I'm not like Athen. I have no family, no magick, and despite that, the Order gave me a home, an education, the promise of a future. I owe the guild a great debt."

Despite having her walls up to block emotions out, Nyssa peeked through, and Reece sensed something different in her: a seed of doubt. "I know what the Order did to you, Nyssa. I know they allowed your peers to torment you."

Her mood grew somber. "I grew stronger because of it."

"No. The *darker* parts of you grew stronger. Your anger and distrust flourished."

Nyssa offered no reply. Reece had reopened old wounds.

When the server brought four mugs of ale their way, Nyssa dropped a couple gold marks in his hand, more than enough for the drinks and a generous tip. He smiled at her and wished them all a happy Winter's Fire.

"C'mon," Nyssa said after taking a sip of the ale, "let's get closer."

The three of them followed her out to the large courtyard. High brick walls enclosed the whole area, with strings of light orbs crisscrossing above their heads, their soft-yellow glow brightening the night. Reece and the others wove their way around groups of people, many nodding and wishing them a happy Winter's Fire. Tables and chairs filled the space, most already full.

Braziers and fire pits provided warmth to ward off the winter chill, and musicians with guitars, violins, and a large string bass started up a song on a small stage to their right. A cheer of approval rose from the patrons.

Nyssa found a table for them, and they crowded around as she leaned in. "Back corner."

Reece took a quick glance, drinking some of her spiced ale topped with creamy foam carrying the aroma of cloves, cinnamon, and a hint of pine. She almost moaned at how good it was this year, enjoying the taste before the night took its turn to official guild business. Their fugitive was sitting alone along the back wall, a drink in her hand, the hood of her cloak hiding her face.

"Are you sure?" Reece asked.

"Everyone else is having a good time. Drinking and laughing. Dancing. She's off in a corner, like she's hiding. And she should be. Why is she here?"

"It's the first night of Winter's Fire. Everyone is out celebrating. Arcton Citadel is tucked far away at the top of a mountain. I daresay she's never seen a Winter's Fire like this," Aryis said, taking a curious sip of her ale.

"I'd be careful with that," Athen warned.

She ignored him and kept drinking before lowering her stein. "My father sends cases of Frosland whiskey to the Conservatory, and it tastes like burned campfire wood dipped in molasses. This is water compared to that. I can handle my drink, Athen."

He grinned, nodding with approval.

Reece didn't need to sense his emotions to know he was smitten with the young woman. He was so damn obvious.

"How long are we going to wait?" Aryis asked.

"Give it a few minutes. I'm curious to see if she's meeting someone," Nyssa said. She looked at Aryis. "What if we not only get our runaway, but an accomplice? That would be quite the accolade, right?" She put an arm around her and pulled her close, smiling and clinking their mugs together. "Listen to my instructions and follow my lead, okay?"

"Okay."

A booming voice came from the direction of the stage.

"Friends of Ocean's Rest! Patrons of The Masthead! I beg your indulgence for a moment."

They turned their attention toward the stage where a large man with deep-brown skin addressed the crowd. He was sharply dressed, wearing a dark, tailored suit and a large, leather coat lined with fur. He looked around the crowd and made eye contact with many of the patrons, drawing their attention to him.

Aryis gasped. "Is that Aleister D'orn?"

"Yes, it is," Reece replied. "Are you familiar with his work?"

Aryis turned toward her, eyes wide. "He's one of my favorite writers. I can't believe he's here!"

"I'll make introductions later. He's a friend of the family."

Aryis beamed back at Reece, who couldn't help but love the young woman's enthusiasm. She also couldn't ignore the spike of excitement coming from Nyssa at the poet.

So, Aryis isn't the only fan.

She smiled at the new information.

Aleister spoke again. "I am pleased to join you here in Ocean's Rest for the first night of Winter's Fire. This is the night we are reminded of our renewal through the biting winds of winter, the ice and snow fortifying our spirit and our will. We gather here to send our desires into the night sky."

On his cue, the tavern workers began moving through the audience to hand out small, red lanterns and fire sticks to everyone.

Athen leaned into the middle of the table. "We should get Quinn now."

A melancholic smile passed over Nyssa's lips while she kept her eyes on their fugitive. "No. Let her light a lantern. Let's give her that."

When all the patrons had lanterns in hand, Aleister continued.

"Before we whisper our hopes into the lanterns' flames and release them, let us remember the winters past and dream of winters to come.

> *"Winter's Children, float into the belly of the sky,*
> *The stars lay in wait, your wishes whispered into their flick-*

ering eyes.
The will of deep winter beckons, breathed to life e'ery year,
Each flame consumed and honored, your songs lingering in the night.
Each wish, suspended in air, silent and fragile.

Ancient beings groan under the frost, their magicks stir, their song calls,
Its lilting melody echoing across the ice of the Unending Lake.
Outstretched arms wait for us as we tumble and fall,
Fate brings to bear what we deeply desire,
A slumber unbroken.

Stirred at long last by a lover's whisper,
Awaken and see what you have become."

Aleister paused for a moment, letting the silence linger. "Now, speak your wishes into the flames and let them fly."

WINTER'S BLOOD

Nyssa dipped her fire stick into their table candle and lit her lantern. The lantern would carry the flame—and her wish—up to the heart of the winter sky and into the belly of the stars.

She glanced at Reece before whispering into her flame, her first Winter's Fire wish that she could remember that didn't include Athen or Eron. "Grant her happiness, always."

Murmured secrets filled the courtyard before solemn silence swept through. After a few moments, the Winter's Fire celebrants began lifting their lanterns, releasing them into the cloudless night, the glowing red flames breathtaking against the sea of stars.

Nyssa leveled her eyes back at their fugitive. Quinn's head tilted upward, watching the lanterns. They could catch her by surprise, capture her easily if they were swift and careful.

Nyssa turned back to the other three. "Reece, stay here. I'll take center; Athen, go left; Aryis, go right. Cut her off from an escape. Watch her hands. Keep them away from your face, it's the only skin you have exposed."

Aryis straightened and readjusted the dagger on her belt, eyes trained on Quinn.

"Aryis, don't be so conspicuous. Stop looking at her," Nyssa scolded.

"Well, how am I supposed to keep my eyes on her if I can't look at her?"

"What did I say about following my—"

Quinn bolted.

Aryis darted to intercept her, both moving fast. Her initiative was impressive, until Quinn crashed into her with a fist that sent them both tumbling to the ground.

Shit-shit-shit-shit-shit!

The one person they couldn't let get hurt was facedown in the middle of the courtyard.

Quinn scrambled to her feet and turned to run. Nyssa followed, closing the distance and catching hold of Quinn's dark cloak. Quinn spun around, and Nyssa surged forward, holding her fast. They sprawled against a table, knocking drinks over.

"Hey! Take your fight outside!" a patron yelled as people scrambled aside to avoid the women.

Angry green eyes peered from under her shadowed hood as Quinn struggled against Nyssa's grasp.

A high-pitched drone filled the air, and Quinn's eyes turned up to the sky. Nyssa followed her gaze. Dark shapes danced between the glowing red flames of the lanterns.

Nyssa squinted, trying to focus.

The shapes drew closer, the drone getting louder and louder—a chorus of unearthly voices shrieking in the night sky. Drawing nearer, the dark figures began to take form.

White-hot fear ignited in Nyssa's gut.

She looked down at the fugitive again. Quinn's green eyes were no longer filled with anger, but sheer panic.

"Wraiths!" Nyssa yelled, one hand still wrapped in Quinn's cloak. She swiveled her head, finding Athen and the other two women. Reece was ghostly white, arm wrapped around Aryis, and she locked eyes with Nyssa.

"Run!"

An explosion of screams erupted, and a large body crashed into Nyssa. She and Quinn tumbled violently to the ground, her abdomen on fire, drawing a strangled cry from her throat. Seconds passed as her mind struggled through the pain. She slowly turned onto her stomach and gulped in air, fighting to breathe.

A blur of feet ran past her. Screams and shrieks filled the air.

She clawed her way toward Quinn, but it was like crawling through mud. Her fingers wrapped around the edge of Quinn's cloak before a hand grabbed her shoulder and savagely yanked her up from behind, forcing her to let go of the other woman.

Stumbling, Nyssa twisted around to shake the hand off her, coming face-to-face with a wraith. It opened its mouth. Red-stained fangs snapped at her as the creature shrieked in her face, the stench of rot burning her nostrils. She gagged and tried to step away, but the wraith grabbed her shoulder with a gnarled claw and pulled her toward its mouth.

Nyssa drew her sword and pushed the blade into the creature's abdomen, shoving upward as hard as she could. The wraith released her and let loose an unearthly, blood-curdling scream before it stumbled backward and fell at her feet.

She stared at the dead creature's once-human form. Milky white orbs with no pupils stared back at her, unblinking. Dark, leathery wings rose out of its back, and ragged clothes still adorned its body, charred flesh peeking through the cloth.

She shook her head and winced at the pain in her side. The beast had likely cracked one or two ribs when it tackled her from the sky. She turned to find Quinn scrambling to her feet, stumbling away from her.

"Quinn, stop!" Nyssa tried taking a step toward her but sank to a knee, her legs failing her. "Stop," she ordered again, her voice weak.

Quinn stared down at her, hesitating for a moment before turning and disappearing into the chaos surrounding them. Men and women screamed as the beasts howled and tore into any live flesh around them. Beating wings filled the air as more wraiths continued to crash into the crowd.

Bodies swirled around Nyssa and jostled into her, making it hard for her to get her bearings. A wraith near her sunk its teeth into the neck of an older man, tearing his head half off his body. Blood gurgled from his mouth, and his eyes, wide with shock and horror, went still. The wraith tossed the dead man off to the side and set its gaze on Nyssa.

Legs trembling, she stood and tried to brace for the creature's attack, putting her sword between herself and the wraith. Before it set upon her, a large plank of wood crashed into its head, caving it in.

The wraith crumpled at her feet.

Athen stood behind it with his makeshift weapon before quickly moving to Nyssa's side and grabbing her arm. She was still trying to make sense of the surrounding scene. As he dragged her along, her legs steadied underneath her, her head cleared. Men and women pushed against them, trying to get into the alehouse. Athen led Nyssa to the back of the courtyard, tripping over bodies and discarded tankards, ale mixing with blood as screams continued to fill the air.

When Nyssa saw Reece and Aryis hugging the back wall of the courtyard, she let out a hiss of relief. Blood matted part of Reece's silver hair and streaked down her face. Nyssa started toward her, and Reece reached out to grab her.

"Are you alright?" Nyssa asked. "You're bleeding."

"It's not mine," Reece assured her. "You're hurt."

Nyssa gingerly pressed a hand to her ribs and grimaced. "Bruised ribs." She turned her attention to Aryis, whose eyes were wide with terror. Nyssa pulled out of Reece's grasp and put a hand on the young woman's shoulder to get her attention.

"You're going to be okay," she said, hoping it wasn't a lie and that they wouldn't die out here tonight, their blood spilled by undead monsters.

Aryis stared at her. Nyssa turned her attention back to the chaos surrounding them. The courtyard was clearing out—the crowd pushing toward the alehouse, though wraiths were following, picking off stragglers and advancing on the back of the group.

"Shit," Nyssa said. Many more people would die as they panicked and pushed to get away from the wraiths. She grabbed Athen's arm. "We need to help them."

He nodded and turned to Reece and Aryis. "Draw your daggers and stay here."

Nyssa took off running to the alehouse, grunting from the shooting pain clawing at her ribs, with Athen close behind her. She shouted to get the wraiths' attention, hoping to distract them and give people time to escape.

A black blur of motion caught Nyssa's attention. She spun, whipping her sword around, its bite meeting a wraith's neck, its momentum slicing through its spine. The body dropped in front of them with a flutter of wings, and its head rolled ten feet past.

Nyssa and Athen continued their advance, yelling at the wraiths. The dark figures turned in their direction, white eyes staring them down. Athen lunged forward and swung his wooden plank, splintering it on the skull of one of the creatures. He continued to barrel ahead, swinging his fists, mowing wraiths down with sheer strength. Nyssa plunged her sword into the chest of one monster while avoiding the claws of another.

The wraiths kept coming, and Nyssa kept downing them, slicing through the air and through their fetid flesh, falling back on the instincts etched into her body through years of training.

A scream from behind made her blood run cold.

Nyssa turned to see a wraith with its hands around Reece's throat.

"Help her!" Athen shouted and moved to put himself between Nyssa and the dark creatures.

She turned to go back to Reece but tripped over a body, falling hard. Dead eyes stared at her.

The ground was littered with death, far more humans than wraiths.

She pushed to her feet, her stomach lurching, and spun back to Reece, stumbling forward. Before she could reach her, the wraith dropped her at its feet before turning toward Nyssa, a dagger's hilt stuck under its chin. Aryis fell backward and scrambled away, blood splattered on her wide-eyed face.

Good girl!

Aryis turned on her side and expelled the contents of her stomach. Nyssa dropped to the ground next to Reece.

"I'm okay," the empath sputtered, grabbing on to her.

Nyssa stood, yanking Reece to her feet before turning to Aryis, who stared at the body of the wraith she'd killed. "Aryis, get up," she commanded, her voice stern and calm.

Aryis blinked at her.

"Get. Up," Nyssa repeated, her breath ragged. She spat out blood, ribs on fire.

Aryis nodded and stood, trembling, blood streaming down her face from a cut on her forehead.

"We're going to be okay," Nyssa said, trying to reassure her, despite the fear clawing at her gut. She turned to find Athen still fighting, knee-deep in bodies, slow and hunched over, but still standing. He was extremely strong and tough, but not immune to exhaustion.

Nyssa grabbed Reece's shoulder. "Watch each other's backs. I need to help Ath—"

A sharp shriek filled the air.

A dark figure dropped to the ground, straightening and turning to the three women. Nyssa raised her eyes to the massive creature, her mouth going dry.

This wraith wasn't like the others.

It towered over them, eyes red instead of white. Two horns protruded out of its forehead, one broken and jagged.

The monster opened its maw and roared at Nyssa.

"Stay behind me," she yelled at Reece and Aryis, moving to put herself between the two and the massive creature. It stalked toward her with a sick, menacing grin. She braced for its attack, her sword at the ready.

The wraith twitched and rushed at Nyssa in a blur of inhuman speed. It picked her up off her feet and barreled through Aryis and Reece, slamming her into the brick wall behind them.

Her ribs gave way with a sickening snap, forcing a cry of agony past her lips. The wraith pinned her to the brick, high off the ground, its forearm against her throat, crushing her windpipe. She weakly clawed at the creature, desperate to breathe. Her hands went numb, feeling detached from her body. Even her fear was a dull thrum in her gut, as if it were at the end of a long, dark tunnel.

Distant shouts pierced her awareness.

Feet pounded on the stone.

Nyssa's body jerked once then fell.

She crumpled to the ground, barely holding on to consciousness.

Get up.

Get. Up.

The world grew closer. Louder. Her eyes began to focus.

She pushed herself against the brick wall. Reece lay unconscious on the ground next to her, and Nyssa dug her fingers into the woman's cloak to shake her, but she didn't have the strength. Aryis stood in front of Nyssa, clutching her sun steel sword in both hands. Beyond her, the enormous wraith fought Athen.

Nyssa watched helplessly as the wraith picked Athen up by his neck and slammed him onto a table, shattering it under the blow. Athen's shout of pain twisted Nyssa's gut. His magick made him hard to injure, but it wasn't impossible.

The wraith turned its head toward Aryis. Athen swiped at the wraith's leg, but it brushed him off, unfazed.

Nyssa sucked in air. *Please let him survive this. Please let them all survive this. This is my Winter's Fire wish. Let them survive this. Please...please...*

The wraith moved toward Aryis, who held her ground, despite facing certain death. Nyssa braced herself against the wall and forced herself to stand. She stumbled toward Aryis, her legs somehow still working, and grabbed her by the cloak, pulling her back. Aryis gasped.

"Run, Aryis," Nyssa said, her voice barely audible. She struggled to move or think through her pain, but she didn't want Aryis to die. She stepped in front of the young woman, shielding her from the massive wraith, trying to force her back. "Run!" she rasped.

The wraith slowly stalked toward Nyssa. She met it with her fists, but the creature shrugged off her punches and kicked her in the chest, sending her flying backward into the wall. She dropped to her knees, doubling over in pain and coughing blood.

Bone ground against bone. She was broken and bleeding inside.

Nyssa raised her head to face her death as the wraith stalked toward her once more.

It bent over and curled a massive claw around her throat, lifting her off her feet. The wraith smiled its terrible smile, its sharp teeth strangely bright white. It held her up and reached inside the rags it wore as clothes, brandishing a dagger. Mouth open, it drew the weapon across its tongue, bloodying the blade.

With a snarl on its lips, the wraith drove the dagger deep into Nyssa's left shoulder.

Hot, agonizing pain ripped through her. She let out a cry that pierced the night sky. Nyssa reached up and grasped the wraith's forearm, desperately trying to stop the dagger from going in further. She gritted her teeth as the creature's forearm tensed and rotated, twisting the knife into her shoulder. Another cry ripped out of her throat, met by a low rumbling laugh from the wraith. Its eyes stared into hers, as if savoring her agony, and it smiled at her, tendrils of blood dripping from the corners of its mouth.

Her head swam with anguish and fear.

Please let them survive this...

Nyssa's hands slipped from their hold, the edges of her vision growing dark, and her head lolled forward.

Someone screamed her name.

She was falling.

Overhead, Nyssa heard a loud rustle of cloth as an icy wind braced her.

The sails are unfurling. I'm at sea again.

THE MORNING AFTER

Nyssa groaned and opened her eyes, her brain struggling to wake.

Alive?

The thought churned, lethargic, in her mind as she became aware of a hand on her forearm.

"Nyssa?"

She turned her head. Athen. There was a healing bruise on his cheek and dark circles under his eyes, but he was alive. Blunt happiness flooded her heart. "Reece? Aryis?" Her voice was a gravelly whisper.

"Alive and on the mend. You got the worst of it."

Nyssa exhaled, relief washing over her. She tried to sit up, but sharp pain stabbed her side, making her wince. She reached down and gingerly touched her heavily wrapped ribs. Her left shoulder, its throbbing pain dull and distant, was heavily wrapped in bandages, restricting her movement. Her wounds had been stitched up, and a familiar energy of healing magick buzzed through her body, still doing its work.

"The healers had their job cut out for them," Athen said. "But my mother employs the best."

"Where are we?"

"The Keep's infirmary."

A white curtain rippled, surrounding her bed and the chair Athen sat in, flecks of purple magick catching Nyssa's eye. It wasn't her first time in an infirmary, a frequent visitor to the healers at the Order. The curtain deadened sound, giving the illusion of privacy, but she saw the shadows of figures moving outside of their small area.

The healers had dressed her in a sleeveless white cotton shirt and loose cotton pants that were cinched at the waist with a simple tie. Nyssa was thankful for the airy coolness of the clothes against her skin.

Athen helped her sit up and slide back against the pillows before he poured her a mug of warm tea and held it to her lips. She took a few sips, then cleared her throat. "Are the wraiths all dead? Where did they come from?"

"Those still alive took to the skies. We don't know where they came from."

Nyssa laid back against the pillows and breathed deep, wincing at her protesting ribs.

"Your shoulder was torn up, your ribs were broken, and you had internal bleeding, but the healers got to your injuries before they became..." Athen cleared his throat and swallowed. "You will be sore for a while."

He reached over to a table next to the bed and picked up a small, dark bottle, handing it to her. "Drink all of this. It will take the edge off the pain."

Nyssa did as she was told, downing the concoction in one go. She winced at the bitter apple taste.

Athen spoke in a hush. "You almost died, Nyssa."

"How am I still alive?" she asked as her pain slid away and her body grew warmer. She closed her eyes.

"Aryis. She stuck that damn thing with your sword, and it fled into the night sky with whatever wraiths remained."

Nyssa opened her eyes and laughed, groaning from the immediate sharp ache in her side. "Aryis saved me? Where is she?" She looked around. "How did we get back here?"

"The city's guards commandeered a tram." The expression on Athen's face grew serious. "Aryis and Reece were here, but they got called up to

Lilliana's office to answer for last night. Vykas is spitting fire because his sister was in danger."

"Shit."

"That's the least of it, Nyssa. The entire city is on high alert. There's a curfew enacted, not that anyone is leaving their homes. Every guard is on duty. The Empress is sending a delegation to find out what happened last night, including a Justiciar. Thu'Dain used wraiths in the Mire War. This has to be them. Only the Rells still practice such magicks."

Forbidden magick.

Nyssa slowly swung her legs over the side of the bed, and Athen clucked his tongue in protest.

"Help me to Lilliana's office," she groaned.

"You need to rest," he chided. "I swear, if you die on me because you got out of bed too quickly, I'll kill you."

Nyssa laughed and grunted in pain. "I can rest after Vykas yells at me."

"I can't talk you out of this, can I?"

She pursed her lips and shook her head.

Athen sighed, then put his arm around her and helped her to her feet. "Okay, but we're taking it slow."

"You're the boss."

"Then why are you telling me what to do?"

"Because you're a smart boss?" Nyssa paused for a moment, a lump rising in her throat. She leaned against him. "Athen, I was terrified you were going to die. I'm so happy you're okay."

"We got lucky," he murmured. "Please don't almost die on me again."

Athen pushed open the curtain and sound and light flooded in, the infirmary busy. Healers and attendants hurried about, tending to the injured from the previous night. In the corner stood a small group of men and women, their faces painted black and white to resemble skulls.

"Who are they?" Nyssa asked.

"Obscuras faction. They tend to the dead."

The eyes of the Obscuras cohort followed them as they left the infirmary and walked out into the hall, unnerving Nyssa. Athen took it slow, keeping an arm around her as support. The Keep was alive with activity, guards armed to the teeth. Upon seeing Nyssa and Athen, people became quiet and moved out of their way.

"Why is everyone acting strange around us?" Nyssa asked.

"The story of what happened last night has spread quickly. Aleister D'orn survived and is here, safe in the Keep. He had quite the tale to tell. We've got a bit of a heroic reputation now, it seems."

"Don't tell Aryis that. She'll likely explode into a billion happy little stars if she thinks her favorite poet is lauding her," Nyssa grumbled.

"Oh, it's too late."

As Nyssa and Athen drew closer to Lilliana's study the muffle of angry voices grew louder. The room fell silent when they entered. Vykas was there with Lilliana, Pol, Eron, Reece, and Aryis. Reece leaned against Lilliana's desk, arms crossed. Aryis had a light-red scar on her forehead. They looked tired, but they were safe. Perhaps Nyssa's desperate Winter's Fire plea had worked.

Vykas pointed a finger at her. "*She's* responsible for this. I told her to keep my sister safe!"

"Nyssa saved my life," Aryis protested. "She put herself between me and those wraiths. She told me to run, but I didn't listen."

"I don't care!" Vykas yelled. He crossed the room to come face-to-face with Nyssa. "Aryis is of royal blood and should be protected at all costs."

Aryis rushed forward and tugged at his arm. "I'm not a child. I don't need protecting."

Nyssa met his angry gaze. "Your sister showed courage in the face of death last night. You dishonor her by treating her like a helpless girl."

Vykas put his face inches from Nyssa's, snarling, "She is the scion of a family that traces its roots back to before this Empire existed. She's not some plaything brought here to amuse you."

"Stop yelling at me if you want to keep that pretty nose of yours intact," Nyssa warned, her voice low. Aryis let out a sharp breath. His yelling was making Nyssa's head hurt. The warmth of the pain-killing liquid was wearing off, replaced by a heat that felt akin to a fever.

Vykas took several steps back, eyes wide, mouth opening and closing like a fish out of water. He looked idiotic, but at least he was no longer talking.

Eron intervened. "Nyssa conducted herself as we taught her at the Order. You will treat her with respect, Master Vykas."

Nyssa waved off the royal. "Quinn. Where is Quinn?"

"Not among the bodies at The Masthead. Right now, she's not our priority," Lilliana said.

Nyssa frowned. "She's my priority. We have to get her."

"I understand your urgency, Nyssa, but you need to rest. We have her book. Aryis can find her again," Eron said.

Nyssa swallowed, a lump in her throat. "Athen, can you get me something to drink?"

Athen left her side, heading toward the tea set on Lilliana's desk.

"There is a delegation headed here from Cardin to investigate this attack," Lilliana said. "Everyone will need to be available to answer their questions."

"Quinn," Nyssa rasped. "When can we go after her? I need to..."

A cold sweat sprang up on her skin, and her vision blurred as her shoulder exploded in white-hot fire.

THE BLOOD CRAWLS

Cups shattered on the floor, making Aryis jump. Reece fell onto the desk and cried out in pain, clutching her shoulder.

Athen grabbed her. "Reece! What's wrong?"

Reece grunted and shook her head. "Not me," she hissed through her teeth. "Nyssa!"

"My...my shoulder, it..." Nyssa fell to her knees, eyes rolled back, and her head sunk to her chest.

"Nyssa!" Aryis cried out, scrambling to stop her from falling forward.

Athen was quick to their side, picking Nyssa up and laying her on the couch. Aryis knelt next to her. The bandage on Nyssa's shoulder turned dark with blood, and black tendrils snaked out from under it, like lightning arcing out from the wound, across her shoulder, up her neck, and down her arm.

I've seen that mark before...

"Poison," Vykas said, and looked at his sister.

Pol was already at the doors, ordering guards to bring the master healer.

Aryis chewed on her thumbnail and muttered to herself, leaning forward to study the creeping poison trails under Nyssa's skin. Recognition tugged at the edges of her brain. For the first time, she cursed being so well-read. There was too much information to sort through; too much to remember and access at a moment's notice.

When the master healer arrived with a satchel of medicines, Aryis moved from Nyssa's side to make room for him. The healer held his hand to Nyssa's chest and examined her shoulder. "Ashweed poisoning, most likely. It lays dormant for hours. Our enemies have used this before," he said, reaching inside his satchel and pulling out a small vial and an injector.

Aryis frowned. Wraiths sometimes coated their claws with poison, and Ashweed was a rather common variety, but the mark on Nyssa's arm wasn't a known side effect.

The master healer pulled the liquid into the injector from the vial. He took hold of Nyssa's hand, turned it palm up, and pushed the needle into the skin at her wrist, slowly injecting the antidote into her bloodstream.

A few seconds passed.

Nothing happened.

The healer scowled.

"What's wrong?" Eron asked, his face dark with worry.

"I— I don't know," the healer said.

Nyssa was slick with sweat and deathly pale. In her mind's eye, Aryis recalled what happened when the wraith picked Nyssa up and pinned her against the brick wall of the tavern courtyard. It was so strange. "It...it sliced its own tongue on a dagger, covering it with its blood. And that poison mark, it's so odd, but I've seen it before." Aryis blinked at them, then gasped. "It wasn't like the rest of them. Blood wraith? Could it have been a blood wraith?"

Lilliana shook her head. "That's impossible. Blood wraiths haven't existed for over three hundred years. The spell to even create one is locked in the Citadel."

Aryis started pacing back and forth, her mind racing. She had to convince them. Nyssa could—no, she *would* die. "It was much larger than the rest of them and had red eyes, not white. And it moved impossibly fast." She stopped pacing and mumbled under her breath. "I can't remember what to do. Which one is it?"

She held her palm up, and the air above her hand began to shimmer with a golden glow, her hand growing warm. A second later, a large, black leather-bound book appeared in her hand, the air surrounding it sparkling for a few seconds with small, white-gold bursts of light before fading.

Aryis frantically flipped through the book. She cursed and threw it to the ground, holding her hand out again and closing her eyes. Another book appeared, this one small with a faded yellow cover. She thumbed through it, growing more and more frustrated and panicked. She wasn't finding what she was looking for.

"I know I read about blood wraiths, but I can't remember which book!" Tears sprang up in her eyes as she let the yellow book tumble to the floor.

Nyssa needed help.

Her help.

Vykas stepped forward and grabbed his sister by the shoulders. "Look at me, Aryis. Look at me!" he commanded, his voice stern and steady. He smiled a familiar smile of reassurance, one she had seen often at the Conservatory when she doubted herself. "You know you've seen this in one of our books. Search your memory. Then reach out and call the book to you. Just calm down and concentrate. Close your eyes and *concentrate*."

He let go of her shoulders and stepped back.

Aryis closed her eyes and let out a trembling breath. She would not appear a helpless and foolish adept in front of these people, not when she could act. She held out her hand again and opened it slowly, reaching out with her mind and memory to find the book she needed. The myths about blood wraiths were scarce and scattered—a smattering of information here, another bit there, spread across books she had read, but one of them had the information she needed—the information about the creature's blood.

Her hand grew hot, and the air above her palm quivered. A book materialized with a shower of sparks. It was large and heavy, and she tipped forward to catch it. Vykas put his arms under the book to hold it open for her, and she began her search. She flipped back and forth through the pages, growing more and more nervous.

Not finding the answer soon meant Nyssa's death.

One more page turn, and she slammed a finger on the book, pointing to a passage. "Here! 'Blood wraiths are rare and dangerous, their blood carrying the Cast of the Grave, a slow-acting poison inducing certain death'."

Aryis continued to scan the page, her lips moving. She gasped. "Mother's Tears!" Aryis looked at the healer. "Do you have Mother's Tears?"

"Yes," he said, glass bottles rattling as he dug through his bag. He pulled out a small bottle. "Are you sure? It will kill her if you're not."

Aryis exhaled. "Give it to her."

The healer stood and trickled the black liquid into Nyssa's mouth. He held her jaw closed and massaged her throat. After a few seconds, Nyssa let out a deep moan of pain and arched her back, her muscles involuntarily tensing.

Her body eventually relaxed back on the couch, but her eyes remained closed. The dark tendrils of poison that spider-webbed across her skin slowly faded from black to dark gray.

"Did it...did it work?" Aryis asked, breathless.

The room fell into silence. All eyes were on the healer as he placed his hand on Nyssa's chest and closed his eyes, reaching into her with his power. He sighed with relief. "Mother's Tears is a potent drug for powerful toxins. It either kills the poison, or it kills the person. Nyssa is still breathing. It worked," he said, "but she's going to be out for days, maybe longer. It takes time to recover from Mother's Tears, not to mention the poison itself."

The entire room seemed to exhale with relief. Eron approached Aryis and took her hand. "You are a wonder, Aryis Devitt. Thank you for saving my daughter."

Heat spread across Aryis's face, and out of the corner of her eye, she saw her brother smile.

"Athen, can you take Nyssa up to her room? It would be more comfortable for her than the infirmary. I will check in on her later," the healer said.

Athen nodded and carefully slid his hands under Nyssa to lift her into his arms.

"I'll come with you," Aryis said, putting her hand on Athen's back. He nodded, mouthing a *thank you* to her.

As they walked out the door, Aryis dismissed the three books she had summoned, and they faded away with a small burst of shimmering light.

RECOVERY

Nyssa's eyes fluttered open, and she let out a groan as she adjusted to the low light in the room. A lone, softly snoring figure sat in a chair a few feet from the bed. She blinked and realized it was Athen. Another body was curled up at the end of her bed like a cat—Aryis, cradling a book.

Nyssa turned her head toward the bank of windows overlooking the city. Reece stood there, staring out at the night sky, a steaming mug in her hand. Nyssa opened her mouth to speak, but she didn't have to. Reece turned to her.

"Nyssa!" she said, a smile exploding across her face.

Aryis shot awake, her book clattering to the floor.

Athen roused from his chair and sat up. "You're awake!"

"Hey," Nyssa rasped, her throat feeling like an ancient door that hadn't been opened in centuries. "How long have I been out?"

"Almost four days," Athen replied.

Reece sat on the bed next to her and offered her mug. Nyssa sat up and hissed at the lingering ache in her ribs. Athen propped her up with extra pillows. She took a sip of sweet, honeyed tea and closed her eyes, savoring the hot liquid that soothed her throat. When Nyssa lowered the mug from her lips, she caught a glimpse of her left arm. The shoulder was freshly bandaged, and jagged, dark-gray streaks extended down to her forearm, resembling lightning.

"What's this?" Nyssa lifted her left arm with a wince. The pattern looked like a tattoo—one she certainly didn't ask for.

"How do you feel?" Reece asked.

Nyssa tested her arm a little. It was sore but not too bad, considering a knife had been shoved into it and twisted. She remembered that vividly—the creature taking pleasure in her pain.

"I'm sore and everything throbs, but not so bad, I guess," Nyssa said between sips. "But what the fuck is this on my arm?"

The three spent the next couple of minutes recounting what had happened after Nyssa collapsed in Lilliana's office, Reece and Athen telling most of the story while Aryis punctuated it with her excited commentary.

After they had concluded their tale, Nyssa looked at Aryis. "You—" She cleared the lump forming in her throat. "You saved my life. Again."

"I did alright."

"Thank you, Little Hawk," Nyssa said.

Aryis's eyes widened and a grin spread across her face.

Nyssa sank back into her pillows. She had been out for four days but was still exhausted. "I just need to rest for a..."

She closed her eyes and drifted off.

Nyssa groaned as Reece pulled thick, gray socks onto her feet. Being looked after made her feel helpless. It had been a day since she woke up in her bed, and she insisted on getting out of bed and moving to hasten her recovery.

"You don't have to take care of me like this," she objected, drawing a shrug out of Reece.

"It's not like I have much else to do with The Feather closed for now."

Nyssa continued to protest, but Reece shook her head and laughed. They sat on one of the leather couches in the library near her room, a book spread across her lap. The healers had her wear infirmary whites to let her bandages breathe, so she shuffled around wrapped in a blanket, trying her best to ward off the winter chill in the Keep.

Across the room, Athen and Aryis were deep into a game of Fire's Light, each examining the array of glowing orbs floating in the air. Aryis talked to herself while she slowly circled the orbs and contemplated her next move, reaching out to touch a piece before pulling back, changing her mind.

A low rumble vibrated in Nyssa's chest. "Aryis takes forever to make a move. It's like watching ice melt. In winter."

"Athen tells me you're—how can I put this kindly—dreadful at Fire's Light," Reece said, chuckling.

"I don't have the patience for it. All that standing and staring and thinking. Do something!" Nyssa yelled at Aryis. The woman shot her a look, but took the advice and pushed one orb deeper into the center of the floating pieces. It ignited with harmless blue flames. Aryis clapped with glee as Athen crossed his arms.

"Gods, I hate that game," Nyssa sighed.

Reece pointed to their two companions. "Those two have taken to one another, but I suspect Aryis thinks you and Athen are sleeping together."

Nyssa burst out laughing. "Athen and I don't fit like that. We kissed once, and it was a disaster."

"Oh, he told me. Said you two didn't talk for a week."

Nyssa cringed. "I don't think we knew what to say to each other." She reached over to twirl a bit of Reece's hair around her finger. "But at least it opened and closed that door really fast for the two of us. Though if I had known he would grow into *that*, I may have tried harder," she laughed, nodding her head toward her large, handsome best friend. The Athen that Nyssa met was clumsy and awkward. It took him a few years to adjust to his size and strength.

The blanket around Nyssa's shoulders slipped, and Reece reached over to trace a finger on the gray marks on Nyssa's arm, pulling her out of her thoughts. "Do you suppose they'll go away?" she asked.

"I can't say, but they haven't faded at all since you were given the Mother's Tears. They might be permanent."

"It'll be hard to cover them on my neck," Nyssa said, frowning. "At least I can wear a long-sleeve shirt, I suppose."

"I think they're beautiful."

Nyssa scowled. "Beautiful?"

"It's a symbol of your strength. And your damn stubbornness."

Nyssa held up her left arm. "This is a mark of my death. Or it would have been if not for Aryis. So just death delayed, perhaps," Nyssa said softly, looking down at the pattern on her skin. She wished she saw the beauty, as Reece did. She lowered her arm, wincing from the soreness. Looking away from Reece, she gritted her teeth. "After everything we went through, I still failed. Quinn escaped. And I wasn't able to save more people from the attack."

"You're being far too hard on yourself."

Nyssa swallowed hard, hesitating. "I was scared to death facing those wraiths. I thought we were all going to die."

Reece remained silent for a moment. "In the panic, I dropped my defenses. Everyone's fear sank into me, and I couldn't move. Then your courage and determination crashed into me like a damn tidal wave. It helped get me off the ground and fight. I would have died if you weren't there."

Nyssa hesitated, cautious about asking her next question. "The night you came to my room, you said you felt me across the Keep. I'm different from other people, aren't I?"

"Yes," Reece confessed. "I don't know why or how, but from the first second I saw you, your emotions were bright like the sun and beat in my ears like a pulse on top of my own. I didn't know how to tell you because..."

"What is it?" Nyssa asked, turning to look at her.

"I've sometimes lowered my walls completely with you and let your emotions sink into every fiber of my being. It's frightening. And intoxicating. I shouldn't do it. It violates your trust," Reece explained, her eyes downcast.

"Were your walls down our first night together?"

"Yes. I'm sorry."

Nyssa felt there was something more to their connection, beyond the physical, and now she knew for certain. "Did you want me that night as much as I wanted you?"

Reece swallowed and looked up at her. "Yes. Never doubt that."

"So, you got a little deeper into my feelings, we had really great sex, and you think I'd be mad?" Nyssa asked, scowling.

Reece opened her mouth and tried to respond, but Nyssa gently cupped her face and kissed her. It was tender and sweet at first, an unspoken forgiveness for a shame Reece didn't need to bear. The kiss turned more passionate, and Reece moved closer to Nyssa—

A throat cleared, soft and polite, and Reece pulled away and whispered, "We have an audience."

Athen smiled and waved with a cocked eyebrow. He walked over and dropped onto the couch opposite them, picking up his mug and taking a deep drink. Aryis came up behind him, wide-eyed.

Nyssa chuckled at her. "You should really see your face right now."

She cleared her throat and stood a little straighter. "I thought...I didn't know you were..."

Nyssa could almost see Aryis making calculations in her head. Athen helped push her along. "Nyssa and I aren't together. We kissed once. It was awful."

"Point of fact," Nyssa said, holding up a finger in the air for emphasis, "it's not for lack of skill—on my part, anyway."

Athen leaned forward. "How dare you? I will not have you insinuating that I am a terrible kisser. I am a wonderful kisser. It's just that we were like two icebergs scraping together."

Reece grabbed Nyssa's thigh and squeezed, shaking with silent laughter.

"Well, this has been a wonderfully awkward conversation. I thoroughly enjoyed it." Athen stood up. "Let's finish this game, Aryis, and leave these two to whatever we interrupted."

"But—but I have questions!" Aryis said.

Athen nudged her toward the floating orbs. "Nyssa is right, you are a strange bird."

Aryis frowned, but let him prod her back to their game.

Reece chuckled. "I like her."

Not ready to admit it aloud just yet, Nyssa silently agreed.

"I've arranged a small Winter's Fire dinner for the two of us tonight. A way to recapture a bit of the holiday," Reece said.

"I should be on a ship chasing Quinn. I don't know if a—"

"You know damn well you're not fit to be doing anything other than healing. Aryis is tracking her every day. She's at sea, no doubt. You'll catch up with her."

Nyssa frowned. She hated the delay—caused by her own injuries—but Reece was right. She was in no shape to pursue Quinn.

Reece ran her fingers lightly over Nyssa's forearm, tracing the poison scar. "I will cancel the dinner if you'd prefer."

"No. I'm sorry, I'm just frustrated. Actually, a private Winter's Fire celebration sounds lovely."

Reece leaned into Nyssa. "Do you have any Winter's Fire wishes?" she murmured.

Nyssa looked at her and smirked. "I can think of a few." She moved closer and whispered in Reece's ear, voice low and breathy. Reece bit her lip and color tinged her cheeks as Nyssa teased where her hands...and tongue...would roam later.

Nyssa laughed at her reaction and stood with a groan, the pain in her side and shoulder reminding her to move with caution.

"I've got an errand to run," she told Reece.

"You want me to come with?"

"I'll be okay. I'll take it slow. Not that I have any other choice. I'll meet you later for that private dinner. And afterward, we'll explore some of those Winter's Fire wishes." She flashed her best roguish smile and hobbled to the door.

Nyssa made her way through the Keep to Pol's office, her pace languid and deliberate. His office was sandwiched between Lilliana's and Reece's. It was a long way from the family wing, and Nyssa's plodding pace, lack of shoes, and cloaked blanket garnered a few odd looks.

Pol kept the door to his office open, and Nyssa poked her head in. The room was neat and sparse and tracked with her impression of the man. He looked up from his desk, a small smile crossing his face. "Nyssa, do come in. How are you feeling?"

"Progressing well, or so the healers say. I'm slow and sore, but I no longer feel like I fell off a mountain and hit every jagged rock on the way down."

"I came to visit you while you were still unconscious, but I'm afraid I've gotten rather busy since then."

"Well, I won't take up much time. Can I send a message to Vane?"

"Of course. Here." Pol pulled open a drawer and handed her a few pieces of loose paper and a quill. "Please, sit." Two chairs faced his desk, and Nyssa settled into one of them with a light groan, pulling the paper, quill, and a pot of ink toward herself.

She spent a few minutes writing her message before signing the letter with a flourish.

"Give it here," Pol said, holding out his hand. She passed the letter to him. "Vane, you said?"

"Yes."

Pol turned to a small golden bowl with intricate carvings on the side, its interior blackened and charred. He picked up a short, thick metal rod and drew it around the edge of the vessel. The bowl began to vibrate and hum, a low rumble that Nyssa could feel in her chest. A few seconds later, the middle of the bowl sparked and ignited into a bright blue flame.

A soft, high-pitched voice emanated from the fire. "Risen and shining. We await. Destination?"

"Vane, in the Ashen Mountain valley," Pol said. "Message for the blacksmith Jo'ahn Wend."

"Bane? You are in error. There is no town of Bane in the Ashen Mountains. Please consult a map before proceeding," the bowl replied, its flame flicking higher.

Nyssa cocked her head and gave Pol a look. He sighed and leaned closer to the vessel.

"Vane. In the Ashen Mountains. V-A-N-E," he said with a raised voice, each letter enunciated clearly.

The bowl's flame flicked higher again. "Please do not yell. We do not like the yelling. Destination: Vane, in the Ashen Mountains. Please give us your message. We will consume."

Pol crumpled up Nyssa's letter and dropped it into the vessel. The flame belched upward, turning the letter to ash, and faint golden wafts of smoke rose above the fire, resembling handwritten words, before sparking and dissipating in the air.

The flame quickly died down, and the bowl spoke again after a few seconds. "We have delivered your message to the Central Post in Vane. It was very toothsome for us. We would be pleased to consume more letters of yours, Nyssa Blacksea. Now, slumber."

She exhaled a soft laugh. "Thank you."

The flame extinguished itself, and the bowl went back to sleep. Pol sat back with an exasperated sigh.

"That one has a bit of a personality," Nyssa said.

"Entirely too mouthy. And it's not hard of hearing. I swear it gets the destination wrong on purpose to vex me."

Nyssa stood and thanked Pol for his time.

He nodded. "I will bring you the response when I receive it."

IT SHIFTS AND STIRS

The beast stared into her eyes.

Nyssa struggled under its grasp, its hot fingers constricting around her neck, scrabbling against her skin. Her blood burned, its poison moving through her with every heartbeat. Red eyes examined her face.

No, this was not how it happened. Something was different. The creature now took its time with Nyssa. The moment was shifting, changing—breaking apart and reforming.

A knife twisted in her shoulder, and she opened her mouth to scream.

Her lungs flooded with ice-cold water.

Panic spiked through her, the fire in her blood fighting against the icy water engulfing her. Red eyes held her gaze, and she struggled to breathe, her fingers clawing at the creature's arm. Her body began to bow and break, her shoulder giving way to the creature's dagger.

She writhed and moaned.

Bones cracked.

Muscles snapped.

Shards of lightning danced across every nerve, sinking into flesh, bone, and blood. The pain was unfathomable.

Nyssa sank, this ancient monster dragging her down. It released her, but she was too deep. She let go of her future and her past and gave herself over to death. Her eyes closed, and she began to unravel.

Before the darkness came, a hand slipped into hers, and a woman whispered...

"Nyssa."

She woke with a start, a strangled cry stuck in her throat.

A hand slipped over her arm. "Nyssa?"

She looked over at Reece, her heart thumping in her chest as she gulped in air.

"Hey, it's okay," Reece murmured, sitting up and putting her arms around Nyssa.

Nyssa curled up in her lap, trying to hide her fear, hoping her heart wouldn't give out as it pounded in her ears. She knew Reece could feel her terror; she saw it in her eyes.

No one had ever seen her like this, not even Athen. Dread clawed at Nyssa—something deep within her couldn't deny the creeping feeling that the blood wraith had been sent for her.

"It's okay," Reece breathed, trying to comfort her. "I'm here."

THE JUSTICIAR

Staff scurried out of the way as Nyssa stalked down the hallway, boots halfway buckled and working the buttons of her loose white shirt. Anger, anxiety, and a sore body had her in a cold sweat.

No one had mentioned the Justiciar's arrival to Nyssa until she heard some attendants in the hallway speaking in hushed tones. Of course Cardin would send a Justiciar to investigate a wraith attack—it was a rare and dangerous thing, exactly what the adepts at Ambershine were raised and trained to deal with. They were Imperial law enforcers and the judgment of the Empress made blood and flesh.

Nyssa had found Reece and pressed her for details. Eron had sent Athen and Aryis to the Justiciar without her due to her recovery. Reece begrudgingly helped Nyssa get dressed when it was apparent that she couldn't dissuade her from seeing the Justiciar.

Reece trailed behind Nyssa, keeping her distance, likely sensing the anger radiating off of her. Nyssa would give Athen and Aryis a harsh talking to as well. They didn't need to protect her—she was recovering fine and could face a Justiciar. Being left behind made the tips of her ears burn. She was an adept, just like them.

Except not in the way it truly counted.

Nyssa stormed into Lilliana's office, not bothering to knock. The Justiciar sat at Lilliana's desk, a skull-like white mask covering the top half of her face. The mask was severe, angular, and the symbol of their Order, designed to intimidate, if Nyssa had to guess. The Justiciar stilled and stared at Nyssa, her expression impossible to read. Her lips parted slightly, as if surprised.

Nyssa had never seen a Justiciar up close before. This one wore a tight, dark-red leather uniform that covered all of her skin, save for her neck and face. Her dark-brown hair was tied up in a topknot, and her temples were shaved, not unlike Aryis's style. She sat with her elbows on the desk, gloved hands folded together, the leather softly creaking when she flexed her fingers.

Nyssa swallowed. The gaze of the Justiciar unnerved her. Disheveled from her haste, her shirt was only half-tucked into her pants, her belt hung loose instead of threaded into a belt loop, and the ends of her pants were bunched up above the boots that were barely fastened. She panted from the exertion of getting to the office, her body reminding her of its pain. Beads of sweat rolled down her back.

She didn't wait for permission to speak. "If you have questions about what happened—"

"Quiet, adept," the Justiciar said, voice low and steady.

She leaned back a bit in her chair, and Nyssa could feel her eyes scanning her up and down, lingering on the gray poison trails on her neck exposed by the loose shirt she wore. The Justiciar unfolded her hands and placed them flat on the desk.

"You have the audacity to interrupt a Justiciar's inquiry?" the woman asked.

"What else would I do?" Nyssa replied. She took a deep breath and slowly let it out, trying to calm her nerves and quell her annoyance. "I should be here. You have questions for all of us."

The Justiciar stood and walked to the floor-to-ceiling window of the office that overlooked Ocean's Rest. She clasped her hands behind her back before turning to them.

"These two have already recounted the events of Winter's Fire. Your narrative isn't required."

"Bullshit," Nyssa replied.

Athen and Aryis whipped their heads toward her. The Justiciar considered her for several long, uncomfortable seconds before her eyes panned to Athen and Aryis.

"Athen Fennick, Aryis Devitt, I think I have a good idea of how everything transpired. You may leave."

"What about Nyssa?" Athen asked.

"Not your concern. Now, leave."

Athen seemed likely to object, but Nyssa glanced at him and shook her head. She could face a Justiciar by herself.

Once Athen and Aryis left, the Justiciar rounded the desk to stand in front of Nyssa. Nyssa was surprised to find the woman's eyes matched the dark-red leather uniform she wore. Nyssa had never seen a human with red eyes before. They reminded her of the blood wraith's, sending a cold shiver down her spine.

"How interesting to meet the Emerald Order adept with no magick. You're quite the talk among the inner circles of Cardin," the Justiciar said. "A curiosity."

Nyssa swallowed. "Certainly there must be more captivating topics of conversation."

"One would think. But since hearing you're actually on an assignment—for the Empress, no less—the gossips took keen interest. I understand becoming an Ashcloak is tied up in the successful completion of this task. If you fail, you'd likely be asked to leave the Order. That would reflect poorly on First Master Greye."

"I don't intend to fail."

"No one ever intends to fail, Blacksea. The Empress is watching, so I will stress the need for care with this runaway adept."

Nyssa stood a little straighter and lifted her chin. "I will bring Quinn back safe, don't doubt that."

The Justiciar held Nyssa's gaze. "Your fellow adepts told quite the story about the wraith attack and your near demise. A blood wraith, no less. I wouldn't be inclined to believe that bit if Devitt wasn't so insistent. And now I see you bear its mark."

The Justiciar's eyes lit upon the poison scar. Nyssa tried not to swallow.

"Tell me, do you feel you upheld your guild oath that night you fought and almost died?"

The question threw Nyssa off. "Yes."

"Recite it for me."

Nyssa paused and took a breath.

"To my brothers and sisters, my bond.
To my guild, my fidelity.
To my Empire, my blood.
Stand fast. Face the darkness. Fall without fear."

Nyssa had recited the Emerald Order's oath almost every day since she memorized it.

"What part of the oath takes precedence, do you think? The part to look after your fellow adepts, or obedience to your guild? Or to the Empire?"

"The oath doesn't mention obedience to the guild or the Empire. Loyalty and obedience are not the same thing," Nyssa replied, her mouth running ahead of her brain.

The Justiciar's red eyes narrowed. "Is now truly the proper time to parse interpretations of the oath? Is that the conversation you think interests me, Nyssa Blacksea?"

The Justiciar's eyes roamed her face, moving from her scar down to her neck and the poison mark left by the blood wraith. Nyssa swallowed hard, unnerved by the examination. The Justiciar stepped away and walked to the desk, leaning back to sit on its edge.

"Since you're so keen on telling me what your guild oath does and does not say, let's speak on it further. Do you believe in your guild and your oath, Blacksea?"

The question confused Nyssa, and she wondered if it was some sort of trap. "I uphold my oath to the Order and the Empire."

"That's not what I asked."

"I believe in protecting the people of this nation," Nyssa replied. "As the Order taught me."

"Yes, as they taught you. Are you willing to die for the Empire?"

"Seems I was the night of the attack," Nyssa replied, her tone terse.

The Justiciar smirked. "Did you 'fall without fear,' Blacksea?"

The question flustered Nyssa. The memory of that night, and of her nightmares, intruded into her thoughts.

"Or," she said, staring at her, "did you feel fear grip every fiber of your being? Could you hear your pulse pounding in your ears?"

"Stop," Nyssa whispered.

"When you gave in to the darkness of pain, what was your last thought?"

Nyssa shook her head.

"Did you feel your life slipping away from you?"

"Stop!" Nyssa snarled.

The Justiciar lifted her chin. "Do these questions vex you?"

Nyssa tried to slow her breathing. She failed. Her shirt stuck to the sweat on her back. "You're intentionally trying to get a rise out of me," she whispered.

What does she want?

The Justiciar cocked her head. "Which was rather easy to do."

Nyssa crossed her arms, saying nothing. The Justiciar was supposed to be investigating the wraith attacks. Why was she questioning Nyssa's resolve? Just another asshole who wanted to poke at her, like Ceril. Or perhaps she was looking for an excuse to disqualify her from ever becoming an Ashcloak.

The Justiciar tapped her gloved fingers on the edge of the desk. "You break the fundamental guild rule of requiring magick to be a member. Your existence is anathema to many."

Ah, there it is, the goddamned disdain.

"I'm more than aware."

"I believe you care deeply about your status with the Order. By all accounts, you have worked harder than most, become a formidable fighter—your failure to capture that Arcton Citadel runaway notwithstanding," the Justiciar stated, pausing to perhaps see if she rankled Nyssa. And she did. Nyssa tensed her jaw despite herself. "Don't you feel your dedication should be rewarded?"

Nyssa took a deep breath. "I have worked hard in service to the Order, not in service to myself. Have I finally earned my place? That's for my First Master to decide."

"That is a very calculated response," the Justiciar said. "Measured and polite, but lacks true conviction. You recite guild platitudes."

"It's what I was taught."

"At some point, you'll have to decide for yourself what's truly important to you. Until that time, everything you do or say feels hollow. And you, of all people, cannot afford to doubt who you are and where you stand."

She spoke as if she *knew* Nyssa, poking at her doubts. "What does that mean? Why are you telling me this?"

The Justiciar pushed herself off the desk and approached, bringing her hand to Nyssa's neck. She gently traced the poison mark with a finger.

"Remarkable," she said, bringing her eyes up to meet Nyssa's glare. She pulled her hand away. "One day, I may need to ask something of you, and I want you to recall my mercy."

"I'm to be your pawn, then?" Nyssa asked, angry at the thought of owing a Justiciar anything.

The Justiciar turned away from her. "We all answer to someone, Blacksea. I am Justiciar Medias. Remember my name." She waved a hand dismissively. "You may leave."

Nyssa left the office, her stomach in a knot, caused by a mix of confusion and anger.

And fear.

Reece, Athen, and Aryis waited for her outside the office. She didn't feel like talking, not knowing how to put into words the unsettling feeling that Medias had imparted in her. A Justiciar reserving a favor was odd. It could only lead to trouble. Nyssa absentmindedly put a hand up to her neck, still feeling Medias's touch. She turned and walked down the hallway, retreating from her friends.

Nyssa withdrew to the isolated courtyard she favored to train in alone. Athen found her leaning in an archway, absentmindedly kicking rocks across the cold stone ground. What could the Justiciar want from her in the future? Medias seemed too familiar with Nyssa, and it unsettled her.

"Hey," Athen said, leaning against the opposite wall. "First experience with a Justiciar and you're unscathed. I'd say it's been a successful day."

"Then lift a glass to my good fortune."

"Justiciars are the only thing I've ever seen that spook my mother."

"You should have told me she was here to question us."

Athen sighed and looked up into the sky. "Eron thought it best not to. Justiciars aren't to be trifled with."

"You, Eron, even Aryis...you have to let me speak for myself, even if that includes me stepping in it with a Justiciar. This overprotective bullshit has got to stop."

Athen sighed. "I didn't do it to piss you off. Eron gave us orders."

"Yeah, well, you need to take a page out of my book and disobey an order once in a while," Nyssa mumbled.

"I'm sorry."

She looked over at him before she grabbed his hand and squeezed. "Thanks for checking up on me."

"You and I have been watching out for each other for fifteen years. It'll be fifty more if you don't do something stupid like choke to death on a chicken bone."

Nyssa nodded, watching her breath hang in the frosty morning air. She tried to smile, but she could still feel the phantom brush of the Justiciar's fingers on her throat.

THE DEPARTURE

Reece sighed, heart heavy, waiting to say her goodbyes. Vykas and Aryis murmured with one another as Athen chatted with his mother and Pol. Nyssa stood with her arm around First Master Greye, kissing him on the side of his head before she joined Reece.

The day to leave Ocean's Rest arrived three weeks after the wraith attack to allow Nyssa to recover from her wounds. She was a bundle of nerves and excitement, fidgeting while they stood in the Keep's massive main foyer. Lilliana's ship, the Sea Stag, was ready to sail in pursuit of Quinn.

"Here, take this with you," Reece said, slipping a book into Nyssa's travel bag before holding up two small, white disks, barely an inch wide. "And these. Two healing disks apiece. In case you run into any trouble and there's not a healer around."

Nyssa examined them. "The Lightway seal. These are topnotch."

"Lilliana only buys the best. They still hurt like hell, but they do a quality job if you need them."

Nyssa slipped the disks into an inside pocket of her jacket.

Reece touched her arm. "The safest of journeys to you, Nyssa. I hope you find a bit of yourself out there on the sea. It's your birthplace, after all." She stepped close and held Nyssa's face in her hands, brushing a gentle kiss across her lips. She had been more than a pleasant distraction for the weeks she had been at the Keep. Reece didn't know how deeply she would become entangled with Nyssa when they first met.

"I will truly miss you," Nyssa said. She claimed she didn't form romantic attachments, but this felt more profound than just two friends saying farewell.

This could lead somewhere. Reece quickly put the notion out of her mind.

Athen and Aryis approached. "We have to go," Athen said. Reece reluctantly pulled away from Nyssa and gave Aryis a big hug. "Keep an eye on him," she said into her ear. Aryis nodded before Reece stepped into Athen's waiting arms. "Safe journey, Athen Fennick. Return these two ladies and yourself to me unharmed."

"You know I won't let anything happen to them."

Nyssa and Aryis followed Athen out the door, and Reece watched them disappear into the bright light of the day, swallowing the lump in her throat.

Nyssa gasped when she laid her eyes on the Sea Stag. The ship was stunning, its wooden hull a deep-auburn color, a couple shades deeper than Nyssa's own hair. A giant, wooden stag head adorned the bow of the ship, its antlers gilded in silver. As they walked up the gangplank, Nyssa marveled at the giant masts, its sails waiting to be unfurled in deeper waters to take the ship out to sea to wherever Quinn was hiding.

A deep chill hung in the briny air, brisk and refreshing. The sound and smell of the sea was alluring in a way Nyssa hadn't expected, as if it tugged at her very bones.

Once on board the Sea Stag, the three of them were met by a tall, thin man. Nyssa couldn't tell if his beard or the hair on top of his head were more sparse. He greeted Athen with a quick, terse nod. "Welcome aboard the Sea Stag. We'll get underway within the hour. Take the staterooms closest to my quarters, if you will."

"Thank you, Captain. Nyssa Blacksea and Aryis Devitt, this is Captain Surk. He's captained my mother's ship for twenty years."

Surk gave them both a small grin. "A pleasure to have House Devitt aboard," he said to Aryis before turning to Nyssa. "And by your surname, I expect you'll be more than at home on the ocean."

"Actually, this is the first time I've been aboard a ship since I was a baby, I'm afraid," Nyssa admitted.

Surk smiled, cracking his stern exterior. "If you were born on the water, it's in your blood and bones, that I can guarantee. Let me get a steward to help you all get settled in."

Captain Surk stuck his fingers in his mouth and let out a shrill whistle. A girl who looked to be a few years younger than Nyssa ran up. "This is Mina, my daughter. She'll be keen to look after you during this trip."

"Oh, you don't have to make your daughter wait on us," Athen protested.

"Nonsense. She's learning every job on this ship, in and out. Gonna take over for me one day, she will." Surk patted his daughter on the shoulder. "I ain't gonna trust you with anyone else."

Mina beamed a massive smile at them. "Let's get you to your quarters."

Nyssa settled into life aboard the Sea Stag, and rather unexpectedly, she loved it.

Once out of the Areshi Ocean waters, they crossed into the Saldurn Sea. Unbound waters, governed by no one. Nyssa liked the idea of it, a free ocean.

Wild and untamed.

The sea and ship were a stark contrast to her insular life at the Emerald Order. Their walls felt like a boundary between worlds, but the sea was endless and wild. The rocking of the boat beneath her feet was like the lilt of an old, familiar song.

They were south of where the Saldurn Sea met the Black Sea, according to Captain Surk, saddening Nyssa a little. She wouldn't mind seeing her namesake.

On their journey, she spent more time with Aryis, learning to appreciate her natural curiosity. It rubbed off on her, too, because after a few days, she sat with Aryis in the mess and asked more about her magick, which seemed to delight the young woman to no end. The Masters had dismissed Nyssa from taking any practical magick courses at the Order, but she at least understood there were two types of magick—corporeal and ethereal—and wanted to know more about Aryis's abilities.

"Like Athen and Reece, I have corporeal magick. My abilities are inherent and fixed."

"But you can do two different things," Nyssa said, confused.

"I suspect it's not different magick, just distinct manifestations of an ability to draw things to myself or to others. Like Athen and his mother—one magick that manifests a few connected abilities. I envy him, to be honest. He never has to think about using his magick, it's just always active, which is rather rare. I have to concentrate. Sometimes I wish I were an ethereal mage instead. There are so many spells they can use."

Nyssa laughed. "You assume you'd be a good spellweaver."

"Truly complex spellweaving requires powerful magick, finesse, and the right spell. I'm afraid those mages are rare nowadays. I compare it to singing. Most can carry a modest tune, some are a cut above, but having a truly transcendent singing voice is rare."

"At least you're guild material. Most born with magick get stuck doing trade work."

"Could you imagine me in a tiny shop, creating enchantments all day to sell?"

Nyssa couldn't help but laugh at the thought. "Or party tricks? Disguise enchantments? Illusions? Day in and day out?"

Aryis shrugged. "It's honest work, at least. And they're not tied to the guilds. They can come and go as they please."

Nyssa frowned and grew silent. Reece had also extolled the virtues of being free, of not being beholden to a guild. Most were never given a choice to stay an adept or leave—it was a decision left up to the guilds and their Masters.

Aryis seemed to sense a shift in Nyssa's mood. "Did I say something wrong?"

"I just...I was wondering why Quinn left the Citadel."

"You're not having second thoughts about this, are you?"

"No," Nyssa said sternly. "Of course not. I'm just curious."

"Curiosity is an excellent trait." Aryis smiled, and Nyssa tried to put their mission out of her thoughts for the moment. Her mind turned to another serious matter.

"We need to discuss what happened at The Masthead."

Aryis straightened in her seat. "Okay."

"I told you to not make it obvious we were there for Quinn, but you looked over at her and gave us away. You need to follow our instructions."

Aryis frowned. "I'm sorry. I just...I get ahead of myself sometimes."

"We can't risk losing Quinn again. Listen to us, and we'll minimize the risk. Minimize mistakes."

"I know how important this assignment is to you. I'll do better."

Nyssa nodded. "You will. You're smart as shit, but when it comes to fighting, there's no book that can teach you what Athen and I know."

Aryis smiled. "I like this. Talking to you is nice."

Nyssa let out a low growl from the back of her throat. "Don't let it go to your head."

"Well, hopefully I'm getting better at holding my own." Aryis beamed.

Nyssa had to admit, she was a quick learner. Nyssa would quietly sit and watch while Athen trained Aryis on deck, teaching her how to at least hold her own. Sometimes members of the crew would sit on crates, passing a flask around, and cheer Aryis on. It seemed to delight her to no end.

The rocking of the boat added difficulty, but Aryis was persistent and had a modicum of natural physical talent. She also had an endless string of questions, and Athen would smile and patiently explain the concepts behind everything he taught her. Nyssa herself even chimed in with advice from time to time, drawing the biggest smiles Aryis seemed capable of mustering.

And it didn't go unnoticed that Aryis and Athen had a growing friendship. Athen tried gently flirting with her, which only seemed to fluster the woman. When he pulled Nyssa aside and asked for advice—she did have a pretty decent flirt game—she merely told him, "Figure it out."

He responded with a low growl.

After a week and a half at sea, Aryis called Athen and Nyssa up to the deck. The red glow of her magick surrounded Quinn's book, and she sent out a tendril, closing her eyes to concentrate. After a minute, the tendril collapsed and Aryis's magick faded.

"Quinn's still a ways off, but we're gaining on her fast. She has to be on land. Here," Aryis said, unfolding a map from her pocket. She pointed to a string of islands in the Saldurn Sea, halfway between the Western Continent that housed the Areshi Empire and Thu'Dain, and the Eastern Continent, home to multiple independent nations and alliances. Nyssa looked closer at the map. The Black Sea lay north of their location, maybe a few days away. It was massive.

"The Basai Islands?" Athen asked.

"Specifically Jejin," Aryis replied.

"Jejin? Good. I know a place we can stay. I'll message ahead. Good work, Aryis. We won't throw you overboard today."

"Wait...you wouldn't actually throw me overboard, would you? Is this some Emerald Order thing?"

Nyssa leaned in. "It was a joke, Little Hawk."

Aryis seemed confused, but offered them a smile, regardless.

"We're in Unbound territory," Athen remarked. "We don't have the protection of the Empire, so we keep to ourselves, find Quinn, and get her back on the Sea Stag. Hopefully, we won't run into any trouble."

"Trouble?" Aryis asked.

"Unbound territory belongs to pirates, brigands, and other unsavories," he explained, glancing at Nyssa. She didn't mind. She knew her parents had lived on the outskirts of lawful society.

"Sounds like my kind of place," Nyssa said with a wink.

When the Sea Stag approached the island of Jejin, two weeks after taking leave of Ocean's Rest, Nyssa, Athen, and Aryis marveled at the city glistening beyond the sea. Its architecture mirrored that of Ocean's Rest, though its colors were more vibrant. A myriad of deep tones—reds, oranges, and blues—shimmered with the movement of people. Tall, skinny spires poked out, reaching to the sky.

Once off the ship, Jejin bustled around the trio, the streets full of people and lined with shops and eateries. Sweet, spicy incense wafted through the air, a widespread tradition that welcomed winter to the islands. Banners made of small, colorful squares of cloth hung between buildings, flapping in the winter winds. Some banners, along with glowing shop signs, were in languages that Nyssa didn't recognize.

Like Ocean's Rest, the corners of many buildings were decorated with wooden carvings of protective demons, wood sprites, and animals. She even spotted a carved Kraken or two, warding away ghosts and unwelcome spirits.

There must be a lot of ghosts and spirits wandering the world, looking for a place to rest.

"Remember, these islands are Unbound lands, so our guild affiliation means nothing," Athen warned. "We need to be careful."

"So many people coming and going, plenty of pirates and thieves. It's the perfect place to get lost in and not draw much attention," Aryis observed. "Quinn would be impossible to find if not for me."

Nyssa laughed. "Don't get cocky. We haven't found her yet."

"Stick close," Athen said. "The Lash should be up ahead."

Nyssa looked at him. "We're staying at a place called The Lash?"

"One of my mother's pleasure houses outside of the Empire."

Aryis perked up. "Oh, I rather liked The Feather. A very interesting place."

Of course she finds The Feather interesting. Nyssa shook her head, wondering what exactly The Lash had in store for them.

THE LASH

The three adepts wound their way through the streets of Jejin, following the captain's directions to get to The Lash. The city teemed with activity and everything seemed so clean and well-maintained, surprising Nyssa. Greenery covered the island, from trees lining the streets to the large parks filled with flowers.

"This isn't at all what I expected from Unbound territory," she remarked.

"Unbound doesn't *just* mean unruly and wild. The Basai Islands has a council government. People pay taxes, much like anywhere else, and that money funds the city workers."

"But this island is still a haven for pirates?"

"Oh, of course. But pirates love their luxury as well, Nyssa."

Athen drew to a halt in front of a large building that took up a city block of its own. The sign above the ornately carved doors was absent of lettering, only donning a black whip on a stark white background that pulsed ever so slightly.

Subtle.

"What odd signage," Aryis remarked. "How is anyone supposed to know what this place is?"

"One doesn't merely stumble inside places like this. The people who want to be here know how to find it," Athen said. "My mother is the majority owner of The Lash. This is the safest place on the island for us," Athen said.

Aryis leaned toward the doors to get a better look at its carvings. The artwork was a mass of men and women in various states of undress and risqué poses that drew a sharp gasp from her.

"Oh," she said, pulling back with a grin.

Athen swung the door open, and they walked inside a warm anteroom, dim light orbs dotting its deep-red walls. Two guards in finely tailored black suits greeted them, slim daggers at their hips, both giving Athen a curious look as he towered over them.

"Welcome to The Lash. State your business," the female guard said with a polite smile. Her eyes darted quickly to Nyssa's and Aryis's weapons.

"We're looking for Mox the Whip," Athen said.

"What's your business with him?"

"Family business. He's expecting us. Tell him his friends from Ocean's Rest are here."

The female guard looked up at Athen and nodded, pulling an orb out of her suit pocket. She whispered into the orb, and it rose out of her hand and darted down the hallway. Athen cleared his throat and rocked on his heels while they all waited for the orb to return with its reply message. When it did, the guard held it up to her ear.

"With me, please," she instructed.

The three of them followed her out of the anteroom, down a dark hallway, and through a set of heavy curtains into a large, noisy salon—part tavern and part gaming room—full of people drinking and socializing.

Hands and lips seemed to roam freely.

Unlike The Feather, The Lash was darker inside, lit only by light orbs and a fireplace—no windows to be seen. Perhaps it was a conscious decision, but the establishment felt sexier, more dangerous, than the bright, warm interior of The Feather. Nyssa quite liked the differences. The Lash was suited to a clientele of pirates and wayfarers.

The guard led them past a sizable fireplace, blazing with a cozy fire, to a large round leather booth in a tucked-away corner of the room, occupied by a man with light-blue skin, green eyes, and cropped black hair. He had two small black horns growing from his forehead, curling back on themselves. They were decorated with silver bands, as was Ashken custom.

The three of them approached, and he stood with a smile, opening his arms wide to welcome them. Nyssa found him to be rather handsome, lithe and sleek, with well-defined muscles revealed by his sleeveless shirt and tight, tan leather pants.

"Welcome to The Lash." He smiled, revealing a pair of short, sharp-looking fangs. "I am Mox the Whip, proprietor of this lovely establishment, and I am honored to have you here, Athen Fennick." Mox extended his hand out to Athen, who gave him a hearty handshake.

Athen smiled. "Pleased to meet you."

Mox stepped around Athen to get a look at the two women, then turned his attention to Aryis. "Aren't you a lovely respite for my weary eyes?"

Aryis nodded at him. "Aryis Devitt."

"A Devitt? I am honored to have House Devitt in my humble presence," he said with a deep bow.

"And this one," he continued, stepping in front of Nyssa and putting his hands on his hips. "You're a bit of a bite, aren't you?"

Nyssa looked Mox up and down. "One you'd likely choke on."

He laughed. "I probably would. You seem like a wild one. Just as likely to fight me as to fuck me, I'd say. I can tell an Order Ashcloak from a mile away. You all carry yourselves the same way."

Nyssa smiled. "Nyssa Blacksea. And not an Ashcloak. Yet."

Mox glanced back at Aryis. "But you, not an Order adept? Which guild are you from?"

"Wayland Conservatory," she replied.

"Ah," Mox said. "Come, sit for a moment, my friends. Your suite is being sorted. You have the top floor, the best room in the house. Very private. Stocked full of drink, freshly made beds, clean linens, and the best bath oils these lush islands have to offer. The very picture of luxury."

They slid into the round booth with Mox, and he motioned for drinks to a barkeep behind a massive wooden bar across the room.

"So, I take it this is a whorehouse?" Aryis asked, her eyes darting about.

Mox smiled patiently. "A pleasure house. You can do far more than just fuck here."

"So, like The Feather?"

"Indeed."

A barmaid arrived and passed tall glasses of spiced ale around the table.

"Thank you, Vanessa," Mox said before turning to the group. "Truth be told, many of us here consider ourselves the spiritual sons and daughters of Lilliana Fennick. She saved many people back in the rough days of Ocean's Rest, including my mother. And when Mum wanted a fresh start away from the aftermath of the war, Lilliana staked her to buy this place. When she passed and left The Lash to me, Lilliana didn't bat an eye and welcomed me with open arms as her partner."

"I'm so glad to see you thriving here," Athen said. "My mother speaks highly of you, as does Reece."

"A testament to your mother's generosity and trust," Mox replied. "And Reece...that marvelous woman. When my mother died and Lilliana and Reece came to pay their respects, Reece stayed an extra two weeks to pick me up off the floor and make sure I was okay. Her heart beats true."

Nyssa smiled. It came as no surprise that Reece had helped when needed. Nyssa cocked her head and smirked. "Wait a minute. The Feather and The Lash—I just connected those names."

Mox nodded his head. "Yes, there is a bit of a theme. And while you can get a taste of the lash at both establishments, there is only one Mox the Whip."

Aryis leaned forward. "Why are you called that, if I may ask?"

He smiled. "Oh, my dear. Usually, people pay me a handsome fee to find out why."

Nyssa wrapped an arm around Aryis's shoulders. "I'll explain it to her later, Mox."

"I understand you expect one more guest?"

"Yes, and we'll need privacy," Athen explained.

"Discretion is of the utmost importance in our business," Mox replied. He stood up and waved a young man over. "My steward will show you to your suite, and I'll have food sent up in an hour so you can get settled in. I hope you enjoy everything we offer."

He held his hand out to Nyssa and helped her out of the booth. "If you're curious about Mox the Whip, come see me later," he said with a wink.

As Athen and Aryis turned to follow the steward, Nyssa hung back. "Actually, I do have a request," she said, pressing her hand to his chest.

"My dear Nyssa, anything you wish."

"Be sure to send up dessert with the meal," she said with a tap of a finger on his chest before turning to follow her companions.

"Is that all you want? We could have a lot of fun together."

She winked. "Only if I'm holding the whip, Mox."

He chuckled and covered his chest with both hands. "You're going to steal my heart, woman."

Nyssa let out a low whistle when she entered their suite. "Mox wasn't kidding."

The loft on the top floor of The Lash was huge, a fireplace blazing on one end of the room, a large kitchen on the other. The expanse between the two contained a dining table and a large sitting area. Slender wooden columns supported wooden beams that spanned the ceiling. The space was cozy, despite its size, with books scattered about on tables and the shelves flanking the fireplace.

Nyssa inspected some of the artwork placed around the loft, much of it erotic. She touched a sculpture of a man and woman in mid-tryst. "This place must have been furnished by Mox."

A large bank of windows with a set of double doors led out to a private rooftop terrace, the space outside almost as large as the interior, decorated with benches, plants, and a fire pit off in a corner. Ivy-covered wooden posts dotted the perimeter of the terrace with strings of lights hung between them. Nyssa wished they weren't on guild business. She wouldn't mind a tea and a book out in the fresh air.

The steward smiled. "I have stoked a fire in the great room for you. I suggest spending some time in the evening on the terrace. The view at night is simply stunning. That hallway leads to the bedrooms and adjoining baths, fully stocked with linens, soaps, candles, and bath oils. We see to every comfort. If you should need anything, including companionship, you have multiple messenger orbs at your disposal throughout the suite," the steward said, giving them a quick bow before leaving.

"My mother has set a high standard of quality. This place is a little rougher around the edges than The Feather, but it's very lucrative," Athen explained.

"Well, let's get settled. When our meal comes, we'll sit down and go over our plan to get our wayward adept back," Nyssa said. The other two nodded in agreement.

Nyssa walked over to the terrace doors and stepped outside, gasping as the cold air rushed up to greet her. Dusk had fallen over the city, and it lit up in a myriad of reds, oranges, and whites as lanterns and orbs illuminated the growing darkness.

She took a deep breath of the early evening air, the scent of the sea and grilled meat filling her lungs, causing her stomach to growl in anticipation of dinner. She flipped the collar of her leather jacket up and tightened her scarf against the chill, eyes roaming the city below, wondering where they would find their lost adept.

Nyssa put another forkful of dessert into her mouth, thoroughly enjoying the crackled layer of caramelized sugar topping the fluffy sweet potato pie infused with cinnamon, vanilla, and other spices. If the food was always this good on Jejin, she never wanted to leave.

As she chewed, Aryis held her hand over Quinn's book. She closed her eyes and concentrated, ribbons of red magick winding around her.

"She's on the island," Aryis said, opening her eyes. "She feels closer than I thought. We can definitely find her within an hour if she doesn't suddenly pack up and leave. I can zero in on her in a couple tries."

Athen leaned back and lifted his drink to his lips. "Good work."

"I wish the Sea Stag stayed in port. We'll likely have her before lunch tomorrow," Nyssa said.

"My mother got a line on some very rare whiskey and a few spell books on the southern-most island in the Basai chain. When she wants something, she gets it. The Stag will be back in a few days, don't worry," Athen said.

Nyssa sighed. Once they had Quinn, it's not like she could go anywhere, but a delay in getting back to Ocean's Rest, whatever the reason, was still a delay in getting Nyssa what she wanted.

"You two need to be careful around Quinn," she said. "If she can dampen your magick with a touch, watch her hands at all times until she's secured. And we've already seen she can get physical when desperate. I'd prefer Aryis not take another fist to the face."

"I agree with that." Aryis smiled. "Her magick is so rare. I hope she's open to talking with me once we get her back here. I would love to learn more about her abilities."

"We treat her as a hostile, Aryis. She's not a friend or even a fellow guildie at this point. You follow our lead, and remember what Athen taught you, okay?"

"You taught me a little too," Aryis replied, smiling at her.

"And you're a good student, I have to admit." The compliment made color rise in Aryis's cheeks. How would she handle what Nyssa had for her next? Time to find out. Nyssa leaned forward. "Will you come with me for a moment?"

Aryis exchanged a glance with Athen, but got up and followed Nyssa to her room.

Aryis entered Nyssa's room, worried. A burgeoning friendship seemed to be building between the two of them, but Aryis still didn't know what to expect.

Nyssa walked over to the bed where a small box lay on top. "Open it."

Aryis looked down at the box, furrowing her brow. "What is it?"

Nyssa sat on the bed. "It's a gift. From me. I've been waiting for a suitable moment to give it to you."

A smile spread across Aryis's face, unable to help it. She rarely got gifts that weren't from her father or obnoxiously extravagant. A small gasp left her when she carefully opened the box.

Inside, on a bed of dark-red velvet, lay an exquisitely crafted dagger, a foot from end to end. The double-sided blade was made of black steel and had a thick black matte oval cross guard with an intricate pattern carved into the top, revealing bright silver underneath the dark surface. A black leather sheath lay tucked in at the side of the box.

Nyssa pointed at the silver pommel. "I had an osprey etched into the side—your house sigil. And there are wings on the cross guard, stretching out from the blade. Go ahead. Pick it up. See how it feels."

Aryis reached into the box and wrapped her fingers around the black leather-clad handle. It felt good, or what she supposed a quality blade felt like. It had heft, unlike Splinter—may it rest in peace. Aryis turned the blade over in her hands.

"This is the least I could do to thank you for saving my life. I had my blacksmith in Vane make it to my specifications. He's the only one I trust to craft a blade for me. It was delivered right before we left Ocean's Rest. I hope you..."

Aryis shook with tears. She hadn't expected to cry, but once started, she couldn't stop.

Nyssa stood. "Oh, no, no, no, please don't cry. I didn't mean for you to cry." She patted Aryis on the shoulder.

"I can't help it," Aryis choked out. "This is the most wonderful gift anyone has ever given me."

Nyssa's face turned red. "That can't be true. You're a scion of a noble House. Certainly you've gotten—I don't know—horses or ships or estates as presents?"

"Yes, but nothing like this. Nothing made just for me." Aryis laid the knife back down in the box and threw her arms around Nyssa, squeezing hard.

Nyssa stood there for a moment. "You're going to finish the job that blood wraith did on my ribs, Little Hawk."

Aryis let up the pressure. "Sorry," she softly said into Nyssa's shoulder.

"You like it?" Nyssa asked with a chuckle.

"I love it." Aryis smiled when she found Nyssa hugging her back.

"You and I didn't get off on the right foot when you arrived in Ocean's Rest. I'm not particularly comfortable with new people. I take a while to warm up," Nyssa explained.

Aryis frowned. "You only met Reece a few days before me, and you seemed to warm up rather well to her."

Nyssa cocked her head at Aryis. "Reece is a special case."

"Because you wanted to sleep with her?"

"Aryis!" Nyssa burst out a laugh.

Aryis knew she was far too forward, her brother admonishing her at times, but the truth was the truth. "Sorry! I don't always say the right thing at the right time, and I get myself in trouble."

"I *always* say things that get me in trouble. You know, I didn't appreciate your spirit at first, but you've grown on me."

Aryis beamed, her heart growing at least two sizes, of that she was sure.

"Do not hug me again," Nyssa warned. "Now, there's a tradition at the Order when you get a weapon crafted for you. Before your blade tastes the blood of an enemy, it needs to taste yours."

Aryis wasted no time. She picked up the knife, held it to her left hand, and drew it across, sucking in a breath. Blood pooled in her palm. Nyssa nodded and went to the bathroom to retrieve a towel.

Nyssa took the knife from Aryis and cleaned its blade, returning it to its box before gently wrapping the towel around Aryis's hand.

"Now that Talon has tasted your blood, it's bonded to you."

"Talon?" Aryis asked.

"Yes. Do you like the name?"

Aryis smiled. "It's perfect."

Nyssa gently squeezed her wrapped hand before pressing it up against her chest. "We'll find a healer to bind up that wound tomorrow, before we hunt down Quinn."

"Oh, why don't I let it heal on its own?"

"You can if you wish, but a cut on the palm is annoying."

"I noticed you have a scar on your hand where I assume you cut yourself with Winter's Bite."

"Winter's Bite?" Nyssa asked, confused.

Aryis blushed. "Oh. I know you haven't named your sword, but after you fought so courageously at The Masthead I thought it was appropriate. I know it's silly."

Nyssa laughed. "No, I...I actually love it. Winter's Bite. It's a good name. Strong and fitting. And yes, I chose not to get my scar healed over. Some scars I leave as reminders, much like this one." She pointed to her face.

"Reminders of what?" Aryis asked.

"Mistakes."

"I...I asked Athen about your facial scar, but he told me to ask you. Will you tell me?"

Nyssa sighed and sat down. "When we were thirteen, the Masters finally put real swords in our hands. I was so excited. I finally felt like a proper warrior. Athen and I set off to spar, and I got cocky, feigning attacks, thinking myself the best swordswoman in the Empire. And Athen caught me. He did exactly as he was trained and sliced right through my face." She folded her hands together. "He carried me to the healers, thinking that I would lose my eye. But they fixed me up. I just never went back to have the scar healed over."

"Why?"

"That's private."

Aryis looked down, sensing she shouldn't push the issue. "Thank you for being patient with me. I don't have any friends back at Wayland. They all made their minds up about me because of my last name."

"I know what that feels like," Nyssa said, standing up. "We're both treated differently because of who we are. Fuck the lot of them."

Aryis tried to muster a smile, but she hated that she didn't have even one friend at the Conservatory.

"Now, go get some sleep. We need to be rested and ready to capture Quinn."

THE CHASE

The crowd pressed around Aryis in the busy square. Stall owners shouted or employed dancing lights made of magick to draw attention to their goods and tease money out of the pockets of customers. The enticing aroma of grilled meats and freshly ground coffee hung in the cold air while a man on a crate advertised his spun sugar treats.

Aryis's stomach growled.

She pulled out Quinn's book and held it in her left palm, running her right hand along the top of it to get the sense of the woman; to feel her presence. The book was one end of a thread, and she waited to find the other end and follow it to Quinn. Aryis closed her eyes and slowed her breathing, trying to shut out the distractions surrounding her. She reached out with her senses, concentrating on the book in her hand, anchoring herself to it.

Aryis opened her eyes and glanced down at the book, now glowing red. She ran her hand along its cover, and it glowed brighter. Thin, red tendrils of light materialized and stretched forward. Using the same trick from Ocean's Rest, she ran her red tendril along the ground, a far less noticeable option than weaving through a crowd of bodies.

Aryis stepped forward, following the threads of light, moving toward a target she could not yet see. Nyssa moved in tandem with her and

Athen. It was risky to take Quinn in a crowd, but it was loud and busy, and they could get her out of the square without making much of a fuss.

As they wound their way through throngs of people, Aryis held her concentration, not letting the tether drop. The red tendril kept sliding toward the center of the crowd. Aryis and Athen pushed past a boisterous group of men laughing at a street performer, coming to a large, round fountain. A lone figure stood in front of it, facing away from them.

The threads of light reached the figure and lazily wound up her legs. Aryis cursed and broke the tether, her magick dissolving into the air, lest she tip Quinn off like she did in Ocean's Rest.

Quinn was dressed in a tattered, dusty cloak with a hood with ratty, mismatched boots sticking out from the bottom. Aryis spotted Nyssa out of the corner of her eye, swiftly moving toward their target.

Just as Nyssa reached the runaway adept, the shrouded figure whirled on her and caught her square in the face with a fist.

"Shit, shit, shit, shit, shit," Nyssa hissed.

She stumbled backward and fell to one knee, grasping her throbbing nose while their fugitive fled. She gave it a wiggle. Not broken, a small tidbit of good fortune, but damn bloody. Athen and Aryis ran to her side.

"Go after her! I'm good."

Not my finest moment.

Aryis took off running after Quinn, and Athen barreled around the fountain, following them. A few gazes turned their way, but no one made a move to stop them.

Nyssa shook her head to get rid of the fuzziness at the edge of her vision. She got caught off guard and caught good. She cursed herself for being so careless as she took off running after Athen.

She exited the town square and turned down a narrow street. Nyssa struggled to keep up—their runaway was fast, that was certain. Hoping

Aryis was just as swift, Nyssa followed Athen, running through narrow streets and alleys, losing track of the twists and turns, moving farther and farther away from the market square, just doing her best to keep her eyes on him.

The scent of brine became stronger, and the sound of the sea grew louder. Quinn was running them toward the docks. Nyssa doubled her efforts, sucking down air and trying to ignore the throbbing of her nose.

Athen disappeared around a corner, and Nyssa followed, almost running into the back of him and Aryis. Up ahead, a group of men and women had paused what looked to be a game of dice. Quinn was among them, pointing back at the three of them.

"Help!" she yelled. "Slavers are after me."

The five men and women, all in dark wool peacoats and looking quite formidable, turned at once toward the threesome. Even in unaffiliated territories, slavers were hated.

Athen held up his hand. "Now wait. She's a fugitive from the Areshi Empire, and we're Imperial adepts sent to return her. Not slavers."

One of the men, grizzled and hairy, stepped forward. He was short, but his broad shoulders more than gave the impression he was a bruiser. "Don't much care if you're slavers or Empire. Girl came to my crew asking for help, we help."

Aryis pulled at Nyssa's arm. "What do we do?"

Nyssa eyed Quinn as she retreated behind the man and his crew. Likely shipmates trying to enjoy a little shore leave, but obviously not a group that backed down from a scrap.

Nyssa would admire them if they weren't between her and her prey.

"Stay behind us," she instructed Aryis, patting Athen on the back. "You want to clear these guys out?"

"I'll mow 'em down, you go after Quinn," he said, voice low. He rose to his full height, cracked his knuckles, and rushed the group of sailors. Bodies went flying as he fought, five-on-one, but nowhere near a fair fight. He could have easily crushed all of them, but hurting innocents wasn't part of their mission.

As Athen waded into the group, Nyssa pulled Aryis along behind her, darting around him.

A hand grabbed at her, and she pushed Aryis in front of her. "Go after Quinn! Hurry, I'll be right behind you," she ordered, turning her attention to the woman who yanked her back.

The woman threw a punch at Nyssa, but she ducked out of the way, not ready to take another unpleasant strike to the face. She grabbed the woman's shoulders, pulled her toward her, and buried a knee in her midsection. The woman collapsed to the ground.

Nyssa pivoted and ran after Aryis. She spilled out into a busy street, bumping into people headed from the docks. It was late afternoon, and the dock workers and ship crews were headed to the bars and card houses, the day's work done.

She spotted Aryis's long ponytail bobbing down the street. The dings of metal against metal and wood, along with the call of seabirds, filled the air as Nyssa gave chase, reaching the inlet that nearly split the island of Jejin in half. Wide footbridges ran from one side of the inlet to the other, joining both sides of the island. Aryis was on the bridge, and ahead of her, their hooded fugitive.

Athen pulled up and stopped next to Nyssa. "Come on, we can't leave Aryis alone to fend for herself," he said, taking off again. Nyssa followed. A few gazes turned their way, but no one made a move to stop them.

The crunch of gravel under Nyssa's feet turned to thumps against wood once they got to the bridge. It was wide enough for five people across and slung low, only a foot above the water, with handrails to cling to after a night of drinking. To Nyssa's relief, the bridge was mostly empty.

Fifty feet ahead, Aryis had caught up with Quinn, and Nyssa's stomach sank when Aryis collapsed to the bridge, a victim of Quinn's fists again.

"Fuck," Athen growled.

Quinn bent over Aryis for a moment before snapping back up and taking off again. Aryis swayed back up to her feet and yelled, "Stop!"

Athen and Nyssa were twenty feet away when Nyssa spotted an orange glow beneath Aryis's feet and slowed to a stop, pulling Athen back. Thick tendrils of magick wove around the wooden slats of the bridge, holding it together.

Ahead of them, a jumble of orange glowing letters floated above the handrails in a language Nyssa didn't recognize. They shimmered and changed to the common language of the Western continent—Caution Bridge Under Repair—before changing again to a series of symbols.

Nyssa eyed Quinn, who glanced down.

"Oh shit," Nyssa breathed.

Quinn knelt at the edge of the repair on her side of the bridge and touched one of the vibrant cords of magick that held the bridge together. The orange glow of the enchantment flickered. Before Nyssa could move, the bridge beneath Aryis fell apart, and she plunged into the icy water.

"Aryis!" Athen yelled, and lunged forward, scrambling to the edge of the bridge. Aryis sputtered and swam toward him.

Nyssa trained her eyes on their fugitive standing across the gap where the bridge used to be. A smile curled Quinn's lips, and she gave Nyssa a terse wave before turning and running again.

Nyssa snarled. "Son of a bitch, I'm going to wipe that smirk off her face. We'll double back and track her again. She won't get off this island."

Athen pulled Aryis out of the water, and she flopped onto the wood, soaked head to toe, her teeth chattering.

"N-Nyssa," Aryis said, "I c-can't track her. She t-took the book!"

"Just summon it back to yourself!"

Aryis held a trembling hand out, a golden glow surrounding her hand. Nothing happened. "I...I don't understand, it won't come. The book won't come!"

Fuck. Quinn would escape and take Nyssa's future with her.

Nyssa turned to Athen. "Can you jump the gap?"

"No, it's too far for me."

"Then toss me over."

Athen blinked at her before looking across the missing section of the footbridge. "Nyssa, that's got to be over twenty-five feet. You'll break your neck."

Nyssa grabbed his arm. "If she gets away, we'll never find her again. I can land that...just aim well, okay?"

Athen shook his head.

"Please," she whispered.

He bared his teeth and hissed, "Fuck, fuck, fuck." He turned his back to the gap in the bridge, laced his hands together, and bent down. Nyssa slotted one foot in his palms and braced her hands against his shoulders. His eyebrows knit with worry, but she nodded at him.

"Okay, big man."

Aryis scrambled to her feet. "Nyssa, this is insane, y-you'll get hurt—"

Athen launched Nyssa through the air over his shoulder, aiming blindly for the other side of the footbridge. Azure water passed beneath her, parts of the collapsed bridge floating in the inlet. Nyssa barely had time to get her feet under her before she reached the other side, landing and immediately collapsing her legs, rolling over on her shoulder once, then twice, her momentum carrying her forward. She flattened out, skidding against the bridge. Her chin bounced viciously off a wooden slat, filling her vision with stars.

She flopped onto her back, her hands opening and closing, grasping at nothing as the world pulled away from her. A loud hum filled her ears. Half-formed curse words floated in and out of her head.

The voices of Athen and Aryis roused her back to consciousness, and she did a slow mental inventory of her body.

Nothing seemed amiss.

She willed herself to stand.

Turning back to Athen and Aryis, she yelled, "Take the next bridge and meet me on the other side."

Nyssa's legs trembled beneath her and weren't good for anything other than a slow jog at first, but her pace quickened when she had eyes on their fugitive again. The bridge was now empty, save for a few people, but if Quinn got to the other side of the inlet and into the crowded streets of Jejin, it would be easy for her to disappear forever.

Gritting her teeth and ignoring the twinge of pain that flared in her ribs, Nyssa pushed forward, breaking into a full run, willing her body to hold out for a few more moments. Through sheer force of will, she quickly closed the distance to Quinn, who chanced a glance over her shoulder. It must have thrown her balance off because she stumbled and nearly fell.

Nyssa took advantage of the blunder to make up the last few feet and launched herself at Quinn, tackling her. They tumbled to the ground, the impact with the hard wood drawing a groan out of Nyssa.

Quinn kicked at her, trying to scramble away, but Nyssa latched onto her ankle and yanked. She needed to get Quinn subdued. A blade flashed in the fugitive's hand, and Nyssa leaned back out of striking range.

Quinn pulled out of Nyssa's grasp, and they rose to their feet in concert. She kept her dagger trained on Nyssa, who took a cautious step backward. Getting stuck in the gut wasn't in the day's plan.

"Whoa now, girl. You don't want to do that." Nyssa ran the back of her hand across her mouth and nose, blood smearing on her face. "You are going to only hurt yourself with that knife."

Brandishing her blade, Quinn shuffled forward a few inches. "I don't have any money."

"You think I'm a thief?"

"Come near me and I'll kill you!"

"That's rude," Nyssa scoffed. "We're not thieves. Arcton Citadel misses you. We're here to take you back."

Quinn narrowed her eyes, a flash of recognition on her face, and she snarled at her. "You can piss right off. I'll kill you before I let you take me back."

The audacity of this woman.

Nyssa lunged, grabbing Quinn's wrist and twisting it to force the blade from her hand. A sharp palm strike to Quinn's chest landed her on her ass with a cry of surprise.

Nyssa kicked the knife away and bent over her, gathering two fistfuls of cloak to pull her to her feet. She reared a fist back and punched Quinn in her nose, letting her drop to the bridge.

"Stop hitting me," the woman weakly mumbled from the ground, blood dripping from her nose.

"You and I are even now." Nyssa pointed to her own bloody nose. She knelt in front of Quinn and pulled a length of rope out of a jacket pocket. "Hands together."

Quinn didn't move.

"Behave or I start hitting again," Nyssa warned.

"Ignorant brute," Quinn spat.

"Arrogant ass," Nyssa shot back. She wound the rope around Quinn's wrists, giving the knot a firm yank.

Quinn hissed.

"Let's get a proper look at you." Nyssa pulled down Quinn's hood to reveal a wavy tumble of dirty, dark hair, bright-green eyes, and—under layers of dirt and grime—cheeks dotted with freckles.

Nyssa pulled a piece of cloth out of her pocket. "Open your mouth." Quinn clenched her jaw tight.

"Open your mouth or I'll break it." Nyssa tapped on Quinn's nose, and she stared back at her in defiance for a moment before relenting and opening her mouth. Nyssa used the cloth as a gag, slipping it between Quinn's teeth and binding it tightly around her head.

She pulled Quinn's cloak open and found the book tucked into her waistband. "I'll have this back," Nyssa said, retrieving the tome and sticking it in her own jacket. "Now, sit tight while we wait." She leaned back against the handrail opposite Quinn, rubbing her sore ribs. "Nice trick with disintegrating the bridge repair. Some spellweaver is going to be pissed at your handiwork ruining their handiwork."

Quinn stared up at Nyssa, murder in her eyes. Nyssa didn't much care. She was just relieved Quinn hadn't escaped, taking Nyssa's shot at becoming an Ashcloak with her.

The adrenaline of the chase wore away and left Nyssa breathing heavily, a dull ache throbbing in her ribs. No doubt the remnants of her injury from the wraith attack, aggravated by her hard landing across the gap in the bridge.

A few pedestrians strolled between them while they waited. "This one owes me money. She's shit at cards," Nyssa lied if anyone eyed Quinn.

It took over ten minutes for Athen and Aryis to reach them. Aryis looked absolutely miserable, her teeth chattering from her time in the water.

"Nice work!" Athen said, beaming at Nyssa and nodding at Quinn. "You okay? You had a rough landing."

Nyssa scoffed. "I was graceful. Like a cat."

"A d-dead cat," Aryis said.

"Rude." Nyssa laughed and clapped Aryis on the back, a loud *SPAK!* ringing out as her hand hit the waterlogged cloak. Nothing could ruin Nyssa's mood now that they had Quinn.

"Here," Athen said, taking off his cloak and wrapping it around Aryis's shoulders.

"Thank you."

Athen leaned over and hauled Quinn to her feet. Nyssa pushed off the handrail and stepped in front of her before pulling the hood back over their fugitive's eyes and poking a finger into the woman's chest. "Don't try to run. Keep your eyes down."

Quinn's eyes blazed with anger, but Nyssa didn't look away. She crossed her arms and waited for the woman to comply. Quinn finally lowered her eyes toward the ground.

"Good girl," Nyssa said. She turned to Athen. "Lead the way."

"Keep hold of her."

Nyssa patted Quinn on the back and locked arms with her. "She's in excellent hands." Quinn glared at her, words that sounded like a string of expletives muffled by the gag.

Aryis fell in next to Quinn and reached across to hand Nyssa a cold, wet handkerchief. "For your nose," she said. "Sorry, it's slightly damp."

"Thank you, Aryis," Nyssa said, wiping the blood from her face, and they started back toward The Lash. She leaned closer to Quinn. "That was quite a nasty punch back at the fountain, I'll give you that. Took me by surprise. But be warned, that'll only happen once."

THE RUNAWAY

A few eyebrows rose when the three adepts walked their new acquaintance through The Lash and to the backstairs. Mox gave them a nod as they passed. Once back in their suite, Nyssa took Quinn by the arm and steered her toward the dining table, pulling out a chair and shoving her down into it. She pushed the hood of Quinn's ratty cloak off her head.

Nyssa sat opposite the woman, fighting back a groan, soreness setting into her body. Athen and Aryis stood behind her while she contemplated her words. Treating Quinn with kindness could go a long way to keeping her calm and contained. But Eron had told Nyssa many times she needed to work on her interpersonal skills.

She shifted in her chair. "My name is Nyssa Blacksea, and the big man is Athen Fennick. We're from the Emerald Order. And our friend there is Aryis Devitt from the Wayland Conservatory. It's our intention to get you back to Arcton Citadel in one piece, and we'd like your cooperation."

Nyssa got up and removed the woman's gag. Quinn flexed her jaw and raised her bound hands.

"No. Not until I have your word that you'll behave," Nyssa said. "My nose still aches."

"As does mine," Quinn croaked, her voice raspy.

Aryis spoke up from behind Nyssa. "Well, don't start a fight with the Emerald Order if you don't wish to get hurt."

Quinn glared at her before her bright-green eyes settled back on Nyssa. "You three are the idiots from Ocean's Rest? I punched that one, as I recall." Quinn nodded toward Aryis.

"Yes, you did," Nyssa said.

"I'm astonished you're not..." Quinn stopped.

"Dead? Yeah, we fought off a legion of wraiths and saved lives while you fled."

Quinn scowled at Nyssa. "Are you taking me back so a Justiciar can kill me? Too good to dirty your own hands? Or do you not have the stomach for killing?"

Nyssa studied Quinn's face. Her eyes still had a spark of anger, but her shoulders drooped. Nyssa leaned forward, touching her knee, and she flinched.

"We are not taking you back for execution," Nyssa said softly.

Quinn shook her head. "Liar. I know what happens to adepts who abandon their guild. A Justiciar will take my head. Or they'll have me marked as Unworthy."

"You have our word," Athen piped up. "You won't face punishment."

"I wish I could believe you, but the world is full of liars who wear kind faces."

Aryis stepped forward and squatted down next to Quinn's chair. "The Empress herself has granted you mercy. Arcton Citadel will welcome you back without question. I give you my word as the first daughter of House Devitt of Frosland."

Quinn looked at Aryis and scowled. "You have a very kind face. They would send someone exactly like you to persuade me."

Aryis opened her mouth to say something in response, but Nyssa laid a hand on her shoulder to stop her.

"Quinn, can we offer you a bath? Get you some clean clothes?" she asked, standing. She held out her hand to help Quinn to her feet, but the woman ignored her, standing on her own. She held up her bound wrists.

Sighing, Nyssa untied her hands.

Athen stood behind her, giving Quinn a once-over. "Could you take off your boots? Your feet are not big enough to fill those," he chuckled. Quinn did as she was asked. Her feet were bare and black. She nudged the boots towards him with a toe.

He bent over before straightening up quick. "Okay, those need to be burned. They are ripe."

Quinn looked down and mumbled, "I'm sorry. I'm not an unclean person, I just..."

Nyssa leaned forward, a spark of pity igniting in her heart. "Let's get you cleaned up."

She escorted Quinn down the hallway, leading her to one of the cozy bedrooms with a small fireplace on one side of the room and a small adjoining bathroom housing a generous tub on the opposite side. Two large windows flanked the bed and looked out onto the terrace.

Nyssa ducked her head into the bathroom. "Wash up. There's a robe here that'll have to do until we get some fresh clothes for you. Leave your old clothes in the corner, they will be destroyed. If you have any belongings on you, be sure to set them aside."

"I have nothing," Quinn said, her green eyes alive with resentment. She set her jaw and seemed about to say something before Aryis joined them in the bedroom. Quinn quickly spun away and headed into the bathroom, closing the door behind her.

When Nyssa heard the water run, she turned to Aryis. "Don't leave this room until I come back. Keep an eye on that door."

Nyssa joined Athen in the great room as he was stoking the fire. "Hardest part is over," he said. "Don't you think punching Quinn in the nose was a little..."

"Over the top? I couldn't help myself, she called me an ignorant brute! She was very punchable at that moment."

Athen stood up and smiled. "Regardless of that little indiscretion, Eron would be proud of his ignorant brute."

Nyssa exhaled. For the first time in a long time, she believed she was moving toward her future. Proving herself worthy.

"Can you go see if Mox has some clothes we can snag? She's about Aryis's size. Five foot five, maybe? She'll also need a good coat and cloak.

We want to keep her toasty warm and happy. Oh, get a pair of gloves. Leather. Something tells me Mox has plenty of leather." Nyssa gave Athen a wink. "Oh, and don't forget underwear! Preferably not leather."

"Got it. Underwear," he said, smiling. He handed her the fireplace poker. "Don't let that fire go out."

Nyssa walked over to one of the big, comfortable chairs by the fire, sitting down with a tired sigh. She laughed to herself before absentmindedly poking at the fire, her thoughts drifting back to Quinn's brilliant green eyes, angry and defiant.

After Nyssa tended the fire for a while and sorted her thoughts, she walked back into Quinn's bedroom where Aryis waited beside the bathroom door. Nyssa lay across the bed, looking at her.

"What do you think?" Nyssa asked, nodding her head toward the bathroom.

"I think if we show her a bit of kindness and compassion, she'll be easier to deal with. I don't like confrontation," Aryis said. She walked across the room and sat on the bed next to Nyssa.

"You did good today."

Aryis groaned in response. "I got punched again. At least you did, too."

"Hey!"

Aryis shook her head. "I meant nothing by it!"

Nyssa chuckled. "She's got quite a fist on her. I can't believe she caught me."

Aryis looked down at her hands. "Is it weird to say that I had more fun today than I've had in the last...I don't know...forever at Wayland?"

"No, it's not weird at all. When I was at the Order, before every sparring session, I could feel my heart beating in my chest and the hairs on the back of my neck rise. It's a dance, exciting and dangerous all at once."

"It's not the physical part—though that was exhilarating—it's the feeling that I actually *did* something. Something important instead of opening a book and writing another endless missive about the nature of magick."

"Now you know what the last three years since I turned twenty-two have been like for me, waiting at the Order, hoping to be named an Ashcloak."

The bathroom door cracked a bit, then swung open, and Quinn stepped out in a dark-blue robe, running a towel through her long dark hair.

"There she is," Aryis said. "My goodness, you clean up well. There's a human under that dirt after all, eh, Nyssa?"

"Yes. Yes there is..." Nyssa tried to think of something amusing to say but found herself at a loss, distracted by Quinn. A chill ran over her skin. "Athen is getting you some clothes, and food should come up soon. There's a hairbrush at the dressing table."

Quinn nodded. She sat down at the table and ran the brush through her hair, catching on tangles. The dark robe was a stark contrast to her pale skin, previously hidden under weeks of dirt. Her cheeks were flushed from the bath, and she cast her eyes down while she brushed her hair.

"Well, I think perhaps we should give you a little privacy," Aryis said, gesturing for Nyssa to come with her.

Nyssa stood and smoothed out her clothes. She cleared her throat after a beat. "Behave," she said to Quinn, then followed Aryis out of the room.

After they closed the door, Aryis turned to her. "Are you okay?"

"I'm fine," she said, walking down the hallway and stopping outside her room. "I need to clean up."

"Okay, I'll keep watch out here."

Nyssa nodded and entered her room, closing the door behind her before she leaned against it and exhaled deeply.

A PERFECTLY PLEASANT DINNER

Nyssa sat in the dark for an hour after freshening up. Quinn cleaned up well, and seeing her without a layer of dirt set off an odd spark of recognition, as if she knew Quinn. Which was impossible.

A gentle knocking on her door pulled her out of her thoughts.

"Nyssa?" Aryis called out.

"I'll be out in a second." Nyssa tried to rouse herself to get up and open the door and get out of her own head. She looked in the mirror, passing her hand over the nearest light orb to illuminate the room. She stood up straighter and smoothed out her shirt, closing her eyes and taking a deep breath.

Sighing, she took one last look at herself, then went to open the door. As she exited her room, Quinn stepped out into the hallway. She was dressed in the new clothes Athen brought her, though they were a little baggy—black leather pants, short boots, and a tan knit sweater pulled over a gray cotton shirt that stuck out at the bottom. When Quinn saw Nyssa, she crossed her arms over her body.

Nyssa pulled her door closed and waited for her. "How are the clothes? Do they fit alright?"

Quinn shrugged.

"Keep those gloves on, please. We don't want any mishaps with your magick," Nyssa said, her voice soft. "You look a sight better now."

"Not being covered in a layer of grime does wonders," Quinn replied, her green eyes meeting Nyssa's gaze, jaw tight. She had a little color in her cheeks, and her raven hair tumbled over her shoulders in loose waves, faintly scented with the cedar and juniper soap.

"It sure does, Freckles—which I can see clearly now. Cute." Nyssa flashed her a lopsided grin.

Quinn scowled, and her face went red. "That's rather forward of you."

"I'm a rather forward person. How is your nose?"

"It aches. And yours?"

Nyssa stuck her lower lip out and shrugged. "It's survived worse."

"Barely, it would appear."

Nyssa raised an eyebrow and grunted out a laugh.

The cheek of this woman.

"Let's get some food in you."

Quinn followed Nyssa out into the great room, annoyed at her forwardness. The woman's manners needed work. When Athen and Aryis saw Quinn, they remarked on how much better she looked. She tried to will the heat from her cheeks but failed. Nyssa stood silent, her gaze unnerving.

Quinn knew the Areshi Empire would pursue her—leaving the Citadel without permission was forbidden. She expected to be chased by Justiciars and branded a traitor to the Empire, probably killed on sight, but these three weren't the cruel pursuers she had imagined. They were adhering to guild rules—all adepts should be treated as brothers and sisters.

What a pile of horseshit.

Athen pulled out a chair at the rustic dining table. Quinn was familiar with his family name, though he didn't put on airs. Aryis puzzled Quinn as well. She didn't understand why a scion of one of the noble Houses of the Areshi Empire was out in the wilds of the Unbound territories.

Then there was Nyssa. The crude woman had an orphan's name, yet the others seemed to defer to her. She was quick to anger and carried herself with a cockiness that rankled Quinn.

Her captors had clothed her and now offered her a seat at their table, unexpected gestures of kindness.

She didn't trust any of them.

The four sat down to the small feast sent up by The Lash's kitchen. Quinn's mouth watered—the roasted chicken smelling divine. Potatoes, carrots, and turnips basted in garlic butter, their outsides gently charred and their insides soft and warm, accompanied the bird, along with thick slices of dark rye bread and butter. Their tankards were full of a foamy, iced winter tea. Quinn noticed Nyssa eyeing the fruit pie while she ate. It was almost bursting with apples, its crust topped with dark caramelized sugar.

Quinn tried to be as mannered as possible, but she was famished and ate with more fervor than the rest of them. Her time on the island had been difficult, her money and bag stolen within the first few days of her arrival, and she'd resorted to begging for scraps of food and clothing.

The entire experience was humiliating.

Fully engaged in pulling every bit of meat off a chicken leg, Quinn hunched over her plate, trying to ignore Nyssa's steady gaze. Finally, Nyssa spoke up. "I'm curious, why did you leave your guild?"

Quinn straightened and took another bite, letting the awkward silence linger.

Nyssa pressed further. "Arcton Citadel, no less."

Quinn narrowed her eyes, unappreciative of the questioning. "They took me in as a baby. No one gave me a choice in the matter."

Nyssa's eyebrows perked up, and she and Athen shared a glance.

"What I wouldn't give to take just a peek at their library," Aryis sighed. "That Citadel is a scholar's dream. All the secrets of the Empire; so many rare books and artifacts I'm dying to see. I could spend hours in the enchanted items collection alone—"

"You romanticize a drafty old mansion full of dust and secrets," Quinn replied.

Aryis spoke up again, undeterred. "But you got an excellent education. You betrayed your mentors and your peers by leaving."

Quinn's blood turned hot. "I betrayed no one! You know nothing about me, girl."

"I didn't claim to. I'm simply making an observation. You're viewed as a traitor because you abandoned your guild. You have to know this."

"I really don't care what anyone thinks of me." Quinn tossed the chicken bone on her plate. "I'm done being a guild slave, a mindless fool like you three."

Aryis scowled. "Your rudeness is uncalled for. And you're not a slave."

Quinn shook her head in frustration and disgust. "You're gullible. A good little adept, aren't you? Throwing out your family name like it's supposed to impress me. Give me the word of a Devitt, like it's precious currency. You're nothing more than a bauble for the Empire to dress up and trot out at state dinners."

Quinn turned her attention to Nyssa. "And this one here. A capable fighter, aren't you? Look at that meandering nose. That scar. You use that as your currency like that one uses her family name, since you don't have one yourself. I'm supposed to be intimidated by someone who punches first and tries to sweet-talk later? You're laughable."

Nyssa opened her mouth, but Quinn moved on to Athen. "And you, big boy, all you likely do is nod and smile and run to obey whatever orders your Masters give you. You're a good little lapdog. Or perhaps to be more precise, you're her lapdog." Quinn nodded her head in Nyssa's direction.

Nyssa shot out of her chair and rounded the table before Quinn could blink, yanking her out of her chair. Quinn put her hands up, not willing to fight back and get another punch in the nose for her troubles.

"How dare you!" Nyssa snarled.

"Fuck off," Quinn snapped.

Athen stood. "Nyssa, let her go."

Nyssa eyed him before shoving Quinn away from her.

"Bit of a hothead, eh? Where's your cute little pet name now?" Quinn smirked at Nyssa. "You don't intimidate me. The guilds must have scraped the bottom of the barrel for you lot." She smoothed the front of her sweater and sat back down at her place at the table.

Nyssa didn't move. "Open your mouth again and see what happens."

Athen turned to her. "Nyssa, let it go."

"Listen to your lapdog, Nyssa," Quinn said. "Let it go."

Athen pulled Nyssa's chair out and pushed her into it, then he sat back down and reached over to pick up Quinn's tankard. He drained its contents, held it up in front of her face, and crushed it with one hand while she looked on, slowly chewing. She made a mental note—corporeal magick, strength—for later.

"You will keep your thoughts to yourself. We will return you to your guild, and it will be good riddance, hope to never see you again," he said, returning the crumpled tankard to its place next to her plate.

Quinn merely shrugged, reached across the table, and stabbed her fork into the fruit pie, dragging the whole thing over to herself. His large hand wrapped around her wrist.

"Let me cut you a piece," Athen said, giving her a wan smile.

Quinn stared at Nyssa quietly seething. The damage had been done. It surprised Quinn that stabbing the pie didn't send Nyssa over the edge again.

Athen slid a slice onto her plate.

"Next time, mind your manners," he cautioned. Quinn ignored him, continuing to stare at Nyssa with contempt as she ate her pie.

It was delicious.

Nyssa pushed her plate away and stood. "I need to wash this day off me," she said, then pointed her finger at Quinn. "If she even looks at the door, tie her up."

A PATIENT GUEST

Quinn found a couple empty sketchbooks on one of the well-stocked bookcases lining the walls next to the fireplace and pulled one down. Gathering a few pencils from the writing desk, she opened the book and began sketching, one of the few activities she had been allowed to keep herself busy back in Arcton Citadel.

She kept her eyes on her two guards. Athen tended to the fire, and Aryis scanned the bookshelves.

"Anything interesting?" Athen asked after a while.

"Oh, I would say there's a lot of interesting material here," Aryis replied. "A lot of, um, racier books. There's one here that professes to contain over one hundred sexual positions. A dubious claim."

Athen choked on his own laughter. "Let me see that one." Aryis looked at him, and he held his hand out, eyebrow arched. She shrugged, pulling the book down for him and handing it over. He sat across from Quinn and started browsing through it.

Aryis turned her attention to Quinn. "What are you doing?"

Quinn pulled her sketchbook closer to her. "Nothing of interest."

"Suit yourself."

Aryis scanned the bookcase until she found a book and sat next to Athen. As she read, she would look aside and move her lips almost imperceptibly.

Talking to herself? Making mental notes?

Very odd.

Aryis held her hand out in front of her, and with a small flash of golden light, a leather notebook appeared in her palm, sparks falling off the book like a small cadre of falling stars.

"What did you just do?" Quinn asked.

"Nothing of interest," Aryis replied with a smirk.

She opened the book and began making notes, but after a moment, she stopped and addressed Quinn.

"Corporeal magick. I can *blink* books to me if I've read them. Of course, I'm writing in my notebook all the time, so..."

"Blink?" Quinn asked.

"That's what I call it. Summoning sounds so serious."

"Just books?" Quinn asked, curious.

"I tried a pet rabbit once when I was a child," Aryis replied, her face growing dark. "It did not go well. I stick with books."

"A serviceable bit of magick, I suppose."

Aryis offered a smile. Quinn didn't completely dislike the woman, but she wondered when the Wayland Conservatory and the Empire would wring the kindness and curiosity out of her. How many years would it take to turn Aryis cold and complacent?

Nyssa interrupted Quinn's dark thoughts upon returning to the great room. Her hair was damp and cheeks red from a bath. She padded across the floor in bare feet, her shirt halfway tucked into her pants. She eyed Quinn as she crossed the room to sit on the arm of Athen's chair, leaning on his shoulder. When she got a look at his reading material, she arched an eyebrow and cocked her head to the side.

"Oh, that's a fun one," she said, tapping her finger on an illustration. She winked at Aryis. "What are you all up to?"

"I was just having a friendly chat with our guest," Aryis said.

"Prisoner," Nyssa and Quinn corrected simultaneously. A smug, self-satisfied smirk spread across Nyssa's face. She got up and rounded the back of Quinn's chair, plucking the sketchbook out of her hands. She stared down at the drawing, a scowl settling on her face. "Seriously?"

Nyssa turned the book toward the other two. Athen tried to keep a straight face, but Aryis was less restrained.

"It's rather good," she remarked with a giggle. "Captures your likeness well."

Nyssa tossed the book onto Quinn's lap. The sketch wasn't complete yet, but the bones were there—a drawing depicting the moment Quinn caught Nyssa with a punch to her nose.

That it rankled Nyssa made it all the better.

"Alright, it's time for bed. I'll take watch out here tonight. Try to sneak out of your room and I'll have your ass," Nyssa said to Quinn.

"I'll relieve you before dawn," Athen said, "so you can get some sleep."

"May I have a book?" Quinn asked. "I promise not to knock you out with it and attempt a daring escape."

"No. To your room," Nyssa insisted.

Quinn stood, and with a dramatic curtsy to Nyssa, she turned and walked back to her bedroom.

"She's got an attitude," Nyssa said, hands on hips. "Arrogant."

"Yes, reminds me of someone," Athen replied.

Nyssa cuffed his shoulder. "Go to bed!"

Athen and Aryis roused themselves and headed off to their bedrooms. Nyssa looked down the hallway and sighed. Quinn's words over dinner stung, but Nyssa still didn't think being disagreeable was the best option, even if the woman intended to test every strand of her patience.

She sighed and took a quick scan of the bookshelves, pulling a book down and heading to Quinn's room. She knocked softly on Quinn's door before entering. Quinn was lying back on the bed, hands folded across her stomach while she stared at the ceiling, her gloves next to her.

"Why bother knocking if you're just going to let yourself in?" Quinn asked with a sigh.

Nyssa walked over to the bed. "Do you mind if I sit?"

"Can I stop you?"

Nyssa sat down on the edge of the bed and placed the book next to Quinn. She glanced at Quinn's hands, surprised to see them peppered with small scars that seemed odd for the hands of an adept at a cushy guild.

"I brought you something to read," Nyssa said, drumming her fingers on the book, considering her next words. "I...apologize if my asking about Arcton Citadel during dinner upset you." She cleared her throat and took a deep breath before continuing, trying not to wince from the pain in her ribs. "I'm also sorry for getting physical with you. But understand this: you can insult me all you want, but those two deserve respect. Please don't speak ill of them again. You don't know them."

"And you don't know me," Quinn said, her voice low, gaze unflinching.

Nyssa nodded. "You're right. I don't." She stood. "Get some sleep. We have a long day of awkwardly staring at each other ahead of us as we await word of our ship."

"Oh, you have jokes. Not just an Order nosebreaker, then?"

"Nope, I have many talents. And if you just get to know me, you'll see I'm quite likable," Nyssa said and walked toward the door.

"I highly doubt that," Quinn replied, drawing a grunt of displeasure out of Nyssa as she opened the door and left.

A gentle knock on her door startled Aryis, and she shot upright, a book tumbling off her chest. She had fallen asleep while reading. Again. Her research into why she was unable to blink Quinn's book to herself had yielded no answers.

She opened the door and Athen stood in the hall. Aryis brightened upon seeing him. He leaned against the doorframe and cocked a smile.

"Did I forget something?" she asked.

"No, I just wanted to say you did a good job today. Better than good."

Aryis grinned. She didn't expect the compliment, though she would take it.

"We make an excellent team, you and I," Athen continued.

"Beauty and brains."

He narrowed his eyes at her. "Am I the brains or the beauty?"

"Maybe both?" Aryis kicked herself for such a dumb answer. For all her studying, the volumes upon volumes of books she read didn't cover flirting. *Wait, is this considered flirting? Am I flirting?*

Athen laughed and leaned forward, his eyes smiling.

Is he going to kiss me?

Aryis panicked, taking a step back into her room.

Crap.

"Well, it's been a long day, and you should get some rest," Aryis said. She held her palm up, and it grew hot, sparks cascading as a book materialized. "I need to get back to trying to find out more about blood wraiths, if you'll excuse me."

Athen nodded, looking a bit confused. And maybe a little sad. "I'll see you in the morning, then."

Aryis closed the door and listened to his footsteps retreat down the hall. She glanced at the book she had mindlessly summoned. *The Dragonfly and the Frog*—a children's book she had read obsessively as a little girl.

She groaned at herself.

Idiot.

AN ORNERY GUEST

Nyssa groaned. A few hours of sleep weren't nearly enough to wipe away her exhaustion. Soft voices accompanied the clank of metal against plates, the muffled sounds of breakfast coming from the great room.

She got up and stood in front of her mirror in her white camisole and tight undershorts, peering at the tendrils of lightning the poison had left on her neck, shoulder, and arm. The scar had not faded at all since it turned dark gray after being cured with the Mother's Tears. Nyssa was losing hope that it would go away at all.

Dishes clattered in the dining room, followed by a loud thud.

Nyssa's blood turned to ice in her veins.

She flew out of her room and ran into the great room to see Quinn bent over Athen's body. "Get away from him!" Nyssa growled.

Quinn's eyes snapped to Nyssa, and she pulled her hand off of Athen's neck. Behind her, Aryis was slumped over the dining table.

Quinn had used her magick on them. She leaped over Athen's prone body, darting toward the door.

Nyssa closed the distance, tackling her, both sprawling to the floor. Quinn scrambled to her knees and spun to face her, grabbing her forearm, bare skin on bare skin. A shimmering darkness flowed across Nyssa's forearm, and Quinn's magick vibrated through Nyssa's body, strange and cold, painlessly arcing through her.

Quinn's eyes flew to Nyssa's face. "What the fuck?"

Nyssa lunged forward and knocked Quinn backward. Quinn hit the floor hard and Nyssa straddled her, pressing a forearm into her throat.

"What did you do to my friends?" Nyssa growled.

"I didn't hurt them! I swear!" Quinn choked out, her fingers grasping at Nyssa, eyes pleading for mercy. Tears rolled down her temples into her hair as she struggled to breathe. "Please," she rasped, squirming under Nyssa, fighting for her life.

Nyssa bared her teeth in a snarl as she lay on top of Quinn with all her weight, crushing her windpipe. Quinn gasped for air, clawing at Nyssa's arms, desperation in her eyes, trying weakly to buck Nyssa off.

I could kill her.

Nyssa sucked in a breath and exhaled forcefully, a cold, dark shiver moving through her. She lifted her forearm from Quinn's throat, and the woman gulped in ragged breaths. Nyssa sat up, her heart pounding in her chest as she desperately tried to slow her breathing.

What am I doing?

Quinn grabbed her throat, sucking in air, locked in Nyssa's

icy blue gaze. The rage on her face splintered and shattered, and she recoiled from Quinn, obviously shaken. Quinn's panic receded, replaced by confusion. Her magick hadn't worked on Nyssa. Had they lied about her being an adept?

"Nyssa?" a weak voice muttered.

Aryis stumbled over and dropped beside them. "Are you okay?"

Quinn opened her mouth, but Aryis pointed an angry finger at her. "You shut up. You don't get to talk."

Nyssa reached up and patted Aryis's outstretched arm. "I'm okay. Her power doesn't affect me."

Nyssa stood and bent over Quinn, yanking her to her feet. Quinn coughed violently and trembled, taking a step back before Nyssa pushed her toward a chair by the fireplace. "Sit down. Try to escape again and—"

"You'll kill me?" Quinn asked quietly so only Nyssa heard. She stared at Quinn, perhaps searching for something to say. Quinn rubbed her throat and ambled over to a chair by the fireplace, trying to draw in a deep breath.

Nyssa turned and picked up Aryis. "How do you feel?"

"Weird and wobbly, I imagine quite like a newborn horse feels when it takes its first step. I have to say, her magick has a fascinating effect. At first, it's like someone turns the lights down really low, and you're disoriented and nothing really works like you think it's going to. Very odd feeling. I believe I spent a good minute trying to grasp hold of a fork. I could see my hand, and I could move it, but not the way I intended. She doesn't just suppress magick, the whole body is affected, which very much supports research that suggests magickal essence is woven into key functions of—"

"Okay, back to the table with you," Nyssa said, scooting Aryis closer to a discarded chair. When Nyssa got Aryis seated, she tended to Athen, who had managed to get back in a chair, holding his head in his hands.

She knelt down next to him. "Athen, you okay?"

The big man groaned and gave a peek at her around his fingers. "I'm trying to keep my breakfast down. Everything is spinning. Just leave me be for a moment."

Nyssa stood and rubbed his shoulder before turning her attention back to Quinn who watched them silently. Nyssa spotted Quinn's gloves on the dining table and picked them up, then walked over and tossed them on her lap. "Put these on. I see them off again around anyone other than me and I will sew them to your goddamn hands. Do you understand?"

Quinn pulled the gloves on and looked up at Nyssa, gaze drifting from her face, down her neck to her left shoulder and arm, lingering on her angry, lightning-shaped scar on full display in her state of undress. Nyssa must have been roused from bed when Quinn tried to escape. If she had been quicker to act, she might have been able to get out the door before Nyssa woke up.

She sighed. "Did you all seriously think I wouldn't attempt to escape? They're going to lock me away in Arcton Citadel until I die. That's what you're condemning me to." She met Nyssa's gaze before looking down at her hands. "The First Master is cruel, and the others are...no one will come near me. They're all cowards."

"We're taking you back," Nyssa insisted.

"Of course you are. Mindless guildies mindlessly following orders."

"Is there anyone in your world who isn't mindless?"

"No, you're all disappointing in the same way."

Nyssa looked down at her, a low growl rumbling in her throat. Her insult had landed. "I don't trust that you won't try to escape again, and since you can't put me on my ass with just a touch, it looks like we're going to be the best of friends until we get you back to Ocean's Rest."

Quinn met Nyssa's gaze and narrowed her eyes. "What exactly are you? You're no Order adept."

"I am. I'm the magickless adept that you apparently haven't heard about. No guild gossip gets up to you in Arcton Citadel?"

Realization hit Quinn. She leaned forward. "Wait, I have heard about you. First Master Anelos mentioned you once."

Nyssa furrowed her eyebrows. "If you've heard of me, then why did you think you could use your powers on me earlier?"

"I didn't know he was talking about you specifically. I never heard a name. He was...unkind in how he referred to you."

The others glanced at Nyssa, who scowled and pushed a pile of books off the chair next to Quinn.

There it is—a crack in her armor.

If Nyssa felt like an outsider, Quinn could use it to gain her sympathy. Maybe she could be worn down, bargained with—Nyssa could be her chance at freedom.

"I've never used my power on anyone like you before," Quinn said.

"I felt your magick move through me. It was so strange," Nyssa murmured.

Quinn caught Nyssa absentmindedly rubbing her left shoulder. A voice from the kitchen startled her.

"Nyssa, go get some clothes on. I'm going to order you breakfast and clean this mess up," Athen said.

Nyssa stood and looked at Quinn. "Don't move from that chair. You try to bolt on us again, I'll break your arm. Don't count yourself too valuable to Arcton Citadel that we won't hurt you if we need to, Quinn. Somehow I think a Justiciar will understand. Aryis, watch her. And I mean eyes on her every second I'm gone, Little Hawk."

Quinn blinked up at Nyssa, and Aryis moved to stand by the front door, taking her duty seriously.

Quinn sank back into her chair and crossed her arms, tucking away every bit of information she learned about Nyssa and the others to use later.

A RESTLESS NIGHT

After a day of being confined to her room, Quinn washed up for bed and pulled a long-sleeve shirt over her head, careful to cover up around Nyssa and the others.

Quinn exited the bathroom to find Nyssa standing at the window, looking up at the night sky, filled with stars and a faint sliver of a moon. Quinn crossed the room to a chest of drawers, found an extra blanket, and tossed it on the chair.

"Here," she offered. "It's going to be a chilly night."

There was no response.

"Nyssa?"

She turned.

"A blanket for you. Winter has taken hold."

Quinn sat on the bed and watched Nyssa settle into a chair and untie her boots. She slipped them off with a heavy sigh and placed them neatly next to her before pulling a small book out of her jacket, opening it up, and frowning down at whatever was on the page. Quinn glimpsed script handwriting scrawled across what appeared to be a notebook.

She glanced up to find Nyssa staring at her, quickly closing her book and storing it back in the interior of her jacket. While curious, Quinn refrained from asking after it, instead considering how best to gain Nyssa's trust and sympathy before their ship arrived back at the dock and her window of opportunity closed.

"How does it work, being an adept without magick?" she asked.

The question seemed to catch Nyssa by surprise, and she paused for a moment, swallowing hard before offering an answer.

"It's like being an adept. But without magick," Nyssa quipped.

"It can't be easy."

"The Emerald Order isn't easy by design. We're warriors. We don't sit in mountainside citadels doing whatever one does in mountainside citadels."

Quinn studied Nyssa's face. She was hard to read and hid behind humor, but Quinn pressed on. Sharing might build trust.

Trust she could exploit.

"I was raised an arm's length from everyone. I had private tutors and a top-notch education that Ceril himself oversaw. The only time I interacted with my fellow adepts was when Ceril wanted me to test the extent of my powers on others. To see how far down I could push their magick, how long it would take to recover," Quinn said. "The others pretty much fear me now."

Nyssa hesitated. "Is it true that First Master Anelos spoke about me?"

"Yes. You're an oddity. Surely you understand that."

"I'm sworn to my guild, just like all other adepts."

"But you're not like other adepts, are you?" Quinn pressed further, taking a guess. "Are you even an Ashcloak?"

Nyssa looked down, her eyes narrowing. The answer was an obvious *no*. How long had the Order strung Nyssa along with the promise of elevating her status? It seemed a rather sore subject by the way she bristled at the question. Quinn hoped the crack in Nyssa's armor was widening so she could worm her way in.

"They treated you differently, didn't they?"

"Kids are cruel, and I got the brunt of it. I was in a lot of lopsided fights," Nyssa said with a frown.

"And the Masters at the Order? They didn't protect you?"

Nyssa looked up, and her expression grew dark, but she didn't answer.

The Masters let her get hurt.

"They didn't stop it, did they?" No answer again. Quinn swallowed. "You and I live in the shadows of our guilds as outcasts."

Nyssa stood, wincing and clutching her side. Quinn pretended not to notice while Nyssa grabbed the blanket off the bed.

"I know what you're doing," she said, pulling the blanket around her shoulders before settling back in the chair. "You think you've found a kindred spirit in me. You get me to pity you so I'll let you go, is that it? It won't work."

Quinn let out a sharp, exasperated breath, standing and walking over to the small fireplace to stoke the glowing embers. "You don't have to take me back."

"I won't betray the Order."

"And I thought Athen was the lapdog."

Nyssa sharply inhaled. "You sound like Anelos. Haughty and arrogant. Above everyone."

Quinn flinched. Being compared to that man was a knife to the gut. She could never be like him.

She turned from the fireplace, meeting Nyssa's inscrutable stare.

"You're a fool. The Order doesn't value you, otherwise you'd be an Ashcloak by now." Quinn huffed and got into the bed.

"When I bring you back, I'll be an Ashcloak, simple as that. You're the only thing that stands between me and my future, so if you think for one moment I would contemplate letting you go, you're insane."

The small glimmer of hope that she could get through to Nyssa faded, and Quinn ground her teeth, setting her jaw. Giving up after how far she'd come wasn't an option.

"Nyssa, you think the other guilds know what Ceril does in the Citadel?"

Nyssa sighed and glared at Quinn. "What is that supposed to mean?"

Quinn sat up in bed, wringing her hands. "The Citadel has the Alabaster Books."

Nyssa gave her a blank look.

Quinn sighed. "Did they teach you nothing at the Emerald Order besides how to hurt people?"

"I didn't take magick classes, asshole."

Quinn ignored Nyssa's insult. "I guess you didn't learn history either. The Alabaster Books are Rell spell books, the ones locked far away in the Citadel. Ceril had me suppressing the magick that protects them so he could study the spells, Nyssa. Those books are strictly off-limits, full of forbidden magick—"

"You are truly desperate," Nyssa said, her tone pointed. "Those are dangerous lies."

"I'm not lying. Ceril's ambitious. In my gut, I know he has bigger plans for himself than being a First Master. He's even spoken about taking me to Cardin with him—and likely not for my scintillating companionship."

"Shut up and go to sleep," Nyssa said, closing her eyes. "And don't repeat what you just said to anyone. You'll get yourself marked as Unworthy for sedition, speaking of a First Master like that."

Quinn sputtered out a frustrated sigh and drew her hand across the light orb on her nightstand to turn it off, plunging the room into a darkness lit only by pale moonlight and the faint red glow of the dying fire. The reflection of the embers danced in Nyssa's eyes.

Quinn quickly got under the covers. If she couldn't win Nyssa's sympathy, she'd have to find another way. She had run from a life she didn't want for herself, trapped and lonely. Only sadness waited for her back at Arcton Citadel.

And First Master Anelos.

Quinn closed her eyes and tried to shut out those thoughts, willing herself to still. She desperately hoped she could find some solace in her dreams. Lately, the one dream she'd had her whole life eluded her, and she desperately wished it would return. It had been her only source of contentment while growing up.

In the dream, she roamed a chill, shadowy forest. Above her, the night sky twinkled with endless stars and she found comfort in the safe presence that took her hand as she sank into infinite darkness.

With a sigh, she slid into sleep, the vast cold of winter settling into her bones.

The nightmare came deep into the night, waking Quinn. Nyssa whimpered in her sleep, struggling against an unseen foe.

"Let them survive this," she mumbled.

Quinn froze and watched Nyssa, not knowing what to do. A gleam of sweat shimmered on Nyssa's forehead, reflecting the last of the glowing embers in the fireplace, and her body tensed up. "Reece," she moaned, her voice soft and weak. "Athen, no."

As she continued struggling, Nyssa's hand shot up to her left shoulder, clutching at the now-healed wound. "What do you want from me?" she hissed, waking with a start moments later, her chest heaving.

Quinn closed her eyes and pretended to be asleep.

A WORD OF ADVICE

The next day, a light rapping on their door disturbed their quiet afternoon. Quinn glanced up, wondering if she could make a break for it. When Athen got up to answer it, any hope slipped away. No getting past the big man. Besides, Nyssa would be on her in seconds.

When Athen opened the door, a small glowing blue orb floated in the hallway.

"Message for Athen Fennick from the Sea Stag. Entrance?" it asked in a tinny voice.

"Yes," Athen said, stepping aside to allow the orb to float in.

It spoke again. "Verify identity."

"Athen Fennick."

"Secondary verification required. Hand please."

Athen held out a hand, palm up, and the orb dipped down quickly, trying and failing to prick a finger for a bit of blood. It tried again with the same result. Quinn bit her lip to stop from laughing. At least these idiots were somewhat entertaining.

"Stop," Athen said. "That won't work. I have to do it. You're not strong enough to get a drop." Athen pulled a small pocketknife and slid it across a finger, hissing at the pain. The orb dipped again and sampled his blood.

"Tastes right. Paper for message?" the orb asked.

Athen walked over to the writing desk and pulled a piece of paper out of a drawer. He placed it on the table, and the orb floated over, positioning itself above it. Tendrils of dark-gray smoke wafted out of it, billowing down on the paper and dissipating quickly as the message appeared.

The orb floated back up and addressed Athen again. "Reply unnecessary. Exit, please."

Athen walked over to the door and cracked it open, and the orb flew out.

He picked up the message and read it. "The Sea Stag will be in port today with plans to leave midday tomorrow. We have our ride home."

Aryis smiled. "I do so enjoy Captain Surk's stories."

"I want to take you shopping today. Explore the city a little before we leave," Athen said.

"What about Nyssa?"

"I have graciously agreed to stay here with our guest," Nyssa said.

Quinn frowned. The thought of returning to Ocean's Rest filled her with dread. She sank further into her chair and pulled her sweater tight around her body. She could feel Nyssa's eyes on her. The previous night was a misstep on her part. She had tried to coax too much out of Nyssa to make her second-guess herself and the guilds, but she pushed too hard.

I misjudged her. She's resolute. And she wants to be an Ashcloak more than anything. They dangle it in front of her. Dangle me in front of her.

Quinn couldn't go back to Arcton Citadel. She drew her knees up to her chest and wrapped her arms around them, trying to think of what to do.

Aryis roused Quinn out of her thoughts when she stood and turned to Nyssa.

"Well, before we leave, can I ask a favor of you?"

Nyssa draped a towel around Aryis's shoulders. This was a bad idea. Nyssa had no experience in such things. "Are you sure about this?"

"Yes. It's too long, and I hate it like this," Aryis replied.

Nyssa warmed the oil between her hands and smoothed it onto Aryis's temples before wiping her hands and reaching for the straight razor.

Aryis turned her head. "Just...just watch the ears and keep as neat as possible? Vykas did this once for me, and it...wasn't good."

Nyssa swallowed and started shaving the sides of Aryis's head, careful to not cut her. Quinn watched from the corner of the terrace, wrapped up in her cloak. Aryis had insisted on having some space to talk to Nyssa while they kept an eye on their fugitive.

"You know, given how we started off rocky with one another, one would think you'd be more cautious about letting me put a razor to your head," Nyssa mused.

Aryis chuckled. "Can I ask you a question?"

"Yes, but don't blame me if I slice off an ear because you're distracting me."

"Would it be impertinent of me to pursue a physical relationship with Athen?"

Nyssa stopped moving the razor across Aryis's temple and put her hands on the young woman's shoulders. "Okay, this is not a conversation I can have while shaving your head."

She walked around, sat at Aryis's feet, and rested her arm across Aryis's knees. "Look, you will not get an argument from me, if that's what you're worried about."

"This is, admittedly, awkward. I'm not well-versed in these matters. No one at the Conservatory pays me a second glance," Aryis confided.

"What? You're gorgeous!"

A shy smile spread across Aryis's face. "You don't have to flatter me."

"Trust me, I have excellent taste, and you're beautiful."

"So, how do you suggest I proceed with Athen?"

"You're way in your own head here. You just need to find a moment and grab it. Grab him if you're feeling saucy," Nyssa said.

"Is that how you charmed Reece?"

Nyssa sighed. "Oh, Aryis. That woman...ah...she flipped me completely on my head. She seduced me, I'll have you know!"

Aryis burst out laughing, and Nyssa threw up her hands. "I'm not usually in that position, but she knew what she wanted, and I was powerless to stop her."

"I thought you weren't great with people?"

"First off, I'm a very charming asshole. And number two, never underestimate the power of being horny."

Aryis smiled and grabbed Nyssa's hand. "You have become an unexpectedly delightful companion over these last weeks. Even if we got off to a shaky start."

"I'm proud to call you a friend, Aryis," Nyssa said, a wave of emotion settling over her. Aryis had surprised Nyssa with her courage, but it was her kindness that was a genuine treasure. Athen deserved someone like her. "And if you have your eye on Athen, then go for it."

Aryis lowered her gaze. "I've never been intimate with anyone."

"That's okay," Nyssa said, giving Aryis's knee a soft squeeze. "I assume, of course, that you've done exhaustive research on the subject?"

"Naturally. I'm a scholar."

A smile crept onto Nyssa's face. Of course. She was well-read. Why would sex be different from any other subject?

Nyssa suspected she knew exactly what she wanted.

"Then you'll be fine. Don't be afraid to talk to Athen about any of this. I can vouch for him, he's a good man."

"He's really been there for you, hasn't he?"

Nyssa sighed. "When I was a kid at the Order, there were a lot of bullies, and I got into plenty of fights. I turned into a little asshole with a massive chip on my shoulder. Athen didn't just help me stand up for myself, he saved me from becoming the worst version of myself. There are parts of you that can die off if you never see kindness."

"I'm sorry that happened to you."

A lump rose in Nyssa's throat. "Well, at least I'm somewhat less of an asshole, thanks to Athen."

Aryis narrowed her eyes. "Somewhat."

Nyssa barked out a laugh, thankful for her humor. "Cheeky!"

Aryis shrugged with a nonchalance that reminded Nyssa of herself.

Nyssa stood and smiled at her. “Remember, you asked to join this assignment—sight unseen—for adventure. So maybe give yourself permission to have a little adventure?”

“I agree.”

“And if that adventure happens to include seeing Athen naked, then so be—”

“Nyssa!”

“I give brilliant advice, you must admit,” Nyssa said. “Now, let’s finish this tragic haircut I’m giving you.”

THE GHOSTS OF WINTER'S FIRE

Nyssa let out a small, slightly embarrassing cry of delight when Aryis and Athen returned to the loft that evening and presented her with a bag of grilled chicken skewers. She pulled Aryis toward her and gave her a kiss on her newly shaved temple.

"I told you she loves meat on a stick," Athen said with a grin.

Nyssa could sense a lightness between them. Maybe Aryis took a little of her advice and just let herself relax around Athen.

She sat at the dining table and waved Quinn over from her seat near the fireplace. "You can join us."

Quinn stood, hesitant, and Nyssa gave her a small, reassuring nod. She was still sore about the night before, Quinn poking at her doubt, but food brightened her mood.

"I'm making a fresh pot of tea. Sit at the table and eat your food," Aryis said, a chipper lilt in her voice.

As they all sat, Aryis told them about their shopping trip and all the stalls they visited.

"They have a tradition on these islands where they celebrate Winter's Fire for an additional month. Isn't it wonderful?" she asked.

Nyssa grimaced. "I don't want to celebrate another Winter's Fire for a couple of years."

"Maybe a small gathering? Celebrate your survival, Nyssa," Aryis said.

"Celebrate your courage," Nyssa replied with a proud smile. She stole a glance at Quinn. Did she feel even an ounce of guilt for leaving them in the lurch at The Masthead? Guildies were supposed to look out for each other, regardless of affiliation—all brothers and sisters in the end.

"I've been meaning to ask," Aryis said, looking at Quinn, "why were you out that Winter's Fire night? Surely you were taking a risk by not lying low."

Quinn swallowed. "I've never celebrated Winter's Fire before. I just wanted to experience it once before I left."

"You've *never* celebrated the holiday?"

"No, Aryis. I told you they keep me by myself. That doesn't include Winter's Fire lanterns or spiced ale or meat on a stick."

"I'm sorry," Aryis said, looking sullen.

Nyssa studied Quinn. Truth was, they didn't fully understand the nature of her situation.

The isolation.

How lonely she must be.

Quinn cleared her throat, hesitating before speaking. "I...I've been meaning to inquire about that night. After I—"

"After you ran?" Nyssa locked eyes with her.

Aryis didn't seem to hold the same contempt for Quinn running that Nyssa did, unable to contain her excitement. "We fought a blood wraith!"

Quinn shook her head and scoffed. "Nonsense. Blood wraiths are myths."

Nyssa pulled the collar of her shirt down to expose her poison scar. "Does this look like a myth?"

"Then explain," Quinn replied.

Aryis enthusiastically launched into the story of what happened that night while Nyssa remained silent. The accuracy and detail of her recounting led Nyssa to believe she had already documented it all.

As Quinn absorbed the story, she would ask them to slow down and repeat parts. When Aryis got near the end of the fight, Nyssa's chest grew tight. She vividly remembered so much of it, but hearing it made a familiar dread ache in the pit of her stomach.

Nyssa tried to occupy herself with picking at a splinter on the dining table, but her mind flashed to images of that night. How the blood wraith moved, its unnatural speed, and her inability to do anything to stop it from hurting her or her friends. The creature treated her like a rag doll, crushing her throat and ribs, breaking her insides. When it plunged its dagger deep into her shoulder, the pain was unlike anything she had ever encountered.

A shiver ran down her body as she broke out into a sweat. Aryis's voice became a distant drone, Nyssa's mind completely occupied by images of that night. The monster's laugh ringing in her ears as it twisted its knife into her, its poisoned blood mixing with her own, its red eyes watching her agony, its lips curled in a smile of pleasure.

Nyssa pushed away from the table and stood, her legs wobbly. She felt hands on her. Athen or Aryis, she didn't know, but she pulled out of their grasp and ran to the terrace doors.

Her heart pounded in her chest.

She couldn't breathe.

She stumbled outside and emptied her stomach onto the ground.

Hot tears streamed out of her eyes, stinging her sight. Voices called from behind her, barely discernible over the white-static roar in her ears. Hands steadied her and swept her hair from her face. A woman's voice was close, murmuring to her—Aryis, her tone soft and comforting, even though Nyssa couldn't make out what she was saying.

The buzz in her head receded, and she straightened, her breathing quick and ragged. Athen rubbed her back, and Quinn looked on, arms folded across her chest. Nyssa sucked in a deep breath and let it out. She had never reacted this way before, trembling and helpless in the face of a memory.

A damn *memory*.

"You're okay," Athen said quietly.

Nyssa reached up with a shaky hand and pulled the collar of her shirt down to expose her poison mark. "Am I okay? Really? Because I don't feel like I'm okay," she choked out, her voice catching. Dread tumbled through her, cold and sharp.

"Nyssa, I'm sorry—" Athen started.

"Do these two know about your nightmares?" Quinn asked.

Nyssa sucked in a breath. "Don't," she replied, her voice low and threatening.

Quinn shook her head in response and persisted. "By the looks on their faces, I suspect not."

Nyssa balled up a fist, staring daggers at Quinn.

"You talk in your sleep."

Nyssa shrugged Athen and Aryis off and lunged at Quinn, grabbing fistfuls of her sweater. "You're lying!"

"*Let them be safe*," Quinn whispered, repeating Nyssa's nightmare plea so only she could hear.

Nyssa reared a fist back, intent on pummeling Quinn, hurting her, but an arm wrapped around her waist, pulling her away. Nyssa hissed in pain as her ribs objected.

"Stop!" Athen said in her ear.

"Back to your room," Aryis commanded, yanking Quinn's arm and walking her inside.

Athen let go of Nyssa. "Calm down. You were going to hurt Quinn."

"She had no right to tell you that," Nyssa rasped.

"Why didn't you share with me you were having nightmares?"

Nyssa turned and sat on a bench, putting her face in her hands. "It's just a dream. I thought I was fine."

Athen crouched next to her, placing a hand on her leg. "Obviously not. And hearing the story of that night...you panicked."

"I couldn't breathe. It felt like my heart was going to pound out of my chest."

"What can I do?"

Nyssa looked up at Athen. His face was scrunched up in an expression of concern she had seen countless times at the Order. She didn't know how to combat a nightmare. It made her feel helpless and vulnerable as her trauma revisited her, night after night, pulling her back into that horror.

"Just give me a few minutes."

Nyssa stood and started pacing, her thoughts pinging in her brain.

"All I want is to get her back and be named an Ashcloak, but that damn woman keeps needling me. I want to..." Nyssa shook her head, not giving words to the violence she wanted to commit. "Do you know she had the audacity to accuse First Master Anelos of studying forbidden magick?"

Athen closed the distance between them and took Nyssa's arm, his face grave. "Please don't repeat those accusations. Just repeating it could get you in deep trouble."

"Do...do you think she could be telling the truth?"

"Nyssa, no. She's desperate and will say anything, playing on you for sympathy. If a Justiciar heard her say those things about a First Master..." Athen exhaled forcefully, "that's treason."

"Quinn just doesn't strike me as a liar." Nyssa looked up at him. "Athen, are we doing the right thing?"

"That heart of yours...you always need to do the honorable thing. And this is the right thing, Nyssa."

She swallowed. "Is it?"

He sighed. "She reminds you of yourself a bit, doesn't she? An outcast?"

Nyssa frowned. He knew her struggles too well.

"Don't let her get to you. Let's just focus on getting her back home, Eron making you an Ashcloak, then drinking ourselves silly to celebrate."

Nyssa looked up at Athen and forced a smile. "You're right. Of course."

"Are you going to be okay to watch her tonight? No more punches to faces?"

"I'll be fine. I promise I won't hurt her."

Quinn took a few steps back when Nyssa entered her room. Nyssa looked over at Aryis, posted next to the door, her arms crossed.

"You can leave," she said, patting Aryis on the arm.

"You sure?"

"Yeah," Nyssa replied, shifting her eyes to Quinn, those blue eyes boring into her. A flutter of fear unsettled Quinn's stomach, but there was something else there—something confusing that made her heart beat faster with anticipation.

Aryis nodded and let herself out of the door.

Nyssa gestured toward the bathroom. "Get cleaned up and ready for bed."

Quinn gathered her bedclothes and walked to the bathroom, closing the door behind her. She leaned against it and exhaled. She kept provoking Nyssa, drawing out the woman's anger. At some point, Nyssa would hurt her if she pushed too hard. Quinn put her hand to her throat, remembering Nyssa's rage when she tried to escape.

The woman bewildered her. Why didn't she tell her friends about her nightmares? Athen and Aryis could help.

Quinn caught herself.

I wouldn't tell them either.

Some pain needed to be kept private, locked away.

When Quinn exited the bathroom, Nyssa was sitting on her bed. She stood and reached down to pull her shirt over her head, revealing a thin-strapped camisole underneath. She stepped toward Quinn and held up her left arm. The dark-gray scar that radiated out from her shoulder was strange and ethereal, almost as if it shifted in the dim light.

"This scar was caused by the Cast of the Grave, the poison carried in the blood of a blood wraith. When it spread from my wound, it felt like my body was being torn apart. The poison somehow hurt worse than the dagger the wraith twisted into my shoulder. It was pure agony," Nyssa said, voice low, her eyes not leaving Quinn's face.

Nyssa's expression changed, anger replacing calm. "When you ran from The Masthead that night, I didn't chase you. I stayed back, trying to save lives. While you slipped away, I watched wraiths spill the guts of innocent men and women. So when you try to draw on my sympathy—to show how we're the same, outcasts from our guilds—know that you and I are *nothing* alike. You are a coward."

Quinn didn't think, her body simply moved, reaching up to flutter her finger across the poison scar that snaked along Nyssa's collarbone. Nyssa's lips parted in surprise, drawing in a breath.

"Nyssa—"

Nyssa blinked and stepped back from Quinn. After hearing about the Winter's Fire horror and seeing Nyssa's reaction, her pain, something in Quinn hurt for her. She carried the weight of that night, its terrors plaguing her dreams.

"I'm sorry for what happened to you," Quinn whispered.

Nyssa exhaled, and her throat bobbed up and down. "We leave tomorrow. Get some sleep."

Quinn crossed to the bed and sat down, watching Nyssa pick up the blanket from the chair and wrap it around her shoulders, her eyes downcast. She stood by the chair for a minute before finally tucking in to get comfortable.

Quinn burrowed under the covers of her bed.

It took a while for her to fall asleep. She listened to Nyssa breathe, thinking how electric her skin felt under her touch.

LEAVING THE LASH

The next morning, Nyssa woke to find Quinn's bed empty. She swore under her breath, afraid that the fugitive had bolted until she heard the soft humming coming from the adjoining bathroom, its door slightly ajar. She sat back with a heavy exhale, the small burst of panic dissipating from her body. Nyssa wouldn't forgive herself if Quinn escaped simply because she was exhausted.

She didn't sleep well the previous night, her mind turning over what had happened with Quinn, dissecting the complete confusion that washed over her when Quinn reached up and touched her scar, her fingers light and electric.

Nyssa covered her eyes with her forearm, willing herself to get a little extra sleep. The water turned off, and the soft humming grew louder as Quinn exited the bathroom.

"Oh, you're awake."

"Unfortunately," Nyssa grumbled. "I'll let you get dressed."

She stood and stretched, her muscles sore and cramped from the chair, and she winced, her ribs twinging with pain, drawing a glance from Quinn. Before anything else could be said, Nyssa left the room, closing the door behind her.

The sounds of breakfast and laughter pulled her to the great room where Aryis and Athen were eating. She leaned in the hallway entrance for a minute and watched them, a small smile on her lips at how well they got along.

"I know I said I'd be Quinn's shadow, but I desperately need a bath before I get on a boat. She's just getting dressed and should be out in a couple minutes. Please watch her carefully. If she so much as tugs at a glove, subdue her," Nyssa said. She didn't add that she needed time away from Quinn, her mind still trying to process the prior night and the tightness in her stomach at her touch.

"Not a problem," Athen said. "Take your time. We have a few hours before we have to get to the Sea Stag."

Nyssa returned to her bedroom and stood in its darkness. She opened the shades to let a little of winter's morning light in and started a few logs burning before running a hot bath.

Stripping out of her clothes, she shivered in the cold air. She moved over to the mirror and examined her naked body, running her hands along her arms to warm up a bit, brushing against the lines of the poison mark on her left arm. Her fingertips lingered on the raised, angry edges of the dagger scar, and she swallowed hard at the memory of the pain.

She ran her hands down her breasts, her nipples hard from the cold air, then turned to get a better look at her left side. The bruising on her ribs had disappeared weeks ago, but the lingering pain frustrated and concerned her. Her eyes trailed down to the dark hair between her legs, feeling a slight ache of loneliness as her mind drifted.

After her bath filled, she slid into the tub and soaked, letting the hot water relieve some of the stress in her muscles. The verbena bath oil soothed her, and she rubbed down her arms and legs, gingerly grazing her ribs. She realized she had been tense ever since they found Quinn, not feeling like she could relax.

Closing her eyes, Nyssa let her mind drift from place to place before settling on Quinn. The woman had been trying to work on Nyssa's sympathy, and at times, had succeeded. But then she would say or do something to anger Nyssa, and that sympathy ebbed.

Regardless of her actions, Quinn's complaints weren't completely without merit, if true. She faced a lifetime of solitude. No friends to confide in. No one to take into her bed. Nyssa wondered where her obligation to her guild ended, and the responsibility to her fellow adept began. She was always taught that the guilds were one entity at their very heart, all adepts brothers and sisters.

Her lips formed the words of the Order oath she recited every day:

> *"To my brothers and sisters, my bond.*
> *To my guild, my fidelity.*
> *To my Empire, my blood.*
> *Stand fast. Face the darkness. Fall without fear."*

Nyssa slid her head under the water, and came up for air, undoing her braids and working soap deep into her auburn locks. She slid back down to rinse the soap out, staying under the water. Only when her lungs burned did she come up for air, gasping in big, deep breaths.

She lingered in the bath for a bit before getting out and drying off, pulling on a pair of dark leather pants and a cotton shirt out of her travel bag. She retrieved her belt out from the pair of pants that lay in a heap on the floor, then packed her things, stuffing everything into her bag.

Athen and Aryis were finishing up breakfast as Nyssa joined them in the great room, dropping her bag on the floor.

"Nyssa!" Aryis said when she saw her. "Your hair! You took your braids out!"

Nyssa grinned and ruffled her hair. "You like?"

"You should wear it like that more often," Aryis said.

Nyssa walked over to get a piece of bread from a basket on the dining table. "Not practical for fighting. It's always in my face."

She frowned at the breadbasket, her loose curls falling around her face, and caught Quinn looking at her before quickly glancing away.

That tight feeling returned to her stomach.

"Where is the heel?" Nyssa asked, picking through the leftover bread. "Is it too much to ask to leave the least desirable piece of bread for me since you all ate everything else?" She sat down at the table across from Quinn, pulling the butter dish to her and settling on a slice of bread with a grumble.

Nyssa watched Quinn while she chewed. The woman seemed distracted, her mood sullen. “You all packed up?”

“Yes,” Quinn replied softly.

When Nyssa finished eating, Athen stood. “It’s time to get going.”

She sighed and downed the last of her tea. “I will miss this place.”

DESPERATION

The Sea Stag waited at the end of the dock, and a weight lifted off of Nyssa, knowing she was just one ocean trip away from becoming an Ashcloak. She smiled and let out a contented sigh.

Quinn slowed to a stop, pale. Nyssa moved next to her and took her bag.

"Athen, will you take these up? We'll be aboard in a minute."

"You sure?"

"Yeah, we need a moment."

Athen and Aryis nodded and took off toward the gangplank.

Nyssa turned to Quinn. "Are you okay?"

Quinn shook her head. "This is happening. You're taking me back."

"Yes. You knew this was inevitable."

Quinn bent over, her hands on her thighs. "I don't think I can do this. Nyssa, I can't...I can't breathe."

Nyssa grew concerned and moved closer to Quinn, gently touching her back. "Listen to me. Just relax, slow your breathing and—"

A sharp jab to Nyssa's ribs brought her down to one knee, and she tumbled forward, catching herself before flattening on the ground.

Quinn sprinted away.

Nyssa opened her mouth to yell, but gasped for air instead. She staggered to her feet and took off after Quinn. Each breath felt like a stab in the side, and she cursed loudly in her head as she gradually gained speed.

The pursuit drew some eyes, but trouble on the docks didn't seem to be a rare occurrence while Nyssa ran by disinterested onlookers.

The fear of losing Quinn made her push past the ache in her side.

Quinn glanced over her shoulder and swerved off the docks into the streets of Jejin. Nyssa followed, narrowly avoiding a collision with a man and his lunch cart. She spotted Quinn veering into a side street and followed, pushing past people who got in her way and cursing under her breath.

Nyssa turned onto the side street, only to realize it was a dead-end alley. A relieved smile crossed her lips when she saw Quinn had trapped herself.

"Fuck!" Quinn yelled, her voice reverberating off the walls and echoing down the alley. She spun around.

Nyssa put her hands on her hips, panting, trying to catch her breath. Quinn had mirrored Nyssa's panic attack, luring her into a moment of concern and sympathy, using it as bait. The plan was cunning, Nyssa could give Quinn that, but it was crass and heartless.

"What were you thinking? We have your book. We'd find you again."

"I don't know. I don't know!" Quinn yelled, pacing back and forth, worrying her hands through her hair. "Please, I can't go back."

Nyssa stalked Quinn. "You don't have a choice."

"But you do. I can find a ship going east and disappear. All you have to do is let me go. You can say I subdued Athen and Aryis and ran."

Fear painted Quinn's voice. She wasn't pretending anymore.

Nyssa didn't care.

"We wouldn't get the lie past First Master Greye, let alone a Justiciar."

Quinn held her hand out. "Nyssa, what do you want?"

Nyssa slowed her gait for a moment. "To get you back and become a fucking Ashcloak. It's what I've worked for. What I deserve. That's it. That's all I want."

"Is that *truly* what you want?"

Nyssa frowned. This felt similar to her conversation with Justiciar Medias. The shadow of a doubt that lived in the back of her mind was spreading, and Nyssa didn't like how discomforting it felt.

"I've worked too hard, I've gone through too much—" Nyssa stopped herself before she revealed more of her past. "I won't betray my guild or Eron."

"They'll use you up and toss you aside."

"You need to stop talking," Nyssa warned. Quinn was poking at her, trying to get a rise out of her, and it was working. Unnerving an opponent was one of Nyssa's tactics, and Quinn was using it to perfection.

But Nyssa couldn't stop her rising anger.

"I deserted my guild. By the rules, a Justiciar should take my head or mark me as Unworthy. But they covet my abilities and will do anything to get me back, regardless of what I've done."

"One would think you'd see that as a blessing. They value you."

Quinn's eyes bored into Nyssa's. "And you? You know what you are to them? An ordinary woman with no magick and above-average fighting skills. You're a fancy mercenary who covets a title you don't deserve. And because of that, First Master Anelos will make an example out of you. He will hurt you."

"No."

"When I overheard Ceril talk about you, he said that the guilds had tolerated the existence of a magickless whelp long enough and you would be dealt with. Nyssa, that's a threat."

Nyssa swallowed and fought to control her reaction, looking away from Quinn. She had experienced Ceril's disdain firsthand.

"Vague threats will not scare me into helping you." Nyssa stepped forward, and Quinn backed up, the wall behind her cutting off any hope of escape.

She locked eyes with Nyssa. "You think men like Ceril will show you mercy? You're utterly *worthless* to them."

Nyssa snarled and grabbed a handful of Quinn's cloak, shoving her back, drawing a grunt out of her as she thudded into the brick.

"And yet your magick is completely useless against this *worthless* woman," Nyssa seethed. "Do you want to see the extent of my above-average fighting skills?"

A flash of steel grabbed her attention, and she caught Quinn's wrist, interceding her desperate attempt to punch her again. Quinn had a bent spoon wrapped around her fist, and Nyssa pulled the metal off and tossed it away, tightening her grip on Quinn.

Quinn fought back, grabbing Nyssa's forearms and burying a knee in her midsection. Nyssa cried out, letting go of Quinn and stumbling backward, dropping to one knee.

The pain in her ribs throbbed as Nyssa gasped for breath.

Quinn pushed off the wall, but Nyssa shot to her feet, ignoring the searing pain in her side, and shoved the other woman hard. She fought the urge to tear into her, to truly hurt her. Quinn shrank back, her previous bravado giving way to fear.

"Go ahead and hurt me," she whispered. "I deserve it." There were tears of resignation beneath her crumbling defiance. She looked ready to fall apart. To give up.

"Okay." Nyssa's fist caught Quinn on the chin, and she crumpled to the ground.

Nyssa leaned against the wall, taking a few moments to catch her breath.

"Fuck," she grunted while pulling Quinn up and over her shoulder. Despite the screaming pain in her side, an unconscious Quinn seemed far less work than the alternative.

Nyssa slowly trudged back to the ship.

Athen and Aryis ran up to her when she approached the Sea Stag with Quinn.

"Take her," Nyssa wheezed, her breath ragged, legs ready to give way.

Athen took Quinn into his arms. "What happened to you two? When we came back, you were gone."

"Bitch tried to escape," Nyssa fumed. She saw no need to mention their argument. "She goes in the brig."

"Is that necessary?" Aryis asked.

"She goes in the fucking brig!" Nyssa snapped, wincing.

Aryis touched her arm. "Nyssa, what's wrong?"

Nyssa put a hand to her side. "My ribs. They're on fire."

"Aryis, take her to her quarters and get the ship's healer," Athen directed. "I'll take care of Quinn."

Quinn's eyes fluttered open, and she groaned, rubbing her sore jaw.

"Where am I?" she mumbled to herself, her eyes slowly adjusting to the low light.

"The brig."

She turned her head, spotting Athen crouching next to her. She sat up and swung her legs off a small cot, peering around the brig—it was tiny and dark with one little porthole to let in the waning light of the day. A bucket sat in the corner, and the air was stale.

"You landed yourself here after the stunt you pulled with Nyssa," Athen said.

"You're not seriously going to make me stay in here for two weeks?"

"Make the best of it," Athen quietly said before standing.

As he turned to leave, Quinn spoke up. "Athen, wait. You need to look out for Nyssa. First Master Anelos is not a good man. The words he used when talking about her...Athen, he will come for her. He'll hurt her."

"Why do you care?"

Quinn leaned her head back against the wooden wall behind her. "I don't. But you should."

Athen put his hands on his hips. "You need to stop spreading nonsense about Anelos."

"Have you met him? Do you even know what he's like?"

The look on his face gave him away.

"You *have* met him. Don't make the mistake of thinking all guild Masters adhere to the rules. Ceril is loyal to one thing—himself."

"As are you, it seems."

Quinn frowned. "What's that supposed to mean?"

Athen walked back to her and knelt down on one knee. "We all took guild oaths. The words may be different, but one thing is common: loyalty to each other. You and I are brother and sister in the Areshi guilds. That means I look out for you. Nyssa looks out for you. But you only look after yourself."

"They are just words, Athen. At some point, the people who make you recite your oath will fail you. And Nyssa."

Athen frowned at her and clenched his jaw. He didn't seem to get angry often, but when he did, it was always to protect Nyssa. A small part of Quinn was envious of her to have such a stalwart friend.

"You know, the night we first caught up to you in Ocean's Rest, we could have ended all of this right then and there, but Nyssa stopped us. She wanted to give you a moment, let you light a lantern and speak your Winter's Fire wish. She offered you grace."

Quinn blinked at him. *Why would Nyssa do such a thing? For a stranger, no less.*

Athen let out a long sigh. "I've seen Nyssa angry. Many times. And not because of a fight. She was at the wrong end of a lot of those growing up. She can let cuts and bruises roll right off of her, but some asshole says something to hurt her and she lashes out. Nyssa came back to this ship seething. So congrats, whatever you said cut into bone. We could have been friends to you when we get back to the Empire, checked in from time to time, but that will not be possible now, will it?"

Quinn leaned forward, doing her best to ignore the throbbing in her jaw. "Go on, Athen. Go back to being her lapdog."

Athen shook his head before standing. "You have no idea what friendship looks like, do you?" he asked, then locked her cell and walked away.

Quinn settled on the bunk, biting back her resentment. What did he care? What did any of them care? After they returned to Ocean's Rest, she'd never see them again, and they would be unconcerned with her fate.

They were her captors, not her friends.

Soon, she'd be back at Arcton, that fucking void collar around her neck. She was out of options, her heart beating faster as she thought of what awaited her at her old guild. Desperation was all she had and it had made her intentionally cruel with Nyssa, raw anger raging in her eyes.

She stood and took her emotions out on the bucket in the corner, kicking it as hard as possible.

"Fuck!" Pain pulsed through her foot, and she limped back over to the cot, dropping onto it. "Fuck," she whispered, lowering her head into her hands, hot tears falling gently onto her cloak.

Aryis looked on as Athen spoke to the ship's healer. He had come back from the brig noticeably upset, so Aryis thought it best to let him simmer down and take care of Nyssa.

The healer handed him a bottle of silver liquid. "She reinjured her ribs, but I've applied some mending magick and had her drink a bit of this to dull the pain and help her sleep. Let her rest now."

The healer let herself out, and Athen sat next to Aryis on the small couch opposite Nyssa's bed. Nyssa's eyes were closed, her soft breathing barely audible. Winter's Bite lay on the floor next to her bed, along with her jacket and one boot. The other was half-unbuckled and still on her foot.

"She's out," Aryis said, thankful for Nyssa's unconsciousness. She was in obvious pain, but it was her mood that scared Aryis, refusing to answer any questions of her encounter with Quinn.

Athen sighed. "We need to keep an eye on Quinn and Nyssa. We'll keep Quinn in the brig for as long as Nyssa wants. With everything we've all been through and Nyssa having nightmares, I think a little break will do everyone a bit of good."

"And what of Quinn in that small, cold brig?"

"I'll make sure she's okay. I'll keep her fed, and I'll take her out on deck a couple times a day for some fresh air. We just need to keep some distance between the two of them."

Aryis smiled. Athen's kindness warmed her. "I can help you with her."

"I would appreciate that." He stood up and unbuckled Nyssa's remaining boot, pulling it off and putting both boots neatly near her bunk, then he tidied up the rest of her belongings on top of her footlocker. Aryis wondered how often he took care of Nyssa like this back in their time at the Order.

After he tucked Nyssa under the covers, he rejoined Aryis on the couch, and she produced a flask from the inside of her jacket. He raised his eyebrows.

"I got this off of Mina when we boarded," she admitted.

"Thank you for staying with Nyssa. I worry about her at times. She puts so much pressure on herself."

"It's not a bother. You two have become good friends to me."

"I've enjoyed getting to know you. You are perhaps the best part of this whole mission."

The compliment warmed Aryis's cheeks. "You're rather kind. I'm awkward and sometimes don't know what to say or do. Especially around you."

"Ah, I'm harmless," Athen said with a low, rumbling chuckle. "And be as awkward around me as you want. I like you when you're just yourself."

Ignoring the nervous fluttering of her stomach, Aryis leaned in and kissed him. After a moment of surprise, his lips smiled under hers and he drew her closer.

She pulled out of the kiss, instantly missing the warmth of his lips. "I just wanted you to know that I'm interested in you."

"You just kissed me, I should hope so, woman!" A deep, warm laughter emanated from him, his dazzling smile making it hard to think. He put his arm around her and she leaned into his massive chest. "I like you too, Aryis. And all your awkwardness."

"I'm glad I forced my brother to let me come on this assignment."

He sighed. "I am too. I'd like to stay here for a bit if you don't mind, keep an eye on Nyssa."

"Of course," she replied, and Athen pulled her a little closer. Aryis leaned into him, and her thoughts quieted for a time as she inhaled the clean scent of his soap.

THE GHOST OF THE SEA

The Sea Stag got underway, headed back to Ocean's Rest. Each day, Nyssa took it slow, trying to heal, and Athen and Aryis looked in on Quinn, ensuring she was fed and got a little on-deck time. Whenever they were on deck together, Quinn was kept away from Nyssa, but they stared each other down.

They were seven days at sea when a commotion on deck roused Nyssa from a nap. She had dozed off reading Reece's book, but quickly shot out of her bunk, pulling her sword over her head.

She stumbled into the hallway, groggy and slow, colliding with a short man with bright-red hair.

"What's happ—"

A hard object bashed her head.

The world went black.

Nyssa groaned and opened her eyes, blinking in the bright sun, her mind foggy and sluggish. She struggled to move and found her hands tied behind her back.

"How's the head, love?" a deep voice asked, a shadow drifting over her. "Get her on her knees."

Rough hands pulled Nyssa upright, propping her on her knees. Her head throbbed, and a low moan escaped her lips. Water dripped from her chin to the deck.

No, not water. Blood.

"I'm invoking the Law of the Unbound Sea. Time to pay the Ghost of the Sea, yeah?" the deep voice said.

"Lilliana will have your head," Nyssa slurred, wincing from the pounding in her skull.

A pair of shiny, black boots stopped in front of her, helping her eyes focus. She lolled her head back, finding a large man looming over her. He wore a tight, white button-down shirt and a heavy cloak lined with white fur. Her eyes drifted to his face, finding a Koja man standing before her. The bluish-white tint of his skin made his race as unmistakable as his golden eyes. His glossy hair hung to his shoulders, its dark-blue hue matching the ocean.

"I've danced with Lilliana before, girl. She honors the laws of the sea, doesn't she, Athen Fennick?"

"Lilliana will honor the Law of the Unbound Sea," Athen said from Nyssa's left. Nyssa's eyes darted about, scanning the pirates to see how many they would have to fight. Her eyes widened. The crew of the Sea Stag were surrounded by pirates.

She struggled against the ropes that bound her hands behind her back. "Let them go!" she growled.

"Nyssa, don't!" Athen hissed. "We're fine, you don't underst—"

"If you hurt them, I'll kill you," Nyssa threatened, her words directed at the Koja pirate.

"Oh, how I love a spirited woman," he said, stepping closer and crouching down to be eye level with her. "You're a bloody mess. Sorry about that, love. Jerrin is a gentle soul, truly he is, but my crew can get a little anxious when people burst out of closed doors."

"What's your name so I know who I'm going to kill," Nyssa demanded, drilling her eyes into the man before her.

"The name I use with your people is Elias. So what's the story here? We found three of you in staterooms and that one there in the brig." He stood and pointed to Nyssa's right. She turned her head and an involuntary scowl settled on her face seeing Quinn staring at her.

"The four of us are together. We're Imperial adepts," Athen said.

"Ah, Fontaine was right! Been trailing your ship for days and patience paid off. Athen, sorry my boy, but I'm taking the four of you as my hostages. Law of the Unbound Sea."

"Shit," Athen whispered under his breath.

Nyssa knew any body of water not claimed by a country was considered Unbound, but she didn't know what the laws pertaining to them were.

She screwed her eyes up. "What the fuck is going on, Athen?"

"The Law of the Unbound Sea," he replied. "Elias has made his claim, and we honor it. Unfortunately, his claim is us. As hostages. Lilliana will ransom us out."

Aryis spoke up. "Wait, you can't claim us. We have to get back to Ocean's Rest."

Elias smiled at her. "Something to do with that woman down there, I reckon?" he asked, pointing at Quinn. "Seems she's with you, but not really *with* you, right? If she's your prisoner, that means extra coin for me, I suspect."

Aryis tried to interject again, but Quinn scrambled to her feet, stumbling forward. She straightened and cleared her throat before speaking. "Whatever ransom Lilliana Fennick would pay you, I will double it if you take me wherever I ask."

Laughter exploded from Nyssa, making her head throb. "Ow," she mumbled. "Elias, this idiot has no money. She can't pay you shit."

Elias took a couple steps toward Quinn, giving her a once-over before sighing and shaking his head. "I'm afraid that your offer is rejected."

Nyssa threw her head back and began laughing wildly, drawing a withering stare from Quinn. She didn't care. The whole situation was absurd, and Quinn trying to buy her way off the Sea Stag was insanely amusing.

Aryis stepped forward and straightened her posture. "I would like a word with you, sir."

Elias smiled and cocked an eyebrow. "Oh, you would?"

Athen shook his head. "Aryis, it's best if we—"

"Athen, let me take care of this," she said before turning back to Elias. "My companions and I need to get this prisoner back to Ocean's Rest as quickly as possible. This is official Imperial business."

A smattering of laughter rippled among Elias's crew.

Aryis frowned.

"Official Imperial business? I suppose we'll just have to let you all go, then," Elias said, spreading his arms wide.

Nyssa strained against her ropes when she heard more laughter from the pirates.

"Sir, I need to impress upon you the importance of returning to Ocean's Rest. We are on a mission sanctioned by Empress Kalla herself."

"I don't give a floating fuck. You'll be my hostage for however long it takes to get your ransom," Elias said, stepping up to Aryis, towering over her.

Aryis scowled and glanced back at Nyssa, grinding her jaw. When she turned back to Elias, she planted her hands on her hips.

"I am Aryis Devitt of House Devitt, first House of Frosland, and the last thing I'm going to do is not deliver on my promise to complete this mission for the Empress."

"I know who you are. No matter your lineage, you are still my hostage."

Aryis exhaled forcefully, her typical cheery enthusiasm gone, frustration now obvious. Nyssa hoped she wouldn't get herself hurt.

"I demand you free us."

Nyssa gritted her teeth, struggling against her bonds. Aryis entering a game of wills against this pirate was not going well. Athen scowled and crossed his arms. Why wasn't he helping?

Elias narrowed his eyes at Aryis. "You realize I'm in control here, right? You don't get to make demands."

Aryis hesitated for a moment. "I don't think you're quite understanding me. I'm Aryis Devitt, the Queen-in-Waiting of Frosland. I demand you let us go."

Queen-in-Waiting? "What the fuck?" Nyssa stared at Aryis, unsure if she had heard right or if she was still in a fog from her head wound.

Aryis looked back at her. "I'm sorry."

"Are you serious?" Athen asked.

"Yes, quite. Athen, I wanted to tell you but—"

"You've been hiding this little secret all along? What if you had gotten seriously hurt at The Masthead? Or when Quinn attacked you in Jejin?" Nyssa asked, fuming.

Quinn piped up. "Attacked is rather dramatic—"

"Shut up!" Athen and Nyssa snapped at Quinn.

"I didn't want you to treat me differently. You were already thinking you'd have to babysit me, Nyssa. I was trying not to be more of a bother!" Aryis explained, her face red.

"You could have been honest with us," Athen said.

Aryis frowned. "Yes, because you are both taking this news *exceptionally* well right now."

"You taking the piss out of us, Your Highness?" Nyssa growled.

"Will the lot of you kindly shut the fuck up?" Elias bellowed. "I've kidnapped divorced couples that natter far less than you four."

He stepped forward, offering his hand to Aryis. When she took it, he bowed before her, lightly kissing her hand.

"It is truly an honor to meet you, Aryis Devitt, Queen-in-Waiting of the First House of Frosland. I truly apologize for the rough manner in which you were treated."

Aryis let out a self-satisfied grunt and smiled down at Nyssa.

The pirate continued, "But alas, your title—or what it may be one day—has no bearing in Unbound waters. And I couldn't give three fucks about your Imperial mission. You are my hostage, and thanks to you, Queen-in-Whatever, the price just went up. Considerably."

A rumble of approval spread through Elias's crew, Aryis's secret turning into their good fortune.

Nyssa rolled her eyes.

"Son of a bitch," Aryis mumbled, shoulders slumping.

Athen let out a heavy sigh. "I tried to stop you, Aryis. You and Nyssa need to listen to me. I know how these situations play out. We have no leverage here. We got caught, and my mother will negotiate our freedom."

"I don't understand," Nyssa said, blinking the sun out of her eyes.

Athen bent over to help her to her feet. "Without the Laws of the Unbound Sea, things get violent between pirates and merchants. The law stops all that. It sounds strange, but it works in its own way."

"We don't have time for this!" she hissed. "We can fight our way out."

"No. You three follow my lead," Athen said. "We're now Elias's guests. That means no fights and no drawing your weapons. Do you understand me?"

Nyssa swallowed back her anger. Aryis nodded. Quinn merely blinked.

Elias walked over to them and clamped a hand on Nyssa's shoulder. She tried to pull away from him, but a wave of dizziness hit her, causing her to stumble. "Ho there, woman," he said as he steadied her. "What is your name, surly one?" He took a knife from his belt and cut the rope binding her wrists.

"Nyssa Blacksea." Shivering, she tried to work blood back into her arms and shoulders, her cotton shirt not doing much against the winter air.

"Blacksea." A frown turned down his face. "With a name like that, I suspect I'll only get a few pennies and some pocket lint for your ransom, but it's better than nothing."

"You fucking—"

"And you, prisoner, what is your name?"

"Quinn."

"Surname?" he asked.

"I-I don't have one."

Elias shook his head and glanced back at Nyssa. "A prisoner with no surname is worth more to me than you, Blacksea!"

Nyssa was ready to burst forth with a string of expletives before Elias quickly spoke again. "I am pleased to meet all of you, though I wish it were under different circumstances. While we are indeed pirates, I am a gentleman and pursue only profit, not pain. You'll find my ship quite accommodating. Sorry, though, two to a stateroom."

"She goes to the brig," Nyssa said, nodding her head at Quinn.

Elias scowled and shook his head. "We don't have a brig aboard Hannah's Whisper, Blacksea. It is a ship for gentlemen and gentlewomen, not ruffians."

Nyssa blinked and looked over at Quinn, gritting her teeth. "Then she's with me. She has to be watched."

Quinn groaned loudly.

Elias smiled and spread his arms out wide. "You see? It's easy to compromise after all, my friends. Ah, I see my people have brought your bags and weapons. Please make sure your possessions are intact. I will not be accused of stealing. And don't think about using your weapons against my crew. I'll have Fontaine bite your fingers off."

Nyssa cursed under her breath as a pirate handed her sword to her and placed her bag at her feet. She grimaced while trying to lift her sword's strap over her head, and Athen helped her sling it onto her back.

Elias hooked his thumbs into his belt, tapping his fingers, running his eyes up and down her.

"Blacksea. Your surname must have been given to you by mistake. You know nothing of our ways out here," he said, bending over to pick up her bag and holding it open for her to inspect its contents. Nyssa scowled at him, begrudgingly scanning her items. She didn't care about anything other than Reece's book and her jacket. Both were there. She gave him a nod, and he closed the bag up and passed it to her.

"Shall we, then?" Elias gestured starboard.

"Where's your ship?" Aryis asked.

"Oh, sorry." He cupped his hands over his mouth. "Fontaine, will you please drop the veil?"

A ship as large as the Sea Stag shimmered into view, its bone-white exterior reflecting the sparkling sea off its hull. The three sails looked to Nyssa like bat wings in stark contrast to the Stag's large, square white sails, and the carved figurehead at the bow was a woman with wings and curled horns.

It struck Nyssa that if she were painted black, she'd resemble a wraith. The thought sent a shiver through her.

The pirate ship seemed in impeccable condition—every bit of brass polished, every piece of wood spotless—and the crew matched the ship. They wore black woolen overcoats and dark-blue denim pants with shiny black boots. The one Elias called Jerrin came over to Nyssa and extended his hand out. "May I take your bag? Ooh, my sincerest apologies for the nasty cut I gave you, good lady."

Jerrin was several inches shorter than Nyssa, with a shock of spiky, red hair on his head and a scruffy red beard to match. He had a pale, kind face and light-green eyes that smiled before his mouth did.

Nyssa found it hard to believe this man had gotten the jump on her.

"Buck will tend to that wound," Jerrin said with a grin. They stepped toward the small gangplank that led to Hannah's Whisper—their unexpected new home for the foreseeable future.

HANNAH'S WHISPER

Quinn stepped on the pirate ship, instantly struck by the unexpected—everything was so tidy and clean. Nyssa hopped off the walkway after her, grumbling under her breath, her face half covered in blood. When Elias and his crew had tossed an unmoving Nyssa on the deck of the Stag, a shiver of dread ran through Quinn, only washed away when Nyssa moaned in pain—a puzzling relief.

When everyone was aboard the new ship, Elias spun around. "Welcome aboard Hannah's Whisper, the most advanced vessel on the seas, if I may be so humble," Elias boomed, spreading his arms wide. Quinn found his flair for the dramatic annoying. "This will be your home now, so make yourselves comfortable. But remember: you are my prisoners. Respect this ship and its crew or I'll chuck you into the sea and we'll take bets to see how long it takes for the gulls to peck your eyes out."

Quinn had never heard of Elias—the so-called *Ghost of the Sea*—but there was an edge of darkness to him despite his smile, inclining her to believe him.

A flurry of white feathers made Nyssa flinch. Quinn snorted, drawing a death glare from the woman. A small chicken flopped next to Elias, clucking at the four new guests.

"Let me introduce you to my quartermaster, Fontaine," Elias said.

"Your quartermaster is a chicken?" Athen asked.

"Not a chicken," Elias huffed. "Old Folk. They stay away from your kind after the Cursed Hunt, so you'll excuse her if she keeps an eye cocked your way at all times."

Aryis brightened, a smile exploding onto her face. "Fontaine! I would love to have a talk with you about the Old Folk. Your people are so fascinating, and I can only imagine the things you've seen. I study all types of magick and—"

Elias held up his hand. "Enough. It has been a long day of piracy, and you four are, frankly, quite draining. I think it best we show you to your quarters. Jerrin, take them down, then go fetch Buck to fix Blacksea up."

"Yes, sir," Jerrin replied. "If you will kindly follow me."

He ushered them below deck, and Quinn eyed the two guards trailing behind them while he showed them around.

Their rooms were cozy and comfortable enough for two people. Quinn was just happy to be out of the brig, even if she had to share the space with Nyssa. Each room had two bunks with large footlockers to secure their belongings and a tall folded screen made of wood and painted paper.

Portholes lined the outside wall, a small desk sitting beneath them. The wood was painted off-white like the outside of the ship, which Quinn found warm and comforting after the dim interior of the Sea Stag's brig.

Athen and Aryis stood at the door to their room.

"I guess this means we're bunking with each other," Aryis said, and Athen cleared his throat.

Nyssa grinned. "This is deliciously awkward."

Jerrin gestured inside the room. "There are privacy screens next to your bunks for the more modest of us. Close quarters don't have to mean giving away all of one's best secrets," he said with a wink to Nyssa.

"This one is cheeky," she said with a lopsided grin. "I just may forgive you for bashing my head in."

Jerrin smiled and continued, "Bathrooms are down the hall. Nyssa, if you would please take a seat on your bunk, I'd feel better if you were off your feet while I get Buck."

Nyssa did as Jerrin requested, and he left to get the healer.

Quinn sat on the bed across the room and tried to busy herself by looking around. She felt Nyssa's eyes on her, so she stared back.

A short old man walked into their room. He was bald save for a thin tuft of white hair on top of his head. Pale-gray eyes looked around from under thick goggles. "I'm Buck. I'm here to patch Nyssa up. Which one of you is her?"

"Perhaps the one with blood all over her face?" Quinn suggested, drawing a soft snort from Nyssa.

She may hate me, but at least she still appreciates sarcasm.

Buck dropped a small bag and stack of white towels on the bed, then grabbed Nyssa's head to get a closer look at her wound.

"Ow, hey! Be gentle!" Nyssa said, swatting at his hands.

"Mmm—this is a nasty one. Jerrin got you good, did he? Gonna be—mmm—twenty or so stitches."

Nyssa winced. "Stitches? I thought you're a healer."

Buck blinked at her. "I'm a medic. I got no magick, girl. This ain't a pleasure cruise."

"That's obvious. Wait, I have healing disks."

Nyssa pulled her jacket from her bag and retrieved a disk out of a pocket. Buck plucked it out of her hand.

"Mmm—Lightway, eh? This here is worth four or five hundred gold. You break an arm or a pack of wolves gnaws at your leg, we use this. Don't waste a perfectly good disk on a mere scrape."

Nyssa mumbled and put the disk back in her pocket.

"Gotta clean this up, though. Girl, get over here and bring that water," Buck said, pointing to a small table pushed up against the wall, a tin canteen sitting atop it. "You clean her up while I get my—mmm—needle threaded."

"The name is Quinn, not *girl*. And I don't think she wants me anywhere near her," Quinn said, bringing the canteen over.

"I don't recall giving a floating fuck about what she wants or asking for your opinion. It has to be done. Or she can just have a festering wound, maybe get a nice—mmm—infection and die before she sees land again." Buck pulled some bottles out of his bag.

Quinn shot him a look and sighed. She sat next to Nyssa, took off her gloves, and poured water on a towel, then turned. "Look at me."

Nyssa complied, and Quinn gently cleaned the blood off. As she worked, she placed her right hand under Nyssa's chin to steady her head. Nyssa grimaced while she worked but didn't make a sound, her sapphire eyes trained on Quinn's face.

"Is that okay?" Quinn asked, not wanting to hurt her.

"Yes."

Nyssa's persistent gaze unnerved Quinn, and she swallowed and licked her lips, trying to concentrate on cleaning the cut. She wondered how many times Nyssa had sat patiently while a healer worked on her.

After Buck got his needle threaded, he narrowed his eyes at the two bottles in his hands. "One of these is to drink, the other is to—mmm—clean the cut," he mumbled to himself.

Quinn sighed, pulled both bottles out of his hands, and uncorked them, giving them a sniff. She handed one to Nyssa. "Take a couple swigs of this."

"Wait, what is it?" Nyssa asked, passing the bottle under her nose. "Oh." She put it to her lips and tossed her head back, taking a few deep swallows. "Ow, that made my head hurt."

"That is for the wound, then," Buck said, pointing at the other bottle. "Gonna—mmm—sting and burn, but it'll clean the wound up 'fore I sew it closed."

Quinn peered down at the antiseptic tonic and thought for a moment before grabbing the rum out of Nyssa's hand. She exhaled, took a swig, and immediately started coughing. The liquid burned her throat and went down hot before settling in her stomach with a not-unwelcome warmth.

"Don't be wastin' the rum. You never had a stiff drink before, girl?"

"No." *But I could get used to it.*

Quinn handed the rum back to Nyssa and pressed a clean towel to the top of the tonic, tipping the bottle until it was soaked. When the potent smell of herbs and alcohol hit Quinn's nose, she winced.

"Ready?" she asked. Nyssa exhaled and nodded.

Quinn pressed the towel against her wound, drawing a sharp hiss out of Nyssa.

"Don't play at cleaning it, girl," Buck said. "Mmm—get in there."

"Shit," Quinn whispered, and Nyssa took a few more swigs of the rum, nodding again.

Quinn exhaled and pressed the towel to Nyssa's forehead, rubbing it across the wound to get it as clean as possible. Nyssa gritted her teeth, looking miserable, but she didn't make a sound.

"Let me see, girl," Buck said, and Quinn pulled the towel away, the blood mostly cleaned up, save for a little at the hairline. The cut itself looked pink and fresh. Buck nodded with approval. "Good job for such a skittery little thing," he said to Quinn, drawing a chuckle out of Nyssa. "You'd think I asked you to stitch her up yourself. You mainlanders are—mmm—soft. Ready for the needle and thread?"

Nyssa sighed and nodded.

"This'll hurt—mmm—too, so drink up."

Nyssa did as she was told. Buck took the bottle from her and had a few swallows himself.

"Hey, aren't you supposed to be sober for this?" Nyssa asked, her voice soft. "That rum is strong."

"It—mmm—steadies my hands."

"Shit, you're half blind *and* you have the shakes?"

Buck shrugged at Nyssa. "You want stitches or you just wanna leave that cut flappin' about for the next few weeks?"

"Fuck," she cursed under her breath and closed her eyes. "Do it."

He diligently used his needle and thread to close her cut, making quick work of the stitches before leaning back with a smile. Quinn couldn't help but be impressed.

"Mmm—great work, I say," Buck said with a nod.

Nyssa looked at him, frowning. "I hardly felt that."

Buck shrugged. "There's such a thing as being really good—mmm—at your job, girl." He took the bottle of cleaning potion from Quinn and put it back in his bag, then retrieved the bottle of rum from Nyssa and took another swig before corking it and placing it, too, in his bag. "I'll give it a look in a day to see how it's—mmm—healing." He gave them both one last glance before leaving the room.

Athen lingered in the doorway. Aryis squeezed by him and entered the room. "How are you feeling?" she asked.

"To be honest, Your Majesty, I'm feeling a little tipsy," Nyssa replied. "I don't have the energy to curtsy right now."

"Nyssa, stop." Aryis scowled at Quinn. "Put your gloves back on."

Quinn complied with a frown. Aryis picked up a clean towel and dipped it in the pitcher, then carefully wiped the remaining blood out of Nyssa's hair.

"Ow," Nyssa whined.

"Oh, stop," Aryis chided. "You seem to love collecting scars, Nyssa."

A throat cleared behind Athen, and he moved aside to reveal Jerrin. "Excuse me, if you will, sir."

"That's the one. He did this to me. Get him!" Nyssa said, pointing at Jerrin and laughing.

He glanced nervously over his shoulder at Athen. "Again, I cannot apologize enough."

"Ignore her. She's slightly drunk," Aryis said.

Jerrin nodded politely. "I wanted to let you all know that dinner will be served in the mess at the other end of the ship. Buck is a skilled cook, and I think—"

"Wait, that blind, trembly little man is the medic *and* the cook?" Quinn asked.

"Everyone here has a multitude of skills." Jerrin smiled at her.

"Oh, really?" Nyssa grinned with an arched eyebrow. "What skills do you have? Anything that might come in handy later?"

"Nyssa!" Athen said.

"What? I'm flirting. Shhh."

Quinn raised her eyebrows at this different side of Nyssa.

She is much easier to endure when filled with rum.

Jerrin cleared his throat. "Hostages are off-limits, though I'm flattered."

"Don't be. I haven't gotten laid in weeks. Wait, aren't you the guy that hit me right here?" Nyssa asked, pointing to her head.

"Anyway, I need to tend to my duties. I hope to see you all in the mess later," Jerrin said, escaping out the door as quickly as possible.

"Nyssa, you are a handful. How did you get drunk so fast?" Aryis asked.

"She drank a lot in a short time," Quinn replied. "I think it was stronger than she expected. I'm feeling the effects myself, and I didn't have that much."

Athen laughed. "If that was Basai rum, that's nothing to mess with. Reece and I got drunk off some a few Winter's Fires back, and I don't remember that night. At all."

Quinn perked up.

Reece. The same name Nyssa says in her nightmares.

Aryis looked up at Athen. "You seem rather casual about our circumstance. I'm not happy about this detour. It reflects poorly on us. I know how important this mission is for Nyssa."

"The First Masters will understand. As will the Empress. These things happen out here, and we have honored the Unbound Laws for years," Athen replied.

"I just don't trust Elias," Aryis said.

"He's a savvy pirate and not in the business of wanton violence. He's honorable, in his own way."

Nyssa snorted. "Unlikely."

Athen narrowed his eyes at Aryis. "While Elias will treat us well, revealing that you're going to be queen was not the smartest move. Elias probably doubled our ransom."

"Did the two of you *want* to be stuck on a pirate ship for who knows how long? I didn't tell you two because my family swore me to secrecy. You've met Vykas. He's—"

"An ass," Nyssa mumbled.

"Yes, among many things. But he's also very protective of me. Keeping my secret keeps me safe."

Athen shrugged out of his jacket and tossed it on a chair. "I get why you had to keep it to yourself. I'm sorry I got a little heated. This isn't an ideal situation."

Aryis perked up. "Thank you, Athen. That means a lot."

"Nyssa?" Athen said, raising an eyebrow at her.

Nyssa pouted, but acquiesced. "Yeah, I guess."

"That's your apology?" Aryis asked, her eyes narrow.

"Yeah, I guess, Your Majestic Highness."

Aryis shook her head, but laughed as the tension lightened between the three of them.

"Look, my mother has dealt with Elias before, and he's the best we could expect in Unbound waters. No ships like to be overtaken by pirates, but they don't fear for their lives with Elias if they give him what he wants. He can be a charmer."

"He's an asshole," Nyssa protested. "A stupid assho' pirate."

Athen sighed. "I'm going to find the mess and see if I can't get some tea and bread to stuff down her throat to sober her up."

The very large female guard stepped in front of Athen, meeting him eye to eye. "I will escort you."

"Seriously? I need a babysitter?"

The large woman glanced around the room, then back to him. "You all do. Orders are orders."

Athen sighed and shrugged. "After you," he said, and they left the room.

Aryis regarded Quinn. "I suppose we should thank you for helping fix Nyssa up."

Quinn shrugged. "I did as I was told by that little man." Truth was, she didn't mind. Time in the brig allowed her to reflect on how she had spoken to Nyssa when she attempted to escape, her words desperate and cruel. Shame burned at her when she thought back on her actions. And pride kept her from offering an apology.

"You're actually not so bad when you're not an arrogant ass," Nyssa said. "But you're an arrogant ass a lot, so..."

Quinn rolled her eyes.

"Take your shirt off," Aryis ordered, waggling a finger for Nyssa to get up.

She stood. "Ho now, I'm flattered, but not with an audience. I'm shy," she whispered loudly, teasing Aryis with a grin followed by an uncharacteristic giggle.

Quinn bit the inside of her cheek to stifle her smile. It was odd seeing Nyssa tipsy after their confrontations in Jejin and their icy time on the Sea Stag. At least Nyssa was a fun drunk, humorous and unguarded.

"There's blood all over it. You need to change," Aryis replied.

"Yes, Your Majesty," Nyssa mumbled and pulled her shirt over her head with a slight stumble. Aryis steadied her.

"Oh, thank gods you're wearing an undershirt. I don't know how to deal with you drunk *and* naked. And stop with the 'Majesty' and 'Your Highness'. I'm just Aryis."

Quinn shook her head and snorted under her breath as she watched Nyssa struggle to aim her arms into a clean pullover. She finally got it on with Aryis's help, then flopped down on the bed.

"We need to keep you out of trouble until dinner," Aryis said. She withdrew a small book from Nyssa's bag, sat down, and pulled her legs up on the bed. "Is this okay?"

Nyssa smiled. "Reece gave me that to read. I love it, yes." She tossed a glance at Quinn. "Yes, the brute knows how to read. I do it a lot. Reading, that is. And I might even write a poem or two in secret."

Aryis perked up, her eyes wide. "You write poetry?"

"Shhh, don't tell anyone!" Nyssa wrapped her arms around Aryis and smiled. "You're warm."

Aryis sighed and thumbed through the book. "I suppose we just need to make the best of this new situation."

Quinn sat back and tried to relax, tucking away Nyssa's secret.

Perhaps not such an ignorant brute, after all.

THE PIRATE AND HIS CAPTIVE

"What the fuck is this?" Nyssa scowled, pointing at a bucket and mop. The sun glared overhead, making her splitting hangover headache worse. Apparently hostages were expected to pitch in and work on the ship, which was a mound and a half of utter bullshit. The last thing she wanted to do was lift a finger to help their captor.

"Every artisan needs their tools. And to scrub the deck, you need a mop," Jerrin said, smiling. "With your help, we can get this boat shiny in no time."

Nyssa's head swiveled. The deck was immaculate, clean and tidy, every piece of metal shining within an inch of its life as the sharply dressed crew bustled about their morning duties. They had put Athen and Aryis to work on the sails while a crewman was showing Quinn how to tie knots.

And somehow she got stuck with mop duty?

"You're kidding me, right? Look around. This boat is already clean. Cleaner than clean," she complained.

With a shrug, Jerrin held out the mop handle. "Orders are orders."

"I don't take orders from you."

The guard charged with watching Nyssa stepped forward—a very large, pale woman with cropped blonde hair who towered over Nyssa by at least half a foot.

"Problem, Jerrin?" the guard asked.

"No problem, Yuha. Nyssa's just getting adjusted to life on our ship."

Nyssa balled up her fists and stepped up to Jerrin. "I'm not mopping the deck."

Yuha put a hand on her shoulder and pushed her away from Jerrin. "Tone it down."

Nyssa wasn't about to be pushed around by this lot. She cocked her head and smirked. "Put your hands on me again and see what happens. I dare you."

Predictably, Yuha took the bait and swung at Nyssa, who sidestepped the punch and grabbed the guard's arm, yanking her forward, using the large woman's momentum to send her tumbling to the deck.

Nyssa danced away with her hands up, grinning. "Didn't I warn you?" she taunted.

Yuha scrambled to her feet. Shouts rang out from the crew, and men and women moved in her direction. Nyssa would soon be outnumbered. She lunged at Jerrin and snatched the mop out of his hands, driving her foot down on the end, snapping the mop head off. She drove the blunt end of the impromptu staff into Yuha's belly, making her double over in pain.

A crewman charged toward Nyssa, but she spun out of his way, twirling her staff and cracking him on the back of his head with it. He fell to the deck, stunned.

"Who's next?" Nyssa growled.

Two crewmen rushed at her, both soon writhing on the deck in pain—one with a very broken nose by the sound of the crunch when Nyssa hit him. She shifted back toward the side of the boat, cutting off an avenue of attack.

"Nyssa, stop!" Athen cried out as he and Aryis ran forward.

"You want to play nice with the pirates, Athen? Or do you want to do what we were trained to do and fight?" Nyssa yelled.

A crew woman lunged forward, and Nyssa sent her reeling, splintering her staff on the woman's skull.

"Well shit," Nyssa mumbled, tossing the broken staff aside.

"I warned you about testing me or my crew, girl," Elias roared, walking through the gathered members of his crew. Fontaine trailed behind him, clucking loudly.

"I'm an Emerald Order warrior. I don't do scut work. And I don't take orders from you, your lackeys, or your damn chicken."

A hush fell over the crew.

Fontaine ruffled her feathers and cooed.

"You really shouldn't have said that," Elias said, his voice low.

The air around Nyssa grew thick and heavy, constricting, dragging her down to the deck. She grunted, struggling against the magick that drove her to her knees. It wound around her neck, tightening.

As Nyssa fought to breathe, Athen and Aryis pushed through the crew. "Elias, please. Don't hurt her," Athen pleaded.

"You were all warned. How hard is it to behave?"

Nyssa gasped for air.

Athen grabbed Elias. "Let her go, or I'll tear through your crew," he growled.

"Fontaine will kill her before that happens," Elias threatened.

Quinn pushed past Aryis and rushed toward Nyssa. She jolted to a stop, frozen in place, a glove halfway off.

Nyssa stared at her.

What is she doing?

"Elias, they don't understand the rules out here," Athen implored. "But if you hurt them, the Empire will hunt you down. And if the Empress doesn't get you, my mother will."

Elias eyed Athen and sighed. "I know she would." He looked down at Fontaine. "That's enough. Let them go."

Nyssa fell forward, clutching at her chest, sucking in air. Quinn stumbled, and Athen caught her before she fell, but she quickly wriggled away from him.

"Get your asses back to work!" Elias yelled at his crew. "And get this blood off my deck, Jerrin."

Fontaine clucked and pecked at Elias's foot.

"You're sure?" he asked her, turning his gaze on Nyssa. He closed in on her and hauled her to her feet.

"I think you best explain yourself, Blacksea. I entered negotiations for your ransom with the understanding the terms were fifty thousand gold for four adepts. But you're no adept," Elias accused, clutching Nyssa's jacket.

Nyssa pulled away from him.

"The fuck I'm not," she rasped.

Athen slid between Nyssa and Elias. "She's an adept. We grew up at the Emerald Order together."

"Then why doesn't she have magick?"

"How do you know that?" Aryis asked.

"Fontaine has many talents," Elias said, eyeing Nyssa. "Sensing magick is one of them. The guilds have one rule above all. How did you fool them?"

Nyssa cleared her throat. "I didn't fool them. They know I don't have magick. My First Master took me in as a baby, raised me in the Order. He defied their rules."

Elias clapped his hands and laughed. Nyssa stepped back, confused.

"Finally, someone breaks rank and does something truly original. I like this First Master of yours, Blacksea!"

"Yeah, well, not everyone feels the same way," she replied.

Elias's golden eyes searched her face. "What should we do about you? I can't take the chance you won't try something like this again."

"I'll vouch for her," Athen said.

"Or I could just tie her to the mast and let the gulls peck at her."

"Don't threaten me with a good time," Nyssa growled.

"Just...give us a minute?" Athen asked of Elias.

The pirate sighed and put his hands up. "Sort this out, Fennick."

After Elias gave them some space, Athen turned to Nyssa.

"What the fuck were you thinking?" he asked, his voice low.

"A guard got pushy with me. I pushed back."

"It got out of hand. *You* got out of hand."

Nyssa bristled. "You don't need to protect me."

Athen straightened up to his full height and shook his head. "I wasn't protecting you. I was protecting Aryis and Quinn. Your actions put us in danger. Do you understand that? And you put the crew in danger. We're stuck on this ship, and you need to get your anger in check. You can't be getting into fights."

Quinn spoke up. "She didn't start it."

"Shut up," Nyssa growled, rounding on her. Quinn recoiled. "This ignorant brute can speak for herself."

"Nyssa, calm down," Athen said. He turned to Quinn. "And what were you doing?"

"She was choking. I thought she needed help, and..." She looked down at her hands.

"You were going to negate Fontaine's magick?" Aryis asked.

"Doesn't matter," Quinn mumbled.

Nyssa stared at her. Their argument in the alley in Jejin told her everything Quinn thought of her. Why would she try to help now?

"We need to get back to Ocean's Rest, not play nice with fucking pirates," Nyssa said.

"This whole situation is out of our hands. But we will get back to Ocean's Rest. It's just going to take a little longer, okay?" Athen asked.

Nyssa stared at him.

"Okay?" he asked again, raising an eyebrow at her. It wasn't the first time he had given her that look. He had plenty of practice talking her down.

Nyssa closed her eyes and nodded. She hated that they were trapped on Hannah's Whisper. Hated Elias and his idiot chicken for taking them hostage. Hated that she would have to spend more time keeping an eye on Quinn. But she had little say in the matter.

Athen waved Elias back over. "We've got things sorted."

Elias turned to Nyssa. "Have we?"

"I'm not mopping your deck," she said.

A low groan rumbled in the back of Elias's throat, and he looked down at her, narrowing his eyes. He stared at her for several moments.

"Jerrin!" he hollered.

Nyssa braced for another confrontation. Jerrin jogged up to them, and Yuha followed, though slower and worse for wear.

Nyssa bit her tongue to stop from smiling at her handiwork.

"Blacksea here needs a job. I'd like her to shadow you and learn how to sail a proper ship. See if we can have her live up to her surname a little before we kick her back onto dry land," Elias said, a pleasant surprise. She expected a lot worse.

"Yes, sir." Jerrin beamed. "No more fights, if you please, Nyssa."

She peered up at Yuha, who met her with a wicked frown. "I'll be perfectly behaved," she said with a smirk.

Nyssa straightened up, her back screaming. Jerrin worked her hard and while she was used to aches and pains as a fighter, manual labor made her hurt in a much different way. But it was oddly satisfying to lower herself into bed at day's end with a grumble and a groan, knowing she had put in a day of honest work. Her slumber was deep and contented, not one nightmare plaguing her since being taken prisoner.

Through it all, Yuha hovered about, watching—not that she posed much of a threat. Nyssa suspected she was merely there for show.

Elias's eyes seemed to always be on her when she was on deck, his gaze disconcerting at first. After a couple of days, it simply became annoying. Nyssa bit her tongue and paid close attention to Jerrin, doing her best to ignore the pirate.

Three days into their journey, as Jerrin and Nyssa took a break, Elias sauntered over to them.

"My dear Jerrin, I would like to get to know our guest better. Quinn is making a mess of that rope over there. Could you show her how to tie a proper knot so she's not completely useless?"

"Yes, Captain," Jerrin said, giving a quick nod to Nyssa before taking his leave.

Nyssa cocked her head at Elias as he approached and reached forward to slide her hair away from her forehead. She didn't flinch, puzzled by his gesture.

"Ah, your injury is healing well," he said, meeting her gaze before dropping his hand. Nyssa turned from him and walked over to the handrail, looking out to sea. Elias joined her.

"Where's your chicken?"

"She is Old Folk. You will show her respect." Anger colored his voice, surprising her.

"Understood. I apologize."

"Good. I would like to avoid another unpleasant experience for you. Despite what you may think of us, we live honest lives on the sea."

"You're thieves. There's nothing honest about that."

Elias scoffed. "We're pirates, not thieves. If we were thieves, I would have confiscated those Lightway healing disks and your fancy sword."

"Is there really a difference?"

"Is there a difference between a back-alley fighter and an Ashcloak?"

Nyssa shook her head. "That's a dumb question. Of course there is."

"If you say so," Elias replied.

She turned to him, her irritation growing. "Whatever you think of the guilds, at least I have a purpose. I know who I am. All of this"—she gestured to the ship—"is rather impressive, but one day your way of life will catch up with you."

"Ah yes, all the freedom I have is positively awful." Elias rolled his eyes. "You're an embellished indentured servant. So I'll take my freedom—and my rather large stash of gold—and let the sea rock me to blissful sleep every night."

"You're a preening asshole, you know that?"

Elias put a hand on his chest and feigned shock. "A preening asshole? I have been called many things, but preening has not been one of them."

"So, you're accustomed to being regarded as an asshole?"

"This audacity coming from the woman who threatened my life as she was on her knees, dripping blood on the deck of the Sea Stag?" Elias grinned. "And got into a fight with my crew the next day over being asked to mop?"

Nyssa narrowed her eyes at him. "You attacked our ship. Your man knocked me unconscious. Yuha over there got pushy with me. Not exactly shining moments of courage by you or your crew."

"My dear girl, I'm a pirate. I don't make money with flattering words and warm hugs. But I can get you a fluffy pillow and sing you a lullaby later tonight, if you so wish, so as to not further offend your tender feelings."

A bit of color rose in Elias's cheeks. He was getting angry. Nyssa smiled. *Good*. "Do people fall for this noble pirate act of yours? You disarm with a smile as you slip your fingers into their pockets and act like you're doing them a favor."

Elias snorted. "I could slit throats and put ships into the deep, but I abide by the Laws of the Unbound Sea. I get a taste, the other ship gets an interesting story, and their rich purveyors—sleeping safely in their beds far inland—breathe a sigh of relief that I took far less than I could have."

Nyssa rolled her eyes at him, watching his irritation grow while she continued to mock him. "A true gentleman thief, then! I stand corrected. Where is the applause and the accolades for such a man? Who would fete you, my dear Pirate Lord?" Nyssa gave him a half-hearted bow before breaking down in a fit of laughter.

A low growl came from Elias's chest, and he took a step toward her. Nyssa didn't know if she had pushed too far, but she was more than ready for another fight.

"You have quite a way with people," Elias said, narrowing his eyes at her. "I suppose some masochists may find you charming."

Nyssa laughed again. "Are you trying to get into my pants, Ghost of the Sea?"

The look of pure frustration on Elias's face delighted her. Quite the change from the cocky pirate who took them hostage days prior. She couldn't stop the grin that spread across her face. Poking at Elias proved to be far more enjoyable than she expected.

With a heavy, pointed sigh, he turned to look out on the water and set his jaw. "We're running north to avoid any ships that might come looking for us. We'll be on the Black Sea in a few days' time. Tumultuous waters to match your tumultuous mood."

Before Nyssa could respond, he turned on his heels and returned to the quarterdeck.

"Everything alright?" Quinn asked. Nyssa jumped a little, roused from her thoughts while she leaned on the rail, looking out to sea. "I saw Elias over here speaking with you."

"He's toying with me," Nyssa replied.

"Can you handle him?"

Nyssa looked at her, surprised by Quinn's concern. "You don't need to worry about it."

"Nyssa, I—"

"We are not friends."

Quinn's actions in Jejin were still raw. Nyssa hated that part of her understood why Quinn went to such drastic measures, desperate to escape and be free. And a deeper part of her felt a pang of compassion. The woman had wormed into Nyssa's brain in a way she couldn't explain.

"If I could just—"

Nyssa turned to her. "You had your say before we got on the Sea Stag. You saw how I reacted to my Winter's Fire memories and used that, used my pain to—" Nyssa shook her head. "You played me. Fuck you. Just...fuck you."

Nyssa made her way back to Jerrin, leaving Quinn behind.

THE BLOOD CALLS

Nyssa flexed her fingers, trying to work the stiffness out of them. The weather had gotten decidedly colder, and she was content, reveling in the chilly air. Some of the crew looked at her as if she were strange, but she couldn't help the smile plastered on her face while she worked, the boat rocking underneath her feet soothing her in a way she had never felt before. It was the only thing that made the delay of getting back to Ocean's Rest tolerable.

Nyssa shined the massive, metal sheath that held the mainmast in place, slowly working her way around it. Yuha stood guard behind her.

A tug on her shoulder interrupted Nyssa's work. Yuha towered over her, nodding toward Elias standing at the handrail of the quarterdeck, looking down at her with a smile. They hadn't spoken for days, which suited Nyssa fine.

"Blacksea! Get your ass starboard and cast your eyes over the water you were named after," he called out.

"Which way is starboard again? I get so confused," she asked, determined to poke at the pirate.

"Fuck you, Blacksea." His smile took all the bite out of his words.

Nyssa stood and strode over to the handrail, gripping the cold metal. The Black Sea was rough and dangerous, even in good weather, but the skies had grown darker throughout the day.

Athen and Aryis joined her at the handrail.

"We're on the Black Sea," Nyssa said, her words turning into puffs of chilled fog as they left her mouth.

"You were born here?" Aryis asked.

"Yes. Somewhere out there."

The dark-blue sea stretched before Nyssa, its white caps rising and falling almost in rhythm with her breathing. Perhaps others found it cold and desolate, but she found it stunning. There was serenity in the chaos.

"It's beautiful."

Nyssa turned towards the voice. Quinn stood a few feet away, pushing her hair away from her face, fighting the wind as it picked up.

Elias stomped behind them, Fontaine tucked under his arm. "This weather came on us sooner than expected. Quite the homecoming you're about to get, Blacksea. We have to batten this ship down. Athen, we need your muscle on the sails. Nyssa, Quinn, and Yuha, you too."

"Of course," Athen said.

"Aryis, please take Fontaine below."

Angry clucking ensued.

"No! I will not hear it," Elias huffed. "You will not be safe up here when the storm hits. Why do we have to have this argument every goddamn time?"

Fontaine let out a few resigned-sounding chortles, and Elias nodded to her. "I will be safe, I promise you, old friend."

He handed Fontaine over to Aryis, who carefully took her. "I apologize in advance for my chilly hands." Fontaine let out a few clucks, causing Aryis to look at Elias for translation.

"She says you're fine." He turned toward the rest of his crew. "Get to it, then! I'm not paying you to lie about and bat your eyes at me!" Elias bellowed.

"I think I should point out that we're not being paid at—"

"My dear Queen-to-Be, shut up and get my quartermaster to my stateroom."

Aryis hurried off.

Jerrin quickly explained they needed to collapse and stow all the sails or the winds and ice would shred them. Nyssa and the others got to work.

The ribbed sails folded like a paper fan, each yard collapsing on the one underneath, but it took coordination and muscle.

As they labored, the weather worsened. Dark clouds overtook the light-gray sky of the morning, and the winds picked up, stinging gusts and bits of ice pricking their faces. The wind drove the sea and cold through Nyssa's clothes, and her fingers went numb.

"Pick up the pace!" Elias yelled.

Nyssa set about securing lines, and Quinn joined her, deftly knotting the rope—a far cry from their first days when she struggled to master even one knot. Aryis reappeared on deck, running to help the crew pull down the last sail. It whipped about violently in the wind on its mast until Athen got to it, helping lower the heavy yards one by one.

"Get r-ready to tie this one d-down!" Jerrin instructed, teeth chattering. It had begun to rain, and his red hair was plastered to his head, water clinging to his eyelashes.

Nyssa left the mast to the others and walked over to the handrail, entranced by the rise and fall of the sea's deep-blue waves. A cold wind cut across her, and she shivered, her clothes soaked from the dark sky dumping freezing water from its fast-moving clouds. She wrapped her hand around a rigging line to steady herself, knocking off already-forming ice.

Staring into the heavens, she smiled.

She was finally on the Black Sea.

Tension and excitement danced across her skin, the surrounding tempest roaring in her ears, howling its dangerous song. Whipping winds pulled her back and forth, mixing ice with rain that struck her skin like daggers. The ocean roiled beneath the ship, violent and tumultuous—the sea's primal fury thrumming in her chest—and she pulled in a deep breath, the crisp scent she often smelled before a lightning strike filling her lungs.

The storm sang to her, tugging at her bones and blood, burying itself into her very being.

Elias shouted Nyssa's name from the quarterdeck, and she ran to the deck and up its stairs. "Are you staying out here?"

"You worried about me, Blacksea? I knew my charm would get to you."

"You think you're charming? That's precious," she yelled through the wind.

"I'll be fine. I'm going to strap in and ride it out."

"You'll freeze out here!"

"You underestimate Koja fortitude," he said, flashing her a smile. "I've done this hundreds of times. Now, get down below. I can't worry about this ship and you at the same time."

Nyssa opened her mouth to say something, but paused, the screeching wind growing louder.

The hair on the back of her neck pricked up.

Heavy, black shadows crashed onto the deck, and Nyssa whirled around to see wraiths landing on the ship to the startled cries of the deckhands. She instinctively reached over her back for Winter's Bite, grasping at nothing.

Shit.

All of their weapons were in their staterooms.

"Get these fuckers off my goddamned boat!" Elias bellowed to his crew.

A wraith landed next to Aryis and Quinn, sending them scrambling along the wet, icy deck. Nyssa vaulted over the railing to the deck below, breaking her fall with a roll before sprinting toward the wraith advancing on the women, barely keeping her footing.

She tackled the creature, and they spilled to the deck. Nyssa clambered over its back and grabbed its head, twisting its chin around, snapping its neck with a sickening *crack*.

It twitched beneath her as she stood up.

"Are you both okay?" she yelled at Aryis and Quinn. Aryis shouted, "Yes," and Quinn just nodded, her eyes wide, water dripping off her chin. She was pale and in shock, staring at the dead wraith at Nyssa's feet.

"To me, men! On me!" Elias yelled, running to the bow of the ship, sword drawn.

Nyssa spun around, looking for wraiths while the deck crew scrambled on Elias's orders. She pulled Quinn toward her out of instinct.

Athen ran over, his arms bloodied up to the elbows. "How many left? I killed two."

"I put one down. I think Elias got one too," Nyssa said.

She heard a roar from Elias's direction, and they turned to see him slice the head off a remaining wraith, a deckhand dead at his feet, the poor man's head partly severed. Nyssa turned her eyes skyward, shielding her face from the icy rain with her hand.

The storm made it hard to pick out anything.

"Elias, do you see any more?" she yelled. He ran toward her with a small group of crewmen. Jerrin's head was bleeding, Yuha had a shallow slash across her collarbone, and everyone was soaked to the skin and shivering. If the wraiths didn't kill them, the weather would.

"No. I think there were only five or six. Eyes up!" Elias commanded. "There could be more. Sound off if you see anything!"

Everyone on deck craned their necks up to the sky, watching and waiting. The wind howled in Nyssa's ears. She scanned the sky, but after a tense minute, only the storm roiled overhead.

She let out a heavy breath before turning to Quinn and gently touching her arm. "Are you okay?"

Quinn opened her mouth to respond when Nyssa's left shoulder ignited with searing pain, bringing her to her knees, a sharp cry wrenching from her lips. Her guts turned to ice.

The blood wraith was near. Nyssa could *feel* the damn thing. She whirled around, searching for it, her hands curling into fists.

The massive wraith landed on the quarterdeck with a loud screech. Athen and Elias sprinted past Nyssa toward the creature. Even with Athen's strength and Elias's sword, Nyssa knew they were as good as dead against a monster of its size and speed.

"Get Nyssa up!" Aryis shouted.

Yuha yanked her to her feet, and Aryis and Quinn each hooked an arm under her, supporting her as she tried to stand. Nyssa groaned. Her shoulder screamed in agony.

How is this happening?

"Run!" Aryis cried. She and Quinn dragged her toward the bow of the ship and away from the blood wraith, but Nyssa resisted.

"No! I'm not leaving Athen and Elias back there."

"Nyssa, please!" Aryis pleaded. "We need our weapons from our rooms."

"I think— I think it's here for me." Nyssa yanked out of their grasp and turned around to face the quarterdeck.

A flash of fire illuminated the blood wraith as Elias showed his magick for the first time since the foursome came on board. The creature cried out in pain, backhanding Elias while he tried to form a fireball, sending him crashing into the ship's wheel. Athen shot up the stairs to help him, but the wraith met him at the top and slashed its claws across his chest, sending him sprawling back down to the main deck.

"Athen!" Nyssa screamed. The blood wraith disappeared from the quarterdeck and landed before her in the blink of an eye. It slowly extended to its full height and furled its wings to its back, dark-red eyes focusing on Nyssa, who stopped in her tracks.

Her heart hammered in her chest, her whole body trembling. The fire in her shoulder flared again, and she stumbled forward, clutching at the old wound.

The blood wraith took a step toward her, and she glanced back to see Aryis and Quinn, along with Jerrin and Yuha, inching forward. "Run!" Nyssa yelled.

Instead of listening, they braced for an attack.

As they advanced, the blood wraith reared up and shrieked at Nyssa, its hot, fetid breath coating her face as its eyes bored into her. Its muscles bulged and rippled under its pitch-black skin, denoting dangerous power.

Nyssa took a step forward, gritting her chattering teeth. "What do you want?" she screamed at it.

The blood wraith stopped and cocked its head.

She took another step forward, almost slipping on the slick deck. "What the fuck do you want?"

The creature snarled at her with a frightening grin before opening its mouth.

"Magickless whelp." Its voice was a low, scraping growl that vibrated in Nyssa's chest.

She had heard those words before.

In a blur of speed, it closed the distance to Nyssa in less than a heartbeat. Its claws scrabbled across her throat and heaved her off her feet. She cried out, digging her fingers into its wrists with her numb, frozen hands.

Aryis and Jerrin shouted behind her.

Nyssa kicked her legs forward, striking the blood wraith's chest. She braced herself against it and pushed as hard as she could while it choked her, trying to get enough leverage to pull out of its grasp.

The blood wraith smiled its bright-white smile again, just like its first attack in Ocean's Rest. It tightened its grip.

Whatever it started the night of Winter's Fire, it was going to finish.

Nyssa's legs trembled and her muscles strained, pushing against its body.

The blood wraith cried out and collapsed to one knee, bringing her down with it. She turned her head to see Jerrin wielding Elias's sword before the wraith backhanded him, sending him flying across the deck.

Nyssa tried to take advantage of its divided attention by prying back the fingers wrapped around her throat, but the blood wraith turned its head to her, constricting its fingers. Despite her struggle, she felt her legs go slack.

The wraith let her slip to her knees as it strangled the life out of her.

"Quinn stop!" Aryis yelled.

Quinn darted next to Nyssa, grabbing the forearm of the blood wraith with both hands.

Bare hands.

Dark, shadowy magick wrapped around the wraith's arm and dove into its body. The creature let out a confused cry, and its face contorted, grotesquely shifting from monstrous blood wraith to a human man and back to monster. It gurgled, losing its grip on Nyssa's throat.

She fell forward and gasped for breath.

"Run!" Quinn weakly cried out. Lightning streaked overhead, illuminating her face—a mask of concentration and pain. She was dampening the blood wraith's forbidden magick, weakening it, revealing its once-human face.

Nyssa had to kill the wraith and kill it quickly.

Thunder boomed in the sky, vibrating through her. She spotted a grappling hook hanging on the starboard rail. Scrambling to her feet, she shot toward the handrail, sliding forward, crashing into the rail. Nyssa snatched up the hook and turned back to the wraith, watching in horror as it violently shoved Quinn down onto the deck.

The wraith stood, shaky and hurt, and it advanced toward Quinn, raising a fist to crush her where she lay.

Panic flooded Nyssa's body.

No!

"Hey, asshole!" she yelled. "I'm right here, you motherfucker. Come get me."

The creature turned its head and lunged on all fours at her. The lingering effects of Quinn's magick slowed it down, and Nyssa wheeled out of its path, sinking the grappling hook deep into the meat of its shoulder. She held fast to the rope attached to the hook as the blood wraith reared up and spun around, trying to claw at her. It lost its balance and slid against the ship's handrail.

Kill it.

The wraith was regaining its strength and speed. It would rip through them all.

Get it off the ship.

Nyssa looked down at the rope in her hands. She wrapped the end of it around her forearm and sprinted toward the monster. Veering at the last moment, she jumped over the handrail, a chorus of voices shouting her name, and tumbled overboard, yanking the rope taut. She feared her momentum wasn't enough to drag the creature over the rail, but the rope gave way a heartbeat later.

The sea enveloped Nyssa, pulling her into its icy embrace. Panic gripped her, the shock of the frigid water numbing her limbs, seizing up her lungs. The blood wraith's body hit her, forcing her deeper into the freezing darkness of the Black Sea.

A cry caught in Quinn's throat as Nyssa jumped overboard. *No!*

The blood wraith toppled off the ship a second later.

The crew scrambled and shouted, and Aryis shot to the rail where Nyssa and the creature fell, screaming her name. Athen stumbled to the side, gripping his bleeding chest, and Elias ran down the deck toward them.

"Nyssa's in the water!" Aryis yelled.

Quinn shrugged off her cloak in the freezing rain, and hopped on one foot, shucking one boot, then the other.

"I have to go after her," Athen said. He dropped to a knee, bleeding.

"I got her." Quinn tore off her soaked sweater and dropped it on deck with a wet slap next to the boots and cloak at her feet, ignoring the icy winds cutting against her skin. She ran past Elias and the others and leapt over the rail, pulling her arms into her body and hitting the sea feet first, like a dagger slicing the water.

The cold shocked her body, stunning her for a moment, and she let that shock move through her, remembering to focus, to get her bearings. After collecting herself, she resurfaced and opened her eyes to see Athen, Elias, and others peering over the handrail at her.

"Quinn, Nyssa can't swim!" Athen yelled.

She ignored her pounding heart and swallowed back her fear, filling her lungs with air and diving below the surface. A distant body sank beneath her, and she swam with all her might, hoping to reach Nyssa in time.

THE SEA CALLS

Nyssa's brain screamed at her seizing muscles to do something. She flailed in the icy water, every movement a struggle.

Her heart beat fast in her chest. Too fast.

Fear took over.

Somewhere in a deep recess of her mind, she realized she had experienced this before. In a dream. Or a dream become nightmare. Her mind tried to grasp at its meaning, but she understood—this was certain death.

The more she tried to fight, the more her body rejected any order to move. The screaming in her brain receded, drifting farther away.

Her heartbeat slowed.

She couldn't struggle against the freezing water; it sapped her strength. Instead, she sank into it and let it pull her down.

The blood wraith had hit the water with her and would suffer the same frozen fate. That was enough for Nyssa.

The sea wrapped its arms around her, and her limbs went slack as she descended.

Nyssa was born on the Black Sea, named for it. And she would come to rest here. Fate had decided for her, and it pulled her further and further into its darkness. She closed her eyes and tried to think of her friends, her parents, and how short a life she had lived. How very little of that life was her own. What did the guild or the Empire matter now, below the waves of the Black Sea?

Every fight Nyssa had been in, every indignity she had swallowed, seemed a waste, amplified and pressed into her while an ache of regret, deep and unyielding, eased her into the darkness.

A jolt of pain assaulted Nyssa, and her eyes flew open, her brain jumping awake. Pulses of blue lightning skittered along her arms and hands, energy arcing from finger to finger. Around her, the water shimmered, dark and infinite, like the sky and the stars beyond.

A hallucination—the remnants of life driving her mind into madness.

Nyssa reached forward, grabbing at nothing. Beyond her splayed fingers, she glimpsed a figure moving toward her, and a prick of fear shot down her spine.

The figure got closer, fighting through the water.

The face was familiar. And impossible.

Quinn?

Nyssa's lungs burned. Her body fought against her mind—it needed to take a breath, desperate for air.

She gave in.

Nyssa convulsed, her lungs filling with freezing water. The shroud of blue lightning around her sparked and flared as she drowned.

Quinn fought to get to Nyssa, her muscles burning and threatening to cramp. Something that looked like blue lightning danced across Nyssa's body, confusing Quinn. Her eyes must be playing tricks, her brain starved for air.

As she reached her, Nyssa convulsed violently.

Quinn caught her hand, and the woman convulsed again, shooting a searing jolt up her arm, almost making her lose her hold. Nyssa convulsed once more, and another burst of pain crashed into Quinn while shards of blue light danced in her vision, hemmed in by an encroaching darkness. She forced herself to not scream—she would doom them both if she did.

Nyssa's gaze met hers, full of fear and cobalt fire. Her mouth opened, and she shuddered once. Then twice, weaker.

Her eyes stilled.

Nyssa had drowned.

No.

Panic surged through Quinn.

No!

She circled behind Nyssa's back, hooking her arms around her chest. Quinn looked up to the surface, its soft, distant glow giving her the smallest flicker of hope, and she started kicking with all her might. If she didn't get air soon, she was going to drown as well.

Her lungs burned and crippling pain rippled through her shoulders and arms, but she held on to Nyssa and kept kicking.

Even as her legs went numb, she kept kicking.

The surface grew brighter.

Almost there, almost there, almost there, almost there.

Don't let go.

THE DEAD

Quinn broke the surface of the water and inhaled a big gulp of freezing air, shocking her lungs. Voices shouted above her, but she couldn't find the energy to look up. She kept her arms around Nyssa's limp body and treaded water, hoping the crew could get to them before her legs finally quit on her and they both sank.

Faces appeared next to Quinn, bobbing up and down in the water, hands steadying her. "T-t-take Nyssa," she said, her teeth chattering uncontrollably.

Nyssa's body was pulled from her arms, and she closed her eyes and let her rescuers work. She shivered fiercely, trying to calm her body as she was pulled aboard the ship and laid down on the deck. Jerrin appeared above her, covering her with a blanket. Light rain pattered around her, a brief respite from the driving downpour of the storm.

She turned her head to Nyssa, whose blank eyes stared up at the sky, her body limp, arms splayed.

She was pale, so very pale.

Quinn reached out and grabbed hold of her ice-cold hand. Elias bent over Nyssa, his hands on her chest, pushing down. As he leaned into her, water spewed up out of her mouth. He pushed down again and again, then pressed his mouth to hers and breathed into her.

"Come on, woman!" he yelled before breathing into her again. Nyssa's chest rose and fell, and Elias breathed one more time before leaning back, slicking away his soaked hair, and putting his palms above her heart. His hands glowed red, and he pressed them on Nyssa's chest, pushing down several times. "Come on, come on, come on."

Every one of Quinn's muscles shook uncontrollably, and her teeth rattled against each other with a violence she didn't know could exist from mere cold, but she didn't let go of Nyssa's hand. "C'mon, you stubborn woman," she whispered, willing Nyssa to open her eyes.

Aryis and Athen stood behind Elias, watching with faces full of dread. Streaks of blood ran down Athen's shirt, but he waved Buck away when the medic tried to look at his wounds.

Elias bent over Nyssa again. "Nyssa, you fucking asshole, don't die on my goddamned deck!" He breathed into her mouth one more time.

Nyssa's body arched, and she sucked in a deep, wet breath, violently coughing as she exhaled. Elias rolled her over on her side and let her cough up the rest of the water in her lungs.

Swallowing hard, Quinn took a deep breath, thankful they were both alive. Nyssa's blue eyes opened and met hers. The strange blue glow was gone—surely a hallucination caused by a lack of air.

"Holy sweet fuck," Elias said, rubbing Nyssa's back. Quinn let out a strangled laugh of relief.

Nyssa closed her eyes, and Elias picked her up in his arms. Quinn lifted from the deck, too, Yuha scooping her up.

"I can't...can't st-stop shaking," Quinn said.

"You are insane. You are both insane," Yuha said, smiling down at her.

Elias and Yuha carried the women down to their stateroom, and Buck helped Athen. Once inside the room, Athen leaned up against a wall and slid down it with a grunt. Aryis crouched next to him. "I'll be okay," he said as he stripped off his shirt.

Elias looked at Nyssa and Quinn. "Not to be impolite, but we need to get them out of their clothes." Yuha disappeared and returned with extra blankets.

Elias and Aryis stripped Nyssa down to her underwear, wrapped her in blankets, and placed her back in bed. Quinn waved Yuha off, preferring to keep her clothes on, and pulled one of the extra blankets around herself, sitting on her bed.

Elias pulled a brazier from one corner and set it in the middle of the stateroom. He held out his hand, igniting a ball of flame over his palm, then winked at Quinn and directed the flame into the brazier. The rocks within glowed red, providing extra heat to the room.

"Who's steering this ship through the storm?" Quinn wondered aloud.

"Jerrin's got it. He's trained for this," Elias replied.

"Stop your squirming, boy!" Buck grumbled, examining Athen's wounds while Aryis hovered over him, her face painted with worry.

"What's the damage, Buck?" Elias asked. Athen had four deep slashes across his chest from the blood wraith, and Buck was doing his best to clean the wounds with the same tonic he used on Nyssa a week earlier. Quinn winced, remembering Nyssa's reaction to the sting of the liquid.

"No sign of poison. He's going to need—mmm—stitches, but no needle will get through that skin," Buck said. "Too tough."

Athen hissed as the medic continued cleaning his wounds. "Nothing's hurt me like this."

"I'm sorry, Athen, that monster was after me," Nyssa croaked from the bed, her voice weak. But she was alive and conscious. Hope flooded through Quinn. "How did it find us?"

Elias sat on the edge of her bed. "That mark on your shoulder, did that big wraith give it to you?"

Aryis put her hand on Elias's shoulder. "I can explain for you, Nyssa, don't try to speak." Aryis quickly recounted the events of Winter's Fire and the next day. Quinn listened carefully. She had not heard the poison part of their ordeal.

"I know Reece Ae'Shen is an empath, but she felt your physical pain?" Elias asked.

"Yes. We have an...unconventional connection," Nyssa replied.

An empath? Their connection...what does it mean?

"I know a little about blood wraiths. You have its blood in your veins, so it can sense where you are."

"Fuck," Nyssa croaked. "What if it's not dead?"

"It followed you into the water. We didn't see it come back out. Nothing survives that sea. Well, nothing save for you two fucking insane women, that is," Elias said, shaking his head. "Blacksea, what were you thinking jumping overboard with a blood wraith in tow?"

Nyssa cleared her throat. "Quinn temporarily weakened it. But it was regaining its strength. I thought the only thing to do was get it off the boat. I took a gamble that it would drown."

Elias crossed his arms and shook his head. "And you would drown with it, girl."

"One person for a ship full of people. It was more than a fair trade."

The room grew quiet.

Elias put his hand on her arm. "I realize you have very little respect for my authority, but this is my ship and you are my hostage. You are to remain aboard this vessel at all times. I'm counting on getting pennies and pocket lint for your ransom. There will be no more noble sacrifices."

Elias patted her arm gently before standing back and turning to Quinn. "And you. I don't know what you were thinking, but that was the damnedest thing I've seen in a long time. And completely idiotic. The same order I gave Nyssa applies to you. No heroics." He smiled, despite his warning.

He then turned to Buck. "Now, how do we get Athen fixed up if we can't get a stitch in him? I cannot hand Lilliana Fennick's son back to her like this, Buck."

"We have healing disks," Aryis said.

"They don't work well on me," Athen replied. "Their magick runs into mine and, well, they're designed for normal flesh."

Aryis cleared her throat. "I have an idea, but I don't think Athen will like it."

"I don't much like these either." He pointed at the slashes on his chest with a grimace.

"Quinn. She can dampen your magick, then maybe a disk will work?" Aryis suggested.

Quinn sat up. "Oh, I don't think that's a good idea. He didn't react well when I—"

"Maybe you can try? A little gentler this time?" Athen asked. He gave her a slight nod.

Quinn looked at Athen and Aryis. They were extending her a great deal of trust. Before, she would have said no. But before, she wouldn't have dove into freezing water to save Nyssa either. "Alright."

"Boy doesn't need a disk. Those cuts are shallow. Hurt a lot less for me to stitch 'em up. You should—mmm—be grateful for your magick. You'd be cut in half if not for it," Buck said.

Aryis frowned. "No, we should use a—"

"No, Aryis, Buck is right. I hate those things, if I'm being honest. They never heal me right. I'll take the needle and thread."

Athen ambled over to Quinn's bed, sitting on the floor beside it. Buck knelt next to him and squinted. "Brave boy."

Athen extended his hand toward Quinn, and she took it. "Sorry, my hands are cold," she whispered.

She closed her eyes and reached out, finding the nexus of Athen's magick—bright and strong, glowing deep in his chest. She concentrated and shrouded his magick with her own, careful to go slow and gentle.

Athen let out a breath. "I think it's working, but it's not like before. I don't feel queasy."

"Mmm—let me give you a poke, then." Quinn heard Athen softly hiss and Buck hummed. "Yup, it's working—mmm—good job, girl."

"Again, my name is Quinn." She focused on the delicate balance of suppressing Athen's magick without causing pain and disorientation. The last thing she wanted was to hurt him.

When she opened her eyes, soft, smoky wisps swirled around their joined hands. Her attention drifted to Nyssa, who watched with drowsy eyes.

"Girl! Keep your concentration," Buck scolded, trying to poke a needle into Athen's skin. It didn't budge. Quinn swallowed and closed her eyes again, tamping down his magick again. Aryis whispered to him, perhaps attempting to keep his mind off his pain.

After a long while, Quinn felt a hand on her shoulder, and she opened her eyes, finding Aryis smiling down at her. "Buck is done. You can stop now."

Quinn let go of Athen's hand, and he stood, his wounds stitched up well. Buck set about wrapping his chest in gauze to keep the wounds clean and dry. Quinn lay back on her pillow, exhausted. Diving into the freezing sea and then using her power for so long to help Athen drained her completely.

"You okay?" Aryis asked, crouching by her bedside.

"I am. I just need to rest."

Aryis put her hand on Quinn's arm. "Thank you. For everything you did today."

"Alright, everyone out," Elias ordered. "These two need to rest." He herded people out of the room before turning back. "Quinn, that was a damn fine thing you did. You have guts, woman."

Quinn fought off a grin, though heartened by his sentiment. "Elias...when I was under the water, I thought I saw something—" She found herself at a loss for words, not quite certain how to explain the blue lightning or the pain when she grabbed Nyssa. "Never mind."

"Being under that long, your mind can play tricks on you. And the sea...well, the sea has tricks of its own," he replied.

Elias gave her a smile and left, closing the door behind him. Across the room, Nyssa breathed softly, already asleep.

Shivering, Quinn stood and stripped off her blanket and damp clothes, letting them drop to the floor while watching to ensure Nyssa didn't stir. By the time Quinn got into dry underclothes, she was practically panting. Her shoulders drooped, and she leaned against the wall. She struggled to get a shirt on, but she needed to cover up before falling into bed.

A soft moan from across the room drew her attention back to Nyssa, who pulled her blankets tighter to herself in her sleep. Quinn couldn't imagine the toll the day had taken on Nyssa. She witnessed Nyssa in the throes of drowning.

The panic in her eyes was haunting.

Quinn dropped into her bed and burrowed under her blankets, her own body beaten and punished by the day's events. She closed her eyes, and sleep claimed her quickly.

She dreamt of walking in a dark, luminous forest, the scents of pine and winter orchids heavy in the air. Coming upon a stream, she lay next to it, and stared up at the umbral sky, a myriad of stars twinkling above. She held up her arm to the sky and thick strands of darkness extended from her blackened fingers, stained from the charcoal pencil she used for her sketches. The darkness enveloped her, shimmering and rippling over her skin, strange, cold, and comforting.

A hand slipped into hers and squeezed.

AN APOLOGY

Nyssa groaned and sat up in bed. The prior day was a blur, and she barely remembered being woken for a dinner of hot broth before falling asleep again.

Her throat and chest hurt.

Every muscle ached.

She swung her legs off the bed and looked across the room to find Quinn gone. There was a small pile of clean, folded clothes on her footlocker along with her boots, freshly polished. She made a mental note to thank Jerrin—it was undoubtedly his work. She appreciated his kindness.

Nyssa wondered where her bunkmate had gotten off to. She owed Quinn her life, and they needed to talk. She needed to understand why Quinn dove into the sea after her.

A soft knock on the door roused her from her thoughts. "Come in."

Elias entered, beaming. "Ah, you're looking better, love. You have some color back in your cheeks."

"I'm still shaky, to be honest," Nyssa replied, pulling her blanket up around her shoulders.

"Of course you are." He retrieved a chair from the corner and sat. "You went through quite an ordeal. I've never seen someone survive in the water that long."

Nyssa hung her head. "I didn't, though, did I? I died."

Elias ran his hand through his dark-blue hair. "You were under for a long time, and Quinn...I don't know how she got you back up. That woman risked her life going after you."

Nyssa looked down at her hands. "I have no idea why."

"In my experience, people will always surprise you. There's conflict between you two, but she deemed you worthy enough to risk diving into freezing waters to fish you out. You owe her."

"Is that another Law of the Unbound Sea?"

"No, you silly fuck. That's just life."

Nyssa swallowed back a lump. "I—I remember drowning down there...the pain...I was so scared."

"At least you weren't alone. Quinn was there with you. Remember that. Honor that."

Elias got up and moved the chair back into the corner. "Take the day and tomorrow to rest, but tomorrow night, I want to see you in my quarters for dinner. I figure you deserve it after saving this ship."

"Is that an order, Captain?"

"Does it need to be?" he asked, raising an eyebrow.

"I suppose not."

As Elias opened the door to leave, he turned around. "My heart is truly glad to see you alive, Nyssa. But if you plan to spend another second on a boat, learn how to swim, woman."

Nyssa smiled as he left. Standing, she stepped toward the small table against the wall, bracing herself against it, and gazed in the mirror nailed above it. The face that looked back at her was a mess—hair wild and dark circles under her eyes. Even the scar that ran down her face looked more severe.

Nyssa stared at it, her thoughts lingering on the day Athen had accidentally cut her. The fear on his face. His tears. The admonishment of Eron, telling her she acted like a fool and not a warrior, her cockiness nearly costing her an eye.

The thing that Nyssa remembered most about that day was her shame. She didn't keep the scar to remind her of Athen's mistake, but of her own. And the pain she caused her best friend. It was a secret she kept to herself, next to her heart.

Her eyes went from the scar on her face to the poison scar left by the blood wraith. She sighed and traced it from her shoulder down her arm to her wrist. That wraith was always going to be with her, whether she liked it or not, the gray lightning evidence of its hate.

A troubling detail tugged at her mind, one she had nearly forgotten after almost dying the previous day.

It had spoken to her, uttering an insult.

Magickless whelp.

The same insult Ceril used to describe her, according to Quinn. Nyssa took a deep breath, trying to order her thoughts. The most plausible explanation was also unthinkable...

The blood wraith had not just attacked Ocean's Rest, it had targeted her.

Quinn had told her about Ceril's interest in forbidden magick, but she'd dismissed it as the accusations of a desperate woman.

Magickless whelp.

Nyssa gritted her teeth, anger simmering, apprehension tugging at her gut. Was Ceril capable of creating wraiths? A blood wraith? If he did, why was she his target?

Nyssa placed her palms on the table and leaned forward, her head hanging. Even after sleeping for half a day and a night, she was exhausted.

The door opened behind her, but she didn't move. She felt unsteady, as if the table was the only thing holding her up.

What if the wraith is still out there, waiting for me?

"Nyssa?"

Quinn appeared in the mirror's reflection. She crossed the room and reached out, placing a hand on Nyssa's shoulder for a moment before pulling back. "Are you okay?"

"I'm just resting," Nyssa said, straightening slowly and turning around to lean against the table for support. Quinn looked tired, but her green eyes were vibrant, studying Nyssa's face.

"You look better."

Nyssa swallowed hard. "Why did you go into the water after me?"

Quinn retreated to her bed and pulled off her cloak.

"Athen said you couldn't swim. One of my few escapes at the Citadel was swimming, and it's always freezing in that damned place. I'm used to cold water," Quinn said, shrugging.

Nyssa sighed and dropped her head. There was something too easy about Quinn's response. "You risked your life for me." Her voice was quiet, close to breaking with the sudden flood of emotions, and she fought back tears.

"It was nothing," Quinn replied.

"It was *not* nothing." Nyssa swallowed. "You are brave, Quinn."

The compliment seemed to throw Quinn off, and she sat down and folded her hands in her lap, fidgeting. "I...I wanted to talk to you." She paused and took a big breath. "What I did before we left Jejin...I'm sorry. I was scared and desperate. Nyssa, I don't think you're worthless. I was an asshole."

Quinn stared up at Nyssa, her eyes unwavering. Others had hurt Nyssa many times in her life with no remorse. She had learned to live with the little indignities, but Quinn had hurt her deep.

Deeper than she wanted to admit.

When Quinn let down her guard just a little, Nyssa could see the person behind the thorny exterior. A frightened woman who didn't know how to trust others—a person Nyssa might befriend in another life.

"I called you a coward for running away from your guild. You're not a coward. You could have run away from the blood wraith or let me drown, but you didn't. I...I don't understand you, Quinn."

"I'm trying to figure out who I am. And I'm having a rough go at it, Nyssa." Quinn looked down at her hands. "Am I an adept? A traitor? Am I dangerous? Can you tell me?"

Nyssa opened her mouth but could offer Quinn no answer.

Tears sprang to Quinn's eyes, and she blinked them away. "I don't understand who I'm supposed to be. I just know I can't be the person I am at Arcton Citadel. That person is hollow and alone, surrounded by darkness." She shook her head and stood.

"I'm sorry, Quinn. I really am. I wish I could—"

"There's nothing you can do. You have a mission. You'll return me to the Citadel, and they'll hide me away, make me small again."

Nyssa exhaled, an ache of helplessness carving through her.

Quinn opened the door and forced a smile. "Let's get you some food."

That night, while Quinn got ready for bed, her exhaustion made her careless. She stripped her sweater off, forgetting that the camisole she wore didn't cover her shoulders. Movement from behind startled her, and she spun around to find Nyssa scowling.

"Show me your back," she said, her voice low.

Quinn's stomach dropped. "No."

Nyssa came closer, her face dark with anger. "Show me your back."

Quinn stumbled back, her knees suddenly weak. "Nyssa, please—" she whispered, her voice breaking. She had been so careful around her and the others, careful to cover up and not let *anyone* see.

Nyssa took another quick step toward her, and Quinn flinched, shrinking away.

"Do you...do you think I'm going to hurt you?" Nyssa asked. She reached forward, and Quinn retreated further, the back of her legs hitting her bed.

Her eyes filled with tears.

Don't show weakness...

Nyssa's face softened. "I'm not going to hurt you, I promise. Please, show me your back."

Her unwavering gaze broke Quinn down. She couldn't run, couldn't lie or hide.

Nyssa had seen.

Quinn clenched her jaw and turned around, trying to hold herself together.

Nyssa sucked in a breath.

Quinn knew what she saw, having stared in a mirror more times than she cared to recall. She'd memorized the thin, red scars of hatred etched into her back, extending from shoulder to shoulder and down to her tailbone. Quinn reached behind her with trembling hands and pulled up the bottom of her camisole to expose her lower back. More healed-over scars.

After a few silent, torturous moments, Nyssa gently tugged the camisole back down. "That's enough," she whispered.

Quinn sat on the bed, and Nyssa picked up a blanket and draped it over her shoulders before kneeling in front of her. Quinn kept her eyes downcast, afraid to look at Nyssa. She began to cry and covered her mouth. She hated how weak she was. Crying wasn't a luxury she indulged in frequently. Ceril never had the patience for it, and it was a part of herself she refused to give him.

"Quinn, I'm so sorry...I—"

She wiped her tears. "You didn't do it."

"Ceril," Nyssa said, cold and certain.

Quinn nodded. "He had me test my powers on others, trying to understand the extent of my magick. One day, when I was sixteen, I decided to find out what a First Master's magick felt like, what made them special. So I touched him to see. Ceril whipped me himself."

"Quinn, your back is full of scars."

She brought her eyes up to Nyssa's face. "He was thorough. The pain was unbearable. I...I passed out." Nyssa's blue eyes teared up. "And the thing is, when I touched him, I felt nothing different. First Masters aren't special, Nyssa."

"This only happened once?"

"Yes."

Nyssa paused, jaw flexed. "And the scars on your hands?"

Quinn turned her hands over, inspecting her palms. "I can only suppress magick through physical contact. Many of the books and relics at the Citadel have wards and traps...most of them trip when touched. So there's a split second when the enchantments geared to inflict pain do their job." Quinn had gotten good at hiding her pain with Ceril, steeling herself against the worst enchantments.

"These scars healed poorly, Quinn. Didn't the healers try to—"

"Ceril never let me see a healer."

A sharp breath left Nyssa. "Fucking prick." She shook her head and placed her hand on Quinn's knee. Its warmth was comforting.

"Ceril kept me in a void collar since that day I touched him."

"What? A void collar? Goddamn it. This is why you begged me not to bring you back...why didn't you tell me?"

"Because I'm ashamed! I let him hurt me." Quinn's voice broke. There was something about Nyssa that weakened her resolve and left her open and vulnerable.

And she couldn't bear it.

Nyssa grabbed Quinn's hand, fixing her gaze on her. "You did nothing to deserve what he did to you. He's a monster. You did the one thing that scares him the most—you took his magick away, made him small, made him nothing, even for just a minute. He's a pitiful man that whipped a child."

"And you'll return me to him regardless."

"I can't—I don't..." Nyssa's eyes dropped away from Quinn's face.

"I understand."

A tear rolled down Nyssa's face, surprising Quinn. Nyssa wiped it away quickly and sat back on her haunches. "I can talk to Eron. We can show him your scars—"

"No. I don't want you to tell anyone about what he did."

"But—"

"No one."

Nyssa opened her mouth, struggling for something to say.

"No one. Promise me, Nyssa," Quinn said. "Please."

Nyssa's face fell. "I promise. But taking you back means this could happen again."

"There's not much either of us can do at this point. Once we land in Ocean's Rest, it's over. You'll have completed your mission, and they'll reward you for it."

"I'm sorry. I wish it wasn't this way."

Quinn sighed and held Nyssa's gaze. "If you knew, would it have made a difference? Would you have let me go?"

Nyssa's face and shoulders fell.

"I know you can't answer that question, Nyssa, so I won't ask you again."

Her loyalty to the Order was strong, her desire to prove herself evident in every action. Returning Quinn was Nyssa's ultimate test of worth to the Empire—an Empire that would never fully value its magickless adept.

Yet there were moments when it seemed like something different drove Nyssa. How else to explain her jumping off the ship to certain death, desperate to save the Whisper, its crew, and her friends?

Nyssa ran her fingers over the scar on her neck, left by the wraith's poison, before looking up at Quinn. "When you're back at the Citadel, if you need me, send a message. Make it innocuous in case someone reads it, but mention punching me in the face the first time we met. I'll understand that it means you need my help."

A lump rose in Quinn's throat. For the first time in her life, she was being offered help—a lifeline. "I will remember that. Thank you."

Nyssa stood and padded back to her bunk. Quinn lay on her bed, staring at the ceiling and wondering if she would ever—could ever—take Nyssa up on her offer of help. She imagined what returning to the Citadel would feel like, the dread that would overtake her as she cast her eyes upon the white stones of the massive guild once again. And how would she feel under Ceril's withering, icy stare.

The day he stripped the flesh from her back, something shifted in Quinn. The emptiness inside her turned into a jagged ball of hate, embedded deep in her core, dark and cold.

An errant tear rolled down into her hair as she tried to will herself to sleep.

AN UNEXPECTED GIFT

Nyssa knocked on Elias's door, taking a deep breath when she heard footsteps within.

He opened the door. "Nyssa Blacksea, come in. How are you faring?"

"Better. Rest helped."

As she passed into the room, Elias smiled at her. "Did you bathe just for me? You smell of verbena."

She suppressed an eye roll. "I bathed for me."

Elias's quarters were spacious, and he had cleared off a large drafting table, setting it for dinner. He walked over to the table and picked up a bottle. "Blackberry wine?"

"Who did you pilfer that off of?" Nyssa asked, raising an eyebrow.

He let out a short laugh. "A Froslandian merchant company. Please don't tell Aryis."

Nyssa chuckled. "I'll have a glass."

Elias poured the wine while Nyssa glanced around his quarters. His book collection was varied, some in languages she didn't recognize. On a shelf near his bed were a few small wooden carvings—a woman, a chicken, a man wearing goggles, and a man with shoulder-length hair. Nyssa smiled. Fontaine, Buck, and Elias. The fourth carving's identity eluded her.

"A toast," Elias said. "To new acquaintances acquired through interesting means."

She turned around and took the glass Elias offered her. She tipped her glass against his and took a sip. The wine was delicious—sweet and dark.

"Did you make those carvings?" She pointed to the shelf behind her.

"No," he said, his mood darkening for a moment. "Let's sit."

They took seats opposite each other, and Nyssa kept her eyes on him as he drank his wine. On deck, he covered up from head to toe to guard against the cold, but in his quarters, he was more casual. His gloveless hands were pale white, shifting to light blue in the middle of his forearms. Koja were known for their unique skin tone patterns, though all were shades of blue and white. A patch of dark-blue hair peeked out of the top of his shirt, a few buttons generously left undone. The effect wasn't lost on Nyssa, nor was the intent.

Elias leaned back in his chair and swirled his wine. "I wanted to thank you in private for your bravery. You saved this ship."

"Your crew stood their ground. Fucking Jerrin and Yuha, I told them to run, and they did the opposite."

"I have good people on this ship. Don't let the piracy be the only thing you see. We're a family here."

"Why Elias, that's almost sentimental."

He smiled at her and drank his wine. "I suppose it is. But in this business, you have to find men and women who will have your back and not stick a dagger in it when it's turned."

Nyssa sat back and tapped her finger on her wineglass. "I don't need this dinner as a thank-you. You saved my life, that was enough."

Elias leaned forward. "I want to get to know you. I'm curious about the magickless adept and why you're so far away from the Empire."

"Nothing nefarious. Quinn ran away from her guild, and they sent us to bring her back. Her magick is rare and valuable to the Empress and Arcton Citadel."

Elias cocked his head. "Arcton Citadel?"

"Yeah. This is partly First Master Anelos's errand."

The look on Elias's face grew tight, dark. "I've had some dealings with him."

Nyssa straightened. "Really?"

"In another life, well over thirty years ago, I used to deal in antiquities and rare items, some of which Ceril had interest in. I have to tell you, Nyssa, many of those items would not be approved by the Empire or a Justiciar."

"Like what?"

He held his hands up and gave her a sly smile. "Now, before you judge me, understand that I pay little heed to rules, save for those of the sea. I sold Ceril rare spell books that dealt with things of a darker nature. Blood magick. Bone magick. Even necromancy. I was very good at getting my hands on items of an illicit nature."

Nyssa blinked. After seeing the scars on Quinn's palms, she knew she wasn't lying about Ceril accessing forbidden books, but this information confirmed it.

Ceril had been breaking Imperial law for decades.

"That man is a hypocrite, Nyssa. No one buys those kinds of spell books just to collect them. I would bet this boat he's at least dabbled in some of those spells, and by the look on your face, that doesn't surprise you."

"The more I learn about that man..." Nyssa stopped herself.

"What?"

She flexed her jaw, remembering how Ceril looked at her.

"Oh, he doesn't like you, does he?" Elias asked, laughing. "You must rankle him something fierce."

"I think he hates me. Really hates me."

"What do you know about him?"

Nyssa shrugged. "Not much at all."

"Did you know he was meant to become the Emperor instead of Kalla?"

She scoffed. "Bullshit."

Elias shook his head and poured them both more wine. Nyssa noticed it was going down smooth. A little too smooth.

"Ceril comes from a middling family, but they had curried some favor with Emperor Nillis. The Emperor declared Ceril his choice for the next Emperor, which didn't sit well at all with the Great Houses on the Sun

Council. Then that damn fool Nillis went and drank himself to death as war loomed. Coward, through and through."

Nyssa almost spit out her wine. "Nillis died in his sleep."

"That's the fakery the historians peddle. Make no mistake, he died choking on his own vomit with his dick in his hand. With Nillis dead, his wishes were ignored. The Great Houses wanted one of their own—Kalla Simac. On the brink of war, they put an eighteen-year-old girl on the throne and tossed Ceril aside, making him a Master at Arcton as consolation. Quite a crushing chain of events for Ceril, considering what he gave up."

"Which was?"

"A fiancée, so the rumor goes. Areshi Emperors are not allowed to marry or have children, and for good reason. For centuries, House Areshi ruled with an iron fist, insisting on their heirs holding the throne. The Sun Council decided on different laws of succession after incest killed the Areshi family off. They played a little too loose when entangling the branches of their family tree."

Nyssa winced and gazed down into her wineglass. Her instructors taught none of this in any of their history lessons. The story was shameful and salacious if true.

"Ceril withdrew to Arcton Citadel and became more secretive. So, from on high—literally the highest mountain in the Empire—he looks down. On everyone. Even I found him unbearable despite all the Imperial coin he had to spend. That man is bitterness wrapped up in arrogance with a healthy dash of disdain on top."

Despite herself, Nyssa laughed. "It's true. He's an asshole. And he has a hard-on for me."

"My guess is simple: he hates you because he thinks you were handed something you don't deserve—your place in the Emerald Order. Be careful around him, Nyssa. A man like him will never be happy with a modicum of power. He lusts for far more. Best to steer clear of an ego like that."

"The more I find out about him, the more I truly dislike him," Nyssa remarked. Her mind wandered over this new information. Just how many books did Ceril have access to in the Citadel? How long had he been collecting forbidden tomes? "Wait. You don't look any older than thirty years old. Thirty-five tops. How could you have known Ceril over thirty years ago?"

"Nyssa, I'm one hundred and sixty-seven years old, and frankly, I'm offended you think I could look anywhere close to thirty-five." Elias gave her a roguish smile.

"Longevity magick?" Nyssa asked.

"Yes. In my bloodline. Blood magick's not exactly looked upon with favor these days, but my ancestors spoke those spells into the world when the Rells still had sway in the Areshi Empire."

A soft knock on the door interrupted her thoughts, and Buck rolled a cart of food in.

"Buck!" Nyssa exclaimed, happy to see the little man. The wine was having an effect.

"Who is it?" Buck asked, squinting in Nyssa's direction. "Oh—mmm—Stitches."

"My name is Nyssa."

"I prefer Stitches," Buck replied, met with a soft chuckle from Elias.

"What have you prepared for us tonight?" Elias asked.

"Neskian chicken and rice with a rum bread pudding for dessert," Buck replied, sliding plates onto the table. He squinted at Nyssa again. "Enjoy."

He wheeled his cart out of the room, leaving them to their dinner. Nyssa bent over her plate and breathed in the spiced chicken and rice. She had never smelled anything like it. She took a small bite and was immediately hit by a medley of flavors—deep, earthy spices with a bright, hot kick on the back of her tongue.

"This is amazing," she said, and Elias laughed before tucking into his own plate of food. While they ate, he asked her what she thought of being on the sea. She found herself unreserved, sharing how much she enjoyed sailing and, oddly, learning how to work a ship as his hostage.

She finished her meal, and Elias offered her more wine. As she drank, she patiently tapped her glass, her thoughts drifting...

"Elias, have you ever heard of pirates named Mikel and Shana and their ship, the Demon's Wail?" she asked, trying to keep the tremor out of her voice. Thinking about them still brought up unresolved feelings.

Elias looked up from his wine, his expression slowly changing. His eyes grew wide. "You're not...are you their daughter?"

Nyssa nodded, struggling to form words.

"I knew of them. And I heard they had a daughter, born on the Demon's Wail on the Black Sea." He exhaled a laugh. "Nyssa Blacksea. I'll be damned."

She swallowed. "Can you tell me anything about them?"

Elias's face lit up. "Shana was a sailor of some repute. People said she was fearless on the water and could put her ear to the sea and listen to it breathe. Rare magick that any sailor would kill to possess. And your father was a master thief. If there was an object you wanted, Mikel could procure it. At a hefty price, of course. They ran a small company of pirates, but they were feared. A pirate queen and her smuggler king. The perfect pairing, if you ask me. They were highly sought-after, even doing jobs for the Empress, I hear. That's prestige." Elias's face grew serious. "I heard the Wail was lost at sea years ago."

Nyssa nodded. "Months after I was born, I'm told."

"So you never really knew them."

Nyssa swallowed back the lump in her throat. "No."

"I'm sorry to hear that, Nyssa. I truly am." He looked genuine, his demeanor a far cry from the pirate she met over a week ago.

"You never met them?"

"No. The oceans are vast, Nyssa. And in my early years, I stayed in safe waters I could easily navigate. Your mother and father sailed seas I didn't dare back in my early days. Hannah's Whisper, well, she's a vessel for an old hand to sail and extremely valuable. The invisibility veil alone is worth more than the wood that built this ship. Add in the water purification enchantment, the internal plumbing magick...let's just say I could sell this thing and retire rich.

"When I first took command, I was new to the sea and still trying to master this finicky beast and not run it aground. Now, the only people still here from those days are Fontaine and Buck, so if you so much as tell a soul how completely in over my head I was as a newly minted pirate, I'll put you in a tender and leave you floating for the birds to pick at."

Nyssa laughed, the tension easing from her shoulders. "I didn't expect to see a different side of you. I like it."

"Are you flirting with me?" Elias teased, cracking a smile and offering her more wine.

She pushed her glass toward him. "We didn't get off to a brilliant start with one another, and I appreciate you telling me a little about my parents. It...it means more than I can express."

He refilled her drink. "You have the sea in your blood. You belong out here in its air, free, not stuck as an Ashcloak, forever serving others."

"Everything I am today, I owe to the Order and Eron. He raised me."

"Raised you as a magickless adept in the guilds where the number one rule is you must have magick."

Nyssa shrugged. "Maybe if I prove myself, show them all what I'm capable of, I won't be the last magickless adept they allow in."

Elias sighed. "Nyssa, you are the first and you will be the last."

She frowned into her wine. "How can you be so sure?"

He looked down and pressed his lips together. "There are plenty of magickless progeny in the richest, most influential Houses in the Empire. How many of them are in the guilds?"

Nyssa sat back. "None."

"That's right. None. I'm sorry, Nyssa. You are a fluke, not the start of a new age."

It was true. No amount of money could buy a magickless person into the guilds. Her inclusion flew in the face of everyone, not just men like Ceril. Some of the richest Houses in the Empire must resent her. And Eron.

Nyssa cleared her throat and changed the subject. "Tell me some juicy pirate stories, Elias."

He was more than happy to share tales of his adventures at sea. He was bombastic and charming, and his stories were entertaining and most certainly exaggerated as he poured more wine for her, which was delicious and easy to drink. By the time he suggested opening another bottle, Nyssa held up her hand and said it was time to call it an evening.

"No, you must stay and drink with me, love," Elias said.

"I'm afraid I know where this leads if I do," she smiled, trying not to meet his gaze. His golden eyes sparkled whenever he laughed, and his roguish personality both entertained and maddened her. It would be easy to fall into his bed, and though it was tempting, she wanted their relationship to remain uncomplicated. And Reece kept entering her thoughts, as did a strange desire to be faithful to their non-relationship.

Elias stood and offered his hand to Nyssa. "Then I will bid you goodnight and see you to the door."

Nyssa took his hand and stood. "I'm surprised. I've been around some rather pushy men who are far less attractive and charming than you who try to get me into their beds."

"I don't take what I am not offered freely. And you just admitted that you think I'm both attractive and charming. The other day, you scoffed at the notion of me having any semblance of charm whatsoever."

"I'd tell you not to let it go to your head, but I see that would be in vain," Nyssa said as they walked to the door. "Thank you for a surprisingly wonderful dinner tonight."

Elias smiled. "You're welcome. Now, off to your stateroom and dreams filled with pleasure, not strife."

A PRIVATE MOMENT

Aryis slipped into her stateroom after taking a quick bath. It had been awkward at first for her to share a room with Athen, and while the privacy screens helped a great deal, there was a nervous energy between them when alone.

Athen was already in their room, sitting cross-legged on the floor, a white cloth spread out with silverware, two cups of ale, and a few covered bowls. He glanced up when she entered the room, a smile lighting his face.

"I thought maybe we could have a private dinner tonight. I hope you don't mind we're somewhat rustic here, but the writing table is too small, and I thought you might—"

"Athen, it's perfect," Aryis said.

His smile grew brighter and his eyes twinkled. "Then join me."

Aryis walked over and sat across from him while he uncovered the bowls of food. "Buck offered us what he made for Elias and Nyssa."

"What do you suppose those two are talking about?"

"Hopefully nothing that causes us further trouble. She assured me she would behave."

"And you believe her?"

Athen laughed. "I have to. I keep forgetting it's not my place to always be looking out for her." He portioned the food out on the plates and handed her one. Her stomach rumbled at the rich, spicy aroma of the food, and sighed happily after her first bite. "This is truly special."

"I'm happy to be sharing this with you," Athen said with a wink.

They fell into a comfortable silence while they ate until Aryis felt the need to be straight-forward. "Athen, where do you see our friendship going?"

Athen looked up at her and put his food down. He put his hands on the floor behind him and reclined with a grin. "What are you thinking?"

"You and I have a rather enjoyable connection and I want to be with you. I don't want to wait until we get back to Ocean's Rest." Aryis held her breath, not knowing how he would react—she was deep into uncharted waters with him—but she prided herself on being straight-forward.

A smile reached Athen's golden eyes, and Aryis's stomach did flip-flops as her heart beat in her ears. He stood and stepped around their dinner, holding out his hand, and she grasped hold. He gently pulled her to her feet.

She looked him in the eye, a bit concerned he hadn't offered a reply. "Did you have a response or—"

Athen bent over and kissed her gently, taking her by surprise.

This is happening.

She closed her eyes and kissed him back, his lips smiling under hers. He smelled like pine and deep, warm spices. He splayed his fingers across the back of her neck, raising goosebumps along her skin as he pulled her closer to him. His kisses grew more passionate.

This is happening!

It wasn't their first kiss, but the tenor and intent certainly had changed. He obviously had done this before and Aryis wondered if her efforts measured up to his past experiences, breaking away from him mid-kiss to ask as much.

Athen's face lit up and he burst out in laughter. "Aryis, you're doing great. And this is something you learn by doing."

"I want it to be enjoyable for you."

He smiled and ran his thumb along her jawline, sending a shiver of pleasure down her spine. "This should be enjoyable for both of us," he rumbled, his voice vibrating in her chest.

"It is," she whispered.

Athen swept a stray hair out of her face, tucking it behind her ear. She laughed, her heart almost bursting from the tender gesture. She pulled his face down to hers to kiss him again, moving slow and deliberate. A playful bite to his bottom lip seemed to take him by surprise, making him smile under her lips.

Aryis grasped his shirt and tugged him towards his bed.

He stopped her. "Aryis, are you sure about this?"

She looked up at him. He was careful and considerate, which she appreciated, but she was past doubt—she wanted to be with Athen.

"People may think I'm naïve, but I just lack experience. I know what I want. So yes, I'm sure about this."

Athen smiled and nodded. "Let me know if anything I do isn't right for you, and I'll stop."

"I have always spoken my mind. I don't think that will change now."

"Sex is different. Not a lot of talking."

"We'll see about that," she teased, pulling at his shirt. His rumbling laugh set her at ease. "Take this off."

"Taking charge? That's sexy, woman." Athen did as he was told, pulling his shirt over his head and tossing it to the floor. Aryis stood back, admiring him. His muscles rippled from the simple act of casting his shirt aside. The short hair on his expansive chest trailed downward to his sculpted stomach, his abdominal muscles descending into his dark leather pants. The sight of his bare chest, new scars and all, made her breath catch and heat rise on her cheeks.

He hooked a finger in one of her belt loops, playfully tugging her toward him with a grin. She swallowed as he started to unbutton her shirt.

"Seems I have to do all the work around here," he murmured, then leaned in to kiss her neck, drawing a moan from her. As his lips grazed her skin, his beard made her neck tingle where it touched.

"Not all the work," she teased, sliding her hand over the front of his pants, feeling his arousal for the first time. He moaned under her touch, the sound of his pleasure intensely exciting. The way his breath quickened as she stroked him through the fabric made her own pulse pound at her neck. Never in her mind's eye, in her deepest fantasies, had she imagined being so bold her first time experiencing such intimacy. But with Athen, she felt safe.

He moved closer and deftly tackled button after button on her shirt, slipping it off and pulling the camisole she wore underneath over her head. His hands moved lower, working at undoing her belt.

"Your hand is delightfully distracting, so I hope you appreciate this feat of pure concentration," he said with a broad smile as he slid her belt out of its loops.

Aryis pulled back, eyes locked on his while she slid her pants down. The hunger in his eyes and his sultry smile sent a shock of excitement between her legs. She didn't know how sex was going to go exactly, but it already far surpassed her research. She wanted every part of him, and it was hard to stop smiling like an idiot with anticipation.

He took a step toward her, gently brushing his fingers across her collarbone. "You're beautiful, you know that?"

"You don't have to flatter me, I'm already naked," she teased.

Athen laughed and kissed her neck, his hand trailing down over her breast. "I'll flatter you as much as I please." His tongue flicked against her collarbone as his thumb found her nipple.

The one thing she could always count on—her brain—stopped functioning correctly. She could barely think. Barely breathe. And she didn't mind one bit.

Aryis smiled at him, pressing her hands on his chest, careful to avoid his stitches, the fuzz underneath her fingertips rough. "Get your pants off and take me to bed," she whispered.

Athen grinned and began undoing his belt, doing as he was told.

Athen stretched before putting an arm around Aryis, pulling her closer. Her skin tingled at his touch. She smiled to herself, discovering that sex was much better than her studies suggested. Gods, she hoped no one overheard them.

"Was that okay?" she asked.

"That was better than okay and I think you know it." Athen smiled, stroking her hair. "Are you alright? Do you need anything?"

"I'm quite alright, thank you," she replied with a smile, giving him a quick kiss on his cheek. "I've done a lot of reading, but putting what you learn into practice is a whole different animal. I wasn't expecting a foot cramp."

Athen laughed. "I will never not appreciate your scholarly pursuits. You knew exactly what you wanted, foot cramp aside."

"Well, I had a lot of time to myself at the Conservatory." Aryis blushed. She sat up. "I'm hoping this isn't a short-lived affair. I would like to see where this leads."

Athen propped himself up on his elbows. "Maybe you could spend some time in Ocean's Rest? I know you're likely headed to Cardin, but perhaps we can visit one another?"

Aryis had given her future post a lot of thought, growing increasingly dissatisfied with the idea of landing in Cardin.

"I've been thinking and I would like to propose a far better solution. I'm going to insist that I stay in Ocean's Rest for a while, specifically to learn under your mother. If she would have me, that is. And if that would not make things difficult for you. I don't mean to come off poorly, but stashing me in some back room in Cardin, shuffling paperwork and running errands, is frankly a waste of my talent and intellect," Aryis said, watching Athen for his reaction.

He laughed. "That's not arrogance, that's just fact. And regardless of whatever this is between us or what it grows into—or doesn't—I think you could learn a lot from my mother. But be warned, her tactics aren't always tactful."

"Oh, Vykas has filled me in. I think I would benefit from seeing leadership from a completely different perspective. Your mother fought for everything she has. If I'm to be queen one day, my people need me at my best, not resting on my family name."

"You're...incredible, you know that?" Athen asked.

"So, it's not a completely insane idea?"

"It's *slightly* insane." He pulled Aryis in for a kiss. "But I would be thrilled to have you in Ocean's Rest."

She sighed, pleased that he was receptive to her idea. Vykas and her father would not be happy, but it was time she made her own decisions. Her father was a practical man. He would understand her choice. And hopefully, so would the Empress—she was a savvy, practical leader.

"Did you want to...go again?" Aryis asked, grinning at him. "I know men need a bit of time to recharge, so it's up to you."

"I'm ready when you are," Athen said with a cocky smile.

"Good, because I thought maybe we could try something?" Aryis held her hand out, and in a flash of sparkling white light, a book appeared. She flipped through it and pointed to an illustration. "I thought this might be fun."

Athen sat up. "Is...is this the book from The Lash?"

Aryis grinned. "Maybe?"

Athen leaned forward to peer at the page and cocked his head at the illustration she had chosen. "Oh, we are definitely going to try that one."

FAREWELLS

Nyssa pushed a potato around on her plate, deep in her thoughts. Learning more about Ceril from Elias added to her growing sense of unease about the man and her mission to bring Quinn back. The sight of Quinn's scars, knowing Ceril had hurt her and kept her in a void collar, filled her with a helpless anger. She needed to talk to Eron, but even then, she worried. Conjecture and suspicion alone might not be enough to sway him.

Nyssa stabbed the potato, splitting it in half.

Usually, she would confide in Athen, but she didn't want to put a damper on his newfound happiness. The shift in his demeanor, and Aryis's, was too obvious to slip her notice. She'd had to pull him aside and let him know to keep their...enthusiasm a little quieter. The big man turned shades of red she had never seen before.

Yuha sat with Nyssa in the mess, keeping watch as always. Even after saving the ship, Elias didn't give her a break, but she had grown used to Yuha's quiet presence. It became a strange comfort.

Elias dropped down next to her. She hadn't even noticed him come in.

"Blacksea! I've told the others, but good news! I have agreed to terms with Lilliana—a little less than I had hoped to get, but such is the dance of negotiation—and we're setting a course to Ocean's Rest this afternoon."

"Should we be offended that she negotiated your price down instead of trying to get us back as soon as possible?"

He laughed. "I would have tried to swindle her blind next time if she didn't counter. It's all part of the dance."

"How long will it take to sail to Ocean's Rest?"

"Oh, about a week," Elias replied. "But don't fret. Most of the journey will be across the Black Sea. It is truly a vast expanse of water. So you will have some time to say your goodbyes to your home."

"Good. I need to get back."

Clearing his throat, he reached in his coat pocket and slid something across the table.

"What's this?" Nyssa picked up a small, reddish gold coin.

"I have friends in the Ivory Triad territory, northern part of Ocean's Rest. Take this to Crae's Alehouse if you ever have need of me. They know how to contact me."

Nyssa looked closer at the coin. It wasn't common currency. It was old and contained writing she didn't recognize rimming the edge.

"Why are you giving it to me?"

"You saved this ship and my crew from certain destruction. That's a favor I can't repay properly, but I can at least give you a little help should you ever need it. Just take it, Blacksea. Tuck it away and maybe look at it fondly every once in a while and remember the good times we had together."

From the other side of the table, Yuha snorted.

Nyssa rolled her eyes. "We'll likely never see each other again once I'm back in the Empire. I don't think Ashcloaks have much use for pirates."

She tucked the coin away in a pocket.

Elias got up and swiped a piece of apple from her plate. "Oh, I don't know about that. You're more pirate than Imperial lackey," he said with a smile. "Say, did you ever find out why Quinn went into the water after you? I'm curious."

"She found out that I couldn't swim."

Elias gave her a puzzled look. "She was in the water before she found out you couldn't swim."

Nyssa blinked at him. "Are you sure?"

Elias glanced over at Yuha. She nodded. "Yeah, your friend was already in the water," she said. "You really can't swim?"

"Quinn's not my friend, she's my prisoner," Nyssa said reflexively. Once the words escaped her mouth, she felt awful.

Elias tapped his finger on the table. "Heh, sure." He turned to leave, but paused a moment. "I'm going to miss you idiots."

Nyssa stared down at her plate and frowned. Quinn lied about why she followed her into the water...

Why did she save me?

RETURN TO OCEAN'S REST

The return to Ocean's Rest went by quickly—too quickly for Nyssa's taste. Facing the prospect of having to make some rather uncomfortable allegations about First Master Ceril Anelos left her anxious. And as they drew closer to the Empire, Quinn grew more sullen.

When they finally arrived near the city, Elias saw Nyssa and the others off, letting Jerrin and Yuha take them back to Ocean's Rest in a tender. Elias wouldn't put the Whisper into port and tempt retribution from Lilliana. He said he hoped to see them all again someday under far better circumstances, then he gave them all hugs—even Quinn, who looked like a trapped animal in his arms.

When they got to the docks, Jerrin helped them out of the tender. "I will miss you lot."

Nyssa opened her arms to Yuha, who shook her head. "What? No hug?" Nyssa teased. The woman stared daggers at her before returning to the tender.

Pol and a small contingent of guards greeted them as they walked down the dock. "Lilliana is relieved to have you back in the city. She was not pleased to hear from Elias. Vykas hurried back from Wayland when he heard you were all taken hostage. That man has worn a rut in the great room worrying over his sister."

Aryis sighed and rolled her eyes. Nyssa suppressed a smile. She wasn't fond of Vykas, but she could respect the man's desire to protect his sister and his future queen.

"Elias was the least of it," Athen replied, and Pol raised an eyebrow. "We'll fill you in when we're all together."

Quinn stood at the window overlooking Ocean's Rest while the others recounted their journey to a gathering of Lilliana, Pol, First Master Greye, Reece, and Vykas. They didn't treat her like a prisoner, though she knew better. It was a façade, despite their kindness. Soon she would be back at the Citadel, her purpose in their lives served.

Her contribution to the story of their journey was sparse, only offering information when directly asked a question. She clenched her jaw as they recalled her two escape attempts, though Nyssa left out the details of their conversation in the alley, for which she was thankful. Not her brightest moment.

As Aryis narrated the first part of the wraith attack, Quinn turned to find Reece watching her, a scowl on her face. This was the woman mentioned in passing in front of her. The woman that drew a bright smile and long embrace out of Nyssa when they'd returned to the Keep.

Reece didn't break eye contact with Quinn until Nyssa spoke, explaining how they'd defeated the blood wraith. How Quinn used her powers against it, weakening it long enough to wound it and for Nyssa to get it off Hannah's Whisper.

Eron interrupted Nyssa when she recounted her tumble into the Black Sea. "You drowned?" he asked, voice strained with obvious concern. Quinn wondered what it was like to feel affection from a First Master rather than haughty disdain. Or hate.

"Quinn dove into the water after me and pulled me to the surface. Elias brought me back," Nyssa said.

Eyes turned to Quinn, and she swallowed, the sudden attention unwanted. She felt Reece's eyes on her again and wondered what the empath sensed in her. She hated feeling vulnerable to this stranger and turned back to the view of Ocean's Rest, wishing she could just slip out of the room and disappear.

"How did Elias bring you back to life?" Eron asked, shaking his head.

"Out on the sea, they've learned to get by without healers," Nyssa explained. "They have old medicine. And really strong rum as a painkiller."

Aryis quickly finished the rest of their story. Quinn noticed she left specific details out, notably anything about the budding relationship between her and Athen. Discretion was difficult aboard the Whisper...it wasn't exactly soundproof.

After Aryis finished telling their story, Eron stood up. "I cannot tell you how relieved I am that you are all safe. I think it best that you get some rest now, and we'll reconvene for dinner. Nyssa and Aryis, your rooms are as you left them. Quinn, you will be taken to a room near the other three. I hope you understand, you'll have guards."

"To ensure I don't escape," Quinn replied.

"You are our guest, adept, until you leave for Arcton Citadel, but you do have a proclivity for trying to slip away, I see. I hope you will put any hard feelings aside and join us for dinner," Eron said.

Quinn glanced over at Nyssa, who drummed her fingers on the arm of her chair, her face unreadable.

Nyssa walked beside Reece, trailed by Quinn and her two guards. Lilliana wanted her kept close and gave her a room next to Nyssa. Reece opened the door to Quinn's suite, and Quinn walked in, her eyes wide. A rather extravagant prison cell, Nyssa supposed as she leaned against the doorway. The two guards took up their post outside the room.

"I'm sorry about the guards," Reece said. "We usually are far more hospitable, but your unique circumstance warrants the precaution."

"Same rules apply, Quinn," Nyssa said. "Gloves at all times. If you want to go anywhere, come to my room and get me. I'm right next door."

Quinn smirked at her. "Will you be by my bedside every night I'm here too?"

Nyssa sighed and shook her head. "Don't be cheeky. Take a bath and relax a bit before dinner." She closed the door behind her and turned to Reece, hoping to pick up where they had left off over a month ago.

"Let's get you a bath." Reece smiled, pulling Nyssa toward her room.

"Join me?" Nyssa asked, arching an eyebrow and flashing a half-smile, hoping Reece couldn't resist.

Reece stopped and grabbed Nyssa, kissing her. "Gods, I've missed you."

ASHCLOAK BLACKSEA

Nyssa rapped her knuckles against Quinn's door, nodding at the two guards standing outside her room. "Quinn, open up. I don't want to—"

The door swung open when Nyssa went to knock again, and she blinked, breath catching in her throat upon seeing Quinn in a long, dark-blue dress, its plunging neckline peeking beneath a black jacket. Her chestnut hair was swept away from her face, loosely pinned back, and her eyes were lined in kohl, a vivid contrast to their emerald hue.

Quinn's outfit was a far cry from the leather pants, cotton shirts, and bulky sweaters they scrounged up for her at The Lash.

Nyssa stepped back to regard her. "You found some clothes that fit, I see."

Quinn nodded. "So I did." She exited the room, with her entourage of guards following closely behind.

Athen and Aryis started down the hallway, and Quinn followed them, her guards trailing behind her. Reece put her arm around Nyssa's elbow and leaned in. "She wears that dress well."

"I'm sorry, she just took me aback for a moment," Nyssa said.

"Don't apologize—at least not to me. You can appreciate whomever you wish, and she is a handsome woman." She paused for a moment. "You like her."

"I—" Nyssa stopped herself. Lying to Reece would be pointless. "She saved my life."

"That engenders gratitude, not affection," Reece laughed.

Nyssa sighed and looked over at her. "Quinn confuses me."

"Confuses or challenges?"

"Both."

They were silent the rest of the way to the dining room where Lilliana, Eron, Pol, and Vykas were waiting, drinking wine and talking, the mood light.

"Ah, there you all are. Looking rested and rather lovely," Lilliana said, smiling at her guests. They had all dressed up a bit for dinner. Nyssa found a tailored jacket in her closet with roses stitched with a delicate, light-gray thread. It was a subtle detail that lent her some elegance. She had toyed with the idea of wearing a dress, but she had never been in clothes as fancy as the ones her closet offered and opted for comfort. And she didn't want to be hitching up her skirts should Quinn try to escape again.

Two servants circulated about the room, handing out glasses of a pale-pink wine.

The moment struck Nyssa as odd. All the dinner guests put up an elegant façade, despite a prisoner walking among them—though she supposed Quinn earned more leeway given her adept status and the fact that the Empress was keenly interested in getting her back.

With a drink in hand, Quinn smiled politely, keeping to herself while her guards hovered at the door.

Nyssa pulled Master Eron aside and kept her voice low. "I need to speak to you."

He reached forward and brushed her cheek before resting his hand on her shoulder. "Of course, Nyssa. Not tonight, though."

"This is important."

"In due time, but tonight you should relax." Eron held her in his gaze, perhaps expecting an argument. He knew her too damn well.

A protest sat on the tip of her tongue, but she held back. "Alright."

She turned from him and spotted Quinn standing alone. Nyssa was about to join her when Reece crossed the room and settled in front of Quinn.

Quinn's eyes searched the room, looking for an escape as Reece approached her with a smile, but there was no way to avoid the woman.

"It strikes me that earlier, in Lilliana's office, no one thanked you for your bravery aboard Elias's ship. You saved lives. You saved Nyssa's life," Reece said.

Quinn swallowed and offered her a wan smile, feeling Reece's eyes drift from her face down to her dress and back up again.

"If I may ask, why did you risk your life for Nyssa?"

This damned question.

A stubborn flicker of annoyance sparked in Quinn's chest.

Reece narrowed her eyes.

Shit.

The empath had to be reading her emotions. There was no reason to believe otherwise.

Quinn stepped forward and met Reece's gaze. "You're the empath, you tell me," she said, her voice low as she watched for Reece's reaction. Her response seemed to surprise Reece, whose dark eyes darted across her face as she quickly exhaled. She glanced over Reece's shoulder, meeting Nyssa's stare across the room, and took a step back.

The soft, high-pitched ring of a bell signified it was time to be seated for dinner. After a quick, polite nod, Reece strolled to the table. Quinn let out a heavy breath and took her place next to Nyssa.

Snippets of conversations drifted to Nyssa. She sat back and sighed, drumming her index finger on the table, barely paying attention to the after-dinner banter around her. Her thoughts stuck to the idea that First Master Anelos was dangerous. A private conversation with Eron couldn't come soon enough. Quinn shifted in the seat next to her. Nyssa could only imagine how awkward it must be to sit there as a prisoner.

Eron tapped his wineglass, the sharp *tink-tink-tink* quieting the chatter at the table. "Now that you are back in Ocean's Rest, it's time for a bit of guild business." Nyssa straightened up, a wave of anxiety hitting her.

Eron nodded to Vykas, who cleared his throat and turned to address his sister. "Aryis, now that you're back from this assignment, your post in Cardin awaits. I will accompany you—"

"I will be staying here in Ocean's Rest," Aryis interrupted.

Heads turned. Vykas gave her a thin smile, his eyes darting around the table. "That is not what we agreed to with our First Master."

A stern expression settled on Aryis's face. "You forget yourselves. As Queen-in-Waiting of Frosland, I answer to two people—my King and the Empress. And you and I know Father will allow me to do as I desire."

The room grew still.

Vykas shook his head. "Aryis, you were willing to take up this post before you left Wayland..."

"Not that I need to explain myself to you, Brother," Aryis said with an edge to her voice, "but from what little I've seen of Ocean's Rest and Lilliana's governance, I feel I'd learn far more under her than being an assistant to a junior advisor in Cardin and far removed from the Empress. That is, Lady Fennick, if you'd allow me to remain here and learn from you, Pol, and Reece."

"Your Majesty, it would be my honor." Lilliana glanced at her son, who tried and failed to contain a broad, satisfied smile. Athen's burgeoning relationship with Aryis was a victory for House Fennick. An association with a Queen-in-Waiting bestowed a measure of credibility that Lilliana could never earn on her own. But moreover, Aryis made Athen happy. Nyssa loved seeing him like this.

Aryis spoke again, addressing her brother. "Please realize that this is the smart choice. There is so much to learn here, and our father will see the prudence of my decision."

Seemingly defeated—or perhaps waiting to unleash his ire in private—Vykas sighed and sat back in his chair. It gave Nyssa pleasure to see his sister exert her will. It gave her even more pleasure to see him uncomfortable under Aryis's gaze.

Eron tapped his glass again. "One more bit of business. Nyssa, if you'd stand and join me." He smiled, and her heart leapt into her throat as she did as requested. "Adept Blacksea, you have served the Emerald Order with honor. It is my distinct pleasure to welcome you into the ranks of the Ashcloaks."

He moved forward, brandishing a small signet pin—a silver disk etched with a wolf's head, the symbol of the Ashcloaks. Eron pinned it on Nyssa's jacket and gently brushed her cheek, whispering, "My daughter."

Turning to the table, he said, "I proudly present to you all, Ashcloak Blacksea."

Applause burst from the attendees, and Athen jumped to his feet, pulling Nyssa into a massive hug. Aryis joined him, along with Reece, congratulating her on the one thing she had been working for all those years. Eron raised his hands to settle everyone down.

"There was a time when our Ashcloaks protected Ocean's Rest and its people, but this city has gone decades without an Order presence. It's time to restore our standing by establishing a permanent Emerald Order unit here again. Nyssa, I want you to lead that effort."

Nyssa blinked at her father. Being in charge of a city's protection was a prestigious post—one she didn't dare dream she would obtain. "I don't know what to say. Thank you." She glanced at Quinn, who still sat at the table, her eyes downcast. She had not participated in the congratulations, not that Nyssa had expected her to. Quinn looked up and gave her a small smile, one that seemed forced out of politeness.

"If I may, I would love to memorialize this moment," Lilliana said. She waved at her attendants, and they opened the doors to a man Nyssa recognized from when she first came to the Keep—the simulachrome imageer. He set up his tripod.

Nyssa stood for several chromoimages and tried to get Quinn to take one, but she begged off. Nyssa kicked herself, remembering that, for Quinn, this was nothing but a forced moment of polite co-existence with her jailers.

Before the simulachrome was packed up, Nyssa insisted on getting an image of just her and Eron. She looped her arm around his elbow and smiled as a wave of red magick flowed out of the device, captured their image, and imprinted it on a wafer-thin, metal square. The imageer handed Nyssa the chromoimage. The look of pride in her father's smile caused a lump to rise in her throat. She slipped the picture inside her jacket, intending to put it in the small notebook she kept hidden away in her leather jacket later.

After the imaging, conversations resumed, and the dinner guests milled about, enjoying glasses of whiskey.

Aryis and Athen talked excitedly about the three of them staying together in Ocean's Rest. Nyssa smiled, but was mostly silent, letting the reality of her new life settle for a moment. She tried to stay engaged in the conversation, but her smile wasn't genuine, despite her effort to feel joy alongside Athen and Aryis.

Finally, she had become an Ashcloak, against the odds and the doubt surrounding her. Yet, it didn't feel...*right*. Her lack of excitement confounded her. This was a better future than she had dared hope for.

What's wrong with me?

After some time, Nyssa slipped out the door, seeking a reprieve from the congratulations and small talk in the dining room. She made her way down the long hallway and kept walking until she found herself back at the Keep's main entrance, taking the chance to step outside for some air.

A few guards and Keep attendants stood around, smoking skinny cigars and pipes, the tobacco smoke filling the air with the scent of sweet spices and pine trees. They glanced toward Nyssa and whispered to one another.

One of the guards walked up to her, his eyes flicking to her Ashcloak pin, and offered his hand. "If I may, Ashcloak Blacksea, I just wanted to meet the hero of Winter's Fire."

Nyssa smiled and shook his hand, thanking him, a bit taken aback. Several of his companions nodded at her.

Nyssa closed her eyes and tilted her head back, taking a deep breath of the frosty night air, hoping it would provide clarity. Perhaps she just needed to adjust to being an Ashcloak. For so long, it seemed like a prize that she could never attain. And now...

She felt someone at her elbow and opened her eyes to find Quinn standing next to her.

"I hope you don't mind me following you," Quinn said.

"They let you escape from the dining room?"

Quinn glanced back to the Keep's doorway, where two guards patiently waited. "No, I brought my two new friends with me. They almost panicked when I broke into a quick stroll."

Nyssa exhaled a quiet laugh.

"I just wanted to congratulate you, Ashcloak Blacksea," Quinn continued.

"Do you really mean that?"

A step brought Quinn closer. She lifted her eyes to meet Nyssa's gaze. "It's what you wanted. Are you happy?"

Happy? Nyssa inhaled a deep breath. "I...I don't know. I should be, but I just feel hollow." She had feigned happiness with Athen, her oldest friend, but with Quinn, she let her honesty spill out. Why?

"You will serve your guild with honor," Quinn said, her breath hanging in the chilly air. "I truly believe that, Nyssa."

An adequate response escaped Nyssa.

Quinn seemed to sense her confusion. "I'm being sincere. I know I've been impossible to deal with most of the time, but I do wish you well."

Her words were unexpected and knocked Nyssa off-kilter. Quinn smiled, her green eyes bright in the golden glow of the moon. A spark of attraction flickered through Nyssa, and her mind seized up, completely thrown by the feeling.

"Quinn, I have been looking for you," a voice said, pulling Nyssa out of her flustered thoughts. Eron approached. "A guild escort has arrived to return you to Arcton Citadel. First Master Anelos is eager to see you again."

Quinn's face darkened, her smile gone at the mention of Ceril.

"You'll be leaving tomorrow," Eron continued. "We're happy to have you back. You're a great asset to the Empire." He turned to walk inside the Keep.

Asset. Nyssa frowned at the word, digging her fingers into her palms.

"I guess that's it, then," Quinn murmured, bowing her head. She turned and walked toward the door before pausing.

"Goodbye, Nyssa." Quinn disappeared inside the Keep, leaving Nyssa in the cold night.

UNSETTLED

Quinn and her escort left Ocean's Keep at dawn the next day to return to Arcton Citadel. By the time Nyssa was told, they'd been gone for hours.

Days later, Nyssa found herself distracted while Lilliana went through a list of personnel she thought should be considered for the new Emerald Order unit in Ocean's Rest. It would be up to Nyssa to train them and turn them into astute fighters. Nyssa made a show of taking notes next to each name, but her mood was dour. Not getting to see Quinn off unsettled her, and doubt gnawed at her gut. She couldn't shake the concern for Quinn's safety simmering deep inside.

As Nyssa poked through the Keep's armory later in the day for something she could fashion into uniforms, she thoughtlessly pawed through the same pile of thick jackets over and over.

She sighed and sat down on a large trunk.

"You want to talk about it?" Reece's voice drifted from the doorway.

"Do you think I can get Lilliana's staff to make something passable out of these?" Nyssa asked, pointing to a pile of clothes.

Reece crossed the room and sat on the trunk next to her. "I wish you didn't feel the need to deflect with me. I can sense your unease. You're distracted."

"I'm not distracted. I'm focused."

Reece sighed. "We need to talk about Quinn. There's something strange—"

"I don't want to talk about Quinn."

"You feel her absence, Nyssa."

"You're being intrusive. I didn't ask you to poke around my feelings."

Reece's face darkened, and she quickly stood up. "I'll let you get back to your work." She turned and disappeared out the door before Nyssa could utter one word of apology for being an asshole.

Nyssa lingered in Reece's office doorway, patiently waiting for her to look up from her ledger. Her Keep office was small by comparison to her space at The Feather, but it still reflected Reece's varied style. Breathing deep, Nyssa savored the light scent of sweet incense that lingered in the air.

As Reece worked, she mumbled to the small succulent plant that sat on her desk. Talking to plants was such an odd habit, and Nyssa couldn't help but smile.

Their disagreement from earlier that day had left her distracted and angry at herself. She tapped her fingers against the leather sword strap across her chest. Winter's Bite hadn't left her side since receiving her commission. The weapon was as much a part of her image as the guild sigil pinned to her chest. She was keenly aware of the necessity to tightly control how others perceived her.

Not looking up from her work, Reece asked, "Ashcloak Blacksea, what can I do for you?"

Nyssa winced at her formal tone. "May I come in?"

Reece leaned back and poured herself some tea from the pot that sat on her desk, sipping on it while she considered Nyssa. She waved a hand toward a chair in front of her desk.

Nyssa entered the office, attempting to smile as she sat. The wood creaked underneath her, as if to signal her discomfort.

"Why do you talk to your plants?" she asked, trying to break the ice between them.

"They are excellent listeners and have no emotions to consider."

Nyssa shifted nervously. "I wanted to apologize for earlier. I lashed out. You didn't deserve my anger. I'm sorry."

"I know when you're in pain, and I cannot help but reach out." Reece paused. "But, I find myself crossing boundaries with you I shouldn't be comfortable breaching." For the first time since they met, Reece seemed withdrawn.

"I feel like I'm putting you in an awkward spot, especially given that I'm...different," Nyssa said. "I'm sorry about that."

"It's not your fault."

"I don't want to jeopardize your position here, Reece. Perhaps I should...perhaps we should—"

"Is this you trying to politely run away from me?"

Nyssa raised her eyes to Reece, who wore a disheartened expression that pained her to see. She opened her mouth to respond but hesitated. It was a valid question, and Reece deserved an honest answer. There was no use trying to create lies or excuses. Reece would suss them out.

Even though her thoughts were half-formed and conflicted, Nyssa spoke her truth. "Becoming an Ashcloak and then being assigned to this city...I didn't expect it. I didn't know I'd be in Ocean's Rest for the foreseeable future. And I don't know what that means for us. I don't want to—"

Nyssa stopped herself, and Reece scowled. She stood and walked across the room to close her office door, then returned to sit on the edge of her desk.

"Finish that sentence, Nyssa."

She shook her head, eyes firmly affixed on her boots. Reece gently nudged her shin with her foot, drawing her attention. A heavy weight of insecurity pressed on her chest.

"Finish the sentence."

Nyssa's jaw moved up and down for a moment before she spoke. "I don't want to be a burden to you. Or Athen and Aryis. I don't want anyone to feel obliged to look after me because I'm now unexpectedly in Ocean's Rest and underfoot."

Reece let out a quick breath of surprise and shook her head. "Nyssa, that's not what any of us feel. Why this sudden doubt?"

"It's not sudden. The doubt is always there. I try not to let being magickless affect me, but it does. And now this doubt is bleeding into everything. Being named an Ashcloak should make me happy, but I'm unsettled and distracted. It feels...empty, Reece. I don't fit in—I never did—and I was okay with that for a time. But what I'm realizing is that I *can't* fit in. I'm a fluke. A piece that never belonged in the puzzle."

Reece sighed. "You and I are alike. We're where we are because of circumstance, not because we chose our lives for ourselves. Eron with you; Lilliana with me. And we're both given these opportunities that we should be grateful for, but there's something inherently unfulfilling about them."

"We're not wrong for wanting more. You have to take what you want, Reece."

Nyssa was met with a frown. "Are you giving me advice you won't heed yourself?"

"I don't know if I can."

"What's making you this sullen? I haven't seen you like this before."

Nyssa kneaded her hands. "Quinn gave me a lot to think about."

"She got to you, didn't she?"

"She said a lot of things that are dangerous to repeat...things I don't want to believe, but I don't think she's a liar."

Reece poked Nyssa in the shin again with her foot. "And if you strip away all the guild nonsense and forget that she was a fugitive, she turned out to be a good person, right? She risked her life saving you. I didn't sense deceit in her, just fear. Pain. And such great sadness."

Nyssa looked down at her hands and swallowed hard. "Bringing her back felt worse and worse the more I got to know her. I just don't know if I can be this loyal and obedient Ashcloak. But how can I tell anyone I feel like this and not appear ungrateful? I've received a great gift, more than I deserve—"

Reece put her hand on Nyssa's shoulder. "You deserve more than they could ever give you. Don't you realize that?" She leaned down until her forehead was touching Nyssa's. "You deserve so much more," she whispered.

Nyssa's breath sped up when Reece's lips parted.

"May I?" Reece asked quietly.

It was a question Nyssa didn't expect, yet appreciated more than she could express. Reece asking permission to use her magick made her feel safe.

Nyssa nodded, and Reece closed her eyes. A scowl passed over her face, though paired with a surprising smile.

"You're chaotic," she uttered, her voice low and gravelly. "Like that night I first came to you. Churning like a storm."

Nyssa gave her a sad smile. "I'm sorry."

"It's intoxicating," Reece breathed, and Nyssa watched her eyes drift down and settle on her lips. Nyssa rose to her feet and pressed herself between her legs, kissing her roughly.

Reece kissed Nyssa back, running her tongue along Nyssa's bottom lip before giving it a teasing bite, driving her crazy. She put her hand over Reece's heart and felt her chest rise and fall under her fingertips as her breathing deepened. Nyssa lowered her mouth to the hollow of Reece's throat, grazing her lips across her neck, drawing a low moan out of the woman.

Reece fumbled at the front of Nyssa's pants, loosening her belt, and Nyssa leaned back, eyebrow raised. "Here? In your office?"

She received her answer when Reece's hand slipped into her pants. Nyssa exhaled a quick, strangled breath that turned into a soft groan, then tried to lift the sword strap off her chest to remove her weapon.

"Leave it," Reece whispered and lowered her lips to Nyssa's neck. Nyssa was certain Reece could feel her throat bobbing as she swallowed and tried to breathe.

Reece's fingers deftly glided between her legs, and Nyssa closed her eyes and tilted her head back, her mind finally focused on one thing for the first time in days.

Nyssa knocked on Eron's door. He answered after a moment, letting her in with a smile. It was strange going from seeing him every day of her life to having been apart from him. She took a moment to take him in, noticing the lines around his eyes and mouth.

Have they gotten deeper? Does he have more gray hairs?

"Are you here for that talk you wanted to have?" he asked.

Nyssa nodded, glancing around the room. She found a comfy chair and sat, fidgeting while she waited for him to join her.

With a shaky exhale, she leaned forward. "Eron, Quinn said some things about First Master Anelos that I dismissed at first, but the more I've learned, the more concerned I am."

Eron rubbed his chin. "Explain."

"Quinn has seen him studying forbidden spell books at Arcton Citadel, and her hands are full of scars from suppressing their wards. I thought it was nonsense, but Elias confirmed that Ceril has purchased illicit spell books in the past."

Eron's eyes roamed Nyssa's face. It was a familiar feeling—when she got in trouble, he would silently study her while he thought about what to do.

He cleared his throat and leaned forward, his voice hushed when he spoke. "Nyssa, you need to understand that people like Quinn and Elias are dangerous. Quinn is desperate and wants your sympathy. I fear she's influenced you."

Nyssa exhaled, confused. Quinn wasn't a bad influence, Eron just didn't understand her. Nor did he know the entire story. "Quinn confided that she overheard Ceril talking about me. He called me a..."

Nyssa's breath hitched, a lump rising in her throat.

Ceril's disdain had cut to her quick.

"Nyssa?" Eron's eyes were full of concern.

"He called me a 'magickless whelp'. When the blood wraith attacked, it called me the same thing. Eron, it used Ceril's words to insult me. What if *he* created the wraiths? I can't stop thinking about it." Nyssa put her hand on her tightening chest.

Eron shifted forward in his chair, his face grave. "You must not repeat this to anyone, do you hear me? An adept speaking like this about the Arch Master is grounds for being marked as Unworthy."

Nyssa blinked at him. "Arch Master?" Ceril was now the head of all the guilds and an advisor to the Empress?

With a nod, Eron let out a heavy sigh. "Yes. He was chosen while you were away."

"What? Why him?"

"It was his turn, Nyssa. A lifetime of service rewarded. The Empire owes him."

Nyssa shot to her feet and stalked around the room. "I don't understand. Wouldn't you be a better choice? You've served with distinction!" Not only was Ceril dangerous, but now he was one of the most powerful people in the Empire.

The look on Eron's face betrayed something unspoken. Her stomach dropped.

"The Empress asked you, didn't she?"

"And I politely turned her down. I still have work to do in the Emerald Order, and unlike Ceril, I have a daughter to look after." He smiled up at her.

"No. Why would you let a man like him ascend to such power?" Nyssa asked, bewildered. "You are a man of principle. You would have served as Arch Master with honor."

Eron gestured to the chair across from him. "Please, sit down, Nyssa. Your energy right now is tumultuous. You need to center yourself."

Nyssa sat back down, and Eron continued, "I'm tired. I've served the Empire since I was ten. Thrown into a war when I was only a year older than you. Those years took much out of me. I want to sit back now and watch you flourish. I think I've earned some rest."

Nyssa hung her head. "What about Ceril? He's dangerous."

"Let me look into it. Quietly. Now that Ceril's no longer leading Arcton Citadel, maybe some tongues will loosen. But this is between us. Do not say anything to anyone, I implore you."

Nyssa met Eron's steady gaze. "I'm scared for Quinn. He'll continue to use her. We have a responsibility to protect her."

"You call me principled, but you are a wonder." Eron smiled softly at her. "You're following your oath, but right now, I need you to trust me and follow my instructions. The Empress spared Quinn. She'll be safe for now."

Nyssa ground her teeth. Eron didn't know the type of monster Ceril was, and she couldn't tell him without betraying Quinn's trust. And so she wouldn't, no matter what.

"Nyssa, I know your heart tells you to do the right thing. Your sense of honor is stronger than any of my other students, but now is when you need to sit back and possess a calm heart."

Anger stirred in her chest. "I'm trying to stay true to myself, but it's getting harder and harder to do. I'm supposed to be loyal to the guild, but I see a fellow guildie in need of my help, and you won't let me help her? It doesn't sit right with me and I don't feel like myself anymore."

"Quinn has wormed her way into your head—"

"It's Ceril!" Nyssa yelled. "He's corrupt. He's likely responsible for those wraiths. All those deaths. I almost died. Why won't you believe me?"

Eron sat back in his chair and sighed. Nyssa used to lash out at him when she was younger, when he didn't stop the other children from hurting her. She didn't understand it then, and she still didn't know why he allowed them to abuse her. As an adult, she never raised her voice to him.

Until now.

"Nyssa, it's not that I don't believe you, but I need to keep you safe. That is my only concern. And you need to be patient and trust that I'll look into this."

"I feel...helpless." A lump rose in her throat, and she couldn't stop her eyes from brimming with tears. Her frustration over Ceril, her concern for Quinn, and now Eron's words were all too much. She buried her head in her hands and cried.

Eron stood up, sat next to Nyssa on the arm of the chair, and rubbed her back.

"I'm sorry for crying like a child," she said.

"That's not something to ever be sorry for, Nyssa." Eron hugged her. "You always try so hard. You have nothing left to prove to me. To anyone. I could not be more proud of you, Daughter."

A DAUGHTER'S FACE

Reece hummed to herself while she walked to the guest quarters, small plant in hand—a gift for First Master Greye, though merely a pretense to have a conversation about Nyssa. And Quinn. He might not have answers, but Lilliana leaned on him for advice throughout the years and he never failed her. Reece thought he might lend her some insight.

The hour was late—work had kept her far later than she preferred—and the dark hallway was empty, pools of light dotting the floor beneath dim light orbs.

Far ahead, Eron's door opened and Nyssa stepped out. She glanced in Reece's direction and grinned. Reece was about to call out to her, but the glaring absence of strong emotions made her stop cold.

Nyssa turned without a word, leaving in the opposite direction.

Reece waited for her to disappear around a corner before breaking into a run. When she got to the room, a bright, desperate fear washed over her from inside, driving all the air from her body. *Eron.*

She threw the door open. Her heart plummeted.

Eron was sprawled on the floor at the foot of his bed, his sword beside him, blood pooling from the hole in the side of his throat.

Reece flew to him, falling next to him. "Eron!" She pressed her hands to his wound, the blood pouring out thick and hot. His hazel eyes shifted to her face, blinking slowly. His emotions crashed into her. Past the fear hummed a hollow sadness that took her breath away in its desolation.

Blood sputtered out of his mouth, voice barely a whisper. "Nyssa..."

"It wasn't her, Eron. That woman wasn't Nyssa."

"I know..." he breathed, blood gurgling from his mouth. "Not...my daughter's...eyes."

Reece choked out a sob. She turned to the door and screamed for help.

Screamed for a healer.

For anyone.

Eron's hand wrapped around hers, drawing her attention back to his unwavering stare. Tears poured out of her eyes as she tried to stem the bleeding.

No. Please, no.

Reece leaned in, applying more pressure to his wound. The pulse of blood against her palm grew weaker. Worse, his emotions receded, fading from her senses.

"I'm here, Eron," she choked out.

"Protect her. Protect Nyssa," he whispered before going still.

Nyssa shot upright, startled awake by loud, frantic banging on her door. She had fallen asleep reading, trying to wait up for Reece. Stumbling out of bed, she swung the door open to find Athen, shirtless, his face distraught.

"Athen? What's—"

"Eron...something's happened," he choked out. Behind him, Aryis looked disheveled, her face streaked with tears.

A spike of fear shot through Nyssa's veins, and she pushed past Athen, sprinting down the hall, the sound of her bare feet slapping against the hard stone and echoing off the walls.

When she reached the guest wing, she slowed and tried to catch her breath. Guards milled about, their voices low. Lilliana stood outside of

Eron's room with Reece—who was covered in blood. Faces turned to Nyssa, all of them grave.

She started toward the room, but Lilliana stopped her, grabbing her arm and pulling her back.

"No, Nyssa. You don't want to see this," she said, her tone low.

Nyssa looked to Reece. Blood caked her hands, wrists, knees. She met Nyssa's gaze and there was nothing but sorrow on the empath's face.

Nyssa pulled in low, shallow breaths, the air tinged with copper and lavender. She yanked her arm out of Lilliana's grasp and hurried into the room, freezing as soon as she passed the threshold.

Eron was splayed on the floor at the foot of his bed. Blood coated his mouth and neck, pooled around his body, his clothes soaked in it. His eyes were mercifully closed, smudges of blood on his eyelids. Nyssa stumbled backward, her breath catching. Her pulse thundered in her ears.

The blood. So much blood. She tried to look away, but her body wouldn't obey.

This can't be real. I can't...

Tears filled her eyes, the red of the blood spreading through her vision. She finally turned back to the door to find Reece standing beside Lilliana, clutching at her chest, wincing.

My pain. She feels my pain.

"Who did this?" Nyssa whispered, barely able to breathe.

"Nyssa, please come outside," Lilliana said, wrapping an arm around her and gently pulling her through the door.

Nyssa couldn't find the strength or the will to fight back. She slipped out of Lilliana's arms and sank to her knees, quaking with cold tremors.

Athen was at her side in an instant, wrapping an arm around her. "I've got you."

"Please take her to my office. Get her away from here," Lilliana said, her voice low.

Nyssa paced back and forth, her mind racing, heart pounding in her chest. "That was Ceril's doing!" she yelled. "I'm going after him."

"Please, Nyssa, you need to calm down and start thinking straight," Athen said. "Eron wouldn't want you to put yourself in danger."

"What do you expect me to do?"

"Keep your head down. Do your job. Let the Justiciars get to the truth."

"The truth is Ceril is corrupt. Dangerous."

"We don't have proof, other than Quinn's word."

Nyssa shook her head. Every nerve in her body was vibrating, like the buildup before a fight, but with nowhere to direct her rage, she felt like she was going insane. "Her word is good enough for me. And she needs our help. I feel it in my gut," Nyssa said.

Aryis spoke up. "You can't risk your life for her, Nyssa. What proof has Quinn offered against Ceril?"

Nyssa shook her head, but stayed silent. Telling them about the Alabaster Books, about her suspicions regarding the wraiths, would only endanger them.

"Nyssa, I know what you're thinking, but you need to stay in the Keep," Athen said. "We can't protect you if you leave, and the Justiciars who come here in the wake of Eron's death will view it as a betrayal of your duties."

She stopped pacing and rubbed her arms. The short-sleeved shirt and light cotton pants she wore to bed were not sufficient to ward against the chill that had seeped into her bones. She considered Athen. She couldn't let him or anyone else stand in her way. Quinn didn't deserve to be imprisoned again. Or worse—Ceril could kill her to keep her silent.

"You can't protect me anymore, Athen."

"The hell I can't. Ever since you met Quinn, you've been...different. And now these allegations against Ceril? It's almost as if you want to fail. You owe it to Eron to honor your oath."

Nyssa trembled, seething. "Don't you tell me what I owe to Eron. Ever."

"Both of you need to calm down and listen to each other. This is madness," Aryis said.

Nyssa rounded on her, blinking back tears. "You're not listening to me! We shouldn't have brought Quinn back. She wanted to be free. She called us all guild lapdogs. Was she wrong?"

Athen stood and came around the desk. "You're taking her word, her suspicions, as fact. You're being gullible."

"And you're being an asshole," Nyssa replied.

"I'm being what I always have to be with you—the one who's looking out for your best interests, even when you don't like it."

"I can look after myself, Athen."

"You're not thinking straight right now." He paused and set his jaw. "Don't leave the Keep."

Nyssa took a step back, shaking her head. "Are you giving me orders now?"

"I don't think he means it like that," Aryis interjected. "We just want you to stay safe."

Shivering in the chill of Lilliana's office, Nyssa searched Athen's face. His eyes, though heavy with tears, were resolute. Arguing would get her nowhere. He wasn't going to listen to her or help Quinn. And if she stayed, she feared things would come to blows.

She turned and headed to the door.

"Where are you going?" Athen asked.

Nyssa paused, hand on the handle, considering a response. Then, without a word, she left.

The moon cast dark shadows in the corners of the small, tucked-away courtyard Nyssa often visited when she needed to practice or think. A chilly wind blew leaves about, and she rubbed her arms, shivering.

During the day, the private yard felt safe and welcoming, the dappled sunlight dancing on the ground. Now, there was little here save for claustrophobic shadows.

It was inconceivable that Eron was dead, and she knew in her bones that Quinn was right about Ceril. That asshole was responsible for Eron's death and Quinn's suffering. But Nyssa also knew her duty, what the Order would expect of her now as an Ashcloak. She was meant to comply. Behave. And if she disobeyed, there wouldn't be a way back for her.

Ever.

"Nyssa?" Reece approached from the shadows of the Keep and crossed over to her, Eron's blood washed away and in fresh clothes. "If you want me to leave, just tell me."

Nyssa choked back a sob. Everything was spiraling out of control, and the one person who could always ground her, help her work through her swirling emotions, was dead.

Reece pulled her into a hug, and Nyssa melted into it. Her anger was sending her down a dark path. Reece's presence, her warmth, pulled her back.

"Nyssa, I saw the assassin."

She exhaled. "Who was it?"

"I don't know...but they wore your face. The assassin had *your* face."

Whatever small modicum of composure Nyssa had regained over the last hour while she tried to hold herself together threatened to come undone. Her legs gave out, and Reece caught her before she crumpled to the ground, directing her to sit on a bench.

"He died thinking I killed him?"

Reece grabbed her face and forced her to look at her. "No! He knew it wasn't you. He told me that her eyes were wrong, they weren't your eyes. Eron knew it wasn't you."

"Are you sure?"

"Yes. And I told him it wasn't you. I wish I had gotten there sooner, I could have—"

"You would be dead too," Nyssa whispered, grabbing Reece's hands and pulling them from her face. "I couldn't bear it if you got hurt too. My heart is already broken."

Reece bent over and kissed Nyssa's hands. "I'm so sorry."

Nyssa lay her head in Reece's lap, pulling her legs onto the bench, making herself small and rubbing her arms for warmth. Reece smoothed down her hair, and Nyssa closed her eyes and wondered how to move forward in the next minute, hour, day without her heart crumbling to dust.

Athen wanted her to stay in Ocean's Rest, to keep her head down, and stay safe. Dread pooled at the base of her spine, setting her on edge. Staying at the Keep meant doing nothing, ignoring her instincts and betraying her honor.

It felt *wrong*.

"I have to leave," Nyssa murmured. "Quinn doesn't deserve what's happened to her. I have to help her."

"I know."

"Am I making a mistake, Reece?"

"Do you believe Quinn?"

"Yes. Every fiber of my being is screaming that Ceril is responsible for the wraith attack and Eron's death. And he will not stop there. He's to be Arch Master. What will he do with that power? What could he do to the Empress? And he'll keep using Quinn. She should be free."

Reece tucked a stray strand of hair behind Nyssa's ear. "Then you're not making a mistake. Trust your gut."

"But I'm betraying my guild. If I leave, if I help Quinn, there's no going back to the Emerald Order."

"You can either betray yourself or betray the guild," Reece said. "I hate absolutes, but I think it comes down to those two choices. If something happens to Quinn, what's left for you in the guild? What's left of *you*?"

Nyssa swallowed. Helping Quinn meant abandoning her future and betraying the Empire. She needed to steel herself to face the consequences. Eron's words rang in her ears and sank into her bones...

When you save others, you save yourself.

Nyssa sat up. "I need to go."

Reece caught her hand. "Wait. Tonight, I went to talk to Eron about you. And Quinn. The two of you...you *both* burn bright. She's like you, Nyssa. I don't understand why."

Nyssa's jaw fell open. "Could she be...could we be related?"

"No. Relations share an emotional resonance...like two people singing in harmony. You and Quinn are very distinct from one another. Whatever connection you have, it's not by blood."

An idea formed in Nyssa's head. "Wait...did you sense the assassin? Could you find her again?"

Reece shook her head. "No, she was out of my range. I only knew she wasn't you because you I can feel from—"

"Across the Keep." A sad smile settled on Nyssa's face, and she stood. Though tired and emotionally spent, the energy of purpose filled her. "I'm going to help Quinn."

Reece nodded. "I'll send word to have a horse readied."

"Thank you." Nyssa choked up. "You can't tell anyone I'm leaving."

"I know." Reece stood and kissed her. "Let's go get you dressed."

It took Nyssa days to find a trace of Quinn and her escort, but she finally had hope of catching them when she got to a busy crossroads along the route to the Citadel.

At a traveling food cart, as she sat over a steaming bowl of soup, the noodle vendor glanced at her Ashcloak pin. "I always welcome guildies at my stand."

She perked up, finally stirred out of her dark thoughts. "Oh? Have you seen any on this road of late?"

The man nodded. "Two stopped by here on their way to the Citadel a few days back. One was a big lookin' fellow, full of himself, talking loud about Arcton like it's somethin' special, puffed up the way guildies are. Uh, no offense, Ashcloak, no offense. Had a woman with him, could kill a snake with a look, ya know? She weren't happy."

The observation made Nyssa chuckle—the first time since she'd left Ocean's Keep that a smile crossed her lips.

"Strange thing, though. The next morning, the man came back for breakfast, alone. Looked like someone pissed on his grave. Dunno what ghost crawled inside his skin to rattle 'im like that, but he sucked down a bowl of oatmeal and left. Back to the Citadel, I guess. Stiffed me on the breakfast, I'll have you know."

Nyssa finished her noodles and left the man with a good tip to make up for the Citadel guard's inconsideration. The vendor pointed her to the trail leading off the main road that Quinn and her companion had taken to camp.

She swallowed hard. What if Quinn had tried to escape and the guard killed her in a panic? What if Ceril had decided Quinn was too much trouble and ordered her death?

What if Nyssa was too late?

After studying the map Reece had given her before leaving, Nyssa followed the trail a quarter hour into the woods, coming upon a dead campfire far enough into the trees to get a bit of privacy.

Far enough in to kill Quinn and leave her body for animals to ravage.

Pushing back her apprehension, Nyssa searched the area. No sign of Quinn, but a set of footprints trailed north, deeper into the woods.

Nyssa followed the tracks as long as she could, camping when it got too dark. She breathed a sigh of relief when she spotted smoke rising from a hole in the roof of an abandoned millhouse next to a small river. It had taken two days to find, losing the trail a few times. While not completely certain it was Quinn, it made sense to wait until after dark to take a closer look.

She tied up her horse out of earshot and crept up behind a tree to hunker down and keep watch. Impatience could get Nyssa in trouble—she couldn't be sure Quinn was alone or if anyone else was stalking her. So, she sat and waited for deep night.

MISTAKES WERE MADE

"Are you here to kill me, Ashcloak?"

Nyssa froze. Quinn tossed her blanket to the side and sank a dagger into Nyssa's thigh. Nyssa stumbled back and fell on her ass with a cry of pain. Quinn's heart almost pounded out of her chest as she scrambled to her feet, shocked she had taken Nyssa by surprise.

"Son of a bitch!" Nyssa wrapped her hand around the dagger and yanked it out of her leg, blood spurting from the wound. She moaned. "I wasn't *going* to kill you, but you may have just changed my mind. What the fuck, Quinn?"

"I'm not going back to the guild," Quinn growled, bending over and gathering her belongings, stuffing them quickly into her rucksack. "Where are the others?"

"What? No—I'm alone." Nyssa tried to sit up but fell back on her elbows. "Please—"

"They're never going to stop coming after me, are they?"

"I'm not...I'm..." Nyssa struggled out, her gaze drifting.

"Sorry, Nyssa. I wish I could trust you, but you returned me to them once already. I'll be gone before you wake up."

Quinn crouched down and opened up Nyssa's jacket, searching her interior pockets. She found a map. It would come in handy—avoiding the roads would keep her safe, but getting lost deep in the woods had become a real fear.

Nyssa tried grabbing hold of Quinn's wrist, but her arm flopped back to the ground. "What'd you do to me?"

Quinn picked up the dagger and tucked it into her belt. Hurting Nyssa churned her stomach, but the woman was an Ashcloak—and dangerous.

"Did you poison me?" Nyssa slurred, blinking long and slow. "You assho—" Her head lolled back, and she collapsed, unconscious.

Quinn rummaged through Nyssa's rucksack, taking out a packet of food. Searching further, she found a shirt and pulled it out of the bag.

After a few minutes, she stood over Nyssa, a strange pang of sadness filling her. Sighing, she gave the unconscious woman one last glance before walking out into the night. "Goodbye, Nyssa."

Nyssa groaned as her eyes fluttered open. Bright light streamed through the hole in the roof, and she cursed the sun's very existence.

Her head throbbed.

When she remembered the previous night's events, she rubbed her face to try to wash the embarrassment away. She had underestimated Quinn. Again.

She propped herself up on her elbows and looked down at her aching wound, now wrapped in a strip of white cloth. With a sigh, she let her chin hit her chest before looking around to get her bearings. The old mill was small, but cozy enough for a night or two, its rough stone floor covered in strands of hay. A stone pit sat in the middle of the room, its fire out for hours.

Nyssa spotted a small bag on top of her rucksack, and she shifted to open it. Quinn had taken half her food.

"Dammit, Quinn," she whispered. If the woman was smart, she would have taken all the food and not spent any time worrying about the injury.

Nyssa stood, taking a few steps to test her leg. The dagger had only gone in a few inches, but it still hurt, drawing an angry hiss out of her when she limped over to pick up her rucksack, then hobbled toward the door.

Stepping outside, she winced at the sun, shading her eyes, and walked back to her horse. She found him munching on snow-covered clover.

"Dammit, Quinn." Another mistake by the woman. Who was this woefully incompetent at escape tactics? Not taking Nyssa's horse would make closing the distance between them far too easy.

She hooked her pack to her saddle and guided her horse back to the run-down mill to search for Quinn's tracks. They were easy to find, headed due north toward endless wilderness. The northern forests of the Empire were vast and dangerous, but the smartest route to shake any followers. The woods could get dense and almost impossible to traverse with a horse.

Nyssa reached inside her jacket, only to find her map missing. "I'm surprised she didn't tear it in half and leave me a piece," she grumbled, limping toward the river with her horse in tow. She would have to cross it to go north, but the water was shallow, only a foot or two deep. She led the horse down to the river and stepped into the cold water, not mounting him for fear of getting thrown if he got spooked.

The icy river swirled around her ankles, and Nyssa shivered as she put her other foot in the river, instantly regretting her decision and dreading having to ride with wet socks and boots.

"I'm going to fucking kill her," Nyssa announced to her horse.

Several feet into the river, a wave of nausea washed over her, and the edges of her vision turned white. The sound of the rushing water receded, replaced by a loud hiss filling her ears. Her legs gave out underneath her.

A soft, warm muzzle pushed against Nyssa's cheek and gently nipped at her nose. She slowly opened her eyes. Flared horse nostrils hovered above her face, and she weakly reached up to stroke the side of his head before letting her arm fall back down, limp as a noodle.

"Thassa good boy," she slurred, her teeth chattering. Gods, she was freezing.

Water lapped against her legs, and she sighed, closing her eyes, thankful she at least had made it out of the river before passing out.

"Imagine how dreadfully embarrassing it would be to drown in less than a foot of water," a familiar voice admonished. Nyssa's eyes shot open.

Quinn sat next to her, knees drawn to her chest. "I couldn't get you all the way out of the stream. You're wet and heavy."

"Dammit, Quinn," Nyssa grumbled. "You're still here?"

"I was waiting for you to follow my trail. I walked half the night to the forest and doubled back."

"Oh, you were going to fool me and head off in a different direction?"

"That was the plan."

"Such a dumb plan."

Quinn let out an amused chuckle. "Was it?"

"Yes." Nyssa propped herself up on her elbows and turned to her. "First off, you should have taken all of my food and my horse. And you certainly shouldn't have bandaged my leg. You wasted time, and you left me with the supplies I needed to follow you. You're *terrible* at escaping."

"And look how successful you were coming after me!" Quinn replied. "Do you really want to debate whether my escape was good enough? Besides, I wasn't going to just let you bleed to death or starve. I figure we owe each other more than that now."

Nyssa sighed. Perhaps the hollow ache in her chest when Quinn was taken from Ocean's Rest was their unfinished business. She was only alive because of Quinn, a debt that she could never adequately repay.

"Whatever you poisoned me with lingered longer than expected," Nyssa said. "My whole body feels heavy."

"I knew Anselweed could put a person on their ass, but I was a little unsure about quantities."

Nyssa moaned. "That's comforting. I finally got over my rib injury and then you stick me in the leg with a damn dagger covered in Anselweed?"

"You keep underestimating me. I got the jump on you. Again."

Nyssa mumbled under her breath while a shiver rippled down her body.

Quinn stood. "Is anyone following you?"

"No."

She helped Nyssa up. Nyssa rocked on her feet as her brain swam in fog.

Quinn grabbed Nyssa's waist to steady her. "Put your arm around me."

Nyssa reluctantly draped an arm over Quinn's shoulders. "Aren't you scared that I'm here to take you back?"

"Yes, but I will not have your death on my ledger. We'll stay here tonight. You need to get out of those clothes or you'll freeze."

Quinn helped Nyssa back inside the mill and sat her next to the extinguished fire pit. She gathered some bits of wood and gave Nyssa the task of restarting the fire while she tended to her horse.

As the flames rose, Nyssa stripped down to her underclothes, and when Quinn got back, she rummaged through her pack and tossed her a sweater. She busied herself with picking up Nyssa's clothes and stringing a makeshift clothesline near the fire to dry out her belongings.

Nyssa lay down to rest, intending to tell Quinn everything that had happened at Ocean's Rest and how she was there to help. Even though she didn't have a plan formulated yet, she was content knowing Quinn was safe.

Her eyes grew heavy. The fire crackled next to her, and she drifted off to sleep.

Nyssa woke to the rich, savory smell of stew, and her mouth watered. She sat up, wincing slightly at the ache in her leg, but thankful her headache was gone. Dusk had already set in. Next to her sat Quinn, slowly stirring a pot over the fire.

"How long was I asleep?" Nyssa croaked, her throat dry and sore. She had been covered with the blanket from the back of her horse.

Quinn tipped a small kettle over a mug and passed it over to Nyssa, who took sips of the hot liquid. She made a face. Unsweetened herb tea wasn't her favorite, but it soothed her throat.

"Half the day," Quinn replied. "Hungry?"

Nyssa nodded. Quinn pulled the pot off the fire and placed it between them. "We'll have to share a spoon."

She handed the spoon to Nyssa first, who dipped it into the stew and enjoyed a big helping. It was hot and delicious, likely made from the dried meat and potatoes in her provision bag.

"I'm not here to take you back to the Citadel," Nyssa said. "I want to help you."

Quinn raised her eyebrows. "You abandoned your post?"

"Yes."

Quinn let out a sharp breath. "Nyssa, that's treason. They'll punish you."

Nyssa bit the inside of her cheek. She hadn't completely thought through the consequences of her actions, but her honor wouldn't allow her to abandon Quinn.

"Have you heard of a man named Sakei?"

"They teach his martial art at the Order, right?"

Nyssa nodded. "Sakei didn't have any magick, but he made a name for himself by being the best warrior and swordsman of his time. I saw him as a role model and spent years studying his writings. He was a true warrior poet."

Quinn smiled. "I guess I was wrong, you did learn something at the Order."

"I told you I like to read. I'm not just a pretty face with muscles," Nyssa teased. She drew her knees to her chest and poked at the fire with a stick, her mood turning serious. "The one thing that always stuck out to me was Sakei's belief in casting your own shadow. To have the courage to be true to your convictions, even if you stand alone. I've been struggling with how to cast my own shadow and still be loyal to the Empire." She turned to Quinn. "You stood up for yourself and defied their laws. You cast your own shadow before I ever did. And they wanted you hunted down, brought back, and made to heel. I can't be a party to that anymore."

Quinn sat silent a moment, her face tightly controlled, before she spoke. "Nyssa, I don't know what to say."

"There's more." Nyssa tried to form the words to tell her about Eron, but a sudden rush of stark sadness overtook her. The ache inside her chest, present ever since Eron's death, grew deeper. She put a hand to her mouth to stifle a sob.

"Nyssa?"

Bile rose in Nyssa's throat and she swallowed hard. "Eron was murdered." The words were like dark ash in her mouth.

"No. Gods, I'm so sorry, Nyssa," Quinn said, putting her hand on Nyssa's knee. A small whimper escaped from the back of Nyssa's throat, and she couldn't stop the tears as she covered her face and wept.

Quinn waited, not rushing Nyssa's grief.

The warmth of Quinn's hand on her knee helped her focus and drew her out of the deep sadness that threatened to engulf her, even though she had no reason to be kind—especially after Nyssa delivered her back to the Empire.

With a shaky exhale, Nyssa straightened. "There's something I didn't tell you. The blood wraith on the ship spoke to me. It called me a 'magickless whelp'."

Quinn's brow furrowed. "That's what Ceril called you." Nyssa nodded, and Quinn ruminated for a while before her face grew dark. "I knew he was studying forbidden magick, but could he have created the wraiths—a blood wraith, no less—and sent them after you?"

"I know he could."

"But why?"

"Eron gave me a spot in the Emerald Order that I didn't earn or deserve, and I think Ceril hates me for it. The Empress was lenient with

Eron and never made him kick me out. I would bet Ceril's jealous of whatever friendship my father had with her. I told Eron my suspicions, and he was going to look into it on his own. And then he was killed."

Quinn sighed and hung her head. "Nyssa, this is much bigger than the two of us. You shouldn't be helping me."

Nyssa grunted. "It's too late now. I'm helping your stubborn ass!"

"*I'm* stubborn? You're one to talk. I just...I don't want you to get hurt."

Nyssa paused and swallowed, her words catching in her throat. "I wish you had that sentiment when you stuck a dagger in my leg."

Quinn exhaled a soft laugh. "I'm going to have to keep apologizing for that, aren't I?"

"Yes." Nyssa handed the spoon back to her. "Here, get some hot food in you. It's delicious, by the way."

Quinn responded with a smile and color rose in her cheeks.

As she ate, Nyssa tried to formulate a plan to get her to safety. "Where were you headed?"

"North. I have a tiny amount of money I took off the Citadel adept, and I figured I could disappear into the Northern Wilds for a time instead of going back to Ocean's Rest."

Quinn pulled a small loaf of crusty bread from the provisions and tore off the heel, handing it to Nyssa. "I know you like the end bits."

Nyssa looked down to hide her smirk. "Why didn't you take your horse?"

"I'm not...good with horses. I figured I'd be safer on my own two feet since I know some tricks to throw a tracker off."

"Doubling back was smart, but rescuing your enemy instead of escaping was foolish."

Quinn frowned. "You're not my enemy, Nyssa."

Nyssa smiled. For days, grief and worry weighed her down, but for the first time since Eron's death, she felt some relief from her crushing sadness. Quinn's unexpected kindness helped.

"How would you like to get out of the Empire altogether?" Nyssa asked.

Quinn chewed on a piece of bread. "How?"

Nyssa reached inside her jacket pocket. "Elias gave me this coin to contact him. We can hitch a ride on the Whisper. We'll have to go back to Ocean's Rest, though."

Quinn took the coin and turned it over in her hands. "Are you sure about this? Ocean's Rest will be crawling with Justiciars after Eron's death."

"Let Elias help. We'll put the Empire behind you forever."

"That's all I want." Quinn said, her green eyes dancing in the firelight. "Nyssa, you're in so much danger now. Will...will you come with me?"

Nyssa looked over at Quinn. There was a stark earnestness to her request, and she couldn't deny the desire to join her. "That's the plan, Freckles."

Quinn smiled, a look of relief on her face. Nyssa stood up and hobbled over to her dry clothes to pull them on, trying to hide her face from Quinn.

"Thank you. For helping me," Quinn said. "You're an honorable person, Nyssa."

A lump formed in Nyssa's throat. She would see Quinn off, but knew she had to go back and face the Justiciars, tell them what Ceril had done, and get justice for Eron. She just didn't have the heart to tell Quinn.

BLOOD ON SNOW

Quinn packed up the provisions and what little belongings they had, reflecting on how drastically her life had changed in the past few days. In an act of pure desperation, she had seized her chance to escape, assailing her Citadel escort. When the man went limp, she collected her things and ran, not looking back.

She didn't understand why he lost consciousness—it had never happened before when she used her magick on someone—but presumed the stress of the moment made her push harder than ever and tried to put it out of her mind.

Quinn stood and rubbed her hands together, the fire doused in preparation for their departure from this place. The old mill had been long abandoned, decay and dilapidation eating away at it, but she felt oddly safe here.

Safe with Nyssa, of all people.

She picked up Nyssa's leather jacket and smoothed it out, draping it over the travel bags. Nyssa had a strange love for winter. Telling her to put her jacket on to tend to the horse had been a futile endeavor. She merely laughed and said the cold would wake her up.

Footsteps startled Quinn as Nyssa entered the doorway.

"I'm almost all packed up," Quinn said.

Nyssa grunted and headed toward the travel bags. As she came closer, the hairs on the back of Quinn's neck pricked.

Nyssa didn't *feel* right.

Quinn took a step back out of pure instinct, and Nyssa lunged at her. Quinn stumbled and tripped over the now-dead fire pit, landing with a thud before scrambling away from the woman.

"Stop squirming, Quinn," Nyssa said, but the voice was wrong.

"Who are you?"

The air around the impostor started to shimmer and distort, and Nyssa's face and hair fell away, dissolving like smoke. A dark-haired woman with black eyes peered down at Quinn.

"First Master Anelos wants you back."

"No," Quinn hissed.

The woman sneered at her. "You should be honored to be at Arcton Citadel. A lowly orphan and you have the nerve to turn your back on your guild? The First Master mentored you himself!"

Quinn shook her head. "You know nothing about me. Ceril locked me away. Put me in a void collar."

The expression on the woman's face changed for an instant before returning to cold certainty.

"No matter." She advanced on Quinn, hatred in her eyes.

The woman cried out, stumbling to the side, grabbing at her back. Nyssa stood in the doorway, sunlight glinting off a blade in her hand. She let it fly.

The woman cried out again and whirled around. Two small throwing knives stuck out of her back.

"Efla." Nyssa reached over her shoulder to draw her sword, but jerked to a stop, clutching at her chest. Green magick billowed off of her, her face pained. "Dammit...where's that bastard brother of yours?" she hissed.

"Behind you," a male voice called.

Nyssa tried turning around, but the man in the doorway smashed her skull with his forearm, sending her sprawling to the straw-covered floor.

Efla stalked toward Nyssa and knelt beside her. A sickening crack of leather against skin accompanied the punch that whipped Nyssa's head to the side. Her eyes lolled in her head from the blow and blood poured out of a cut that split her eyebrow open.

Quinn shot to her feet, drawing out her dagger.

"What are you going to do with that?" the man asked, smirking at Quinn.

"Tann, will you subdue her? I already have enough blades in my goddamn back," Efla spat. She grimaced and reached behind her, pulling out Nyssa's throwing knives with a loud hiss. The blades *thunked* against the floor.

Tann stalked toward Quinn, his eyes trained on her hands. Not just the dagger—her hands.

He fears me. He knows my magick can stop him.

Quinn tucked the dagger back into her belt and stripped off her gloves. She could do more harm with her magick than a blade she didn't know how to use. She just needed a bare inch of skin.

Tann's eyes darted to her face—they were filled with pure hate. Not knowing what else to do, she rushed him, hoping to catch him off guard.

Intense, burning pain seared through Quinn's chest. She seized up, crying out and falling to her knees. Tann's fist slammed into her chin, and she collapsed, her face hitting the cold stones of the millhouse floor. A hand buried itself in her hair and yanked her back up onto her knees. She clawed at Tann's arms, but his clothes and gloves covered him completely, not an inch of bare flesh within reach.

"Stop struggling, bitch. I imagine the First Master would enjoy his upstart adept brought to her knees."

"Fuck...you!" Quinn gritted her teeth. "Nyssa, wake up!"

Nyssa roused back to consciousness. Blood, slick and hot, ran into her eye.

Efla's face came into focus over her, a sneer curling her lips.

Efla. The woman who had murdered her father.

Nyssa grabbed her left hand, wrenching a finger back until it snapped. Efla cried out in pain, slamming a fist on Nyssa's head. She straddled Nyssa and wrapped her hands around her throat, bearing down with all her weight.

"You really thought you got the better of us back at The Feather, didn't you? You're nothing but magickless trash."

Nyssa snarled and tried to peel Efla's hands off, but Efla leaned closer and smiled a wicked, predatory grin. "Yours was the last face Eron saw before I slit his throat. His own *daughter* betraying him."

A guttural roar ripped out of Nyssa's chest, one last desperate burst of energy rippling through her. Clawing at the ground beside her, she dug her fingers into the cold, cracked floor and pried loose a stone, smashing it against Efla's temple. The assassin toppled off of her, landing with a thud and a groan.

Nyssa's chest rose and fell as she took in quick gasps of air, her eyes meeting Tann's.

"I'll peel your skin off of you strip by strip before I kill you," he growled.

Nyssa scrambled to her feet and listed to her left, her balance not right. "You murdered Eron. I'm going to tear you both to pieces."

Tann violently jerked Quinn's head, and her cry of pain cut into Nyssa. "Not today. You've escaped death one too many times."

Nyssa's blood ran cold. "What does that mean?"

Tann cocked his head and smiled. "Great winged death from above," he said, waving a hand in the air.

The wraiths.

Nyssa sucked in a breath. Her suspicions were right. So many innocent people dead because of Ceril.

Tann smirked, his hand glowing green. Searing pain spread through her chest, and she stumbled forward, grabbing Tann and smashing her forehead into his nose.

Bone crunched under her blow, and she fought to stay upright. Blood spurted from Tann's nose, but she could no longer feel his magick jabbing into her. She reached over her back to draw Winter's Bite.

With surprising speed, Tann closed the distance between them and kicked Nyssa in the ribs. She flew back into the wall of the mill, its brittle wood shattering from the impact. Splinters rained down on her, and she found herself outside, staring into an overcast sky, fighting to draw a breath.

She rolled over and pushed herself onto her hands and knees. Drops of blood fell into the pristine snow.

"You're going to die today, Blacksea," Tann said from inside the mill, his voice drawing closer. Nyssa willed herself to stand. He stepped through the shattered wall, and Efla followed, pulling Quinn along by the back of her jacket. Half of Efla's face was covered with blood.

"Let Quinn go, Efla. Fight me," Nyssa growled.

"Gladly, whelp." Efla smiled, her teeth bloody.

Whelp. Ceril's insult. It ignited a flame of indignation within Nyssa.

Efla threw Quinn down in the snow and kicked her in the face. A shock of fear surged through Nyssa when Quinn went limp. She backed up to create space, drawing the siblings to her and away from Quinn.

Fat snowflakes began falling with a hush to the ground.

Tann and Efla matched her steps as she retreated, the snow giving way with each step. A stiff wind hit Nyssa, and she shivered. She had always loved winter more than any other season. The snow, the icy air, made everything sharp and present in her world.

She needed that sharpness, that focus, now.

"Two against one, huh?" she asked. "Seems unfair to you two, but if you both want to die, I can accommodate you."

"Oh, how I've wanted to shut that smug mouth since we met," Tann snarled.

Nyssa stopped and set her feet, grinding them into the snow, settling into her stance to wait for the attack, just like Eron had taught her as a child—*a solid stance is your foundation, your root system. Extend your body into the ground and draw your strength from the earth.*

Nyssa relaxed her body and drew her sword. Tann and Efla split up, flanking her—exactly how they should attack. Nyssa had trained against multiple fighters in one endless training session after another at the

Order. She lowered her head and kept each sibling in the corners of her eyes.

She exhaled and waited.

Efla sprang forward, and Nyssa slid back, deflecting her knife. A flash in the corner of her eye alerted her to Tann joining the fight.

The siblings tried to box her in, but she twisted around Efla to put her in the path of her brother and whirled her sword toward Efla's back. Steel clashed against steel as Efla barely deflected the blow. Winter's Bite still found flesh, though, drawing a shallow cut across her lower back.

Efla retreated, kicking Nyssa in the leg. The sudden pain pulled a loud grunt out of her, Efla's strike aggravating her stab wound. She limped back, cursing under her breath. Blood seeped into her eye from the cut on her head and she swiped at it with the back of her hand.

The smirk of satisfaction on the other woman's face burned at Nyssa.

Tann moved past Efla and charged. Nyssa set her feet. Winter's Bite arched down and struck his forearm. Instead of cleaving his arm in two, the sword clanged against metal and vibrated in her hands.

What the—?

Tann rammed a knee into her midsection, sending a shuddering pain through her ribs. Nyssa teetered back from the blow, confused. Winter's Bite could easily cut through his arm and body—Tann should be dead.

She glanced up to see silver peeking out from under his sliced-up jacket.

Metal bracers.

Nyssa backed up, grimacing from the pain in her leg. The shimmer of blood on her pants let her know her wound reopened.

The siblings stalked her again, Tann taking the lead. He twirled his knife in one hand, extending his other arm out and inching toward Nyssa. Small, claw-like blades protruded from the bracer. It was a shield *and* a weapon.

Nyssa gritted her teeth, waiting.

After a few seconds, Tann struck, slicing his knife at her midsection. She blocked the blow with her sword and countered, her blade striking his bracer.

As Nyssa shifted away from Tann, Efla sprang forward, her knives a blur as she moved. Nyssa slid back, dodging the knives. She slashed Winter's Bite down at Efla, cutting into her shoulder. Efla barely got her blade up to block, saving her from losing an arm.

Nyssa lashed out with a stiff kick to her chest, knocking her to the ground. She closed in on Efla, intent on ending her. She whirled Winter's Bite around, reversing her grip, and reared up to drive the tip of the sword into Efla's chest.

Eron's face stared up at her, and Nyssa jerked her sword off its target, glancing across Efla's ribs.

Efla let out a pained laugh. "You're pathetic." The visage of Eron's face contorted, and a second later the magick dissolved, revealing Efla's face.

Hate ripped through Nyssa, and she reared up again, determined for Winter's Bite to strike true.

She cried out.

Searing pain gripped her heart, and she sank to her knees, Tann's magick tearing through her, forcing the air out of her lungs. The edges of her vision went white as she fought to stay alert, conscious. She ran her trembling fingers down the sword strap across her chest, finding a throwing knife and slipping it out of its sheath, then flinging it at Tann.

The knife found its target with a meaty *thunk*. Tann yelped, the small blade sticking out of his upper chest. It wasn't enough to kill, but it broke his concentration. His magick slipped off Nyssa, and she pushed herself to her feet. Efla slunk away from her, pulling herself along with one elbow, blood trailing across the snow.

Tann gritted his teeth and yanked Nyssa's knife out, letting it drop to the ground. His cheeks billowed in and out with each deep breath, and he glanced at his sister trembling in the snow.

"Efla?"

She turned her eyes up to him. "Finish her."

Nyssa retreated a few steps, bracing for Tann's attack. She shifted her weight and switched to an underhanded grip on Winter's Bite, pressing the back of the blade against her forearm.

The drag of fatigue pulled at her. Her head throbbed and as much as she tried to slow down and control her breathing, she couldn't stop sucking in air. The dull, pulsing ache in her ribs from Tann's kick made it harder to move and breathe. Hot, stinging blood trickled from the cut in her eyebrow, marring her vision.

Tann took long strides toward Nyssa and lunged forward with his knife. She spun Winter's Bite around to block, but his move was a feint, and his bracer's claws ripped across her forearm, its two sharp blades cutting deep into flesh.

Nyssa kicked wildly at Tann, catching him in the ribs. She scrambled away from him, tucking her arm into her body. The cuts were deep, the pain shocking.

Her hand went numb, and Winter's Bite slipped from her grasp.

Tann shot forward, pressing his advantage, driving his clawed fist into her right shoulder. Nyssa cried out and instinctively lashed out, burying her knuckles in his throat. The strike forced Tann back, and his mouth opened and closed like a fish on dry land.

The blinding pain drove Nyssa down to one knee, her right arm dangling at her side, blood dripping in the fresh white snow. Winter's Bite lay out of reach.

With a grunt, Tann choked out, "Do you yield?" He rasped out a snide laugh.

Nyssa panted, grimacing through her pain, and willed herself to stand. She staggered, her body wobbly beneath her. As sweat pricked up on her brow, a cold fear settled in.

A broken body could only be pushed so far before it failed and fell.

And if she fell, she was dead.

Efla rose to her feet, holding her injured arm steady. Nyssa shifted her eyes to Tann.

He wiped his forearm over his face, smearing blood from his broken nose across his cheek, and started toward Nyssa. She slid back.

No weapon and only one working arm made her easy prey. She swallowed a cold lump of fear forming in her throat. Death's grip was far too close. Her only chance was to avoid more injury—to buy time to think. Tann lunged at her, but his strike was slow. His confidence betrayed him, made him sloppy. Nyssa dodged to her left and landed a vicious kick to his groin.

Fighting with honor was no longer an option.

Tann hissed out a string of curses and lashed out with his bracer, slicing into her abdomen before retreating, his hands cupping his crotch.

Nyssa lurched back, hand flying to her stomach. The cut was shallow, a small mercy.

A scream pierced the air.

"Get off me!" Efla yelled. Arms encircled her throat, and a hand clawed at the assassin's face.

Quinn!

Scrabbling on Efla's back, Quinn tried to choke her from behind, dark shadowy magick flowing from her hands.

A spark of hope pierced through Nyssa's pain.

Tann whirled around and started toward his sister. Nyssa lunged, throwing her body into Tann as he reached Efla and Quinn.

The four of them tumbled to the ground in a tangle of limbs.

Nyssa fought to get on her knees. Tann grabbed at her, and she threw a punch, spilling forward as it connected with his face.

She lay facedown in the snow, panting, trying to will herself to move.

Her body wouldn't obey her.

Tann stirred next to her with a pained groan.

Get up. Get up. Get up. Get up.

Get. Up.

Nyssa moved her left arm underneath her and pushed herself up. She screamed, her right shoulder protesting even the smallest movement. Her head lolled forward.

"Nyssa!" Quinn appeared in front of her and grabbed her, keeping her upright. "Oh gods," she whispered, her eyes darting from one blood-soaked injury to the next.

Picking her head up, Nyssa pulled Quinn close. "If they kill me, fight like hell to survive. And if you do, get the coin out of my jacket. Take it to Crae's Alehouse in Ocean's Rest. They will contact Elias. Get away from the Empire and never look back."

"Nyssa, please—"

She pushed Quinn back and cradled her injured right arm close to her chest. Numbness spread across her body—undoubtedly a slow-acting poison. The tools of the assassin's trade. Gods, she hated the Rule with a passion. A small flicker of anger pulsed through her—her indignation taking its last stand.

She pushed to her feet, swaying back and forth. Tann staggered upright. Efla lay still on the ground.

"You and your sister have no honor. You don't know what it's like to fight with your eyes clear and your head held high like a warrior. You're fucking roaches that kill in the dark and scatter when the lights come on," Nyssa spat.

Tann laughed. "What good is honor when you're lying dead in a pool of your own blood?"

"Let's finish this, assassin."

Tann sneered and ran at Nyssa, his anger driving him forward. Instead of moving back to defend herself and parry his knife strike, Nyssa stepped into him, ducking under his blade and ramming the dagger she took off of Quinn into his chest. One last surprise.

A strangled breath escaped his lips, the warmth of it hitting her face. His arrogant smirk disappeared.

"No..." he whispered.

"This is for my father." Nyssa shoved her dagger deeper into him, slow and deliberate, staring into his eyes. Hot blood splashed over her hand.

"Wait..." he pleaded, eyes widening in panic.

A soft whimper escaped his lips, and Nyssa thrust the knife, sinking it to its hilt.

His eyes narrowed. Then stilled.

She pushed Tann away, and he fell to the cold, hard ground. A small puff of air left her lips, and she stumbled away from him, her eyes shifting to Quinn.

Her legs gave out as darkness descended.

Quinn's heart leapt into her throat when Nyssa collapsed. She ran over, dropping to her side. For a second, she feared Nyssa was dead, but a low groan made her grasp at hope.

"Nyssa!" Quinn breathed, eyes darting to her injuries. She gingerly pulled the blood-soaked shirt away from Nyssa's right shoulder, exposing two oozing puncture wounds.

Quinn stole a glance at Efla, still flat in the snow. She fumbled for the knife at her belt. It was gone. *Shit.* Her eyes darted frantically for her only weapon, finding it after a few frenzied seconds.

Her dagger was buried in Tann's chest.

A hand grabbed Quinn, and she jumped. Nyssa's eyes were open.

"My jacket..." she murmured.

A memory of Buck stitching Nyssa up on the Whisper struck Quinn. "Your healing disks!"

She stood, eyeing Efla's unconscious body, before running to the mill, grabbing Nyssa's jacket, and sprinting back, falling to her knees.

Nyssa's eyes rolled into her head, and Quinn grabbed her, slapping her cheeks. "Stay awake! Come on, Nyssa, you stubborn asshole, wake up!"

Nyssa jolted and moaned. Quinn riffled through her jacket and pulled out two round, flat disks.

"How do these work?" she asked.

Nyssa looked over at her injured shoulder. "B-bend the disk until you feel it snap and press it against my shoulder. Hold it there for as long as you can...no matter what I say or do."

Quinn exhaled, following the directions. She palmed the disk and pushed her hand down onto Nyssa's shoulder. Nyssa groaned at first from the contact, and a second later, when the disk turned warm in Quinn's hand, Nyssa began struggling before a scream ripped out of her throat. Quinn centered herself above her shoulder and kept pushing down while the disk grew hotter. It started to sting, forcing her to pull her hand away.

The disk dissolved as its power took root, working on Nyssa's injuries. Her shoulder glowed red, threads of healing magick weaving in and out of her wound. The muscles and skin began to stitch back together.

Quinn leaned down into Nyssa's elbow and chest to hold her as still as possible, clenching her jaw tight as Nyssa struggled against the pain.

It took minutes for the magick to complete its work, the red threads slowly dissipating. Nyssa's body shivered under Quinn's hands.

"My arm. I can't feel my hand. How bad is it?" Nyssa asked, her voice trembling.

Quinn ripped the rest of Nyssa's sleeve to get a better look at the injury. The skin and muscle were flayed open. She had to look away when she realized she could see bone.

"It's bad, Nyssa."

"Use the other disk, Quinn. Please...I don't want to lose my arm."

The look on Nyssa's face hollowed Quinn out. There was no bravado, no cockiness. Just a scared woman in unspeakable pain.

Quinn laid Nyssa's arm on the snow and pressed her knee onto her hand to keep the limb as still as possible. She took a deep breath, snapped the disk, and held it down on Nyssa's forearm. Nyssa grabbed her, twisting a fist into her sweater, and cried out, tears streaming down her face.

"I'm sorry, Nyssa," Quinn hissed through her teeth.

She bore down on Nyssa's arm as long as she could, knowing she needed to keep it still to heal correctly.

It was Nyssa's dominant arm.

Her sword arm.

Nyssa's hand fell away from Quinn. She had passed out. A small blessing.

When Quinn finally let go, she shoved her hands into the snow beside Nyssa to soothe the burning from the disk. Red magick surrounded Nyssa's forearm, the cuts stitching together, the bone and muscle disappearing as the wound healed.

Quinn was never allowed to visit the Citadel's healer—not even after Ceril flayed her back. She knew human healers could mitigate pain, but healing enchantments were akin to using a boulder to smash a fly. It was strong magick focused on solving one problem, but lacked the elegant human touch needed to avoid unnecessary pain.

Soft, fat snowflakes fell relentlessly. Quinn set her jaw and stood, letting the healing magick finish repairing Nyssa's arm. She looked around for a weapon, spotting Nyssa's sword, and hurried to pick it up.

Quinn swallowed at the heft of Nyssa's sword in her hand as she eyed Efla in the snow, blood seeping from her wounds. It would be easy to kill the assassin, but she recoiled from the thought of murdering a wounded, unconscious woman. She had never taken a life and doubted she ever could, even now.

A groan sounded behind her, and Quinn knelt back down next to Nyssa. Her breathing was shallow and quick, and she clutched at her chest.

"Nyssa, what's wrong?"

"I...I can't breathe."

"Fuck."

"Poison..."

"No," Quinn breathed.

She grabbed Nyssa's hand and closed her eyes, reaching out with her magick, diving into Nyssa, desperately hoping the poison was arcane. Her breath caught when she realized she could sense Nyssa's whole body, not just her essence. *How strange...*

Dark green magick glowed and spread from all of Nyssa's wounds, winding toward her heart and lungs. The sickly green poison pulsed with energy.

Quinn exhaled and calmed herself. She pinpointed each instance of poison and wrapped her power around it, snuffing out the deadly magick, targeting the tendrils closest to Nyssa's heart first. Each time she destroyed the foul toxin, Nyssa squeezed her hand and moaned.

It took Quinn several minutes to find every remnant of poison in Nyssa and destroy it. Once she was done, she slumped forward, fatigued from the effort. She had destroyed simple spells before—wards and such—and was surprised to find herself able to quell the poison.

"Quinn?" Nyssa whispered. "You used your magick on me?"

"I think I got all the poison. But I don't know how..."

Nyssa squeezed her hand and pulled her close. "You saved my life. Yet again."

Quinn exhaled a strangled breath. "You have an annoying habit of almost dying around me. I don't much care for it."

Nyssa grunted softly, her blue eyes not leaving Quinn's face. "Thank you."

Quinn looked down. Her hands, stained red with Nyssa's blood, trembled. She balled up her fists to tamp down her nerves. "Think you can stand?"

Nyssa nodded, and Quinn wearily stood up before helping Nyssa to her feet and wrapping an arm around her. "Let's get you to the mill and cleaned up. How's your arm?"

"It's numb. I'll need a sling," Nyssa said, leaning against Quinn.

When they got back inside the mill, Quinn pulled a shirt out of her travel bag and soaked it in water from her canteen. Nyssa hissed while Quinn cleaned and dressed her wounds with strips of cloth, trying to be as gentle as possible.

Nyssa's intense blue eyes did not leave Quinn's face. How disarming it was, the warrior giving herself over, trusting Quinn to take care of her.

It would have been easy to steal Elias's coin and leave. Before she got to know her, Quinn would have left Nyssa behind, not trusting her life to anyone, least of all an Emerald Order Ashcloak. But now, the thought of leaving Nyssa was untenable. The same instinct that drove her to pull Nyssa from the Black Sea prodded her forward now.

Their lives, for the moment, were inextricably entwined.

After Quinn cleaned and wrapped Nyssa's wounds, she pulled a sweater over Nyssa's head and made a makeshift sling out of the last remaining strips of a cut-up shirt.

Nyssa put her hand on Quinn's shoulder and stood. "I need to settle things with Efla."

Quinn nodded, grabbing Nyssa's sword. They stepped outside.

"Fuck," Nyssa breathed.

Efla was gone. A bloody trail led to a grove of trees where one horse stood. The assassin had run.

Quinn swallowed. "Nyssa, I'm sorry."

"It doesn't matter. We're still alive. Bring that horse and mine to the mill."

"What about Efla? She could follow us."

Nyssa shook her head. "She's in no shape to chase us. She's doing what the Rule do when they've lost...running away like a goddamned coward."

"They knew you, Nyssa. How?"

With a grunt, Nyssa nodded. "Ran into them in Ocean's Rest before we came after you. Got into a scuffle. I thought they were just trying to test me, some guild dick-measuring contest, but now I know they wanted to get close to me. Efla...I remember her studying my face. Now I know it's so she could get close to Eron." Her eyes filled with tears.

"Nyssa—"

"Don't say you're sorry about Eron again. If I break down crying now, I may not stop."

Quinn drew closer to Nyssa. "No, I was going to say we'll get Efla one day."

A sad smile crossed Nyssa's face, and Quinn left her to bring Tann and Nyssa's horses up to the mill, tying them to a tree next to the small, meandering stream. Quinn refilled her canteen and plunged her hands into the cold water, washing the blood off until they were numb.

Nyssa bent forward and held herself steady on her horse's reins as it gently nuzzled her. She smiled and gave him a kiss, looking utterly exhausted.

"I don't think I can trust you to not fall off a horse in this condition," Quinn said. "I'll ride behind you."

She hoped she could keep Nyssa upright on the horse's back. Nyssa was at least six inches taller and muscular. She would be impossible to get back onto the horse if she fell off unconscious.

"Bacon's a good boy. He'll get us back," Nyssa murmured.

"Your horse's name is Bacon?"

"They didn't tell me his name in Ocean's Keep, so I improvised."

Quinn affixed their bags to the second horse and helped get Nyssa onto Bacon.

"What should we call this other horse?" Quinn asked, tying the horse's lead to Bacon's saddle.

"Eggs, of course. You and your silly questions," Nyssa mumbled. Even in her condition, she didn't seem able to resist being a smart ass.

Though she hated to admit it, Quinn enjoyed the woman's wit.

She laid her hand on Nyssa's leg and held Winter's Bite up to her.

"You wear it," Nyssa said.

Quinn hesitated at first, but slung the sword over her shoulder. How odd it felt to have a weapon on her back. Exhaling, she gave Bacon a pat on his flank, hoping he couldn't sense her fear, and mounted him.

She took the reins in one hand, wrapping her left arm around Nyssa's waist to keep her upright and steady. As strange as it was to wear Nyssa's blade, odder still was holding on to her. Physical closeness had always made Quinn uncomfortable, knowing that others shrank from her touch out of fear. But with Nyssa, the discomfort melted away.

She peered over Nyssa's shoulder and gave Bacon a gentle nudge with her heels. As the beast moved beneath them, Nyssa held on tight to her arm. A hint of verbena from Nyssa's hair filled Quinn's nose, and a small grunt left her chest as she inhaled the scent.

She pressed up against Nyssa as they rode, the woman's body radiating heat, reassuring her that they were, somehow, still very much alive.

GOOD INTENTIONS

Nyssa pulled the collar of her cloak up, wrapping her dark-gray scarf tighter around her neck and chin, moving as fast as her healing body would allow. Large snowflakes lazily fell on her and Bacon. She tried to keep her teeth from chattering, missing Quinn as a riding companion. She had gotten used to the heat from Quinn's body keeping her warm.

Nyssa had assured Quinn she could ride on her own after they camped the first night out from the mill. A hot meal and a night's rest had done wonders. Though her body was sore, relief had flooded through Nyssa when she gingerly moved her right arm and hand without much issue. They had mended properly—and Nyssa had to bite the inside of her cheek to keep from crying. Losing use of her dominant arm would have devastated her.

As they rode, she stared down at the ring she wore on her left hand, slowly rotating it as she replayed her argument with Athen. In the moment, she had forgotten that he lost Eron too. She swallowed hard. The two of them always stuck close to one another, of one mind about most things. How disappointed in her was Athen now?

Running her thumb along the Kraken engraving, an ache for the sea overtook her. She wished she could go with Quinn, escape to wherever Elias could take them, but now she had to stand on her own.

The journey back to Ocean's Rest was slow. The terrain was harder to navigate as they followed the stream eastward. Bare trees swayed and creaked above them while they rode, the lonely Blackcherry Forest the only witness to their travels.

Nyssa had taken off her Ashcloak insignia and slipped it into her jacket, sad to have only worn it less than a week before betraying the Order. As they traveled, she planned out what to do when they got to Ocean's Rest, filling Quinn in on the essential details, but not telling her she intended to stay and make Ceril answer for his crimes. Nyssa had honored her guild's oath. The Justiciars would have to listen to her.

She *needed* them to listen.

Her first instinct was to ride to Arcton Citadel and kill Ceril. She wouldn't have gotten far at all, forfeiting her own life at the altar of her anger over Eron's death. And in retribution for the scars on Quinn's back. The intensity of her feelings for a woman she had known a little over a month made no sense, but Nyssa never had anyone in her life that she had to protect. Quinn fit her need to be the woman Eron raised her to be: a warrior who faced danger on behalf of others.

But there was something more—a pull to the dark-haired fugitive that Nyssa couldn't explain.

As dusk fell on the third day of their journey back to Ocean's Rest, the two women settled in for the night. Quinn made tea from the needles of skull brush, plentiful at the base of trees in the forest. It tasted like dirt and moss, but it dulled Nyssa's lingering pain.

Nyssa took her small, leatherbound notebook out of her jacket and opened it to the page where she had tucked the chromoimage of her and Eron. The smile on his face made her chest tighten with grief. When she felt Quinn's eyes on her, she closed her book and put it back in its inner pocket, safe and secure.

"How are you feeling?" Quinn asked.

"Sore as fuck, but alive. You saved my arm."

Quinn smiled, her face soft. She was beautiful, unguarded. Though stunning when surly as well—Nyssa remembered Quinn's fury in Jejin, her green eyes blazing with indignation, ready to challenge Nyssa at every turn. There was an excitement to being challenged. She liked being kept on her toes.

Quinn poked at the fire, Winter's Bite lying across her lap.

"You know how to use a sword?" Nyssa asked.

Quinn shook her head. "Not in the least. I'm scared I'll slice my own fingers off."

Nyssa chuckled. "Winter's Bite looks good on you. You should learn the basics—to preserve your fingers and all. And a woman who knows how to handle a sword is a turn-on. I guarantee I'm at least fifty percent sexier with Winter's Bite in my hand."

Color rose on Quinn's cheeks, and Nyssa grinned in satisfaction. Flirting with Quinn had its small pleasures. She lay back, resting her head on her pack, pulling her cloak around her to stay warm.

"I wouldn't mind learning," Quinn said quietly. "How to use a sword."

"I happen to know a pretty decent swordswoman who could give you a pointer or two." Nyssa caught a sly smile from Quinn out of the corner of her eye. "Let's get some sleep. We should reach Ocean's Rest tomorrow. We'll go in the north gate and find Crae's Alehouse."

Quinn nodded and stoked the fire before lying down, softly humming under her breath.

After a moment's thought, Nyssa asked, "Hey, can you do me a favor?"

"Hmm?"

"If I start...talking in my sleep again, will you wake me?"

"Of course."

Nyssa watched the stars through the bare branches of the trees above her, and when she fell asleep, she dreamt of water quietly lapping against the hull of a ship.

Nyssa and Quinn entered Ocean's Rest through the north gate and found Crae's Alehouse near the docks. The bar had the look of an old fishing boat, its paint worn and sun-beaten. The interior was warm and ruddy, smelling of pine and cedar. And roast chicken.

Nyssa's stomach grumbled as she sidled up to the bar and slid Elias's coin toward the bartender. The place was empty, but it was midmorning. No doubt it got crowded at night, the drinks flowing. She swallowed. A cold beer sounded wonderful.

"Eh, what's this?" the bartender asked, glancing at the coin. "That ain't Imperial currency."

With a frown, she picked it up. "It's not for drink. I need to contact Elias."

"Lemme see that again, girl." The man furrowed his giant, bushy white eyebrows at her.

Nyssa tossed him the coin. He caught it and took a closer look. "Ah. I haven't seen one of these in a while. Friends of Elias are welcome here. Follow me."

The bartender moved down the craggy bar, which looked as if someone had cut it from an oak tree, given it a light sanding, and set it up in Crae's Alehouse. Hundreds of bottles lined the shelves behind the bar, their colors deep and rich. Nyssa turned and nodded for Quinn to follow. The man stepped out from behind the bar and continued toward a back room, opening its door and waving the two of them through. Nyssa limped after him, her leg still healing from Quinn's dagger.

The small room, filled with shelves holding bottles of liquor, had a tiny desk in the back corner. Nyssa spotted a gold bowl on the desk, its interior charred with ash. A messenger bowl, like the one in Pol's office.

"Sit, sit," the man said, waving her over. "You two looking to get out of here on the sly? You seem a bit sketchy, if I do say so. Looking over your shoulder every second is a dead giveaway."

"Something like that. You'll keep that to yourself."

"Eh, your business is your business. I know enough about Elias and the company he keeps not to ask questions. He pays me well to keep my mouth shut. I'm Crae." The man smiled at Nyssa. He was missing a good amount of teeth.

"So, how does this work? I want to get out of here quickly."

"That coin there moves you to the front of the line with Elias. He'll sail back as fast as he can. Thing is, he won't dock here. A bit of heat in Ocean's Rest for ol' Elias, yeah? He'll send his men to pick you up in a tender."

Crae pulled out a piece of paper and began writing. "Names?"

Nyssa looked back at Quinn. They had no other option but to trust him. "Nyssa Blacksea, and Quinn."

He nodded. When he finished the message, he let Nyssa read it before he lit up his messenger bowl.

A low, growling voice emanated from the flame. "A bit early to wake. We await. Destination?"

"It's almost noon, ya lazy twat."

"Rude. Destination?"

"Elias on Hannah's Whisper."

"Elias on Hannah's Whisper. Please give us your message. We will consume," the bowl replied, its flame flickering back and forth.

Crae dropped the letter into the vessel, and the paper turned to ash in the flame, its writing rising in smoky tendrils above the bowl before the fire died down. "We have sent your message. Back to sleep."

Crae nodded at the women and rubbed his hands together. "Now, you two look like you could use a room and some food and drink. I've seen half-dead cats with more life in 'em."

Quinn let out a chuckle.

"How much for one room for a night?" Nyssa asked. She didn't know if their money would last for their stay.

Crae frowned. "Elias's friends stay for free. Eat and drink for free. He pays well for accommodations and discretion. And a sword or two at your back if you need it. Though by the looks of it, you can handle yourself in a scrape, yeah?"

She smirked. "Barely. You know any healers? I need a little pick-me-up."

"Yeah, you look rough. Ivory Triad's got healers. I'll send for one. They're discrete. C'mon, let's get you up to a room. I've got a girl who can get you food and some whiskey and fresh clothes," Crae said. "No touchies, though. My boys and girls aren't for gropers. I'll cut yer fingers off."

"Crae, do I look like a groper?" Nyssa asked. She caught a slight smirk on Quinn's face out of the corner of her eye.

He looked from Nyssa to Quinn and back. "I give everyone the same warning. Ol' Crae runs a tight ship. Hard to keep good help if you don't protect 'em."

As Crae called for one of his employees, Quinn turned to Nyssa. "When we're back on the ship, where should we go?"

Nyssa paused. She had planned to stay and answer for her actions, but it wasn't the right time to let Quinn know. *That's a fight for another day.* "Well, I suppose we ought to let Elias give us some guidance on that," she said, avoiding eye contact with Quinn.

"Good idea," she replied.

Nyssa nodded and looked down at her hands. As long as Quinn was safe, she could face the Justiciars and make Ceril pay for Eron's death.

Nyssa and Quinn holed up at Crae's Alehouse to rest and heal. The Ivory Triad healer did a good job reforming and restitching Nyssa's shoulder and forearm to remove the scars. The whole process was extremely painful, and the healer had her bite down on a wooden spoon that had its fair share of teeth marks on it. A dose of painkiller and a good bit of rum helped after the healer left.

Her leg, however, still nagged at her.

When they heard back from Elias, they found that Hannah's Whisper was only a few days away from Ocean's Rest. Quinn welcomed the news, eager to leave, and Nyssa did her best to mirror her relief, but she secretly dreaded what she had to do.

Days later, when Elias was scheduled to arrive, Nyssa put on a brave face, doing her best to hide her sadness. And fear.

As they gathered at the end of the bar to say their farewells to Crae, they thanked him and his people for their hospitality. He and his staff treated them well, keeping them safe and their bellies full.

"It was our pleasure. They'll be waiting at the single boat slips, end of the northern docks. When you see Elias, tell that old twat that I'd like to see his face around here again before I die," Crae said.

Nyssa took a deep breath. "One more thing. Can you get a couple of your men to take Quinn to the docks and watch over her while she waits on the tender?"

Quinn turned to Nyssa, confused. "What's going on?"

Nyssa met her gaze. "I'm not going with you." It was surprisingly painful to tell Quinn the truth.

Concern overtook Quinn's features. Then came the anger. "What the fuck are you talking about?"

"I have to answer for my actions. And make Ceril answer for his. He had Eron killed."

Quinn grabbed Nyssa's arms. "Are you insane? You'll be answering to a Justiciar and leveling accusations against Ceril that you can't prove. You're forfeiting your life, do you understand that?"

Nyssa swallowed hard. "I upheld my oath to protect a fellow adept. That has to count for something."

Quinn shook her head, her eyes filling with tears. "You still don't get it, do you? That oath you took is meaningless. They pick and choose how to honor oaths, which laws to follow, which adepts to value. Please, don't do this."

Nyssa looked to Crae. "Have your men get her to the docks."

"Don't you fucking move, old man," Quinn hissed, shooting him a look that could still a ghost before turning back. "Nyssa, don't make me beg. Please. They'll kill you. I can't—" Quinn shook her head, her emerald eyes piercing into Nyssa. "What are the right words to convince you to come with me? Tell me what they are and I'll say them!"

Nyssa braced Quinn's face between her hands, her stomach tightening. "I have to do this. I'm sorry. It has—"

She stopped cold when Quinn's expression changed—her eyes widened as her gaze shifted over Nyssa's shoulder. Nyssa let go and spun around. A small group of Justiciars stood in the alehouse's doorway, their stark white masks sending a spike of cold fear down Nyssa's spine.

A woman she recognized stood in their company.

"Reece?" Nyssa gasped, stunned.

A bright flash of light hit Nyssa and Quinn, knocking them off their feet. Nyssa clawed at the floor, blinking the stars out of her eyes, trying to get her bearings, her ears ringing and thoughts tumbling. Hands grabbed at her, dragged her to her feet. Someone removed her sword from her back. They pushed her into the bar and wrestled her arms behind her. Quinn struggled and cursed beside her. Nyssa tried to fight her attackers, but they shoved her face down and held it down on the top of the bar.

"Let her up," a deep voice said from behind her.

A hand threaded into Nyssa's hair, pulling her head up and yanking her away from the bar. A tall male Justiciar stood before her, and next to him was Reece. He had his hand on the back of Reece's neck, and he turned to her and spoke. "You have done well, empath. Your suffering was worth it."

Nyssa looked at Reece. Her face was streaked with dried tears, but her eyes were empty, staring into nothingness. The Justiciar took his hand off her neck, and she crumpled to the ground in a heap.

"Reece!" Nyssa yelled, struggling against the Justiciars restraining her. "What did you do to her?"

"What I needed to do to find you, adept. You have taken something that didn't belong to you," he said, his eyes moving to Quinn. "Let me see her."

A Justiciar pushed Quinn forward, and Nyssa turned to look at her, her eyes immediately drawn to the collar around her neck. A void collar. The sight of it made her tense, hating it after knowing how long she had been forced to wear one.

"What a troublesome adept you have proven to be." The Justiciar gave Quinn a cruel smile, and it made Nyssa want to slide her sword across his throat. "It took us a couple days to find you two once we suspected you were here, Blacksea. Your empath friend can only sense you when you're relatively close, and Ocean's Rest is a large city. She wouldn't cooperate at first. Such a spirited woman. She made it more painful for herself than it needed to be."

Nyssa struggled again, attempting to lunge at the man, and he grabbed her by the throat. "Here's a taste." A tearing pain assaulted her brain, as if it was being pulled apart, and she felt the Justiciar in her head. Nyssa cried out, and the Justiciar leaned forward.

"What a good friend she must be to fight so hard against me," he breathed in her ear before releasing her. A wave of bitter cold streaked through her body, and her stomach lurched. She couldn't stop the whimper that escaped her lips.

"Master Justiciar Elken, we're ready for transport," a familiar voice said. Nyssa looked up to see Justiciar Medias's red eyes staring at her.

"Good," Elken replied. "Take these three."

Justiciars surrounded Nyssa, and she glanced over at Crae, who cowered behind the bar. Elken turned toward him. Her heart jumped in her throat.

Please don't hurt him.

"Good afternoon to you all," Elken said with a slight bow. A coin flashed in the air and skittered across the bar. "For your troubles."

A large Justiciar picked up Reece and slung her over his shoulder while the others pushed Nyssa and Quinn to move. Nyssa mouthed, "I'm sorry" to Crae as they were prodded forward.

Elken turned to the women. "Let's get you back to Ocean's Keep. You have much to answer for."

THE UNWORTHY

The main courtyard of Ocean's Keep was silent while the Justiciars removed Nyssa, Quinn, and Reece from the carriage used to transport them. The Keep's guards and attendants stood straight and still, their eyes downcast. Justiciars walked Nyssa and Quinn through the front door, pushing them along.

When Nyssa saw Lilliana, Athen, and Aryis standing and waiting with grim faces, her breath caught in her throat.

Athen approached the Justiciar carrying Reece. "Give her to me," he demanded. He gently took her in his arms, and she let out a low moan.

Nyssa gritted her teeth. How she would love to hurt the Justiciars for what they did to Reece.

Elken spoke up. "Take her to her room. She needs rest now. She served me well."

Athen shot Master Justiciar Elken a look full of fire and murderous intent, and Nyssa was glad Elken seemed to miss it. Aryis followed him, looking after Reece.

"You have caused everyone a great deal of trouble, Nyssa Blacksea," a voice said. Arch Master Anelos strode down the hall toward them. "You took my adept from me. It's time to answer for your crimes. Come."

The Justiciars pushed them forward, following Ceril to the Keep's Great Room. It was empty, tables and chairs moved to the side to clear an ample space in the center. Nyssa had spent a night or two here in a raucous game of cards, taking money from the Keep's friendly residents. Now, the room was void of any cheer.

Afternoon light streamed through the giant windows, dust floating in its beams, but Nyssa didn't feel any warmth. Here they would face judgment, amidst old tapestries, eclectic artwork, and worn books that rested peacefully on the bookshelves that lined the side walls. Even the homey smell of dried flowers and scented candles was missing, all manner of comfort squeezed out of the room by the Justiciars' purpose.

Lilliana stood off to the side, her face inscrutable as Elken and Medias stepped aside to confer with one another—Medias's red eyes unwavering from Nyssa. The other Justiciars fanned out on both sides, flanking Nyssa and Quinn.

Nyssa looked over at Quinn, who was paler than usual. "I'm sorry," she whispered.

Quinn offered a wistful smile. "No one else would have come for me, Nyssa. Thank you."

Several excruciating minutes passed before Ceril walked toward them, and a ball of dread formed in the pit of Nyssa's stomach, weighing her down, growing heavier at his approach. His pale-blue eyes scanned her up and down before glancing over to Quinn.

"Why Eron?" Nyssa asked. "He didn't deserve to die."

Ceril drew closer to her and smiled, his voice low so no one would overhear. "He deserved worse, choosing you over his duty."

The small measure of restraint within Nyssa threatened to snap until she felt a hand on her arm, pulling her out of her murderous thoughts. Quinn looked up at her. "Don't."

"Enjoy what remains of your short, crude life," Ceril whispered before backing away from them to join Elken and Medias.

Elken looked past the two women. "Come. I want the scions of this Empire to see what Imperial justice looks like."

Nyssa turned to see Aryis and Athen hovering in the doorway.

"I said come forward," Elken commanded.

Athen and Aryis moved quickly, joining Lilliana off at the side of the room. A Justiciar closed the doors and glided his hands across their surface. The etchings of a ward sprang to life, shimmering with light. The air hissed for a moment before the ward faded into the doors, sealing them in the room without chance of interruption. Or escape.

Master Justiciar Elken stepped forward. "Ambershine and the Emerald Order, the two oldest guilds in the Areshi Empire, the only two who bestow titles of honor upon their members when they come of age. Justiciar and Ashcloak. It gives me no pleasure to stand here in judgment of you today, Ashcloak Blacksea." He looked around the room. "Seven Justiciars—the eyes, ears, and will of the Empress—all here because of one magickless girl and one very lost adept. You have both betrayed your guilds, broken your oaths. Blacksea, do you even remember the words?"

Nyssa scowled at him and spoke.

"To my brothers and sisters, my bond.
To my guild, my fidelity.
To my Empire, my blood.
Stand fast. Face the darkness. Fall without fear."

"Do those words mean anything to you?" Elken asked.

"I've repeated them to myself every night since I could understand their meaning. I upheld my oath." She held her head high.

"Well, that will go on your gravestone," Ceril scoffed.

"I honored that oath. Can you say the same for yourself?" Nyssa asked, digging her nails into her palms.

The Justiciars around the room looked at one another, a low rumble of anger spreading among them.

"You should measure your words carefully, Ashcloak. You're speaking to the Arch Master," Elken warned.

She didn't give a floating fuck about his new title. "Ask Ceril about the wraith attack. Ask him about sending Obsidian Rule adepts to assassinate Eron." The words tumbled out of her, inelegant and desperate. But they were the truth.

"You are leveling very serious charges against the Arch Master," Elken said.

"Ask him!"

"I will not justify your—"

Ceril held up his hand. "I have nothing to hide. And I assure you, I don't order Rule adepts about. Are you accusing me of sending wraiths to attack you? Of assassinating a First Master? Eron was my friend."

Disavowing any knowledge of Tann and Efla was expected. But claiming Eron as a friend burned at her. *That* was the lie that made her tremble.

Quinn took an unsteady step forward. "Do they know you study forbidden magick?" She looked at Elken. "I know this because he used me to suppress the wards on the Alabaster Books."

The Justiciars around the room remained silent, but they glanced at the Arch Master.

Ceril laughed. "I welcome any of the Justiciars present to question the Masters or adepts at Arcton Citadel. Question the vault wardens. Ask them if they've ever seen me so much as touch a forbidden book or relic. Arcton Citadel protects the Empire by locking those items away, keeping them from the world. I take that responsibility seriously."

Nyssa shook her head. He had a lie for *everything*. "The wraiths…you created them! The blood wraith called me a 'magickless whelp.' Those are *your* words."

Ceril's eyes flicked over to Quinn.

"These accusations, do you have proof?" Master Justiciar Elken asked, stepping forward.

Part of the proof lay on Quinn's back, evidence of Ceril's cruelty, of breaking a guild rule that forbade physical punishment, but Nyssa would not break her promise to Quinn.

"There are too many coincidences that don't—"

"So no," Elken said.

She opened her mouth, feeling the eyes of everyone on her, but couldn't give them what they asked for.

Quinn spoke up, pulling at the bottom of her sweater. "I have proof."

Nyssa reached out and stopped her. "They won't care. I see that now. Don't give them this."

"I have to try," Quinn replied before addressing Elken. "The guilds have laws against physical punishment. Ceril broke those laws. He kept me in a void collar from the age of sixteen. And he took a whip to me."

Quinn turned around and lifted the back of her sweater, revealing the scars crisscrossing her lower back. Across the room, Aryis let out a gasp.

"Do you have a witness to this act?" Elken asked.

"A witness?" Quinn asked, her voice strained. "Who else would do this?"

Elken shook his head. "Then you make another baseless accusation."

Quinn turned to Nyssa, her eyes filling with tears as she searched Nyssa's face, perhaps for hope, for a solution.

She could offer none.

Ceril sighed and crossed his arms, shaking his head as if he were sad. Nyssa knew it was a show. This spectacle must've delighted him.

"Quinn is obviously lost and confused. I take responsibility for her welfare. But the other one...Blacksea, I had hoped you would prove of some value to the Emerald Order, to save face for Master Eron, but you betray your guild and the Ashcloaks. You dishonor your First Master's memory," Ceril said.

Nyssa sucked in a breath. "Don't you dare speak about my father," she spat, balling up her fists.

"Father? You are an orphan he took in, nothing more. You proved to be what we all feared—a failed experiment. Your lack of magick was problem enough, but your betrayal of the principles Eron taught you is the most striking disappointment."

Swallowing back a lump in her throat, Nyssa met Ceril's stare. "I've put up with everything that's been thrown at me, enduring the insults, the bullying, the pain. I did everything I was asked to do, and I excelled. I earned my place, me, the magickless whelp. And do you want to know what I felt when I was finally recognized and rewarded, becoming an Ashcloak? *Empty*. It was meaningless."

Ceril shook his head. "The guilds are a shining example of Imperial excellence. You ignore our laws and buck against the system that gave you everything you have. You could have served with a small modicum of distinction, but you threw it all away instead of knowing your place."

Nyssa exhaled a rueful laugh. "My place? What place? I never fit in. I never could. And I don't care to anymore. I learned too late that what the Empire wants of me is not who I am." She lifted her chin and squared her shoulders. "Eron taught me to protect others. This whole corrupt system would have me hurt a good woman to prove my loyalty. If that's what you want, someone who will betray their own honor, you're surrounded by bootlicks who will do just that. But that's not me. It will *never* be me."

Nyssa exhaled and looked over at Quinn. "I should have let you go in Jejin. I'm so sorry," she whispered, choking on a sob. "What have I done?"

"I'm glad you didn't let me go," Quinn said, a sad smile on her face. "That blood wraith would have killed you if I weren't there. You obviously needed me."

Nyssa expelled a surprised laugh. *This woman...this strange woman...*

"It's time for judgment, Nyssa Blacksea," Elken announced. "Justiciar Medias, you have dealt with this one in the past. What say you about her fate?"

Medias approached Nyssa, her red eyes boring into her. "When we first met, I remember telling you that one day you'd have to make a choice about what's important to you. I think now is the perfect time."

Nyssa swallowed as Medias circled her.

"One of you dies and one of you lives. You decide, Blacksea. Who should die so that one of you may survive this day?"

Quinn gasped. Nyssa blinked, her mind reeling.

"This is not what we agreed to!" Ceril protested. "Blacksea dies and I get Quinn back."

Medias stood behind Nyssa and let out a long sigh. "Justiciars do not answer to you, Arch Master. What you want isn't relevant."

"Quinn's magick is rare," Ceril said. "We shouldn't waste—"

"This is not your decision," Elken said. "Proceed Justiciar Medias."

Ceril stared at Elken, the muscles in his jaw twitching.

Medias's hand settled on Nyssa's shoulder, making her flinch. "Choose, Blacksea. One of you dies today."

The choice was impossible. Cruel. "Why are you doing this?" Nyssa asked.

Medias stared at her. "What is your decision?"

Nyssa's heartbeat pounded in her ears, and she closed her eyes, willing herself to become still, drawing upon what Eron had taught her. She tried to remember the moment of her death under the waves of the Black Sea. Amidst the panic and fear, there was a strange, fleeting calm, like the embrace of an endless night. She drew the moment back to herself and in it, she found peace. And freedom.

Exhaling, Nyssa looked over at Quinn and offered the bravest smile she could muster despite the fear writhing in her guts. Quinn's eyes went wide. "Nyssa, please don't!"

"I won't betray you. Or myself," she said to Quinn. Swallowing the hard lump in her throat, Nyssa uttered words she could never take back. "I renounce my allegiance to the Emerald Order and to the Empire. I renounce the Empress. I renounce every single one of you. I choose death."

"No..." Quinn whispered.

Athen and Aryis raised their voices in protest, their words falling away from Nyssa as the weight of her decision made her legs tremble. Medias smiled and squeezed her shoulder. Nyssa wanted to tear her apart, wishing she could take Medias with her in death.

"Satisfied, Medias?" Justiciar Elken asked.

"Stubborn to the end," Medias remarked, taking leave of Nyssa and walking back to join Elken. "Ashcloak Blacksea, step forward."

Nyssa did as Medias asked, hoping her legs wouldn't give way.

Medias clasped her hands behind her back. "Nyssa Blacksea, you are a traitor to your guild, the Empress, and the Areshi Empire. You have asked for death, but for your crimes, death is a kindness. Instead, you will serve as a living reminder of the price of betrayal. You shall be marked Unworthy."

Unworthy.

The word lashed at her, like plunging into the Black Sea all over again, cold and shocking. No one had been marked in over a century. Unworthy were scorned and hated, abandoned by all. Not even Athen or Lilliana could offer her refuge.

"I-I don't understand," Nyssa whispered.

Medias approached her. "I wanted to see if you had learned anything from your mistakes. To see if you would choose to live, to give yourself back to us, back to the Empire. But you didn't. Now you will be punished as a traitor."

Nyssa balled up her fists. "You fucking monster."

With an unwavering stare, Medias held out her hand. "Surrender your guild sigil."

Nyssa reached inside her jacket and fingered her Ashcloak pin. Taking it out, she flicked it at Medias. The pin hit the Justiciar in her chest and fell, clinking against the cold marble floor. Medias picked it up and slipped it in a pocket, training her red eyes on Nyssa.

"Nyssa Blacksea, orphan of the Emerald Order and fallen Ashcloak, under the gaze and authority of our Empress, I declare you Unworthy. Your service to your guild and to the Empire has come to an end. On this day, you become a shadow, and you will live as such until you pass from this earth."

Medias stepped toward Nyssa. "On your knees."

"Please don't do this!" Athen yelled.

Lilliana put her arm around him. "They will kill you if you interfere."

Nyssa looked at Athen and Aryis, scared for their safety if they defended her. "I'll be okay." She tried to give them a reassuring smile, but her voice betrayed her fear.

"Nyssa..." Athen's eyes pleaded with her.

She shook her head, tears forming. "Athen, please. Don't give them a reason to hurt you." She looked at Aryis. "You too, Little Hawk. I'll be okay."

She turned back to face Justiciar Medias.

"On your knees," Medias repeated.

Nyssa clenched her jaw, her hands forming fists at her sides, refusing to comply. She wouldn't willingly bow to these monsters.

Elken gestured to her, and two Justiciars stepped forward. Nyssa glanced at Quinn. Her emerald eyes were full of anger.

The Justiciars grabbed Nyssa's arms, and she tried pulling out of their grasp until an invisible force pushed down on her. A Justiciar held his hand out toward her, palm facing downward, and Nyssa grunted when he forced her to her knees. The other Justiciars braced her shoulders.

Medias reached inside her dark-red jacket and revealed a short knife. Nyssa struggled again, and the Justiciars tightened their grip, their fingers digging into her shoulders.

Medias stalked toward Nyssa until she loomed over her. "Look at me."

Nyssa tilted her head back, staring at her, breath quickening. She would not flinch. Justiciar Medias gazed down at her. "This will be painful. Ready yourself," she said. Medias lifted her eyes to the other Justiciars. "Hold her still." Fingers laced themselves in Nyssa's hair to hold her firm.

Medias leaned over, placed the dagger beneath Nyssa's lower lip, and pushed the tip in. Searing pain exploded from her chin and radiated throughout her body, magick mixing with the sharp splitting sting of the knife. As Medias slowly carved the blade down her chin, Nyssa cried out. The cut burned, not unlike the poison of the blood wraith. Pain radiated through her body, forcing her to tense up, until all her bones felt as though they'd snap. Tears stung her eyes, and a shrill, high-pitched drone filled her ears as warm blood spilled down her chin and neck.

When she finished cutting, Medias straightened up. The blade of her dagger glowed white-hot, streaks of blood sizzling on the bright metal. She reached in her jacket and pulled out a black cloth, running it along the dagger. As she did, the pain from Nyssa's cut receded, replaced by a cold sensation, like dipping glowing hot metal into water to temper it. All of her muscles relaxed, a chill washing over her, and she exhaled, her head lolling forward, thankful to be free of the pain.

The Justiciars yanked Nyssa to her feet, and she stumbled, her legs and arms numb as if pulled from freezing water. She tried to reach up and feel her chin, but her limbs wouldn't cooperate with her brain. An arm hooked around her, steadying her.

"You're okay," Quinn said. The reassurance helped drag Nyssa out of her daze, and she fought to center herself.

"And now for you," Justiciar Elken said to Quinn.

Ceril cleared his throat. "I would have her returned to Arcton Citadel. She still has use."

Elken shook his head. "Quinn is no longer your adept."

Ceril stepped to Elken. "The hell she isn't. She belongs to me!"

Elken let out an amused laugh. "She belongs to the Empress, and we are her judgment. Quinn's magick is unnatural. Dangerous. And you've proved you can't control her."

"I am the Arch Master now. I have a say here."

"I assure you, you do not. This order comes from the Empress herself." Elken turned to the women. "Quinn, orphan of Arcton Citadel, under the gaze and authority of our Empress, I sentence you to death."

Quinn cried out. Justiciar Elken gestured at her, and two Justiciars grabbed her arms. Nyssa rushed forward to stop them, but Medias pulled her back.

"I have spared your life," she said, her voice low. "Would you risk that for someone you barely know?"

Nyssa turned to her, meeting her gaze. "Yes," she whispered. A maddening smile curled the Justiciar's lips, and Nyssa exhaled, her thoughts racing, her pulse pounding in her ears.

The Justiciars pushed Quinn to her knees, and Elken drew the sword he wore at his waist. Nyssa's life had been spared, but Quinn would die for daring to stand apart and escape her oppressors.

"Please don't do this!" Quinn yelled. Her head swiveled to Nyssa, eyes filled with tears and rage.

Elken raised his sword, poised to plunge it into Quinn's chest. Nyssa shoved Medias aside and hurled herself toward him.

The Master Justiciar jolted backward, mouth falling open, sword clattering to the floor. Nyssa held fast to the blade stuck between his ribs, swiped in a blur from the scabbard of one of Quinn's captors. Elken raised his head to meet Nyssa's stare. She snarled and shoved the blade deeper into his chest.

The light drained from Elken's eyes as his hot blood splashed Nyssa's hands. She yanked the blade out of his body and pushed him away from her. He collapsed to the floor with a dull thud. The Justiciars holding onto Quinn let go of her and backed away, stunned by their Master's death.

Nyssa held the stolen weapon up and whipped her arm down, forcefully flicking the tip toward the ground. The blood on its blade spattered the white marble floor.

She captured Quinn in her gaze. "You will not beg for your life." Rage surged through every last inch of Nyssa. She knew she was dead, but she had to fight. *Needed* to fight. It was the only power she had left. Everything Nyssa believed in had crumbled and fallen away.

There was nothing left but herself.

"Both of your miserable lives are forfeit," Ceril spat.

Nyssa stepped back toward Quinn and reached down to pull her to her feet.

Quinn grabbed hold of Nyssa's arm and shook her. "What did you do? They were going to let you live!"

"I couldn't watch you die," Nyssa replied. Out of the corner of her eye, the Justiciars shifted slowly to surround them.

She turned toward Ceril. "I'm going to kill you next." Her voice was cold and steady, the opposite of the fear quaking in her bones.

Nyssa scanned the Justiciars' faces, noting their distance from her and how they held their weapons. She was prepared to fight, but against six Justiciars, she maybe had a chance to fell one or two of them before they killed her.

She sighed and dropped her head. Blood stained the front of her shirt and stuck to her skin. She wiped the back of her hand across her chin, surprised that the mark had already healed over.

"I'm sorry I couldn't save us." Nyssa turned her gaze to Quinn, the lack of fear she saw surprised her. Quinn stood tall, resolute.

A fine way to meet death.

Nyssa straightened.

Quinn reached out, gently touching Nyssa's marked chin. Her touch was light. And exciting. *Electric.* "You didn't deserve this," she said, her eyes drawn to the mark.

Justiciars moved around them, collapsing the circle, and Nyssa closed her eyes and exhaled.

"When the wraiths come again—and they will—there will be a part of you that wonders if Ceril is responsible. Because now he knows he can do anything and you'll protect him." Nyssa opened her eyes and glanced from one Justiciar to the next.

"You're going to die today," Ceril said from behind the safety of the ring of Justiciars.

"You are fucking pathetic, Ceril," Nyssa growled. "A small man who lusts after power he never deserved nor earned."

"And you are the worthless child of lowlife criminals. You should have followed your mother and father to the bottom of the sea."

Nyssa exhaled, her rage turning cold inside her, obliterating her self-control. Quinn gripped her arm.

The Justiciar behind Nyssa sprang toward her, drawing her attention and fury away from the Arch Master. A strangled, anguished roar left her chest and echoed throughout the Great Room. She whirled, flicking her blade across his throat, and he hit the floor, blood pulsing out of his neck. Another Justiciar rushed toward Quinn, her blade poised to strike.

Nyssa yanked Quinn back by the collar of her jacket and parried the Justiciar's sword. Nyssa stepped inside the Justiciar's guard and rammed the tip of her sword into her torso, then pushed the Justiciar away from her and watched her crumple to the ground.

Another Justiciar raised his hand toward Nyssa, and the air surrounding her constricted. Magick tightened around her throat, and she stumbled, trying to suck in a breath.

Quinn shouted as Nyssa's sword clattered to the ground. Nyssa reached for her throat but felt nothing, invisible bonds quickly choking the life out of her.

Justiciar Medias pulled Quinn away, and a second Justiciar forced her to her knees and unsheathed his sword, looking to make quick work of her execution. He loomed above Quinn and raised his sword.

Nyssa tried to move, to stop him, but magick bonds held her in place. As the sword arced toward Quinn's neck, Nyssa let out a cry of fury.

REBIRTH

Something deep inside Nyssa shifted and howled, as if all her bones shattered at once and released her fury. Every nerve ending crackled with raw, feral energy.

The Justiciar poised to kill Quinn stopped mid-stroke, his blade inches from Quinn's neck. Tendrils of lightning flowed from Nyssa's fingers into the Justiciar's chest. She gasped, bewildered.

Crackling bolts of blue energy stuck out of his chest, and he cried out, his face collapsing in pain. Nyssa closed her fist, and the lightning violently exploded, dropping the Justiciar where he stood.

She held up her hands, her mouth agape. Lightning arced between her fingers. Power, chaotic and unrestrained, coursed through her. The magick bonds holding her in place slipped away.

What is happening to me?

Voices rose around her, coming from all directions. Anger, fear, confusion.

Nyssa flicked her gaze to Justiciar Medias. A brilliant white orb glowed from the center of her chest, as if Nyssa could see inside the Justiciar—life and magick jumbled together, somehow visible. Nyssa rushed toward Medias to get her away from Quinn, and a burst of blue light erupted from her hands. Medias flew off her feet and tumbled across the stone floor.

"Nyssa?" Quinn gasped.

Nyssa extended a hand to her and hauled her to her feet. She touched the void collar circling Quinn's neck, its very existence a reminder of what Ceril had done. Its lock glowed blue and sparked, snapping open and falling from her neck.

Quinn grabbed Nyssa's hand, and a shock wave of power surged from Nyssa into Quinn and back again. A warmth, strange and comforting, spread through Nyssa's chest. Gasping, Quinn let go and stepped back. Her pupils glowed bright green, unlike anything Nyssa had ever seen.

"I'm sorry, I can't control this...are you okay?" Nyssa asked.

Quinn shook her head and turned her palms over. Shadows billowed out of her hands, flowing out of her like smoke, their tendrils coiling around her body.

"What's happening?" she asked, her eyes wide. Ethereal darkness rippled off of her, drifting in the air like drops of black ink in a glass of water, enshrouding her in shadow.

Nyssa's thoughts tumbled uselessly, jagged and confused. Nothing made sense, least of all how her body thrummed like a plucked string. She wanted to run, escape. But another desire pushed to the forefront.

A desire to see Ceril on his knees, begging for his life.

She bent over and picked up the sword she had taken from one of the Justiciars. Spinning to look for the Arch Master, she found him lurking behind two Justiciars.

"Stop them!" Ceril shouted.

A vibration crept across Nyssa's skin as the two Justiciars braced to attack her. She could feel something flare up inside them, a hum that reverberated in her gut, though she did not know how that was possible. A soft glow of pale green and yellow pulsed in their chests like fireflies.

Nyssa broke into a run toward them.

A brilliant flash of light burst from one of the Justiciar's hands, and Nyssa dropped, sliding under the large spear of pale green light that would've impaled her. It exploded against the wall, splintering wood.

The Justiciar balled his fists, rallying his magick to strike again. Nyssa sprang to her feet and closed the distance between them faster than he could respond. She drove her sword into his gut, shoving him to the ground, and he choked on the blood filling his mouth, his eyes wild with fear. Nyssa pushed herself to her feet, her breathing heavy and ragged, unable to look away from the man while he shuddered and died.

A hand grabbed her neck, and the world fell away from her, dropping her to her knees. Her stomach lurched and the room spun. She tried to grab her attacker, but her arms wouldn't obey.

She collapsed to the floor. The cold stone shocked her, and she rolled onto her back. A Justiciar knelt over her. Quinn stood behind him, one hand on his neck, her other pulling his arm away from Nyssa. Her eyes glowed with emerald light. The dark ribbons of magick that swirled around her hands dove into the Justiciar's body. She gritted her teeth, her face hard and cold.

A soft whimper left the Justiciar, and when Quinn lifted her hands off him, he dropped to the floor, his eyes blank.

Quinn's shoulders slumped, and her gaze shifted to Nyssa, who got to her feet despite the exhaustion wracking her body.

"Ceril," Nyssa said, her voice low and steady. He needed to die. She grasped her sword, turning her eyes to the Arch Master. Straightening, she took a deep breath and started toward him, her mind on revenge. His eyes went wide as he began to chant in a language she didn't understand, his hands weaving patterns in the air. A hum similar to the Justiciars' magick resonated in her gut.

The floor in front of Nyssa cracked and splintered, stone and marble erupting out of the ground as Ceril wove his spell. A titan formed in front of Nyssa's eyes, eight feet of hulking stone whirling into the rough shape of a man. Its featureless head turned to Nyssa, and it began ambling toward her.

She stumbled, and it reared up and swung a fist into the ground near her, smashing the floor with such force the ground trembled. Small bits of rock peppered Nyssa's face.

"Shit," she hissed, scrambling back. That thing could crush her with ease if it got closer.

Quinn stepped next to her, and the warm glow pulsing in Nyssa's chest intensified. Quinn grabbed her arm and started pulling her away from the stone construct lumbering toward them. The startling sensation of her touch made Nyssa gasp—their skin vibrated off of one another, electric. Quinn exhaled, scowling.

She must feel it too.

Quinn gestured at the stone titan. "That thing will kill us."

The stone monster took another step toward them, fast for its size, and swung its giant arm at them.

Quinn held up her hand. A spike of solid black shadow flew into the monster, shattering its arm, and Quinn yelped. Shards of rock splintered off. "How did I do that?" Quinn breathed.

The stone monster slowed, listing to the side of its missing arm. Ceril began weaving again, pale-gray magick twisting around his hands. Pieces of shattered stone floated up, re-forming the titan's arm.

"We need to go," Quinn said, pulling at Nyssa. "I don't know how to stop that thing."

Ceril stepped forward and shouted, "Run now, but you won't get far. You can never escape the reach of the Empire."

Nyssa snarled at him. "I'll kill every person you send after us. And then I'll come for you."

His confidence wavered, a flash of fear staining his features. He tried to hide it, but she knew uncertainty would gnaw at him, make him look for her in the shadows.

Good.

Nyssa backed up toward the Great Room's massive wooden doors, letting Quinn pull her along, keeping her eyes on Ceril and his stone creation re-forming its arm. They needed to get out fast.

Nyssa turned and ran to the door, locked down by a ward. She could see the magick, its intricate lines and symbols glowing red, but its structure continually shifted, changing patterns.

"There's a ward keeping it closed," Nyssa said. "I can see it, but I don't know what to do."

"I see it too." Quinn hurried past Nyssa and touched the door. Shadow wafted off of her and the colors of the magick faded, its patterns falling away like dying stars.

Nyssa turned to Athen and Aryis. Lilliana had a hand on both of them, holding them back. Protecting them. "I'm sorry," Nyssa said quietly before whirling back to Quinn.

"Go!" she ordered, shoving Quinn toward the door and pushing it open. The two of them spilled out into the hallway, then Nyssa grabbed Quinn's arm and ran toward the Fennick family wing of the Keep. "Get to my room. There's a way out on the balcony." Nyssa hoped she could remember the path to the north side of the city. If they could get to the docks, they might have a chance to catch Jerrin.

As they ran, the people they encountered flattened themselves against the walls, their mouths open in shock. Nyssa moved as fast as her leaden body could, bolting up the main stairs and down the hallway to their old suites. By the time they got to the door of her room, she couldn't catch her breath.

Quinn opened the door and pulled her inside.

"Are you okay?" she asked.

"I just need a moment...to rest," Nyssa replied. "I feel like I'm about to drop."

She held her trembling hands in front of her face, turning them over, watching blue arcs of lightning jump between her fingertips. "What is happening to me?"

"It's magick," Quinn said, walking over to her. "You're pulsing with it. Your eyes, Nyssa..."

Nyssa stumbled to the floor-length mirror next to the bed, her breath catching in her chest.

Impossible.

Her eyes glowed bright blue like they were on fire, and the scar down her face blazed with sapphire magick, like the lightning sparking off her fingers. Nyssa frantically pulled the collar of her shirt down. The poison scar glowed and pulsed with soft-blue radiance, and faint, cobalt sparks of lightning crackled along the surface of her skin.

Nyssa's eyes returned to her face, resting on the black line carved from her lip to the tip of her chin. Her once-white shirt was soaked with blood, her own mixed with the Justiciars' she had killed.

A wave of nausea hit, her stomach twisting at the thought of what she had done. She had killed. Struck out with a power she didn't understand.

Quinn stepped in front of the mirror, taking herself in. "What the hell is happening to us?" she whispered.

"We can figure out what the fuck is going on later. We need to get out of here before Ceril finds us." Nyssa looked back at herself in the mirror, staring at the mark on her chin forever branding her as Unworthy.

The door to the room clicked shut, and Nyssa and Quinn spun toward the noise. Reece slumped against the door, breathless, her eyes wide.

"Reece!" Nyssa said, rushing toward her. "Are you okay?"

Reece stared at Nyssa in awe. "I...I'm exhausted, but I'll be fine. This explains the explosion I felt in you."

"I don't know what's happening to me," Nyssa said, her voice breaking. Reece stepped forward and reached to take her hand.

Nyssa recoiled from her. "Stop! I could hurt you."

Reece shook her head. "I trust you." She took another step and grabbed Nyssa's hand, sending a jolt of energy through Nyssa at her touch. "The power. It's amazing," Reece gasped.

Her eyes moved to Nyssa's chin, and she gently caressed Nyssa's face. "Oh, Nyssa. I'm so sorry." She squeezed Nyssa's hand for a moment, her expression pained.

"What's wrong? Are you hurt?" Nyssa asked.

"You don't understand how bright and loud you are to me right now. I feel you vibrating through my whole body." Reece's eyes shifted to Quinn. "Both of you."

"What does that mean?" Quinn asked.

"Nyssa can explain later. Now, you have to get out of here. Come on." Reece pulled Nyssa out to the balcony, and Quinn followed. They hurried over to the hidden passageway, and Reece pushed the stones on the wall to open the entrance as Athen had the first night of Winter's Fire.

"Stop!" a voice commanded.

FATE UNRAVELS

Justiciar Medias stood at the balcony doors, a sheathed sword in hand. Nyssa closed the distance between them, throwing a fist across her face. Medias crumpled to the cold stone ground, her Justiciar's mask clattering next to her. Nyssa hissed and shook her hand out, hoping she didn't break a knuckle on the hard mask.

She knelt over Medias and studied her face. Her features were softer than expected. She was just a woman. A normal woman.

Nyssa pulled the sword scabbard from Medias's hand and scowled, confused.

Winter's Bite?

She drew her sword and held it to Medias's throat.

"Not very grateful to have your sword returned," Medias grunted.

"How many more of you do I need to kill?"

Medias coughed and grabbed Nyssa's wrist, sending a jolt through her. It had to be Medias's magick humming against her skin. "I foresaw today. What you'd become. And this, the moment of my death."

Quinn knelt next to Nyssa, rubbing her arms against the cold of the balcony. "You're a seer?"

Medias nodded. "Among other things, though no one knows of my foresight, save for my mother and now you three." Her red eyes shifted back to Nyssa. "Remember when I told you I might ask a favor of you?"

That moment had deeply unsettled Nyssa. "Yes."

"I've seen you kill me in my visions. On this balcony on this day, you draw your sword across my throat. But I'm begging you to change our fates. Spare my life."

"You can't change fate," Quinn countered.

Medias smirked. "In the sea, I watched Nyssa slip out of your grasp, lost forever to the deep, and somehow she's still alive because of you, her sword now at my throat. I witnessed your death at the hands of Master Justiciar Elken, and yet here you stand because Nyssa saved your life. I've seen fate unravel and re-form many times. It's fickle. You can bend it. Break it." Medias trailed her gaze to Nyssa. "And I'm asking you today to change your fate, Nyssa Blacksea."

Nyssa bowed her head, her thoughts in disarray. Leaving Medias alive posed a great danger. She could tell the others that Reece helped them escape. She could tell them which passageway they used to get out of the Keep. Trusting a Justiciar was risky—more than risky, it was insane. Yet, Nyssa couldn't get Medias's slight smile out of her head when she chose to sacrifice herself so Quinn could live.

She knew. She knew who I would choose.

Nyssa pressed her sword against the Justiciar's throat, small beads of blood dotting the blade. "Why did you give me a choice to live or die?"

"To see if you had grown to become the woman in my visions. And you did, Nyssa. You both did."

"You orchestrated what happened?"

"I could only do so much. I couldn't stop the mark. In the visions where you lived and saved Quinn, you bore the mark. Always. I couldn't risk changing that variable."

Nyssa clenched her teeth, remembering the burning pain of the mark. What it meant. The fear and derision it would carry with it.

She closed her eyes and exhaled, calming herself. Something inexplicable in her gut told her she could trust Medias. It was a huge risk, but one she had to take.

"I took lives today to save another, and I will continue to kill if I have to. But I'll spare you if you promise to protect the people I have to leave behind. Athen, Aryis, and Reece. As a Justiciar, you have power and influence. You cannot let the consequences of my actions touch them. And you must continue to keep them safe after this." Nyssa exhaled. "Give me your word and I'll let you live."

Medias peered at Nyssa. "I know what it's like to be different from everyone else, the pain it can cause. You have my word as a Justiciar. And as a woman who believes you did the right thing."

Nyssa scowled, surprised at Medias's words. She glanced up at Reece. "Is she telling the truth?"

"Justiciars are altered when they take the mask by some sort of drug. I can't read their emotions," Reece replied.

Nyssa stood and sheathed Winter's Bite, offering the Justiciar her hand and pulling her to her feet.

"I have no choice but to believe you. Never make me regret sparing your life. I'm entrusting my friends to you. I will kill you if you don't protect them."

Medias gave Nyssa a small smile, and she noticed the Justiciar's slight chin dimple for the first time. "I would wholly expect you to. Now go. The Keep's guards won't betray you, but Ceril will come searching for me if I don't return soon."

Nyssa looked to Quinn and pulled her sword over her back. "Ready?"

Quinn responded with a nod.

Nyssa felt a hand on her shoulder, and she turned to Reece.

"Here, use this to cover the mark." Reece took off the scarlet scarf she wore and wound it around Nyssa's neck and chin, then pulled Nyssa's jacket closed to cover her bloody shirt.

Nyssa touched the scarf and smiled sadly. It smelled of lavender. "I can't look like...well, this." Nyssa held up her hands, lightning dancing across her skin. "How do I make this stop?"

Medias spoke up. "They taught you everything you need at the Order. You use meditation as a warrior, but it's for magick too. Center yourself, regain your focus. Imagine drawing your magick back inside of you. Collapse it into the core of your being."

"You make it sound easy, and I have no fucking idea how to do it. Can you do it?" Nyssa asked of Quinn.

Quinn held a trembling hand up, and the dark tendrils floating around her withdrew, the green glow in her eyes receding.

"Figures," Nyssa mumbled.

Reece took her hands and squeezed. "Just concentrate and trust yourself."

Nyssa swallowed, but Reece's face was calm, reassuring. She exhaled and closed her eyes, trying to calm her mind. Doing as Medias said, she imagined the sails of Hannah's Whisper being furled, collapsed, and tied down, picturing the same with her newfound power. As she concentrated, she could feel her magick separate from the world and grow tighter, smaller, receding into her chest. The sensation was bizarre.

"Open your eyes," Reece whispered.

Nyssa slowly opened her eyes. The world looked normal again, and her hands were still and calm. Reece smiled at her. "Good girl."

"Reece—" Nyssa started, but her voice caught. "I'm so scared."

"I know."

Nyssa tried to smile. "Of course you do."

"I'm going to miss you, Nyssa. But we will see each other again, of that I am certain."

Reece stepped close to Nyssa and kissed her, pulling away as tears filled her eyes. Nyssa wrapped her in a hug. She didn't want to leave. She was scared of what came next. She didn't know what the future held for her without her friends, without the Order. Without Eron.

"Please tell Athen and Aryis I'm sorry," Nyssa said quietly.

"I'll tell them. You need to go," Reece replied, looking down at the entrance to the passageway in the balcony floor.

Nyssa started down the steps that led to the tunnels below the Keep. Quinn began to follow, but Reece placed a hand on her arm. Quinn turned, a puzzled look on her face.

"Protect Nyssa," Reece said softly. "And don't let her run."

"Run?"

Reece took in a big breath. "Just...be safe."

Quinn met her gaze and nodded. "I will."

The two women disappeared down the stairs. Reece took a deep breath and exhaled, wiping tears from her face. She turned and bent over to pick up the Justiciar's mask, handing it back to Medias.

The Justiciar reaffixed her mask. "I fully intend to honor my promise to Nyssa."

"Good. Because if you don't, I'll kill you myself," Reece replied coldly, crossing her arms. The idea of a Justiciar betraying her duty to the Empire to protect the friends of a marked traitor was unthinkable, but she had to trust Nyssa's judgment—even after the Justiciars made her track down Nyssa, subjecting her to pain that Medias was complicit in.

Anger simmered in her chest.

"You cannot tell anyone that I'm a seer. It's a secret that would get me killed," Medias said.

The gravity of that knowledge hit Reece—it gave her power over the Justiciar. But she would make no promises. "I know."

Medias grunted, and Reece clenched her jaw. Her inability to read Medias's emotions set her on edge. She could feel her presence, strangely soft and warm, but there were no emotions behind it.

Medias cocked her head, studying Reece. It was unnerving. After a moment, she spoke. "Do you know what they are?"

Reece blinked. She had guessed Nyssa was somehow different, but didn't understand why. And when she felt Quinn's presence as strongly as Nyssa's, she struggled to make sense of it. But seeing them together, with their glowing eyes, it became clear. Magick didn't manifest like that in anyone.

Not for a thousand years, if the stories were true.

"I can't believe..." Reece mumbled, peering down the dark stairwell that Nyssa and Quinn had descended before meeting the gaze of the Justiciar. A maddening sense of self-assuredness oozed off the woman.

Medias let a small smile alight on her lips, a strange sight for a Justiciar. They were all so very dour.

"My visions have shifted and changed in unexpected ways, often conflicting with one another. Those two defy fate. Refuse to be pinned down by it. They held true to the one vision I've had since I was a little girl—the violent birth of two Cursed Gods into the world," Medias said.

Cursed Gods...

Reece shook her head. It had been a millennium since that kind of Ancient Magick roamed the earth, chaotic and primal. The last of the Cursed Gods had been nightmarish pricks—arrogant, selfish, and deadly. She had read stories, knew the danger. The lore of god turning against god. Reece wondered if the two women were destined to furiously crash into one another and bring the world to its knees.

Another smile crossed the Justiciar's face.

"Why do you look so pleased with yourself?"

Medias sighed. "We fractured a strand of fate today, empath. It's now up to Nyssa and Quinn to shatter the rest."

Reece scowled. The woman spoke in annoying riddles. Reece turned to the switch in the wall and pressed her palm against it. Stone scraped against stone, and the dark tunnel Nyssa and Quinn had escaped down sealed shut.

"Let's sneak you back downstairs and make it look like your search for Nyssa came up short, Justiciar," Reece said.

Medias wiped the thin line of blood from her throat. "After you, empath."

Quinn lifted a lantern while she and Nyssa moved through the tunnel beneath Ocean's Keep as it grew wider, allowing them to walk side by side. Nyssa did her best to remember the way to the north side of the city, the one that she had taken with Athen, Aryis, and Reece the night of Winter's Fire to capture Quinn the first time. There was a sad irony to using the same tunnel to escape Ceril and the Empire with Quinn.

So much had happened in a short few months, the change in Nyssa startling. *What would Eron think seeing me branded a traitor and declared Unworthy? Would I have broken his heart?* Nyssa pushed the thought away and tamped her sadness down.

As they approached an intersection in the tunnel, a faint light bobbed up ahead. Quinn exhaled sharply and pushed Nyssa to the side of the tunnel, pressing her against the cold stone wall, and turned their lantern off, plunging them into darkness.

Nyssa tried to still her breathing, but she couldn't, her heart beating too fast.

"Nyssa?" a voice called out.

Athen.

She let out a deep sigh and leaned her head back against the wall, thankful to hear his voice.

"Can we trust him?" Quinn whispered.

The answer should have been immediate, but Nyssa hesitated, and she hated herself for the pause. "Yes."

Quinn switched the lantern back on, and Athen and Aryis approached them, cautious.

"I hoped you might remember the tunnels. Are you okay?" Athen asked.

Nyssa hung her head. A simple question with no good answer. "I don't think so. I have no idea what's happening."

"Nyssa, we can help," Athen replied, his golden eyes pleading with her—a look she had seen countless times. Whenever she got in trouble or in a fight, whenever she was close to her breaking point, he would try to pull her back, implore her to stay calm, rational.

She put her hand on his chest. "No, Athen, you need to be as far from me—from us—as possible. They'll kill both of you if they suspect you're helping us."

Athen shook his head. "I have to do something."

"No. I need to protect *you* now. Let me do that, Athen."

The look on his face broke Nyssa's heart. It was probably the last time they'd see each other for a very long time, and they both knew it.

"Come here." He pulled her into a hug. "I'm sorry for everything. You stay safe. Both of you. Take care of one another."

Aryis stepped forward with something in her hand. She held it out to Quinn. "Your book. I thought you might want it back."

Quinn reached for it, but stopped. "No. Keep it. You can use it to find us if you need to."

"Are you sure?"

"I'm not sure of anything," Quinn confessed, "but just keep it. Hide it."

Nyssa watched Quinn, knowing it must be hard for her to leave her book behind. The trust she was placing in Aryis went unspoken.

Aryis turned to Nyssa. "I wish this awful day didn't happen, but you did the right thing. I'm sorry I didn't believe you."

Nyssa teared up and gave Aryis a hug. "Take care of him, Little Hawk," she whispered into Aryis's ear before letting go and wiping at her face.

"We have to go," she said, hating the words as she spoke them. Hating that she needed to leave. "And you need to get back before Ceril starts asking questions."

Athen took a deep breath. "Goodbye, Nyssa." He put his arm around Aryis, and they walked back down the tunnel, their light diminishing until it disappeared around a dark corner.

Nyssa leaned back on the wall, willing it to hold her up, and she touched the mark on her face. Quinn reached forward and pulled her trembling hand gently away from her chin.

"That mark isn't who you are. You cast your own shadow today, Nyssa Blacksea. With great honor."

Even in the low light afforded by the lantern, Quinn's emerald eyes blazed with life.

Nyssa pressed off of the wall and grabbed Quinn's shoulder to steady herself. "You ready?"

Quinn nodded. "Yes."

They headed down the tunnel toward the exit that would lead them to the northern docks of Ocean's Rest. Nyssa just had to push herself a little further, not just for her sake, but for Quinn's as well—their fates were now tangled up together. They had to survive long enough to escape and get back on Hannah's Whisper.

Get back to the sea.

EPILOGUE

Suvi Rell tapped her fingers on the table as she read the note a messenger had given her, a small gasp escaping her lips. Her brother fidgeted in his chair, watching her. It had been weeks since the murder of six Justiciars in Ocean's Keep, and details were still trickling to her. Suvi's spy network was doing its job, though slower than she would prefer.

"The girl they stole from me and raised in Arcton Citadel is one of the Cursed Gods foretold by the Whitepeak Mystics after all," Suvi said. She kept her voice even, but she resented the news.

She should have been mine.

"What of her parents?" Matthys asked. "Should we seek them out, tell them the wonderful news that their daughter is alive?"

Suvi chuckled. "Dead in beggar's graves. You're welcome to dig them up and have a chat."

"You're a morbid beast." Matthys flashed a sly grin. "What is this girl's name?"

"She's a woman now, and she's called Quinn. No surname."

Matthys reached over the table and poured her a thick, dark coffee. "This is rather interesting news, Sister."

Interesting news, indeed.

Suvi sipped on the sweet coffee. She had long given up on the White-peak Mystics' prophecy, only for it to unfold in blood and fury in her old enemy's home.

"What of the other god? They come in pairs, don't they?" he asked.

"In the strangest twist of fate, I believe it's the daughter of the pirates who smuggled Quinn out of Thu'Dain. She bears the same first name as their child and is the right age. The lore does say the lives of Cursed Gods are *forever entwined*."

She laughed, rapping her knuckles on the table.

"Suvi, you're downright giddy over this turn of events," Matthys observed.

"This girl was promised to me, and the Areshi Empire stole her out from under me. Only to have her bite their hand. They don't control Quinn anymore. Therein lies opportunity."

"What do you intend to do?"

"Quinn is from our nation, and I am her queen. She belongs to me."

"What of this other god, the child of the pirates who stole Quinn? What is her name?"

Suvi peered down at the note in front of her. "Nyssa...Blacksea." She reclined in her chair, grinning. "I think I'll make her an offer. See if she will bend a knee to a new queen. And if she doesn't bend, then I will watch her break."

ACKNOWLEDGEMENTS

Writing a book is no small feat. Inspiration comes from a myriad of sources. For me, it's a weird mix of kung fu movies, Miyazaki's films, Radiohead, powerful women, the sound of falling snow, and the gentle, warm hue the light takes on just as the sun is setting. Aside from inspiration, writing a book well takes far more than just the lone author. A number of people contributed to this book being written, edited, and out in the world.

Max Gorlov – First and foremost, I'd like to thank Max of First Book Coaching. You're more than just a book coach. You're a cheerleader. A brainstormer. A hole-poker. A voice of reason. A therapist. And a genuinely good guy who pushed me to do my best in the loveliest English accent. Visit FBC at www.firstbookcoaching.com.

L.R. Friedman – My critique partner. My sounding board. And most importantly, my friend. It's critical to find someone who not only pushes you, but understands the Herculean undertaking writing and self-publishing a book is all about. You are that person and you pushed me to make *The Blacksea Odyssey* sing. Oh, and your mom, Lois, is pretty awesome too! Thanks Lois, for proofing *Unworthy*! Check out Lauren's books on amazon.com.

Chinah Mercer – Editor extraordinaire at The Editor & the Quill. You're no normal editor – you're invested in every word, turn of phrase, and idea. Thank you for going above and beyond. Your commitment to the work is unparalleled. Site: www.editorandquill.com.

Zoe Markham – Proof reader and the one who puts my mind at ease that the finishing touches are complete and the manuscript is in tip-top shape. Site: www.markhamcorrect.com.

Chris Yarbrough – I feel truly lucky to have you in my orbit because you're truly a massive talent. Chris is the fantastic illustrator responsible for my book covers, the interior art, and many of the character studies you see me using on social media. Instagram: @the_illustrator_yar.

The FBC Crew – I signed up for book coaching but came away with a community of writers and pudding enthusiasts, which means the world.

My friends, close and far, especially Duy, Lucia, Cal, Scott, Dan, Niecy, Merritt, Jo, Aimee, Meagan, Kirsten, Cristina, Brandi, and Dani. The support and encouragement (and beta reading!) is priceless. Love all of you guys! And for the Space Monkeys: *You are walking through a red forest and the grass is tall...*

Joe – My big brother and mentor, both personally and professionally. A lot of who/what I am is due to you, your brotherly love, and guidance throughout my life. You were a constant bug in my ear who always said "you should be a writer." Well, big bro...here we are. I love you.

Lisa – I dipped my toe into the shark-infested dating pool and there you were, the most unexpected thing to happen in my life. You took a chance on a clueless woman who needed a kind and giving heart. I look forward to years of us sitting on the couch, with me writing and you knitting beside me, while some garbage TV plays in the background. I love you, weirdo #2!

WHAT'S NEXT FOR NYSSA?

The second book in the trilogy, ***Unbound***, is coming July 24, 2024. Preorder at amazon.com.

The third book in the trilogy, ***Unyielding***, is coming October 23, 2024. Preorder at amazon.com.

What were Nyssa and Athen up to before the events in Unworthy? Download my free short story, Whiskey and Wagers, and find out.

Stay updated on the latest *The Blacksea Odyssey* series news by signing up for my newsletter at www.javodvarka.com. The newsletter provides all the latest book and author news, free giveaways, deleted scenes, sneak peeks at my works in progress, and the opportunity to join my ARC (advanced reader copy) team. This trilogy isn't all you'll see of this world or Nyssa Blacksea...more adventures for our heroes (and villains) await.

And finally, a request. Reviews from readers like yourself are the life blood of indie authors, so if you would kindly take a moment and leave a review for this book, I would be eternally grateful.

Find me on social media: https://linktr.ee/javodvarka.

Made in the USA
Middletown, DE
01 September 2024

60152340R00231